# Between Silk and Sand

Also by Marissa Doyle

*By Jove*

*Skin Deep*

The Leland Sisters series:
*Bewitching Season*
*Betraying Season*
*Courtship and Curses*
*Charles Bewitched*

# BETWEEN
# SILK AND SAND

## Marissa Doyle

BETWEEN SILK AND SAND
Copyright © 2018 by Marissa Doyle

Published by Book View Café Publishing Cooperative
P.O. Box 1624
Cedar Crest, NM 87008-1624

ISBN: 978-1-61138-717-9

Cover design by Dave Smeds
Interior design by Marissa Doyle

www.bookviewcafe.com
www.marissadoyle.com

To all my friends
who would not let this story die

And, always, to Scott,
who lent it more than he knows

THE SMALL BOY WAS awakened suddenly. Not, as usual, by one of the nursery maids laying a fire in his big carved fireplace, or even by his governess's loudly cheerful sweeping back the bed curtains. Instead he had been roused by something he'd never heard before in the palace—loud, angry shouting.

Early morning light just peeped around the edges of his curtained windows, like it did when he went with Papa and Lord Drass and their friends to hunt fowl in the great marshes south of the city. Maybe there was a hunt that morning, and people were angry because nobody had told them about it and they didn't want to miss it. He didn't want to, either.

He climbed out of bed and padded to where his small hunting bow hung on the wall. If he got ready quickly and didn't fuss, Papa might let him go. He dressed himself in sturdy leggings and a leather jerkin and put on his wool cloak, for it was autumn and his governess would be cross if he tried to sneak out without it. As he pulled on his boots he listened to the strange sounds that seemed to be growing louder. They didn't sound very nice.

The door to his room flew open. The boy jumped, but it was only his governess, the countess. He ran to her. "What's making all that—"

"Praise be, you're awake," she interrupted, and hurried over to his wardrobe. Flinging open the doors, she stuffed a bag she carried with his clothes.

He watched her rush round the room putting things in her bag. Why hadn't she told him to wash his face and comb his hair the way she did every other morning? "Is there a hunt?" he asked tentatively. "Can I go too? Look, I'm all ready—"

"Yes, I'm very glad you are." She snatched a mostly shapeless and balding stuffed toy from his bed.

He tried to wrench it out of her grasp. "I don't want to take Poofa on a hunt. I'm almost five, you know. They'll laugh at me!"

For an instant she looked at him with a funny look on her face, as if she wanted to cry. Then her usual calm smile slipped back into place.

"Quickly, now. We don't want to be late." She pulled the hood of his cloak over his head. "Best cover that hair of yours. No one else's is quite that shade of gold," she muttered, then took his hand.

The shouting was louder now. It sounded as if it might be at the end of the hallway. But he didn't have time to stop and listen because his governess was pulling him through the connecting door into her room.

Her bedroom was very untidy, which was odd—she was never untidy. Clothes and papers were strewn about, and she had packed another bag that she slung over her shoulder. Then she did a funny thing. She poked at two or three places in the carvings around one of her bookcases, and the bookcase slid aside. There was a dark, narrow hallway behind it, and a flight of stairs leading down. Heya! This was even better than a hunt. He followed close on her heels into the secret passageway.

The countess slid the bookcase-door shut behind them, grunting a little with the effort. Then, fumbling in the dark, she struck a spark with a flint and lit a small lamp. Shadows danced around them as she knelt down and gazed into his face.

"I want you to follow me and do exactly what I tell you. No questions. And above all, keep as quiet as you possibly can."

Her face looked a little scary, lit from below by the lamp. "Is this part of the hunt?" he whispered.

The countess's eyes took on an odd expression again. Was she angry or sad or—or scared? "Yes, dear. Now, quietly!"

They went swiftly down the dark stairs. The shouting sounds had faded. He heard the countess counting under her breath and saw by the flickering light of her lamps that they were passing doors set at intervals in the wall. At the sixth one she stopped and set down their bags, then slid it open a crack. "Your Majesty— Elladis—" she called urgently.

"Wha—?" said a sleepy voice. The boy caught sight of blue silk hangings and realized that this was his mother's room. Mama was still asleep; she had to sleep a lot because the new baby made her tired, wanting to eat all the time. Would Mama and his new little sister go hunting too?

He tried to squeeze past the countess but froze when the real door burst open and the shouting sound he had heard before filled the room. Men waving axes and pikes poured in, shouting his father's name. One of them—a young man with sleek black hair and a narrow, pointed face—bent over his little sister's cradle and picked the baby up, grinning unpleasantly.

The boy opened his mouth to cry out. Before he could, the countess yanked him back and slid the door closed, but not before he saw a tall, burly man with a blood-red feather on his hat bring a heavy axe down on his beautiful, sleepy, terrified Mama's head. Blood exploded onto the sea-blue bed hangings, turning them dark and ugly. Blood everywhere—

Through the door the shouts in the room grew louder and even more frenzied. A thin, fretful cry was cut off in a dull thud, and the boy saw the countess close her eyes and scrunch up her face as if the sound hurt her.

"Maaaamaa!" he started to wail, but the countess lifted him with a small grunt, muffling his sobs in her shoulder, and began to hurry down the passage, away from the door.

"Hush, my darling…please be quiet or they'll find us too," she panted. "I don't think—please the gods, let them not have seen us!"

She kept going until the light from their lamp was no longer visible behind them, then knelt in the darkness and set him down, holding him tightly, till her breathing was less ragged. "Can you walk, child? I need to feel my way from here," she whispered, close to his ear.

The darkness around them felt like it was reaching toward him with grasping, greedy hands, but right now the only light and color he could think of were the gold of his Mama's head and the glint of the axe as it fell, and then— "Mama," he whispered. His legs went all wobbly as the dark climbed into his head, blocking out the red—

But the countess shook him. "No, darling! You can't faint now. Your mama…" She swallowed hard. "The bad men can't hurt her anymore. Now we have to find your papa."

Papa—the men said they were going to get him. Would they hit him too? "I want Papa!"

"We'll look for him, right now." He felt the countess pull him close again and lean her forehead against his. "I will always be here to protect you, but you must help me by being brave. Remember what Papa calls you."

"'Brave as the lions in the Adaiha,'" he said dutifully, trying to swallow the sobs that threatened to choke him.

"That's right. Come, my little lion." She rose and took his hand. He clutched hers tightly and they moved slowly through the darkness, in the secret passage in the great palace by the sea.

Twenty years later

# One

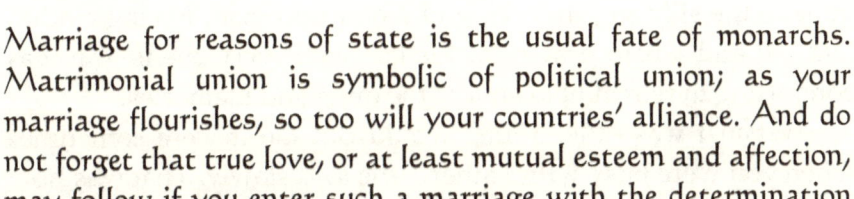

Marriage for reasons of state is the usual fate of monarchs. Matrimonial union is symbolic of political union; as your marriage flourishes, so too will your countries' alliance. And do not forget that true love, or at least mutual esteem and affection, may follow if you enter such a marriage with the determination to make it succeed.

*—The Flower of Royalty Blossom'd; or A Manual for the Instruction of Future Monarchs, with Especial Emphasis on the Moral and Spiritual Development of their Intellects as well as the Nurture of their Practical and Political Instincts* by Count V. Ebroian, Regent of Mauburni

"YOU'RE GOING TO WEAR that book out, you know. The ink will rub off from being read so much."

Saraid jumped and clapped The Book closed. "Pox it, Nin, don't do that to me. And I wasn't really reading. Just…thinking." She casually slipped it behind the cushions on the window seat where she was curled. It was true, really—she *had* been thinking more than reading. Thinking about the fact that in just a matter of days, it might be years before she'd see this room again. Or anything in Thekla, *ever*. She pushed that thought hastily aside.

"Hmm." Nin leaned past her and fished her book out of the cushions. "Ah, *The Flower of Royalty*. Just as I thought. Do you ever read anything else? I'll grant you that it's fairly good, but we studied a lot of other good books, too."

"Careful!" Saraid snatched it back. "That's Mama's copy."

"I wasn't going to hurt it, silly." Nin sat down next to her. "You've been coming in here a lot, haven't you?" she asked in a gentler tone.

Saraid glanced around the large bedchamber with its faded green silk hangings and cushions and delicately carved furniture. Father had left the room as it always had been, though he hadn't gone to the silly lengths a king of Nolor once had, having clothes laid out and a bath drawn for his late wife every evening. It was comforting to retreat here amidst the quiet and memories.

"When I was little, Mama would call me in here sometimes when you were busy with Father," she said slowly. That was how they'd always been: Nin was Father's favorite, and she'd been Mama's. "We used to talk about how one day I would go away to marry in a foreign land because that's what kings' younger daughters did. Mama said they became living bridges to link countries together. We would look at maps and talk about where I might go someday."

Nin patted her arm. "I understand."

Saraid turned away so that Nin wouldn't see her face. No. She didn't understand. She couldn't. Nin would stay in Thekla and become queen when Father someday went to rest with Mama in the Fields of the Dead. She would never have to leave Thekla, never have to learn to call another place home.

"Don't you have something you're supposed to be doing? Ambassadors to receive or some such thing?" she asked. The Book said that "Deflecting unwanted conversation is an art well to be cultivated in any situation, but especially in the confines of a royal court." She thought it might be on page seventy-seven, somewhere near the bottom.

Unfortunately, tactics like that didn't often work on Nin. After all, she'd read The Book, too. She put an arm around Saraid's shoulders. "No. Don't turn away and go all stiff on me. You've been an utter pincushion lately—pointy and prickly all over. In a little while we'll have to dress for the dinner with the council, and then there's the ball, and then later you'll be packing all your last-minute necessities—" She tugged on The Book. "We won't have any time to just talk. C'mon, Sardy. I'm your big sister, remember?"

The childhood nickname wormed its way through Saraid's carefully constructed defenses. She looked down at her hands, where faceted rose-pink tourmalines sparkled on the bracelets Varian Mutrand, Lord Protector of Mauburni, had sent her. *Be a queen!* they seemed to signal up to her blurring eyes. In a few weeks' time, she'd no longer be a Theklan princess but the wife of the ruler of Mauburni. Revealing any of her doubt and anxiety was not queen-worthy behavior.

But this was Nin.

"I...I'm afraid," she mumbled.

Nin reached out and touched one of her bracelets. "What are you afraid of? The Lord Protector? That he'll be horrible or something?"

Saraid thought of the portrait miniature the Mauburnian ambassador had given her. As far as she could tell, the Lord Protector of Mauburni was as handsome as any prospective bride could wish. She wore it on a chain under her tunic, next to her heart, but Nin didn't need to know that. "No, not really. But—" She took a deep breath. "Mama may have talked about living bridges and all that, which was fine when I was little. But she didn't talk about what it was like to be married."

Nin shifted uneasily. "You, um, do know what happens on your wedding night, yes?"

As a matter of fact, she did know. A couple of the older ladies of the court had taken her aside to talk about it. *That* part of being married didn't scare her, though it sounded somewhat improbable. Still, they'd said it could be very pleasant if done correctly. Both had been married for a long time and ought to know.

"That's not what I'm talking about." She looked down at her bracelets again, then back at Nin. It wasn't queen-worthy to worry about anything so trivial as her feelings, either. Thekla *needed* her to make this alliance with Mauburni. But still— "What if he doesn't like me? What if we don't have anything to talk about? I know that's not what's important…"

"You've been writing to each other for months now, haven't you?" Nin asked.

"Y-yes. He seems nice enough. At least, I like the letters that I've actually gotten from him. Keranieth knows how many might have disappeared on their way across the Adaiha."

Ninieth cleared her throat. Saraid followed her glance out the window that overlooked the gardens drowsing in the late afternoon sun. Bees hummed busily above the last of the summer flowers, soon to be felled by the first frost. That was another thing she would miss: the gardens of Thekla, where everyone had a green thumb. But maybe the gardens in Mauburni would be as lovely —

Nin cleared her throat a second time. "Ah, yes. The Adaiha."

Saraid turned from the window. Nin always saved that exaggeratedly casual tone for cajoling her into doing something she wouldn't like. "What about the Adaiha? Is there something wrong? I mean, something more wrong than usual?"

That was the only drawback to marrying a Mauburnian: in order to get there she would have to cross the wide, desolate desert of the Adaiha. When the last king of Mauburni had been deposed twenty years ago, the Adaiha had declared itself free of Mauburnian rule. Now it was held by feuding warlords who could only agree on one thing: that anyone traveling through their land was fair game. Months had been spent negotiating the preparations for her crossing the Adaiha safely.

"No-o-o…" Nin hesitated. "Not wrong, exactly."

"Which means that something is not quite right, either. Stop being mysterious."

"I'll tell you the good part first, shall I? I know you'll like it."

"What makes you so sure?"

"Don't interrupt. What would you say if I told you that you won't have to travel to Mauburni in the horse litter after all?"

That *was* good, if surprising. Since a coach or wagon of any sort would be useless in the sand of the Adaiha, Father had taken it into his head that she should journey as befitted a royal princess of Thekla in an elegantly upholstered and curtained horse-borne litter all the way to Madariv, capital of Mauburni. Saraid had ridden in it for a circuit around the courtyard in front of the stables and had nearly thrown up all over the lovely silk interior. She'd asked, then demanded, then finally begged to ride horseback instead, but Father had been adamant.

"Very well. So what's the 'not exactly wrong' part?" she asked warily.

Nin didn't answer. Instead she regarded the toes of her kidskin slippers with a sudden deep interest.

Saraid sat up and pulled her round to face her. "Nin, what don't you want to tell me?"

She looked up from her shoes. "It's not that I don't want to. I'm just trying to figure out how."

"Tell me *what*?"

Nin sighed. "That you'll be traveling to Madariv in disguise with a small guard, a minimum of belongings, and a minimum of comfort, too, probably, at least between oases."

"You're making that up." There was no way that would happen—not after all those weeks of fussing about the hundreds of horses and pack mules to ferry her retinue and her wedding clothes and gifts for her husband and a thousand other things.

"I wish I were. The Mauburnian ambassador told Father and the council that news of your marriage seems to have spread across the Adaiha, no matter how careful messengers have been, and now every warlord out there is on the watch, hoping to kidnap you for ransom. When Father wanted to enlarge your guard, they said that wouldn't work because none of the oases could accommodate that many people and animals. So between them they came up with a plan: send the bulk of your luggage and people across with as much fanfare as possible to serve as decoy, and send you separately, traveling fast and light—just you, a maid, a handful of guards, a few pack animals. You'll dress like Adaihans and ride Adaihan horses—oh, I wish Father had told us about this sooner, so that you could have prepared for it! When was the last time you spent any time on horseback? Three summers ago, when the water sickness was so bad in the city that we stayed in the country till after harvest?"

"Two summers," Saraid corrected her. "Why didn't he tell me sooner?"

"I don't know. *I* didn't know till just now. Maybe he thought you'd worry less if you didn't know beforehand." She took Saraid's hand. "No wonder you're upset."

"But I'm not upset. It's wonderful news!"

Nin stared at her. "It is?"

Saraid shook off her hand, jumped from the window seat, and began to pace. "Think about it. Instead of lying in that litter either throwing up or going cross-eyed with boredom, I'll be—oh, I don't know. Riding in the fresh air, helping keep watch, and not having a chance to feel bad." Or homesick or worried about her upcoming marriage and the impressions she'd make or any other behavior unworthy of The Book. "It'll be fun!"

"Fun?"

"Fun, exciting...I don't know." She stopped pacing. "Tell me, would you rather be stuck in that litter?"

One corner of Nin's mouth quirked. "Not so fast, Sardy— you'll still have to travel in it until you get to the border."

Saraid shrugged airily. "Pfft. That won't take long."

"Saraid, I'm serious. Are you sure you don't mind? It'll be hard riding, mostly by night, and you'll be camping between watering places...not that most of them are supposed to be luxurious by any means, but at least they have beds."

"I'm not completely soft. It'll be just like when we used to take our blankets to the barn at Great-Aunt Yareth's country house. Remember that? You were always the one who wanted to go back to our room because the hayloft wasn't comfortable enough, not me."

A distant bell rang. Nin glanced once more at the setting sun visible through the window and rose. "Time to get ready for the dinner. I'm glad you're taking it so well, though I still think —"

"Don't worry." Saraid took her arm and propelled her through the door.

As soon as she was safely out of sight, Saraid let the grin she'd been holding back spread across her face as she turned back into Mama's room. Now she would have stories to tell her children, just as Mama had—but hers would be even more exciting, all about how she'd ridden in disguise across a wild, bandit-infested land in order to marry their father. They'd love it.

She fished inside the neck of her silk tunic and pulled out the miniature of Lord Protector Mutrand on its slender silver chain. Would their children have his dark eyes or her green ones? Her rather long nose or his high forehead? She hoped they'd have his sleek black hair and not her rambunctious, leaf-brown locks that were only well behaved when restrained in a braid down her back. Ambassador Rathal said he was tall, like her, so that would be good.

"I think we shall suit each other quite nicely, Milord Varian," she whispered, tracing the shape of his neatly pointed beard with her finger. "At least, I hope...no, I'm *sure* we will."

After all, there was no real reason why they shouldn't. Yes, he was nearly twice her age—but she didn't want a callow youth for her husband, not when she could have a mature man, experienced in both ruling and in...in other things. She only hoped that he would not find her too young, despite all the practicing she'd done recently at being dignified and regal. The Book hadn't had anything to say about age differences between husbands and wives, but maybe that meant it wasn't anything of importance — yes, that must be it. She brought the miniature to her lips and kissed it, then let the chain slither back inside her tunic and picked up The Book from the window seat.

The Book. Nin could tease all she wanted, but it wasn't going to change how she felt about it.

Mama had given her her own copy of *The Flower of Royalty Blossom'd; or A Manual for the Instruction of Future Monarchs, with Especial Emphasis on the Moral and Spiritual Development of their Intellects as well as the Nurture of their Practical and Political Instinct* not long before she died, during one of those talks about Saraid's leaving Thekla someday. It was a beautiful book, with exquisite illuminations, but Saraid hadn't really paid much attention to it until after Mama's death. Then, reading the book that had been written three hundred years ago for a little orphaned king, she'd been struck by a feeling of kinship with him.

Admittedly, she wasn't really an orphan. But with Mama gone, she felt like one. Father had never had time—nor inclination—to be a *father*; he'd always been awkward and uncomfortable with them. He'd only overcome that with Nin once she was well on her way to being grown, and probably only because she was his heir. So it had almost felt that the author of The Book, Count Ebroian, was talking not only to the young king who had lost his parents but also directly to her. She was a future monarch, too, wasn't she?

When the delegations had first started arriving from Mauburni a year ago, seeking her hand, she'd been delighted. To go to Mauburni, the land of her beloved Book? To marry a man named Varian, which had also been Count Ebroian's given name—a fact which delighted her no end? No matter that he was only a Lord Protector, nephew of the man who'd overthrown the last king. He held all the powers a king did, and the delegations had confided that the alliance with Thekla would almost certainly result in his being acknowledged as king by the Mauburnian Council of Lords. The new King Varian would owe his crown to her, which would give her a power not held by many princesses in arranged marriages. No empty life eating sugared *listhra* petals and

14

ordering new gowns for her—no, she would be there right next to her new husband, being the perfect enlightened monarch as described in The Book.

Although envoys from the King of Nolor had also come to Thekla to woo her at about the same time, bearing jewels and gifts from that strange, faraway land, she had barely noticed them. Instead she had spent weeks calling on each of Father's ministers in turn, discussing the benefits of both alliances but making it abundantly clear where her preference lay. Count Ebroian would have been proud of her, she was sure. And it had worked; they'd all supported the alliance with Mauburni, and Father had acceded to their wishes. If it was her fate to leave her home, then at least she'd had a hand in choosing her new one.

There was only one problem. The Book was regrettably silent on the topic of being a wife, of how she should go about becoming both lover and friend, of being all to her husband and knowing he was all to her. If only Mama—

But she couldn't think about Mama now, or she'd end up at the reception later with red eyes and a swollen nose. She would just have to make that part up as she went along.

With a last look around the dimming room, she left to take her bath and go to her final farewell party.

# Two

An intelligent ruler comprehends that he oft must rely on others to do his work. The problem lies in finding the best person to perform the task at hand. Think long and well about whom you choose to perform any task for you, and decide what might be worse: a deficiency in their loyalty or in their ability.

*—The Flower of Royalty Blossom'd*

"'STRONG AND STURDY' MIGHT have worked for your Count What's-his-name in that book of yours, but it ain't workin' for me." Talnith, Saraid's temporary maid, shifted in her saddle and pouted.

"I'm sorry, Talnith." Saraid was *trying* to be understanding— truly she was. "Can't you give it a little more of a chance?"

She had left home five days before in her gorgeously hideous litter, waving to the crowds and trying to stem the tears that she'd sworn not to shed. She'd managed to keep dry-eyed even while saying good-bye to Papa; her tears were all Nin's fault. If her sister hadn't started crying as they embraced for the last time at the eastern gate, then she certainly (well, possibly) wouldn't have. The

Book didn't approve of kings—or queens, she assumed—showing personal sadness or anger in public.

They'd ridden past fields of ripening grain and groves of *lumox* trees, home of the moth larvae that were the source of the famed Theklan silk. The groves were busier than she'd ever seen them; they swarmed with workers planting wagonloads of saplings to replace old, neglected trees, all because she was marrying the Lord Protector.

Mauburni—the greatest seafaring and trading power in the world—had once been Thekla's chief market for its oils and perfumes and, above all, its famous silk. During the years of unrest in Mauburni, though, that trade had all but vanished—and Thekla had suffered.

But that would change, thanks to her. Thekla's acknowledgment of the Lord Protector would lend him legitimacy—and that would stabilize Mauburni. Trade with Thekla would resume, and Thekla's fields and gardens—and its people—would flourish. She sat up more proudly in her litter. She wasn't just getting married; she was *rescuing* Thekla. It was something that not even Nin, the future queen of Thekla, would be able to do.

Their first few nights had been spent at the country estates of Theklan nobles, for which Saraid was grateful: it allowed her to say good-bye to Thekla in stages, one place at a time. But once they had caught sight of the craggy hills bordering the Adaiha, Saraid had packed the small bag she'd been allowed by the captain of her guard: a few Theklan silk tunics and leggings so she'd have something proper to wear if, as was likely, they arrived ahead of the rest of her luggage, her carved *lumox*-wood brush and comb that were the only ones capable of taming her hair, and, of course, Mama's copy of The Book. She'd tucked the letters Lord Mutrand had written her in the back of it and laid it on top of the small silk-lined box that contained her favorite jewelry—several pieces that had belonged to Mama and Lord Mutrand's tourmaline bracelets.

Then she'd said good-bye to her comfortable old maid, Jora,

who would stay behind to help perpetuate the charade of Saraid's still being there. A girl of about her own coloring and build had put on the gauze veil most people wore when traveling through the hot, dusty Adaiha and would huddle in the litter, pretending to be her for the rest of the trip. Saraid hoped the poor girl had a strong stomach once they left Thekla's roads and set out into the desert.

Leaving Jora behind was difficult—maybe it was temporary, but it still hurt to have to let go of yet another piece of home right now. It also meant she had to bring some female to fill in. That someone else had turned out to be Talnith, a niece of Jora's who had promptly agreed to go, citing her devotion to princess and country. Saraid suspected her motives had less to do with patriotism and more with the prospect of having eight sturdy soldiers all to herself. She hadn't stopped flirting since they'd started out.

"I been giving it a chance," Talnith was saying. "But the blisters on my bum ain't helping none. Why couldn't we have took that little house thing to ride in? There's enough soldiers what could have carried it." Her flaxen curls, which she carefully wrapped in rags each morning before they slept, bounced in indignation.

Saraid ignored her own saddle-weary muscles and tried to look on the bright side: listening to Talnith's grumbles about her bottom as they walked their horses along the nighttime roads was infinitely preferable to Talnith being litter-sick. She'd been quoting bits of The Book to the girl in hopes that it would comfort her and maybe inspire a little fortitude—after all, it was helping *her*. But to her chagrin it had not had the same effect on Talnith. Perhaps a new method was in order. She leaned closer to Talnith and murmured, "Maybe you ought to ask one of the soldiers to bandage your blisters when we stop for the morning."

It worked; Talnith giggled. "Oooh, listen to you! And you the king's daughter! You shouldn't be talkin' that way!"

But she didn't say anything more about her sore bottom.

Saraid smiled and murmured, "'Respond not to petty complaints, but speak gently and with good humor, and you will turn them aside as a cloak does the rain.'" The Book had an answer for everything.

They were high in the hills near the border now. Captain Zamas, the head of her guard, had said that they would reach the hills' end by morning. One more ridge, and then a steep road led down into the Adaiha. If it hadn't been the middle of the night, she could have looked back at the verdant Theklan plains, spread like a fading green silk coverlet splotched with the brown of approaching colder weather. But she didn't turn. She didn't want her last view of her homeland to be one of flat darkness.

A cough beside her interrupted her thoughts. "Ahem. Your Highness."

"Captain Zamas," she acknowledged. In contrast to Talnith's breezy familiarity, Captain Zamas was almost painfully correct. But he'd crossed the Adaiha twice last year as part of the delegations negotiating her marriage and seemed to know what he was doing.

"Your Highness will have noticed that we are on a downward incline. We should reach our intended campsite by sunrise. I understand there is a spring nearby, so we'll replenish our water supplies and be ready to leave as soon as the sun is low tonight."

"This traveling by night ain't natural. I'd give my best petticoat to know how we're supposed to know where we're goin' in that desert if we ain't got the sun to see by. It's been bad enough trying to follow this road in the dark," Talnith put in, a little tartly. Captain Zamas had so far proved impervious to her charms, and she bounced between sulky and servile when he was near.

"Most travel in the Adaiha is by night, when it is cooler. I thought it wisest for us to accustom ourselves to it before we set out to cross it. We will navigate by the stars, just as sailors on the ocean do." The captain smoothed his large black moustache with a smug air.

"Well, how you can tell one little twinkling bit from another,

I've no idea." Talnith was in sulky mode tonight. "And what about this curse I've been hearing about on the Day-har? I don't like the idea of ridin' in no cursed land."

"Don't worry, Talnith," Saraid said quickly. "The curse—if you believe in it—won't affect you. It's supposed to be on the Adaihans only. We're perfectly safe."

"That's what they say," Talnith muttered darkly. "How long's this curse been around?"

Hmm. Maybe a bit of storytelling would take Talnith's mind off her bottom—and everything else. "It was three hundred years ago when the curse turned the grasslands of the Adaiha into a great desert waste," she intoned.

"Three hundred years ago?" Talnith frowned in concentration. "That's when my Gran was born. At least that's what she says."

Saraid struggled to keep a sober expression. "Who knows? Maybe she was. Anyway, it was three hundred years ago that the Kingdom of Nolor—"

Talnith squealed. "Oooh, I know about Nolor! They're always wanting to take over other kingdoms on account their own land is so beastly hot. And their king is seven feet tall and eats Theklan babies for breakfast, because they're plumper. Gran told me so."

Saraid abandoned her struggle and grinned. "I don't know about the babies, but Nolor does have a history of trying to push its borders. Three hundred years ago, they tried it on Mauburni and were more successful than they usually are."

"Maybe they liked Mauburnian babies better back then," Talnith interjected.

"Maybe. Anyway, the king of Mauburni was hard-pressed to drive them back with his own men and called on the Adaihans to help him. The Adaiha was part of Mauburni then, and the Adaihans were famous horsemen. They were supposed to meet the king and his army and together send the Nolorish invaders back to their own lands. But for some reason the Adaihans never came, and the king was killed in battle."

Captain Zamas cleared his throat. "Soldiering should be left to soldiers, if I may be so bold, Your Highness."

"Probably." Her father certainly never had ridden out at the head of his army—not that it had ever been necessary, but *still*—was the age of royal heroes truly dead? Would the Lord Protector ride out to battle if Nolor attacked Mauburni again, wearing her emblem as his badge of honor? She certainly hoped so: it was how a real king should behave.

"Now, this is where the curse part happened," she said to Talnith. "The king's cousin, Count Varian Ebroian, was a great soldier, but he was also reputed to be a wizard. He led the Mauburnian army and defeated Nolor, then was made regent for the late king's young son. Count Ebroian had loved the king and grieved deeply for him, and when the new little king was being crowned in the palace at Madariv, he made a speech to all the gathered nobles, including the Adaihan ones. He asked why the Adaihans had been able to come to see this king but not the old one. When they wouldn't answer, he said that Mauburni lived by the sea and was guarded by the water gods, but sometimes even the gods needed help protecting it. Since the Adaihans had refused to come to Mauburni to help, then the gods would do likewise with them. And after that, it never rained in the Adaiha again."

"Never?"

"Never." Saraid made herself sound appropriately solemn. "Wizard Ebroian had given his word. Within months, the grasslands of the Adaiha had withered. Within a year, sand had started to creep across the hills, turning them into enormous dunes. After five years, the Adaiha was a desert."

Talnith shot her a suspicious look. "No rain? Is that true, Captain?"

Now Saraid knew where she stood: Talnith would take her Gran's word that the king of Nolor ate grilled babies for breakfast, but she wouldn't believe Saraid that no rain fell in the Adaiha.

"Never to my knowledge," Captain Zamas told her, "though I cannot vouch for all the region—"

"*But*," Saraid said dramatically. "Count Ebroian also told the Adaihans that one day, if they heeded the king's call and came to his aid when he needed them most, the curse would be lifted, and the Adaiha would be green once more."

"Then why haven't they done it yet? Do the Day-hans like living with all that nasty sand?"

"Maybe it's because the king hasn't called them. Or the need wasn't great enough if he did. I don't know. It's just a story." Saraid yawned on the last word and immediately wished she hadn't.

"I regret Your Highness's weariness, but the sky seems to be lightening. We will break for the day shortly and have our rest." Captain Zamas drew a little closer, as if he were afraid she'd doze off in the saddle and fall from her horse.

Saraid was glad it was still too dim for him to see her embarrassed flush. Did he think she was completely soft? "I'm fine. Thank you, Captain," she murmured. Miraculously, he noticed the faint dismissive tone in her voice and excused himself.

Talnith watched him ride away. "So I was wonderin'," she said, not troubling to lower her voice. "Does he always sit on that horse like he's got a stick up his—"

"Talnith!" Saraid muttered from the corner of her mouth.

The girl didn't even blink. "Oh, he didn't hear. That sort never does. That was quite a tale you come up with there, Your Majesty." Talnith hadn't quite grasped the proper use of titles yet. "You'd think that king what got kicked off his throne a few years back would have been needful enough of the Day-hans' help."

Sometimes Talnith was downright surprising. "Yes, you would, wouldn't you? Maybe he forgot."

"Or maybe there weren't no truth to the story to begin with. I reckon you was pullin' my leg a bit saying that Count What's-His-Name was a wizard." She snorted, then glanced behind her apprehensively. "Do you really think it's nonsense?" she whispered. "About him being a wizard and all?"

"I don't know. Do you believe in magic?"

Talnith looked doubtful. "I dunno...there's my Gran. My sister, once she got this enormous boil on her—well, Gran just looked at and said, 'It'll go,' and blame me if it weren't gone next morning. She charms for warts, too. But that ain't like some wizard turning a whole country into the cat's sandbox. Good thing those Day-hans didn't help that king, or else you wouldn't be goin' off to marry your Protector Lord."

"Lord Protector," Saraid corrected.

"Right. What you said." Talnith had caught sight of her current favorite soldier, the one with brown hair and a gap between his front teeth, a short distance to their right. She casually sidestepped her horse until they were riding knee to knee.

Saraid smiled to herself. Much as Talnith claimed to be afraid of horses, she seemed to have learned to handle them well enough when the need arose.

Ahead of her, Captain Zamas had ridden down into a little hollow. Evidently it was time to camp. Saraid glanced up at the stars, fading now in the early dawn light. Right now they still shone over Thekla. Tonight they would shine over the Adaiha, and they would lead her to her new home.

"Princess? Wake up, princess. Captain says we have to go."

Saraid blinked up at Talnith, who was shaking her shoulder none too gently. "Thank you, Talnith, I'm awake," she mumbled, stretching and sitting up. Usually she was awake before Talnith, but she had fought off sleep for as long as possible—her last moments in Thekla.

"Captain says we have to start wearin' these." Talnith's voice was deeply disapproving as she shoved a sand-colored bundle at Saraid.

"What are they?" Saraid shivered slightly—the early evening air was cool—and unfolded the bundle.

"What those Day-hans wear. Not proper clothes if you ask me,

24

but I suppose they make some sorta sense if you're soap-brained enough to want to live in a great sand pile, waitin' for a king to take a curse off you."

Saraid shook out two garments, a loose underrobe of a very fine, soft woven material and a looser outer one of coarser fabric, as well as a very long gauze scarf to wrap around her head and face. No wonder Talnith had asked her a few days ago if the Adaihans were male and female and not just one uniform sex. Wrapped in these robes, it would be almost impossible to tell them apart. She hoped she'd be able to change back into Theklan clothes before the Lord Protector saw her; her figure was elegant, if her unruly hair wasn't.

But the underrobe was smooth on her skin and the layered garments welcome in the approaching chill of a desert night. Practicality was what was important just now; besides, the Adaihan clothes might offer them some camouflage as they traveled.

They ate a quick breakfast and refilled their water bags at the spring. After filling hers, Saraid took a long drink and let the cool water at the spring's mouth bubble over her fingers. Her last taste of Theklan water. What would the water in Mauburni taste like? Would it be sweet or bitter?

Behind her, Captain Zamas cleared his throat. She touched her wet fingers to her lips, then rose.

"Well! Shall we go see the sunset over the Adaiha?" she asked, trying to sound bright and cheerful as she accepted a leg up onto her horse.

Talnith gave her a dubious look but followed docilely enough as they left the campsite and climbed the short distant to the top of the last hill between Thekla and the Adaiha. She hadn't gone to take a peek at it when they camped this morning. Somehow it had seemed more fitting to wait.

As they crested the rise the setting sun shone full in her face, blinding her momentarily. She held up a hand to shade her eyes and sat transfixed on her horse, trying to make sense of the undulating patterns of red-gold sand and black shadows before her. She was used to open vistas of farmland back in Thekla that stretched as far as the eye could see, all under an open dome of sky. But that was static, orderly, square green block upon square green block. This was a commingling of curves, dunes and valleys, glowing in the setting sun. Even as she watched, the patterns changed and the shadows shifted as the sun sank further. She felt the air grow chill and shivered, though not entirely from the cold. The unsullied purity of the desert fascinated her, its beauty and indifference. She knew that though they might leave footprints, the moving sands and wind would obliterate them even as they were made.

"It's beautiful," she breathed.

Talnith was less impressed. "That weren't quite the word I was thinkin' of. I'll bet it ain't half dusty. How's we supposed to keep our faces clean?"

"I wouldn't worry about that too much. We'll have other things to keep our minds occupied—" Oh, pox. Talnith's face had taken on an expression made up of equal parts of fearfulness and mutiny. "But let's leave worrying to Captain Zamas, shall we?" She gave Talnith a reassuring smile and turned away, this time to cast one last look behind her. It felt like there should be some way to acknowledge this new stage of her journey, her leaving her homeland: a fanfare blown, a ceremony observed. But the guards simply took up their accustomed places around her and Talnith and the pack animals, and they set off over the crest, down a long, stony incline, and into the Adaiha.

Saraid was sure she would never, as long as she lived, forget those first nights of riding in the Adaiha.

It wasn't that it was particularly beautiful; it was, after all, night, and the details of the landscape were indistinct now that the sun had set. But she felt exquisitely aware of everything around her: the undulating hills of sand interspersed with hard rocky ribbons of packed earth that she realized must once have been rivers and streams, the still, very clear air, the muffled tread of their horses barely disturbing the silence, the cold glitter of the stars overhead. Captain Zamas rode ahead of them, pausing frequently to consult the sky and look for easier paths around dunes that would still keep them on course. They camped on the north side of a large dune at daybreak, and Saraid lay in her small tent alongside a snoring Talnith, exhausted but unable to sleep, still feeling the rhythm of her horse's gait through the sand.

Their second night, as her excitement at the novelty of the Adaiha faded, she felt a strange, disembodied feeling come over her. She had left Thekla and her old life but had not yet come to Mauburni and her new one. She was in transit between two places, two lives, carried on a dark sea of sandy nothing. It was comforting, in a way, to have this time in between, to create a buffer between her past and her future.

In the middle of that night, her serenity shattered. The dark sea of the Adaiha was not as empty as it felt.

Captain Zamas had gone to the top of a dune to better see the easiest path in the right direction. Saraid closed her eyes for a few moments as they waited for him. A few yards away Talnith murmured to one of the soldiers, the blond bearded one this time, and beyond them, a harness jangled as someone's horse bent its neck to rub its nose against its foreleg. So when the captain suddenly slid into their midst, she jumped.

"Stay still, all of you!" he hissed.

"Why? What's wrong? What is it?" Talnith burst out. "Oooh, is it something dangerous?" She somehow managed to crowd against her current favorite and threw her arms around his neck. "You'll pertect me, won't you?"

"Quiet!" Captain Zamas commanded.

They stood still, listening. Slowly, Saraid became aware of a thudding rhythm above the sound of Talnith's muffled sniffling. Somewhere not far from them, a group of horsemen cantered across the desert, heading northwest—toward Thekla.

She sidled over to the captain. "Did they see you?" He would have been easy to see on the top of that dune.

"I don't believe so. I dropped to the ground as soon as I heard them. If they had seen me, they would have come over to investigate," he muttered.

They waited, unmoving, till the last hoofbeats died away. Before they moved on, Captain Zamas sent one of his men to examine their trail. "Fifteen horses, maybe twenty," the man reported on his return.

About the size of an Adaihan raiding party. Or so Saraid had read during her whirlwind of research before she left. They were probably on their way to patrol the Theklan border, looking for a merchant party to attack, or maybe to see if her train had started out. Hopefully they wouldn't run across their trail before the restless sands smoothed it out. She looked at Captain Zamas and knew he was thinking the same thing.

Not much later, a second party passed them by, headed in the same direction. This near-encounter was much closer; if they'd been a little farther along, they might have actually met. Saraid did not like to think about that.

Talnith was nearly hysterical. "They're coming," she murmured to herself as they made camp just before sunrise. "Those Day-hans are goin' to find me and make me slave to some chieftain with nasty habits, and I'll never see Gran again."

Saraid bit back a scold—it would not help matters—and tried to make light of the situation. As soon as Talnith seemed appeased, she went to talk to the captain.

"What do you think?" she asked him.

"I don't like this. Passing two other groups in one night—" He shook his head. "I've been rethinking my plan to pause at the Dorsii oasis tomorrow morning. It might already be full of people we don't want to meet."

"Could we send a scout to have a look?"

"We could—but I don't like to divide our force. What I would rather do is strike farther south and travel one more night, which will bring us to a smaller but much less frequented oasis."

"That might be the better plan. Have you been there before?"

"No, Your Highness. But I am confident I can find it. My only concern is for your comfort."

She felt herself bristle slightly. "My comfort isn't what matters just now. Will the men be all right?"

"They know their duty, as do I."

She glanced at the still-muttering Talnith. Telling her would be the only problem, it seemed. She sighed, then wished she hadn't. Talnith couldn't help...well, being Talnith. "Then I'll leave you to it, Captain. Thank you."

They set out earlier than usual that afternoon, before the sun had quite set, to allow Captain Zamas to get his bearings by both sun and stars. Amazingly, Talnith hadn't complained about their change of plans. "If it will keep me safe from those Day-han brutes, I'll go anywhere!" she'd declaimed, clasping her hands over her heart. "That captain's a hero, he is!"

Her words seemed justified. They didn't have any more near-meetings with other travelers that night, or the next. But as dawn approached on the second day, it didn't seem as if they would encounter any oases, either. The captain kept them riding well after sunup, certain that the small inn they sought, built beside its spring of drinkable water, would be visible just beyond the next dune. The sun was halfway to noon before he conceded defeat and called for camp.

Saraid pretended to yawn hugely as Talnith spread out her blanket in their tent. "I don't think I'll bother washing my face, I'm so tired," she commented.

"But you always wash your—oooh, you're thinkin' we're go-ing to run short of water if we don't get to that oasis soon, aren't you?"

"No, I'm tired and want to go to sleep," Saraid said a little more loudly than she'd intended. "We'll most likely be up early, so I suggest we both get some sleep."

"We're lost, aren't we? I don't know what's worse—being taken prisoner by the Day-hans or dying of thirst in the middle of their rotten desert." Talnith picked up Saraid's hand mirror. "Look—are my eyes getting sunken? They say that's what happens when you start to die of thirst. My tongue's gone a funny color, too—" She tilted the mirror, trying to get a better view of it. "And my horse—it'll die an' I'll have to walk the rest o' the way—

Before speaking, Saraid counted to ten. It was barely enough. "We are not dying of thirst, or even short of water, and these horses are desert-bred and can endure a lot more than you think. Now go to sleep." She pointed sternly at the blankets.

Talnith's lower lip quivered, but she lay down and closed her eyes. Only several sighs, deep and dramatically drawn out, betrayed her mood.

Saraid ignored the sighing and settled herself for sleep. The captain had studied navigation by the stars and crossed the Adaiha several times. Surely he could get them safely to this oasis, if it was really there—

Of course it was there. It probably was just over the next dune, or the one after that.

But it wasn't. That night they rode long again, pausing frequently so that Captain Zamas could peer up at the stars. They also rode strung out in a line, with only two guards sticking close by her, and Saraid guessed it was to maximize their chances of finding the oasis. When they camped at dawn, Talnith didn't even complain but rolled up into a miserable ball, her face to the tent wall.

At first it seemed like an improvement. But it was amazing how loud and eloquent Talnith's silences could be. Saraid longed for a full water bag to pour over her head, and then for another to pour over her own. Her eyes felt gritty and dry, and even her teeth seemed to crunch together.

When she awoke that evening, however, she noticed that the water bags carried by the packhorses were alarmingly limp. A little whisper of panic caught in her throat, but she turned it into a cough and straightened her shoulders. What good would her stories be for her and the Lord Protector's children if they were all about rainbows and butterflies? A spice of danger and hardship would only make them more exciting.

That night seemed interminable. Talnith didn't even bother looking at their guards, much less flirt with them. She rode with her head down and whimpered when her horse stumbled, which it did with increasing frequency as the terrain changed from sand to hard-baked earth, littered with stones.

"They're Adaihan horses," Captain Zamas explained shortly when she rode up by him to ask why the animals seemed to find the firmer land more difficult. "Look at their split hooves—they've been bred to walk in sand."

Saraid bent over her mount's withers to look at its feet by the light of the captain's faint lamp. Unfortunately the animal chose that same moment to jerk its head sharply to the side, directly into her face.

"Ow!" Saraid cried, and for a moment the darkness around her grew darker. Pox it, had she bloodied her nose? Her horse snorted as if it, too, were startled, and broke into a trot.

Captain Zamas's mount raised its head and let out an answering cry as it picked up its pace. "They smell something," he said, rising in his stirrups to peer ahead into the night. Off to their right, the other guards' horses whinnied to each other and surged forward.

"Hope I still can," Saraid muttered, feeling her nose. No blood, at least not yet. Maybe it would be all right after all. "What do you think they smell?" she asked, more loudly.

A moment later she had her answer as the eager horses nearly broke into a run down a shallow slope. At its bottom was a cluster of low buildings with oddly peaked roofs and a handful of taller, stick-like things standing out against the stars that she realized were trees.

They'd found the oasis.

# Three

Forget not who and where you are, even at rest and among those you consider friends. Idle confidences, related in an unguarded moment, have an unpleasant way of coming back to haunt one.

—*The Flower of Royalty Blossom'd*

SARAID WAS BARELY ABLE to slide off her horse before it made a final dash to the spring at the heart of the oasis. She might have liked to follow it and drop to her knees at the water's edge and splash the sweet water over her head until the grit and dryness were washed away. But princesses weren't supposed to do things like that, so she waited while Captain Zamas directed the guards to water the horses slowly and carefully so that they didn't make themselves ill, then let him precede her to the largest building.

A man with tousled dark hair had come out its door, rubbing his eyes. Evidently they had roused him from a sound sleep. "How many?" he asked, blocking their entrance.

"Eleven," the captain said. "Myself, my daughter and her maid, and eight of my men. Fifteen horses, too."

Saraid played her part, nodding politely then looking down at her feet as if overcome by shyness when the innkeeper glanced at her. This was her first test...

"My house is small," the man said apologetically. "I have only two rooms for travelers, and one is already taken."

Captain Zamas shrugged. "Then my daughter and her maid will take the room. The rest of us have tents."

"Eleven, plus fifteen horses." The inkeeper looked doubtful.

"We will pay first, of course," Captain Zamas added, judiciously jingling a money pouch at his belt.

He brightened. "In that case, please come in." He opened the door and motioned them inside.

The captain nodded to Saraid. "I must see to the others, Your Hi—" He frowned. "Go in."

"Yes, Father." Saraid passed him with averted eyes and entered the inn with a sinking heart. They'd just met their first Adaihan and already were having a hard time maintaining their masquerade.

The main room was long and narrow, mostly filled with an equally long and narrow table. At one end of it a woman lit lanterns and a brazier of what must be *faarv*, a strange, strong-smelling, oily substance that Saraid had read about that bubbled out of the ground in many places of the Adaiha and was used for fuel. The soft yellow light revealed her—Saraid assumed she was the innkeeper's wife—as small and lithely built, with dark hair and delicate features.

"Please sit. I will bring you drink and food," she said, smiling shyly at Saraid and turning to a door set in the long wall. Like the innkeeper, her Adaihan accent was soft, the esses slurred and the vowels elongated.

"Thank you." Saraid resisted the urge to beg the woman to hurry about the drink part and sat down at one end of the table, which was of a pale, smooth wood that looked as though it had been well scrubbed with sand. It would have been nice to relax against the high-backed chair and close her eyes now that the anxiety of the last few days was over, but somehow it seemed better to stay on guard, at least until she was in her room.

Talnith slunk in, carrying their saddlebags. "This is an inn?" she sniffed, dropping into a chair. "Don't see no kitchen. Do the Day-hans cook their food?"

Saraid looked around the room. The walls appeared to be of baked mud, smoothed and polished and red in the lantern light. Hangings made of dyed string knotted into elaborate patterns decorated the walls, and carved beams supported the high, rounded roof. It was foreign but attractive in a spare, simple way. "Things are done differently in different places, Talnith. I expect the kitchen is elsewhere so that it doesn't get too hot in here during the day."

"A clever observation," said a voice, "which happens to be correct."

Saraid managed not to visibly jump—probably because she was too tired to do so—and turned. A man dressed in Adaihan robes, his hood drawn partly across his face, leaned against the door the innkeeper's wife had vanished through, though far back enough that she couldn't get a good look at him. "It seemed to make sense," she replied.

The man inclined his head, then stepped into the room from the shadowed doorway. He was tall, much taller than the innkeeper. "And yes, the Adaihans do cook," he said to Talnith. "This inn is known for its good food."

Talnith looked at him appraisingly. "How would you be knowin' that, then? Are you the cook here? And what do the Day-hans eat, anyway? Sand and rocks?"

He laughed. "No, I'm not the cook. And they don't eat sand. Adaihan cooking makes use of plants and animals that can survive in the desert. Sheep and goats can live here, so expect to see them on your plates."

His accent was different, crisper, though with a trace of the Adaihan vowels she'd heard in the speech of the innkeeper and his wife. Was he the traveler occupying the other room? Whoever he was, chatting with a stranger hardly seemed proper. "I am sure whatever we're served will be quite edible, Talnith. Thank you," she said to the man, trying to sound pleasantly dismissive.

He turned toward her. Saraid got an uncomfortable feeling that he found her amusing. She'd mentally scolded Captain Zamas for nearly calling her "Your Highness" a few minutes ago, and now here she was, acting like one. She took a deep breath and said, "Pardon me if I was ungracious, but it has been a long ride. Won't you sit with us?"

"My thanks." The man sat in the chair across from her, putting back his hood as he did.

Oh. Whatever she had expected him to look like, it hadn't included bright gold hair worn long and a little shaggy, curling around his ears, and the bluest eyes she'd ever seen. His skin was dark, the weathered tan of someone who had spent years in the bright, hot sun. Not that he seemed very old. Somewhere in his twenties, a few years older than she. His brows and eyelashes were the same gold as his hair, and his smile was open and sunny despite the lines around his eyes and forehead that somehow seemed older than the rest of him.

Next to her Talnith sat up straighter. "So tell me more about this Day-han food," she said, pouting her lips in a way that probably was supposed to be enticing. "How good is it?"

"Very good indeed, though it can vary depending on local customs." Saraid caught a twinkle in the young man's eyes as he looked at them. "I've heard that some Adaihan women down by the Nolorish border make soup by putting a live *hainsh*-fowl and several *hatsuan* peppers in a kettle of water and setting it out in the sun at midday, so that by nightfall it's nicely simmered."

Saraid tried to match his solemn tone. "It gets that hot down there, does it?"

He glanced at her sideways, and the twinkle deepened. "It does. Though if your fowl is large, you're best putting it out earlier, right after you rise in the morning."

"Ah." Saraid nodded. "Of course. I should have guessed as much."

Talnith shot her a suspicious look, then turned back to the young man. "That's just plain *nasty*. What about the feathers and all?"

"Oh, the feathers dissolve into the broth, thanks to the peppers. They give it a distinctive flavor, so it's said," the young man replied. "And the feet stew up nicely, so that they're quite tender. The mothers save them for their teething babies to chew on."

Saraid just managed not to giggle. Talnith looked queasy. "That ain't true...is it?"

The innkeeper's wife came back into the room, carrying a large pitcher and cups of glazed red clay. She paused when she saw the man, then set her tray on the table and bowed, looking anxious. "I'm sorry, sir. I didn't mean to wake you—"

"Water! I thought I'd never see it again!" Talnith nearly lunged across the table for the pitcher. She poured herself a cup and gulped it down, then another.

"Cold palm-mint tea, actually." The man took the pitcher from her, poured a cup, and handed it to Saraid, glancing quizzically at Talnith as he did. "Thirsty, were you?"

"We was *dyin'* of it," Talnith said dramatically, wiping her mouth on her sleeve. "Old Captain Stick-up-the-Pants got us lost when we was hiding from those Day—" She broke off into a grunt as Saraid kicked her foot.

"We were somewhat delayed and running low on water," Saraid said blandly. "Talnith, when you've drunk your fill, could you bring our packs to our room?" Where later on maybe Captain Zamas could fit her with a muzzle. Pox it, she'd *warned* Talnith about watching what she said! The fewer details anyone learned about them, the better. And double poxes on her for ruining the silly conversation they'd been having with him. She hadn't had such fun in weeks.

Talnith glowered but didn't dare argue. "Yes'm," she said, and chugged down a last cup of the tea, then followed the innkeeper's wife through the door.

Saraid glanced at the young man. His liveliness seemed to have left the room with Talnith; now he was pouring himself some tea, staring at the cup with a concentration that the simple act didn't seem to require. Was he thinking about what Talnith had just said?

She leaned back against her chair and closed her eyes as she sipped her tea. Maybe if she drank it slowly, instead of slurping it down the way she really wanted to, the man would think that Talnith had been exaggerating. What had he said it was? Palm-mint? Whatever it was, it was delicious—cool and fresh, like the essence of green. If the Adaihans had created this, they probably did know a thing or two about food.

When she opened her eyes again, she saw that the young man was gazing at her with a thoughtful frown on his face. His eyes really were an amazing shade of blue, weren't they? Or was their intensity just due to the contrast with his tanned skin? Maybe—but they looked as though they were used to looking into far distances and had absorbed the hue of a wide cloudless sky.

Then she realized that they were staring at each other.

"I should go see that Talnith is all right." She scrambled to her feet, suddenly afraid. By Keranieth, she'd been ready to drown in those eyes, and he'd been ready to let her. "We've been riding all night, and she's, um, a little..."

He stood up as well. "I think I know what you mean," he said, making a wry face, and she felt absurdly pleased. And then wanted to slap herself. They were anonymous travelers in a tiny, out-of-the-way oasis in the Adaiha. He'd more than likely be gone by nightfall, and she'd never see him again.

"Good ni—or, er, good morning, I suppose." The inversion of night and day was starting to get to her.

He smiled. "Sleep well and peacefully."

She hurried through the door and ran full tilt into the innkeeper's wife, who listened to her stammered apologies with a bemused expression on her gentle face and showed her to her room. Talnith was already stretched out on a pallet on the floor.

Saraid wasn't at all troubled by her sudden, ostentatious snores as she tiptoed past. The last thing she wanted now was conversation with Talnith.

A bowl of gently steaming water, strewn with fragrant herbs, had been set on a small table. Saraid gratefully washed her face and hands and collapsed onto the bed, not even bothering to unbraid her hair. As she slid into sleep, she could still see in her mind's eye blue eyes gazing into hers.

Late afternoon sunlight was filtering through a small window high in the wall when Saraid woke. Talnith still slept, but a jug of warm water had been left by the door. Saraid quietly stripped off her dusty robes and washed as well as she could. It wasn't a proper bath, but she'd have those for the rest of her life. This was all part of the adventure she'd spin stories around for her children someday, when she'd forgotten what it was like to have sand in her hair and only two changes of underclothes.

A tantalizing smell of grilling meat began to drift into the room as she re-braided her hair. She'd run off that morning before the innkeeper's wife had a chance to bring her anything to eat, hadn't she? Maybe she could get a snack to tide her over till the evening meal. With a quick glance at Talnith's still form, she slipped through the door.

Three doors that she only vaguely remembered from morning confronted her. Behind the one to her right she could hear a low murmur of conversation and guessed it might be the room she'd sat in with the blue-eyed stranger. The memory of him made her feel uncomfortable. Had he left yet, or was he still sitting at the table in there?

To her left, a sliver of light caught her eye. The door there was ajar, and she hurried toward it and out into the open air.

Outbuildings were clustered nearby: a stable almost half again as large as the inn and a cookhouse open on one side to the elements, where she could see the innkeeper's wife basting something cooking on a spit. Tents had been pitched beyond the cookhouse; a few of her guards stood near them, scratching their bristly chins and talking. And beyond the stable —

Saraid stared, then walked as if mesmerized to the small pool of glittering water that reflected the sinking sun, flanked on one side by a scrubby patch of trees and undergrowth and on the other by a tidy kitchen garden. A sharp stab of homesickness went through her at the sight of the greenery.

She knelt down next to the pool and just touched a fingertip to the water's surface. It was cool, much cooler than the air. "A spring," she breathed, and scooped up a handful of water and brought it to her lips. It was sweet and fresh.

"You know, if you go inside and ask, they'll be happy to give you a cup."

Saraid started and made an inarticulate squeak.

"I'm sorry. I don't mean to keep sneaking up on you." The young man with the impossibly blue eyes stood next to her, smiling. He wore a cloak over his Adaihan robes that seemed almost the same color as the desert, tan and shadow-brown commingled. It was thrown back over his shoulders and lined with cloth as blue as his eyes.

"Where did you come from?" She scrambled to her feet, trying not to look completely inelegant in the process. The Book stressed the importance of maintaining one's composure at all times, but especially in front of strangers — at which she had just spectacularly failed.

"Over there." He nodded toward the little copse. "It's my favorite place here. If you sit in a certain spot and half close your eyes, you can pretend you're not in the Adaiha but off in some forest in Choder. Or Thekla."

Had she imagined that he'd slightly emphasized the last word? "H-how interesting," she faltered.

"Not that I've ever been to either of them. But I read a lot." He grinned and looked at her, head tilted to one side. "Did you sleep well? Hursnam's beds are quite comfortable."

"Yes, thank you, er…"

"My name is Kayn. What's yours?"

Saraid hoped she wasn't staring at him too stupidly. The Theklan court was not a formal one, but even so, she wasn't used to strangers introducing themselves and asking her name. She *had* to stop thinking like royalty and stick to their story if she was going to maintain her disguise. "Um, I'm Nin. My father is Zamas, the tall man with the moustache."

Kayn nodded and held out his right hand, palm up. She hesitated, then pressed hers against it. It was the traditional Adaihan greeting, used between strangers when first meeting, or between equals when known to each other. Thank Keranieth she'd read up on Adaihan customs as well as Mauburnian. The feeling of his skin lingered on hers.

"Let's walk around the spring and watch the sun set. Food won't be ready for a while. I just checked." He grinned again. "So where are you traveling to, Nin trel-Zamas?"

Saraid looked at the water as they began to stroll around it. She and the captain had decided that a story based on truth would be easier to remember—and carry off—than a complete fabrication.

"I'm going to my future husband's home. We're to be married in a few weeks," she said, and looked down at her feet, as if overcome with shyness.

He sighed and shook his head regretfully. "Alas. I've only just met you and already must relinquish you to another."

Why, was he *flirting* with her? No one had ever dared flirt with her before. Should she be pleased or offended? A quotation from The Book popped into her mind. "'Words that ring like bells, however sweet and silver in tone—'"

"'—are often as hollow,'" he finished for her. "Well chosen. So you've read *The Flower of Royalty Blossom'd*?"

He knew The Book? "Read it? I practically know it by heart! I love Count Ebroian. He's got an answer for everything. I've been reading him since I was nine, when my mother died."

"The same age as the orphaned king he wrote it for."

She glanced at him. No one had ever picked up on that fact before. "Yes, exactly. That's why I started reading it." She knew she was getting carried away, but how likely was it that a stranger in the middle of the Adaiha should be so familiar with The Book? "The king had Count Ebroian to guide him, even though his parents were dead. So why couldn't the count help me too?"

"'Help oft is where you find it, if only you will look,'" he quoted, looking at her sideways with a hint of a smile.

"That's on page twenty-three in my copy." She couldn't help beaming at him. This was almost as good as having her sister around. Except that Nin wasn't tall and broad-shouldered.

He looked at her a moment longer, then turned away. "I lost my mother at an early age, too." His voice was quiet.

"I am sorry." She reached out and touched his arm, a fleeting touch. Another thing she and this young man shared. "It's—it's not something that ever goes away, is it?"

He shook his head. They were both silent for a few moments. Saraid was surprised to realize that it wasn't an uncomfortable one.

"Is that when you first read The Book?" she finally asked. "When your mother died?"

"I was a little young for it at the time," he said. "So—did your brothers and sisters become devotees of Count Ebroian as well?"

"I have no brothers. Only an older sister. She read it, yes, but she had a lot of other studying to do."

"Studying?"

Mmm, she'd better be careful...but how could he guess who she was from such a silly little detail as that? "To, um, take over our father's business some day."

"Ah." Kayn was silent for a minute. "Is that why she's not here?"

"What?"

"To be at your wedding with you. If your mother's dead,

surely you'd want your sister with you. But if she had to stay behind and take care of your father's business—"

"Yes. Yes, she did. I wish she could have come." No need to hide her wistfulness there. This whole trip would have been so much more bearable if she'd had Nin with her.

"And it's a long journey from Thekla to Mauburni."

"Oh, I know it. I didn't think it would be—" Wait! How had he figured that out? "What makes you think I'm going to Mauburni?"

"Are you?"

Her mind raced. "Not really. We're going to the north of Nolor by way of Mauburni. I'm marrying one of my father's business associates." She hoped he wouldn't ask exactly what business her father was in until she'd been able to come up with one with the captain.

He didn't. Instead he walked in silence beside her, head down and lips pursed, as if in thought. The last rays of the setting sun made his hair shine like molten gold, and she felt an irrational desire to touch it to see if it were hot.

"What about you?" she asked. The Book said that the best defense was often offense. If she asked him questions, he couldn't ask them of her. "Where are you from?"

"Oh, around." He shrugged. "I travel a lot."

"In the Adaiha?"

"Yes. I know it like my father's face." For just a second his mouth tightened, then relaxed into its usual smile.

"Isn't it dangerous?" She shivered. The sun had slipped below the horizon and the Adaiha, purple with shadows now, seemed to loom behind her.

"Not for me. Here, you're cold." He shrugged off his cloak and put it over her shoulders. "Let's go back. Where's your cloak? You should know by now how cool it can get at night in the Adaiha."

"I know. But my cloak—it's not really appropriate..." *Because it makes me look too obviously foreign.* "I've tried to do without it when I can." His cloak was warm, far warmer than hers would have been. But it was also still warm from his body and smelled of fresh air and Adaihan dust and Kayn.

Captain Zamas was in the inn's main room. To her surprise he didn't seem troubled by her arriving with Kayn. Indeed, he looked as pleased as he ever permitted himself to look.

"Very good! I see you've met our new guide." He nodded to Kayn.

"Guide?" She looked from one to the other of them. "What guide?"

"I do not know this part of the Adaiha well enough to feel safe leading us." He reddened slightly, and she realized how difficult it must be for him to admit that. "The innkeeper suggested that we hire a guide and recommended this young man."

"I see." She wasn't sure whether to be pleased or annoyed. Both, just now. "Why didn't you tell me?" she asked Kayn.

One of his brows rose. "You didn't ask."

She opened her mouth to snap at him—then closed it as an astonishing thought came to her. Why, was he *teasing* her?

No one had ever teased her apart from Nin, and even Nin hadn't very often; she was too busy with Father. When she read stories in which people teased each other, she'd been fascinated: properly done, without the intent to hurt but only to laugh together, it sounded like it might be great fun. She'd often wished she had someone to tease her and whom she could tease back.

But she shouldn't be thinking about such things right now: there would be time enough in Mauburni to find such a friend— Lord Murtand, she hoped. And anyway, now she knew how Kayn knew they were going to Mauburni. She'd been worried for a minute that somehow he knew who she was. Only she'd told him they were going to Nolor; how would she explain that when Captain Zamas had surely told him they were bound for Madariv?

Or did it even matter? She didn't have to tell him anything. He was a temporary companion, a hired guide. In another few days, she'd never see him again.

And besides, this meant she'd have someone other than

Talnith and Captain Zamas to talk to. Hadn't she just been missing Nin? After all, he'd read The Book. Maybe the rest of the trip
through the Adaiha wouldn't be so bad. And maybe she could
learn to tease properly from him.

They were up early the next afternoon, getting ready to leave.
Kayn seemed to be everywhere: talking to the soldiers and
Captain Zamas, checking that their water bags were full, even
pausing to smile and wink at Talnith, which made her giggle and
blush and made Saraid wonder if they'd have a moment to talk
about The Book without Talnith trying to divert his attention back
to herself. Hiring him seemed to have put heart into everyone—
with an experienced guide to lead them, they wouldn't have to
worry about getting lost again. And there was just one of him,
which posed no threat.

Just before they were ready to leave she ran down to the
spring for one last look at the water under the setting sun. As she
passed the stable, she saw Kayn near its far door. He was talking
earnestly to a pair of strange men swathed in Adaihan robes,
holding horses already saddled and bridled. Kayn finished what
he was saying, nodded when they bowed, and turned away as
they mounted and rode off at a fast walk. She tried to step back,
but he'd already seen her.

"Come to say good-bye to the spring, Nin trel-Zamas?" he
called out cheerfully. "I always do that, too. The water spirit likes
the attention, they say."

She ignored his question. "Who were those men? They weren't
here earlier today. Where did they come from?"

He came to stand before her, his face calm and unruffled.
"They're friends of mine, passing through. I asked them to deliver
a couple of messages for me."

"To whom?" Maybe she was rude for asking, but something
felt not quite right about the scene she'd witnessed.

This time he smiled slightly. "One to my friends, to let them know I'd be a few days late returning. The other was to a man I owe money to, letting him know I'd be able to repay him, thanks to you." The smile widened. "So shall we get going so I can begin to earn my fee?"

She nodded and turned back to the inn, feeling him fall into step behind her. There wasn't much she could say to that, was there?

But still, something bothered her about the air of surreptitious urgency that had hung over the three men as they spoke, and the unmistakable deference the two riders had shown him. Just who was this Kayn, anyway?

# Four

Knowing one's true friends is never an easy task, even in the best of times. Those who seem to be friends might suddenly become enemies, and just as suddenly friends once more. Even the wisest man can sometimes be mistaken.

*— The Flower of Royalty Blossom'd*

"IT'S PRACTICE. THAT'S WHAT it is," Saraid said to herself the second night out from the oasis. "It's instructive."

The night was clear, with a half-moon low in the sky that kept dipping behind dunes as they rode. Riding next to her, Kayn leaned toward her. "Are you talking to him?" He nodded at her horse.

"Yes, but he hasn't answered yet."

"Well, I flatter myself that I'm probably a better conversationalist than he is, so you could talk to me. Some more."

Despite Captain Zamas's glowers, talking to Kayn was what she'd been doing ever since they left the oasis. Ambassador Rathal had warned her — delicately, of course — that the court at Madariv was a little, well, more sophisticated than Thekla's — at least, that's what she thought he was trying to imply. So if she was going to be able to hold her own in social situations, she should practice her conversational skills now, by talking with Kayn at every opportunity.

Not that their conversation was inappropriate in any way — just continual. It seemed that as soon as they set out, they would somehow end up riding side by side. Kayn had started it by pointing out a short stump of stone emerging from a dune a short distance from the oasis. In the rays of the setting sun even its squat shape cast a long shadow.

"According to the Adaihans, that stone is actually the height of six men. It was a boundary marker between two families' grazing lands, set up by their ancestors hundreds of years ago," he said, gazing soberly at the stone as they passed. "But when the Adaiha became a desert, it was all but swallowed by the sand."

She twisted in her saddle to stare back at it. "Where did all the sand come from? Surely it had to be here all along?"

"I don't know. The stories say it was almost as if it happened by night, when no one could see it — that Count Ebroian called it up from the bottom of the sea and sent it here."

A mental picture of rivers of sand oozing out of the sea and snaking across Mauburni to smother the Adaiha painted itself in her mind. Talnith would love that. "I thought it had just stopped raining. So the Adaihans do think he was a wizard?"

He shrugged. "It seems as reasonable an explanation as any other for such a catastrophic change, don't you think?"

Kayn told her, too, about the few — very few — plants and animals they encountered, and a few she was glad they didn't. Like the scorpion rat, which had scales instead of fur and the female of which had a bite that could be lethal, and the *sahrr* vine of the northern Adaiha that grew longer than twenty man-lengths and could coil around an unsuspecting victim with stealthy, frightening speed. They discussed books — for someone who had spent his life in the Adaiha, he seemed remarkably well-read. And of course they talked about The Book. He seemed amused by how well she knew it, and liked to test her memory on quotations from it. After a few nights, Saraid realized she'd not felt homesick at all; Kayn's conversation kept her from missing Thekla too much.

And then eventually they talked about other things.

Saraid wasn't quite sure how he did it, but something about Kayn—the way he looked at her? his expression?—made her want to confide in him. Not specific details about her life, of course, like being the younger daughter of the king of Thekla. But plenty of other things, big and little: from how she missed Mama and what Nin was like, to hating spiders but liking snakes and going bare-footed whenever she could. There was an almost contradictory freedom in her disguise: Kayn didn't know who she was, so it felt safe to tell him things that she never told anyone else.

And no one had ever listened to her the way he did, seriously and thoughtfully, as if what she said truly mattered to him. She hadn't realized how much she'd needed...well, a friend. She certainly couldn't talk to Talnith or to Captain Zamas the way she could talk to Kayn. Keranieth, she'd barely talked to *Nin* the way she talked to him. And to her joy, he sometimes teased her—gently and humorously—and she was learning how to tease him back.

Once, a few nights after they'd left the oasis, she'd been seized by doubt. "I'm not boring you, am I?" she asked suddenly, after she'd been talking for rather a long time about Thekla. The Book said that too much speech about oneself was one of the worst forms of selfishness, and she didn't want Kayn to think her self-absorbed. "I should not talk so much of myself."

"You are anything but boring me." He smiled, but there was no laughter in his voice. "I *want* you to talk of yourself. I want to know everything about Nin trel-Zamas of Thekla. You are exploring my country. Why can't I explore you?"

She felt sudden heat in her cheeks. "There's not much to know, despite how much I've been talking."

"I disagree. I think there's a great deal to know."

An odd note in his voice made her look up at him. He was

frowning at his horse's ears, an abstracted look on his face. She felt a frisson of fear. He hadn't guessed, had he? Despite all her talking, she'd been very careful not to give away any clues.

"Why would you possibly want to know everything about me?" She strove to make her tone light.

"'In learning about others, we learn about ourselves.'" He raised an eyebrow.

She nodded appreciatively. "Beginning of chapter two."

"Correct. I am learning a great deal about myself, talking to you."

"Good or bad?"

"Let us say…unexpected. It serves me right, too," he added under his breath. "Just when I was sure everything was under control…"

She was about to ask him what he meant, but he still wore that abstracted look. Then he looked up at her and smiled, a real smile this time, and it was as if morning had come early. She could almost feel herself melting under the force of that smile, and felt something else inside her, some emotion she wasn't sure of, burst open like a seedling's leaves unfurling and breaking through the soil.

Almost as interesting were the times when they didn't talk. Silence between them didn't need to be filled. Saraid wasn't sure there was anyone else in her life with whom she could share a comfortable silence, at least not since Mama had died.

He did not volunteer much about himself, though he mentioned that he had also lost his father not long ago. One curious thing she observed was that though he had lived there almost all his life, he never referred to himself as Adaihan: it was always "them," not "we." So where was he from? Choder? Mauburni? Nolor? She never asked; she had no desire to inspire him in turn to ask *her* more questions.

And besides, what did it matter? If they were being more frank and familiar than was perhaps proper, what did that matter, either? At this journey's end, they would part. She would miss him, but she'd soon have her husband to fill his place. Surely Lord Protector Mutrand would be as good a companion as Kayn. Better still, they would be married and be able to share more than just words.

Would the Lord Protector find her attractive and fall in love with her the way she had already determined to do with him? In the heat of the day, when they all rested in their tents, she would lie curled on her side and wonder what it would be like to touch him, to hold him, to let him love her. Varian was an experienced man, approaching forty, and would know how to initiate her into those pleasures of marriage that the ladies at court had told her about. She just hoped he wouldn't find her too young and naïve for his tastes. It might have been nice if he were a little younger. More like Kayn, perhaps—

No. He would be perfect just the way he was. She was sure of it.

The hardest part of each night's journey was just before dawn, when they were all tired and the first ghostly light of the coming sun would sometimes create shadows that fooled the eye and made riding difficult. At those times, Saraid had noticed, conversation with Kayn would either fade away entirely or spark up to unexpected warmth. It was then that the few words that she regretted usually came out.

This morning seemed as if it would be a silent one. Kayn rode beside her with his shoulders slightly hunched, and she got the feeling that he was deep in thought, turned in on himself. So when he suddenly spoke, she was startled.

"So you're not the only one leaving Thekla to get married," he said. "I hear one of your princesses is being sent to marry in Mauburni, just as you are."

Saraid drew in her breath. "Oh, no," she corrected. "I'm going to Nolor, not Mauburni."

"Ah, yes — Nolor. So is Thekla happy about this marriage? It's a long way to send a young girl."

"She's not that young." Saraid frowned. He made her sound like a child. "Eighteen is a perfectly reasonable age at which to marry. And Thekla couldn't be happier. It's...it's been bad there, since trade with Mauburni nearly dried up. The silk growers suffered worst of all — a lot of trees were lost because the farmers couldn't afford to maintain them. The same thing with the flower growers: they had to turn their fields to grain to survive because there was no market for their perfumes and oils, and then the grain farmers complained because there was too much grain on the market. I know that doesn't sound like much of a problem — more than enough grain for everyone. But entire lineages of silkworms and flowers were nearly lost because the growers couldn't afford to keep them flourishing, and the growers — it sounds odd to outsiders, I expect, but their silkworms and their flowers are part of their families. They've tended them for generations, so it's almost a — a sacred trust."

He nodded. "I've read about your Theklan silk growers. They're somewhere between farmers and priests."

"Not quite priests...well, maybe a bit. More like guardians of what makes us Theklan. So if they'll be able to restore their crops again because trade with Mauburni is coming back — it means everything to us. I saw some of them setting out *lumox* saplings as I left — and they were singing. There hasn't been much singing in Thekla over the last years."

"You know a great deal about it." He watched her shrewdly.

"My father is a trader, remember? Of course I know a great deal about it." She was proud of the way the words slipped glibly from her tongue. "And yes, it's important to me. Better trade is good for my father's business. But it's good for a great many people beyond my father. I...care about them, too — the growers and their families, and the weavers, and everyone. Thekla *needs* this marriage. So yes, we're all very happy that Princess Saraid is going to Mauburni."

On his face was an expression she couldn't quite decipher. "Don't you feel sorry for her, marrying a stranger? Marrying *him*?" His lips curled as if in disgust.

"No, I don't. Doesn't The Book say, 'Everyone—man and woman, high and low—has a duty somewhere, whether they are born to it or choose it of their own free wills'? I should think she feels honored and privileged to be the instrument of helping heal her country, even if it means marrying a stranger. It's what princesses have to do, sometimes, isn't it?" She paused and regarded him through narrowed eyes. "And what do you mean, calling her bridegroom 'him' in that way? What do you know about him?"

"More than you probably want to know."

"What? Tell me!"

"Why do you care?"

Saraid caught herself. It wouldn't do to sound too eager, but if he'd heard something about Lord Varian, she wanted to know. "I'm...interested, that's all. Most Theklans are. What do you know about him?"

He shrugged, his expression closed, and she knew it would be worthless to try to get him to say more. Hmm, interesting. She should have tried to talk to some of the lesser members of the Mauburnian delegation about the Lord Protector, but The Book thought that too much attention paid to gossip with one's inferiors was harmful and unworthy of a perfect ruler. Still, a *little* bit might have been worthwhile.

"What about you?" he said after a long silence. "What do you know about your husband-to-be? Have you met him before?"

Saraid pretended to yawn, as if the question was unremarkable. "No, I've never met him."

"You mean he didn't come to woo you before asking for your hand?"

"It was not...possible under the circumstances."

"The pressures of business, I assume."

There was a slightly odd note in his voice; in fact, this whole conversation was odd. And unsettling. "Yes. But we've written to each other several times, and I have his miniature."

"If he's your father's associate, he must be much older than you."

"Somewhat," she agreed cautiously.

"What's he like? Do you like him?"

Perhaps at another time or place when she wasn't so tired, she could think of a cleverly evasive answer. But not right now. "I...don't know."

"But you've corresponded with him," Kayn persisted.

Saraid remembered the letters tucked in the back of The Book in her saddlebag. "Of course. He seems to be everything that he ought to be—"

"Assuming he wrote them."

She frowned. "Who else could have? Why should he try to be something he isn't to me?"

"I don't know. What do you think?"

If she hadn't been riding a horse, she would have crossed her arms on her chest and tapped her foot. "I think that this is my future husband we're talking about. Yes, I like him from his letters. I'm sure that we shall come to care for each other very quickly."

"A man you'll just have met?" In the growing light she could see him raise his eyebrows skeptically.

"Yes, a man I've just met. Why not?" She realized that her voice had risen, and lowered it before continuing. "What do you think I should do? I'm promised to him, and that's that. So if I must marry him, I might as well do my best to love him."

His voice was pitched almost too low to hear, but every word sounded loud as a mourning bell in her head. "What if you don't fall in love with him? What if he doesn't deserve your love?"

"I don't know," she whispered. Pox it, she *wouldn't* cry. "I'm trying not to think about that."

He suddenly pulled his horse closer, so close that his leg pressed against hers. "I'm sorry. That wasn't fair. You're a courageous woman, Nin."

She bowed her head. No, she wasn't. If he could see inside her right now, he wouldn't think that at all.

But he was still speaking. "It's just...I couldn't stop myself. Your future husband..." He took a deep breath. "I envy him."

Saraid's breath caught and she looked up at him quickly. But he'd already spurred his horse ahead to ride alongside Captain Zamas, leaving her to wonder exactly what he meant—and how she should feel about it.

That evening as they prepared to set out, Kayn took her aside. "It will be cold tonight. Can't you feel it?" He nodded toward the sunset.

Actually, every night had been chilly. But she was almost used to it by now. "It won't kill me."

"I know it won't." He slipped his cloak off and put it over her shoulders, inside out so that the blue fabric was showing, and fastened it at her throat. "Because you'll be wearing this."

"Why isn't mine good enough?" Saraid protested. She tried to ignore how much she liked the feel of his cloak around her again even though it was too large and hampered her movements. "What will you wear?"

"I have my winter robes on. And I'm more used to the cold than you are. Humor me. Please?"

He smiled down at her as he brushed a stray wisp of hair back from her face. His fingertips just skimmed the sensitive edge of her ear and her heart began to beat faster.

"I'm just trying to keep you safe and sound for your husband," he continued. "It's what I'm being paid for. In another two or three nights we'll be at the Harnu oasis. Your father should be able to guide you from there to the border, and I'll be on my way."

Her heart seemed to skid to a halt. Only two more nights? She forced lightness into her voice. "So you can go home and repay your debts."

"Exactly." He bent to pick up her saddlebags.

She watched him buckle them onto her horse's saddle and check the girth. Was that all this trip meant to him? All *she* meant to him? Just another job, to be forgotten as soon as money had exchanged hands?

But what else could it be? In a few days they would never see each other again, and a few more days after that she would meet her new husband. Forgetting Kayn's eyes, his voice, the way her breath quickened when he smiled at her — forgetting *him* — was far safer.

As they rode through the deepening night, they were all quiet. Talnith had switched favorites twice since they'd left the oasis and, to judge by her shifty glances, was about to once again. Saraid wondered if she was trying to circulate through all of the guards before they arrived in Mauburni so that she could concentrate all her powers of fascination on the one she liked best for the homeward trip.

But tonight even Kayn seemed inattentive. Distracted, even. Or was she just seeing her own mood reflected in him? How could he make such fuss about her being warm enough one minute, and the next cheerfully talk about their imminent farewell as if it meant nothing to him?

Or was she reading too much into everything he said and did, because her feelings for him were more than they should be?

She glanced briefly at him. It was time to look at the matter analytically, the way Count Ebroian would have. She'd lived a sheltered life and never had much to do with the young men at court. There was never any point for her to get to know them, because she was fated to marry away from Thekla. So maybe it was inevitable she'd fall in love — er, into an infatuation — with the first presentable young man she spent more than a few minutes' conversation about the weather with. Especially one as good-looking as Kayn.

But it wasn't just his searingly blue eyes and easy smile and that shining gold hair she was dying to touch, the opposite in almost every way to the appearance of her husband-to-be. Would she have begun to get flutters in her stomach over Kayn if he hadn't read The Book as much as she had (or almost) and been able to discuss it intelligently with her? If he hadn't had that quick yet gentle wit that could tease without hurting? If he hadn't had that sunny, lighthearted temperament? Maybe it would have been better if he'd been surly and uncommunicative. Then she could have gone to her marriage without having someone to compare her husband to.

On the other hand, she could be pleased with how she'd handled the situation. At least she hadn't openly made a fool of herself over him—

"This will do." Kayn's voice broke into her thoughts. "Let's stop here."

They generally stopped shortly before midnight, in order to rest their horses and have a brief meal. Kayn usually chose sheltered hollows for their pauses, hopefully safe from view, and tonight was no exception: they were in the trough between two dunes, like a narrow valley. She followed him to the end of it and halted. Behind her she heard the guardsmen swinging off their horses and loosening the girths on their saddles, just as they always did at their rest times.

Saraid stretched and yawned, waiting for Kayn to dismount first as he usually did and help her down. She'd secretly come to look forward to these brief instants of contact, though she was loath to admit it even to herself.

But he hadn't moved. He had frozen in place and was staring at something ahead of them. "Stay still," he murmured. "Don't move."

"What is it?" She glanced up and saw why Kayn had frozen.

A group of horsemen was standing at the end of the little valley nearest to them, where just seconds before had been nothing. They were cloaked and masked in black; contrasting with all that darkness was the cold starlit gleam of their drawn swords.

Saraid gasped. "Kayn!"

"Whatever happens, stay on your horse. Please." His voice was low and urgent.

More masked horsemen appeared from around the dune, more than double their number. Behind her, Talnith screamed.

An instant later, chaos erupted as the riders swept toward them, bellowing a weird, ululating cry. Saraid heard it through an odd calm that descended on her, making everything around her seem slow and distant, as if it were happening to someone else and she was watching it from afar. They were being attacked by a force that far outnumbered theirs. Fighting them off was impossible. Only escape remained.

"Kayn!" she tried to shout over the tumult. "This way!"

With fingers that had grown clumsy and numb she tugged her mount's head around and tried to turn and flee. The poor creature tossed its head and rolled its eyes, as did most of the other horses, snorting and whinnying. The attackers' eerie wails had thoroughly spooked them.

But even if she'd been able to control her horse, more riders galloped toward them from the other end of the hollow. They were trapped.

Captain Zamas shouted a command. The guardsmen were already lunging for their weapons, but they were mostly on foot and didn't have time to re-tighten their saddle girths — and fighting off mounted men from on foot was nearly impossible.

Just before someone caught at her bridle and yanked her around again, Saraid noticed from within her bubble of calm a curious thing: the raiders were not killing or even wounding the guards. Instead, they were using the flats of their blades like clubs to stun and disable them.

Then masked riders surrounded her. They crowded close and forced her trembling horse to go forward. Her calm shattered. "No!" She tried to turn her horse's head aside.

One of the riders nearest her pulled out a knife. She gasped, but he only leaned over and cut away her reins. Another rider on her other side knotted a lead onto her horse's halter, and they hurried at a canter into the dunes. Saraid hung on to her horse's mane to keep from falling.

What had happened to Kayn and to the rest of them? She tried to turn and look back, but there were too many of the masked riders behind her to see what was happening. Wasn't there some way she could escape these brigands? Surreptitiously sliding her feet out of her stirrups, she took a deep breath and tried to fall sideways off her horse. If she hit the ground just right, she could roll and then make a run for it—

But the rider who'd cut her reins was too fast for her. "Heya! Slow!" he called as he grabbed a handful of her cloak and pulled her back. "Please don't do that, Your Highness," he said to her, more quietly. "The only thing that will get you is trampled."

Your Highness? Then they knew who she was? "Let me go, p-pox you!" she stammered and tried to yank her cloak out of his grasp. Kayn's cloak. Dear blessed Keranieth, was he all right? She'd lost sight of him when the riders surrounded her. "Who are you? What do you want?"

"Please don't worry. You're safe."

"Safe!" She swung angrily at him, but Kayn's cloak got in the way again. The rider sighed.

"I would respectfully request that you don't try to resist us," he said. "I'm under strict orders to make sure that you're safe and comfortable, in that order. If, for your own safety, I must restrain you, I won't hesitate to do so."

They would tie her up, like—like a common prisoner? Saraid gulped. That's exactly what she was, wasn't she? "Under orders? So there's someone else in charge of this—this insult? Where is he? I demand to see him at once."

"We'll see him as soon as we can, Your Highness, but it's going to take some riding."

"What about my people? What are you doing with them? If you hurt any of them—" That sounded silly, as she was in no position to make threats right now.

But the man didn't seem to notice that. "Your companions will not be harmed if we can help it. Please don't worry about them."

"One of them is an Adaihan. Will you treat him the same as my people?"

"I give you my word no one will be harmed."

"Your word," she repeated sarcastically. "How nice. I feel *so* much better."

The man didn't reply but urged his horse forward again so that Saraid was forced to concentrate on hanging on. They rode in silence for another few minutes, until ahead someone shouted. They were joined by yet more riders, also masked, and came to a halt.

"Is everyone well? How did Milord Cadel fare?" one of them called.

"All's well and according to plan," the man who'd ridden beside Saraid replied. "It may take some time. Their horses panicked."

"Besides, nothing can harm Lord Cadel," someone else added from behind her. A murmur of agreement greeted his comment.

For the moment, no one was paying much attention to her. Saraid sneaked her hand up to her throat to unfasten Kayn's cloak. If she were fast enough, she could slip out from underneath it and run before they could turn their horses. Leaving it behind would be a wrench, but it would give her a chance to shout for Kayn and attract the attention of Captain Zamas and his men.

To her surprise and fierce glee, she made it off her horse and managed three paces. But she'd forgotten that these Adaihans were famed as horsemen. Three of them wheeled around in what should have been an impossible amount of time and space and had boxed her in before she could move any farther. A second later the man who'd ridden with her was beside her.

"I'm sorry, Your Highness, but you leave me no choice," he said grimly and reached for her hands. She wrenched away from him but he was much larger than she, not to mention trained as a warrior. He pinned her arms to her sides and nodded to another Adaihan who dismounted and swiftly tied her wrists together in front of her. Then, to her horror, he produced a scarf and tied it over her eyes.

"No!" She jerked her head and tried to shake it off. Her sudden blindness had made her aware of how vulnerable she was. And how afraid.

He didn't answer. Someone put something over her shoulders and fastened it under her chin. Kayn's cloak. If only she could pull it more tightly around her and bury her face in it, to breathe in his scent. "Now what?" She hated the way her voice trembled.

"We wait a few moments, and then we will be off."

"To go where?"

Again he didn't reply, but she felt him bring a horse close to her. "It's hard to stand while blindfolded and bound. You might be more comfortable leaning against Silbe here while we wait. He won't move. Do you wish a drink of water?"

"Yes," she whispered. A moment later, a waterskin touched her lips and she realized it was her own. That nearly did her in. She'd been kidnapped and tied, but her captors were being almost too considerate.

It was hard to judge how long they waited there. The horses around her shifted and snorted or stomped one foot occasionally; their riders now and again exchanged brief, muttered comments but for the most part remained silent. Saraid leaned against the horse, which bore her weight patiently. Its warmth and solidity were comforting.

How had this happened? Had the innkeeper at the oasis figured out who she was and sent someone after them? That hardly seemed plausible; he and his wife had been quiet, gentle people. But as The Book frequently noted, appearances were just that—an outward guise. They could have been criminal masterminds, for all she knew.

"Captain Zamas won't let you get away with this, you know," she said, trying to sound confident. If she couldn't escape, maybe she could talk her way out of this. The Book said that everything was negotiable.

"Your guard is in our custody by now," her captor replied. "You were eleven. We were thrice that number."

"This is outrageous! If you know who I am, then you know that you'll have the combined armies of Thekla and Mauburni coming to hunt you down. You won't even have a chance to ask for a ransom."

"Please, I'm only carrying out my commander's orders. Will you wait and discuss these matters with him?"

"If you let me go now, you'll save yourself a world of trouble."

"I don't think so, Your Highness." His tone was flat and final.

She huddled in silence under Kayn's cloak. What was happening to the others? Was Talnith all right? Were they treating her as politely as they were her? And Kayn—would they let him go since he wasn't Theklan and probably couldn't afford a ransom? Not that it mattered—she'd make sure that he was freed when she was. Would she ever see him again?

A dull thunder of hoofbeats told her that another group of riders approached. No words were exchanged, at least that she could hear, but someone touched her arm. "It's time to go, Your Highness," said her captor. "You'll ride on Silbe here."

"I want to ride my own horse, please."

"I'm afraid that's not possible. Our orders are that you remain blindfolded, and you can't ride alone. We're only concerned for your safety. Please trust me."

"Do I have a choice?" she couldn't help asking.

No one replied. Someone steadied her by the elbow as Silbe was led away, and she heard a swish of robes as someone mounted him. Then hands tightened on her waist and lifted her up as another set of hands grabbed her from behind under her arms and pulled. It was dizzying and disorienting, but before she could even gasp she was seated sideways on a horse's back, in front of a rider who put one arm around her and held her snugly against him. She squirmed in protest, but he would not loosen his hold.

"Are you all right, Your Highness?"

It was her old "friend" who'd been doing all the talking, now somewhere to her left. So she wasn't riding with him. Who was she with, then? "What do you think?"

The rider who held her remained silent, but she felt him shake slightly and realized he was chuckling to himself. "It's not funny!" she snapped.

The shaking stopped.

Surprisingly, the unaccustomed sensation of riding sideways on a horse while blindfolded was not as bad as she'd feared. Her rider's hold on her was secure, and Silbe's gait was steady and strong. These Adaihan horses were marvelous animals. It would have been nicer to find that out in some other way than this, however.

"How long must we ride?" she asked.

"Till well into morning." The speaker was still close to her left. "Try to rest, if you can."

As if she could take a nap while bound and blindfolded and being carried off to who knew where. She ran through The Book in her mind, looking for a suitable retort, but Count Ebroian had somehow never addressed what to do in a situation like this. The only bit that did come to mind was hardly comforting just now: *When circumstances are beyond your control, wait and watch until they aren't.*

# Five

It is impossible to expect the unexpected. But working to achieve flexibility of mind can save you from being too disconcerted when the unexpected occurs, as it inevitably will.

—*The Flower of Royalty Blossom'd*

THEY RODE UNTIL THE sun was high in the sky. Its heat was oppressive on her cheek and hair until her rider reached up and pulled the hood of Kayn's cloak over her head. But the day's warmth was in every breath she took, making her dull and sleepy despite her fear. She was so tired…

Only after she'd heard it for a while did a new sound register: voices—many of them.

"Heya! We thought you'd be back home sooner, snails!" one called out nearby. "Did you come by way of Nolor?"

"Yes, and Choder, too. So don't call us slow!" someone behind Saraid retorted cheerfully.

Back home? "…R'we there?" she mumbled.

"Is everyone well?" someone else shouted—a woman's voice this time.

"Dadai! Up, up! I ride!" a small child piped.

Women and children? At a brigands' camp? Saraid lifted her head—blessed Keranieth, she'd fallen asleep, despite all her efforts not to. Whoever her rider was, he'd patiently held her cradled against him, her head nestled into the hollow of his shoulder and neck so that she wouldn't be jarred awake. She sat bolt upright in an agony of embarrassment.

"Look, it's her!" someone nearby said in a loud whisper.

A sibilant murmur arose, and she caught the word *princess* several times. They'd been expecting her? She bowed her head to withdraw under the hood of Kayn's cloak, but the rider pulled it back, exposing her to the crowd's view.

"What are you doing?" she demanded indignantly.

"Welcome, Princess!" a voice cried. The others took it up.

Around her she sensed the other riders halting and dismounting. But her rider walked on, away from the babble of voices and shouts of greeting. He rode for a few minutes, turning five or six times as if negotiating streets or passageways, then stopped and easily lifted her down off the horse.

Hands caught her as her toes touched the ground. She wanted to jerk away from them but instead swayed and nearly fell over, only vaguely hearing the retreating dull thud of hooves.

"Careful, Your Highness," a voice said—her captor again. He steadied her by the shoulders. "You're probably a little stiff just now."

Stiff didn't even begin to describe it. She tried to stretch, but her hands were still bound in front of her.

"Can't she be released?" said a woman's disapproving voice. "The poor child must be thoroughly miserable." Someone fumbled with her hands, untying the cord that bound them, then rubbed her wrists gently. "There, I'm sure they're quite numb." There was kindness under the woman's scolding tone. "I've got some warm water to soak them in, and we'll see that you have a bath later on. Seinu, take that blindfold off her at once!"

"Yes, ma'am!" Someone moved behind her and quickly untied the scarf.

The morning sun dazzled her long-covered eyes, so that for several seconds she could only squint and blink back tears. Then gradually she was able to focus on the figures near her.

The woman was tall, taller than she, and very slender. She had gray hair drawn back in a loose knot, a slightly hawk-like nose, and narrow pale blue eyes that seemed to see everything, but the lines of her thin face were not hard ones. She wore Adaihan robes of pale gray. "Now then," she said. "I'm sure that must feel better. Let's get you inside out of this sun. Are you hungry?"

They'd never had a chance to eat their midnight lunch last night before the attack, but Saraid was loath to admit that she was starving. "No." The word came out in a croak. Her throat felt dry and scratchy.

The woman snorted. "Didn't you heedless *vehdrooni* think about feeding her at all? I'll be having a word with Cadel about that."

The man she'd called Seinu—her captor—had pulled off his mask. He had tired brown eyes and a shadow of beard and a pleasantly ordinary face—a far cry from the ugly, leering bandit Saraid had half expected.

"I'm sorry, Lady Perrin." He twisted his mask in his hands. Was he the cool, collected figure who'd managed her capture? This Lady Perrin must be formidable indeed. "We were, uh, a little distracted."

"You were downright addled, if you ask me. Now go home so your poor wife doesn't worry about you. Come, dear." She put an arm around Saraid's shoulders and started to lead her toward one of the several tent-like structures nearby, all made of sand-colored canvas.

"Lady Perrin," Seinu called anxiously. "Lord Cadel requests that Her Highness be brought to him as soon as possible."

The woman paused. "She will, Seinu. As soon as she's had a chance to eat and drink and rest and wash and—by the gods, man, did you even think to stop and let her relieve herself?" She looked at Saraid.

"I couldn't," Saraid replied in a small voice. It had been horribly embarrassing.

Lady Perrin rolled her eyes skyward.

"You—go." She dismissed Seinu with a wave of her hand. He obeyed with alacrity. "And you, come on."

She propelled Saraid to a small tent next to the larger one, waited while she used the privy, and then steered her toward the larger structure. As she did, Saraid looked around her. They appeared to be in a village made of tents, beyond which an area of scrubby green vegetation was visible: an oasis then, like the one where they'd met Kayn.

Kayn. Was there any chance he was there? Would they let her see him? She swallowed and turned to Lady Perrin. Maybe she would know. "Excuse me...my companions—were they brought here, too?"

Lady Perrin shook her head. "No. This is a temporary camp because the water here is seasonal. We're preparing to leave it until spring, when the winter rains near the coast have replenished its source, wherever that is. You were brought here because Cadel is here, but your companions were taken elsewhere, as far as I know. They've probably been sent to Callest, which is where we'll be going eventually."

She spoke briskly, with no trace of an Adaihan accent. It reminded Saraid of someone else she'd met recently, back at home. Ambassador Rathal, from Mauburni? Could this Perrin be Mauburnian? But if so, what could she possibly be doing here in an Adaihan camp? "You're not Adaihan, are you?" she observed aloud.

"Not originally, no." Perrin nodded toward the tent. "This will be your home while we're here. I hope you'll be comfortable."

"I hope I won't be here long enough for it to matter," Saraid said under her breath.

Perrin inclined her head but did not reply as she held the door flap open. Saraid ducked inside.

The tent was small, but someone had obviously tried to make

it comfortable and attractive. There was a small table in its center, flanked by cushioned wooden folding chairs, and a quilt-covered bed tucked behind a curtain to give it some privacy from the rest of the space. Pale blue Nolorish carpets were scattered on the canvas floor, and there was even a small dressing table and mirror near the foot of the bed. Tears came to Saraid's eyes when she saw her saddlebags and the one larger bag she'd been allowed by Captain Zamas. Somehow she had thought they were gone forever. She started toward them, but Perrin had already pulled out one of the chairs.

"Why don't you sit, child, and let me wash your face and bring you some food. You'll feel better," she said kindly.

It was on the tip of her tongue to say that brooding over her possessions would do a better job of consoling her, but those had sounded more like commands than suggestions. This Perrin did not seem to be someone easily gainsaid.

So Saraid sat down and let the older woman dip a washcloth in a bowl of warm water and wash the dust and grime from her face and neck. Her touch was gentle but businesslike. Then she brought a plate of grilled flatbread brushed with oil and seasoned with salt and something that tasted like rosemary, and some kind of tart yellow fruit cut in slices that was luscious but drippy, and little balls of goat's milk cheese rolled in chopped, toasted nuts. Saraid wasn't sure if it tasted like the best meal she'd ever had because she was so hungry or because it really was. She washed it down with an entire pitcher of cold palm-mint tea and finally sat back in her chair, feeling almost normal.

Except for the fact that she'd been kidnapped by Adaihan brigands.

While she ate, Perrin bustled around the tent. She showed Saraid how to open smaller flaps in the wall to let more air in, and fluffed cushions that were already quite fluffed. A faint air of unease underlay her busy-ness, as if she weren't quite sure what to do or say.

"Well," she said when Saraid had finished eating and washed

the sticky fruit juice from her hands and chin. "Let's get you ready, shall we?"

"Ready for what?" Saraid regarded her through narrowed eyes. Oh, yes, her fight was definitely coming back. As pleasant as this Perrin seemed, Saraid was not about to let her roll over her the way she had Seinu.

"Ready for you to see Cadel. He may be a thoughtless *vehdron* sometimes, but that doesn't mean —"

"No." Saraid planted herself more firmly in her chair and crossed her arms.

"Your Highness." Perrin sighed. "I'm not very happy about this…this situation, either. I think bringing you here was a mistake we may all regret, and probably sooner than later. But Cadel is my master. I've known him since he was born, and if he thinks this is the right thing to have done, then I can't dispute him. Right now he wants to speak with you, and I think you should go and listen to him. I'm sure you have questions, and he's the one to answer them."

"Then why can't he come to me?"

Perrin frowned. "These are his lands. You may be a princess in your country, but when he summons you, it is expected that you will go to him." She glanced toward her bags. "Would you like to change your clothes first?"

"No."

Perrin sighed once more, and Saraid got the impression that she was humoring her but not very willingly. "Very well. Can we at least comb your hair and make it tidy? Or would you rather go roll in the sand and make yourself quite dreadful again so he'll feel guilty for doing this to you?"

Saraid stared at her haughtily, but she couldn't help feeling ashamed and a little silly. Perrin might as well have called her a spoiled brat and been done with it.

What would Count Ebroian have done in this situation? Probably not have continued to antagonize Perrin. It was clear that she held a position of respect here — Seinu had called her

70

Lady Perrin—and could become a valuable ally. And beyond that, she just didn't want anyone to think of her as a self-absorbed little girl.

"I'm sorry. That was childish. But it's... I'm..." She trailed into silence and stared down at her clenched hands.

"You're frightened and confused, not to mention exhausted." Perrin knelt by her chair and looked at her earnestly. "All the more reason, then, to appear strong and dignified."

"You make it sound so easy," Saraid muttered.

"Notice that I said 'appear.' Pretending it will work just as well, you know."

Saraid looked at her in surprise. Perrin smiled. "Believe me, it works. So let's make you presentable, shall we? It will help you pretend."

Saraid got her brush and comb from the saddlebag and let Perrin brush out her hair, leaving it down as Perrin suggested instead of coiled into its usual braid. But she still refused to change—all her other clothes, apart from the good ones she'd been saving to wear on her arrival in Madariv, were dirty, and changing from one dusty, sweat-stained set of robes to another hardly seemed worthwhile. Perrin agreed and promised to have them washed for her.

Nor would Saraid leave off Kayn's cloak. "It belongs to...to someone I care about a great deal." She pulled it close. "I'd rather not take it off."

Perrin gave her an odd look and opened her mouth, then closed it again. Saraid thought she knew why. The sun was just past its zenith and cloaks hardly seemed necessary in the midday heat, but surely it was her choice to wear one. It made her feel better to have this reminder of Kayn so near.

She followed Perrin back out into the sun and looked about her curiously. They passed tents laid out in neat rows like houses in a town, though it was clear from gaps between them that there had been more. Many had awnings set before them where people—again, women and children as well as men—were occupied in various activities. They all watched her pass in silence, bowing their heads respectfully if she looked at them. It made her feel oddly confused. If she was a kidnap victim, why were they being this way? Shouldn't they be shouting and jeering and gloating at their prize?

"Is it far?" she asked Perrin.

"No. Cadel likes to be in the center of the camp, in case anyone needs him. Right there. The large tent with the smaller awning in front of it—heya, Meyric!" She waved.

A man sat at a table covered with books and ledgers and stacks of paper held down with stones under an open-sided tent in front of the larger one. Next to him was a girl. The man was shorter than Perrin and slightly rotund, with curly gray hair and green eyes. The girl looked about her own age and bore enough of a resemblance to the man that Saraid was sure they were related.

"Perrin!" The man jumped up and hurried around the table to meet them. "Thank the gods you've finally come," he said under his breath. "He's been pacing like a lion in there. I thought he might explode, he's so anxious to see her."

"This is Meyric, Lord Cadel's secretary," Perrin said to Saraid.

Meyric bowed low to Saraid. "Your Highness. Welcome. May I present my granddaughter Belet?"

The girl rose and curtsied, but her eyes never left Saraid's face. She was small and very pretty and made Saraid feel enormous and awkward in contrast. "How interesting to meet you, Your Highness," she said in a high, clear voice.

Perrin raised an eyebrow and turned back to Meyric. "Cadel should have known better than to expect her sooner," she said. "She needed a little while to recover."

Meyric shook his head. "I tried to tell him that, but he was in no mood to listen."

He, too, looked at Saraid's cloak, and she saw the same peculiar expression cross his face. He glanced at Perrin, who replied with a shrug. What did they find so odd about her unwillingness to be parted from her cloak? She tugged it closer and looked at him defiantly.

"Well..." For a moment Meyric seemed at a loss for words. Then he shrugged and said, "Right through here, Your Highness. I'll announce you."

Would she have to face the man who'd engineered her kidnapping, this about-to-explode Cadel, alone? She turned back to Perrin. "Aren't you coming with me?"

"I'll go," Belet volunteered.

"I don't think that's necessary, Belet. Go on in, child, and don't worry, he's not going to bite you." Perrin sat down in Meyric's chair and folded her hands on her lap.

Saraid bit her lip. Too bad that Perrin had been so quick to stop Belet; at least she would not have to walk alone into the tent. She turned to Meyric who was standing at the entrance of the larger tent. He pulled aside one of the door flaps and announced, "My lord, Her Highness the Princess Saraid is here."

There was no answer but a rustle of papers.

Meyric gestured with his head. "Go in," he mouthed at her.

She took a deep breath and stepped inside.

The interior of the tent was dim after the noontime sun, and it took a minute for her eyes to adjust again. But someone—a tall someone in crisp, cream-colored Adaihan robes—had risen from a paper-laden table toward the back of the tent and walked toward her, grinning.

Saraid blinked at him. She knew that grin, didn't she? Or was she really seeing it? Were her eyes still dazzled by the sun?

"Your hair," the someone said. "I've never seen it down like that. It's beautiful, like a river rippling over your shoulders. Why did you always keep it braided away?"

No, there was nothing wrong with her eyes. But there was with her feet. They seemed to have taken root in the geometric Nolorish carpet beneath them, when all she wanted to do was turn and flee.

The large someone now stood very close to her, his blue eyes bright under his gold brows. He'd obviously found time to wash and shave, and his robes had an edge of embroidery that just matched his eyes.

"No," she whispered.

"Welcome, uh...Nin," he said.

The dreaded Lord Cadel, kidnapper of princesses, was her Kayn.

# Six

The hardest lessons for most men to learn are those of keeping one's eyes open and unblinkered by assumption and prejudice, and one's mouth from spouting the same. Learn these, and you will have mastered the most important lessons a monarch can learn.

*—The Flower of Royalty Blossom'd*

"NO," SHE SAID AGAIN. It couldn't be. There was a coincidental resemblance between them...or they were cousins, or—

"Or can I call you Saraid now? I have all along in my mind. Sometimes it was hard to remember not to out loud. I'm glad we can both drop the pretence and use our proper names." He reached up to tuck a loose strand of hair behind her ear and let his fingertips linger near her cheek. "I like your real name. It suits you better than Nin—"

She jerked her head away from his hand. "Stop smiling! You lied to me!"

"About what?" His smile slipped.

"About all of it! Who you were and what you were doing—"

"I didn't lie. I just didn't tell you all of the truth. There's a big difference. Count Ebroian recommends it as a technique in The Book. And if you recall, you were less than truthful about your identity as well."

Saraid clenched her fists and ignored the twinge his last sentence gave her. "Leave The Book out of it. I was worried sick about you when we were attacked. About you and Talnith and Captain Zamas and the guards—I was afraid they'd hurt you—"

The amusement in his eyes faded. "I'm sorry. I didn't mean for you to worry about me. And everyone is fine. Zamas may be a bit of a fool but he knows when it's smarter to surrender and save his men, and Talnith had stopped blubbering and was already making eyes at my riders by the time they'd started on their way—"

Her breathing had become shallow and short, and heat seemed to be moving through her in waves. "You tricked—no, you betrayed us! You got us to trust you...you got *me* to trust you—" She'd been right to feel uneasy back at the oasis when she saw him talking to those men. He'd arranged the whole scheme right there under their noses.

He was all seriousness now. "No one says you have to stop trusting me. I swear on my mother's soul that I will never, ever hurt you. Your safety and happiness are the most important things in the world to me." His hand strayed up to her cheek again.

She slapped it away. "So what do you call laying a trap for me and then kidnapping me? I *trusted* you..." The thought twisted like a knife in her throat. All their talks about their reading, about what they liked and didn't liked, everything she'd told him about her deepest hopes and dreams—it hadn't mattered what she'd told him, because they would never see each other again and her secrets would be safe. But now here he was, smiling at her like he knew her—because he *did*. And she was at his mercy.

And it was worse than that. She'd not only trusted him. She'd started to fall in love with him. Had he realized that? Had he read in her eyes the way she'd been struggling with that, keeping up her constant everything-will-be-fine-when-I-get-to-Mauburni refrain while underneath she was wondering if the Lord Protector would be half as attractive as Kayn? And under that, so deep inside her that she hardly admitted it to herself, wishing that *he* were the one she was journeying to marry?

"Why?" she demanded. "Why did you do this?"

He didn't reply, but reached out and touched her arm. "My cloak. You're still wearing it." There was a soft, curious note in his voice. "Why?"

His cloak...*his*! No wonder Perrin and Meyric and Belet had looked at her so oddly. And she'd told Perrin it belonged to someone she cared deeply about—

"Oh!" she gasped, too angry to say anything else, and tried to rip it from her shoulders, but the clasp was too sturdy. After a brief, frantic struggle she got it unfastened and threw it on the ground between them.

He stared down at it.

"I thought it was Kayn's cloak, but I seem to have been mistaken." The heat in her felt as if it threatened to burst out through her pores. Would she erupt into flame and take all of Cadel's tent—and Cadel—with her? It was nothing more than he deserved.

"Saraid, I *am* Kayn," he said quietly.

"No. No you're not. Kayn's gone. I'm not sure if he even really existed. There's only someone who looks like him, but he's a liar and a—a..." No! No tears. No raging. She had to be icy cold and controlled now. "Now perhaps you'll be so kind as to tell me the meaning of this...this *insult* and what you intend to do with me. How much of a ransom are you demanding?"

He was still gazing at his cloak on the ground, a frown on his face. At the word *ransom* he stirred and looked up. "You misunderstand what is happening here."

She gave a high-pitched, brittle laugh. "Oh, I don't think so."

"I do. There will be no ransom. And while your arrival here

may have resembled a kidnapping—I do apologize for that but could see no other way, given the circumstances—the resemblance ends now. If you wish, you are free to go."

Saraid was aware she was staring at him and probably wearing a very foolish expression as she did so. "Wh—what did you say?"

"I said that you are free to go—with one restriction." He gestured toward a pair of chairs set before a low table laden with cups and a decanter. "Please, Saraid—why don't we sit down and talk about this like rational people?"

"Because this isn't a rational situation!"

He smiled—actually *smiled*, the beast. "Well, perhaps not entirely. As I said, some amount of improvisation was involved. But now that we are here—"

"We won't be for long. As soon as they realize what's happening, my father and the Lord Protector will cover the Adaiha with their men, and they'll find me...and you. I should be very concerned about that if I were you."

"I don't think so. If things go according to my plans, none of them will even know you're missing. We have weeks—months, possibly."

Months—he intended to keep her here for *months*? She fought down the panic-tinged anger again and asked, "What are you talking about? Why did you kidnap me—or whatever you did," she amended at his frown—"if you don't want something in exchange?"

"I didn't say I wasn't deriving anything of value from the situation," he said calmly. "Come, let's sit."

"I would rather not sit with you." She half turned her back to him.

"The Saraid I know—or thought I knew—did not disdain to sit with an impecunious guide. Why refuse to sit with me now, in my own lands?"

"A half-empty village in the middle of the Adaiha," she sneered. "Am I supposed to be impressed?"

"Well…it's all the Adaiha, actually," he said mildly. "I've just recently received the allegiance of the last clan. Down to a man, they're mine."

Saraid snorted. "Why should I believe that? No one's ever been able to unite the Adaihans. When they're not busy attacking travelers, they attack each other."

"That is no longer true."

He said it so flatly that she knew he wasn't lying or even stretching the truth to impress her. She schooled her face into indifference, but inside she was shocked. Who was Cadel that he'd been able to unite them under his name? And *why*? "Will you force me to sit with you, then? Will you call Perrin and Meyric and your men and have them make me sit?"

"If necessary, yes. Do you want me to?" There was no smile in his eyes at all now, only a cool sternness that made it easier for her to understand how he might have been able to subjugate the Adaiha. "Or I can assume that you're still the intelligent young woman I thought you were and expect that you'll behave like a rational person and sit down when you're invited to?"

His words stung her into silence. She hesitated, then sat down in one of the chairs.

"Thank you." He seated himself in the other, poured them both cups of liquid, and offered one to her. She contemplated refusing it but, after their discussion about the chair, knew there wasn't much point. She had to restrain her emotions, to pretend she had Count Ebroian on her shoulder whispering in her ear. If only she really did. She accepted the silver cup from him and took a sip from it…and nearly dropped it.

"Theklan wine?" she sputtered.

"Yes. From the southwest, near Ardath. I thought you might like it. This was a good vintage as I recall." He sipped and nodded. "Perfect. Tiruus knows exactly how to chill it."

"Where did you get it?"

"I have my sources."

Sources? Where would a warlord in the Adaiha get Theklan

wine? "You stole it," she said. "You stole it from a Theklan—"

He raised one hand. "No. I don't bother Theklan merchants, and now that the Gesanthu Clan follows me, no one in the Adaiha will. We only harass the Mauburnians. Now drink your wine. It'll help."

In spite of herself, Saraid was getting more interested. "Why just Mauburnians?"

"I don't think I'll tell you just now. And besides, we have other matters to discuss." He leaned back in his chair and looked at her in silence for a moment, as if meditating on how to start. "First, you are my guest here. You will be treated as befits your station as a visiting royal princess. In return I expect that you will treat my people with the courtesy one usually associates with princesses."

"A guest is usually free to decide where and when she comes and goes."

"And so you are—quite free. I thought I had made myself clear on that point? You are welcome to stay in this camp with us for as long as you wish. Or if you'd rather, I'd be happy to show you more of the Adaiha, from border to border. It is a beautiful land in its own way, as I think you have already seen. Or..." He hesitated. "Or at your word, I will see that you are returned to Thekla in as expeditious a manner as possible."

She stared at him. "I certainly don't want to traipse around the Adaiha in your company, and I don't want to go home. I want to go to Mauburni!"

His face grew smooth and still. "No. That is the one place I cannot permit you to go."

"This is ridiculous!" She gripped the arms of her chair to keep herself in it. "I am to marry the Lord Protector in a few weeks' time. You're preventing me from doing my duty."

"I know that."

"Then let me go!"

"No, Saraid. You will not go to Mauburni while I have a breath in my body." He looked down at his wine cup for a moment, then said, in a voice as smooth and flat as his expression,

"I had hoped that you would consider staying here, but the thought appears to be too distasteful to you. If you will allow me a day or two to catch up on a few matters here, we will be on our way back to Thekla. There are swifter routes we can take than the one your party used—Zamas led you on quite a twisting path—"

"No!" Her cry sounded anguished, even in her own ears.

"No?" He looked up at her inquiringly.

She couldn't—simply *couldn't*—go back to Thekla. How could she become the perfect queen she'd vowed to Mama's memory she would be, a queen Count Ebroian himself would have approved of and written about in The Book, if she were bundled back home like damaged goods returned to the store? What would Nin think of her? Or her father or his ministers?

Or the workers she'd seen planting trees, singing as they worked because better times were coming soon?

She fought to steady her voice. "No. I will not go back."

"Then you will be staying here, because I will not allow you to go farther."

"This is—oh!" Her frustration threatened once again to choke her. "So I *am* your prisoner."

"Not at all. Right now it sounds like you're your own prisoner. I am quite serious about sending you back to Thekla if you don't wish to stay here."

One deep breath, and another. And another, until she felt less close to explosion. The Book stressed that excesses of emotion when negotiating never helped one's argument. "No. I choose to stay here and make you change your mind."

Cadel set his cup down on the table and looked at her. "I see," he said. To her surprise, a small smile lurked in the corners of his mouth. "Very well, if that's your wish. You are free to try to change my mind about letting you go to Mauburni. Of course, you understand that it works both ways."

"What do you mean?"

"I mean that I may strive just as hard to change yours about wanting to stay."

She straightened in her chair. "I should like to see you try!"

"Oh, you will. You will."

An uneasy shiver rippled through her, leaving a vague disquiet in its wake. He seemed so sure of himself. Whereas she—

Cadel suddenly became very brisk. "Now that that's settled— is your tent comfortable? I sent detailed instructions but couldn't check—do you have everything you need? You'll have to take care of yourself—I couldn't bring myself to take Talnith, too, I'm afraid. Perrin has said she'll look after you in general, but she's not your maid. I'd more intended her as a companion for you. In addition to me, of course."

Had the wine gone straight to her head or was it the way that he'd changed subjects that made her dizzy? "You, my compan— What are you talking about?"

"You are my guest. It is my duty as your host to bear you company when I am not otherwise busy. You'll be taking your meals with me, by the way. It will make everyone's lives easier if you do. It will certainly make mine more pleasant."

"Why, you—I'm your prisoner, not your dinner entertainment."

"I thought we had put that 'prisoner' business to rest? Saraid," he said softly, shaking his head. "We spent every waking moment in each other's company for several days and you didn't seem to mind."

"That was...different."

"How?"

She couldn't look at him. "You—you wouldn't understand!"

He sighed. "No, I'm afraid I do. Very well—I'll give you tonight to settle in. Beginning tomorrow, you will come to my tent for the morning meal. Perrin will bring you at the proper time."

"But—"

Cadel rose and stretched. "And as much as I'd like to keep you here with me right now, I think that's enough for one day. Go rest. I'll see you tomorrow."

A short time ago she would have done anything to escape.

Now she wanted to dig her heels into the carpet and clutch the arms of her chair. "You haven't told me everything I want to know yet."

"I know. Wretched of me, isn't it? You'll just have to come back tomorrow morning and try to coax more information out of me." He went to the entrance of the tent. "Meyric, will you please escort Her Highness back to her quarters?"

Saraid stood. "Am I going to be guarded day and night?" She knew she sounded like a sulking child, but right now she couldn't help it.

"Of course not. Meyric's accompanying you is merely a courtesy."

That made her pause. "Aren't you afraid of me running away?"

He turned and looked at her. "There's nowhere for you to run to. I suppose you were blindfolded on the way in and couldn't see, but take my word for it. This camp is like an island, surrounded by the sea. Only our ocean is one of sand. Yes, you could run away. But you'd be dead inside of a day. Please believe me. Perrin, tell her."

Perrin had ducked her head inside the tent. "He's right, Your Highness. Only experienced travelers can move freely in the Adaiha. I'll bring her back, Cadel. Meyric's got his hands full with Kursa for the moment."

"Ah." Cadel nodded. "Rest well, then, Saraid." He made no move to touch her as she passed him, but stood close enough to the open tent flap that she had to brush against his robes. "Tomorrow will be a busy day."

Perrin mercifully did not ask her any questions as they returned to Saraid's tent, which was just as well: it took all of Saraid's willpower not to burst into tears, and one word from anyone, even a kind one, would have sent her howling.

While she had been with Cadel, Perrin had been busy. A small tub filled with hot water awaited her in her tent. The sight of it made her eyes fill with the tears she'd been struggling to hold back, but Perrin pretended not to notice them as she set out soap and towels for Saraid and then left her alone to soak in peace.

It was wonderful to scrub the dust out of her hair and ears and the stale, salty sweat from her body. If only there were some way to soak the anger and bewilderment from her brain.

This shouldn't have happened. She was supposed to sneak across the Adaiha, have one or two brushes with danger and perhaps a mad dash across the desert to the Mauburnian border, pursued by angry, screeching Adaihan brigands, and then arrive safely in Madariv. Eventually news of how she'd crossed the Adaiha would leak out, and everyone in the city would praise her for her bravery and pluck. The nobility would be so overcome with admiration that they'd decide it was time to make her and the Lord Protector, who in the meanwhile would have fallen madly in love with her, king and queen in name as well as fact. She'd written the whole story in her mind while lying in her tent listening to Talnith snore, down to how she'd modestly deny that her trip had been anything extraordinary and how she'd blush becomingly at the Lord Protector's fervent protestations of eternal devotion. It was going to be perfect.

But it hadn't turned out that way.

How could she have been fooled by Kayn—no, Cadel? Obviously he'd gone out of his way to earn her trust by being charming and attractive and interesting to talk to—and she'd fallen for that charm. They all had, Captain Zamas included.

Why hadn't she seen through him at once? Hadn't she studied every book she could get her hands on about how to read men and determine their inner motives and goals? Hadn't she read The Book over and over again till she'd practically memorized it? And she'd *still* read Cadel completely wrong.

It was embarrassing.

A bathtub was a safe place to give into tears, at least for a little while. But only for a little while. From now on she would have to be strong and keep her anger and frustration well in hand. No matter what Cadel and Perrin said, there had to be some way for her to get out of here. She'd just have to keep her eyes open and look for it—because she was *not* going to admit defeat and let him return her to Thekla.

She had climbed out of the bath and was putting on one of the clean sets of clothes she'd brought from Thekla when she heard a brief rat-a-tat from just outside her tent's door flap, followed by a tentative, "Your Highness?"

It was the girl she'd seen outside Cadel's tent with Meyric—Belet, was it? "Come in," she called, and finished pulling her tunic on over her head.

Belet slipped inside. Closer up, Saraid was even more struck by her delicate prettiness. Her hair was dark and straight and her eyes golden in her tanned face—Adaihan coloring, but with her non-Adaihan grandfather's features. Interesting. She filed the information away for later consideration and turned to a more immediate puzzle. "How did you knock?"

"There's a wooden disc and mallet hanging by the flap. All the tents have them. You probably didn't notice it earlier. I came because I wanted to talk to you more than I could at Del's tent." She looked at Saraid appraisingly. "Are those Theklan clothes?"

Saraid smoothed her tunic. "Yes. Who's Del?"

"Hmm? Oh—Cadel. That's what I called him when I was little. We've been friends practically forever." She put her head to one side. "Those look like what Adaihans used to wear before the sand came. But what they wear now makes more sense in this climate."

They? "Aren't you Adaihan?"

"Only part. On my father's side." Belet straightened her shoulders, and Saraid couldn't help noticing her robes, dyed a soft gold that harmonized beautifully with her skin and hair and cut so that they didn't conceal but enhanced her figure. In a green tunic and leggings and with an extra eight inches of height, Saraid felt like a tree next to her. And not a graceful, shapely one, either.

"The Adaihan robes I had were quite comfortable," she said politely.

"Oh, they are." She looked at Saraid again. "But they didn't look right on you. Your Theklan clothes suit you better."

Had she just been insulted, complimented, or both? Just now, she was too tired and emotionally wrung out to decide. "Please sit down," she said. Years of training by her governesses could hopefully get her through this visit.

"Thank you." Belet perched on one of the chairs. "In the Adaiha water goes away fast. You might want to comb out your hair before it dries funny."

It was said in a perfectly friendly way. But once again Saraid felt put off-balance. "Yes, I will if you don't mind," she said, and seated herself at her dressing table. Maybe over-politeness wasn't what was called for here. "Did Cadel send you? Or Perrin?"

"Of course not!" Belet sounded affronted. "*I* sent me. I've never met a Theklan princess before—or any princess, for that matter. Besides, Del's too busy to think of such a thing, and Lady Perrin just wouldn't." She placed an emphasis on "Lady" so that Saraid felt slightly reproved for not having used it herself. "How old are you, anyway?"

"I'll be eighteen at year's end."

"I'm eighteen and a quarter."

There didn't seem to be much to say to that, so Saraid concentrated on combing.

"Your tent is nice," Belet said after a few moments. "Lady Perrin has made it very pleasant."

"Did she do it? Cadel said he'd sent directions—"

Belet laughed. Even her laughter was pretty and delicate, like a peal of small silver bells. "Del said that, did he? Just like a man, taking all the credit. No, he's busy with much more important things than your tent. Why, I always need to make sure he remembers to eat when Ha-dadai and he get busy."

"You seem close, you and Cadel." Saraid did not look at her but at a tangle caught in her comb.

"Well, when you've grown up with someone and spent almost every day of your life with them, you can't help knowing them well. *Very* well. In fact, he and I—but I'm sure this must be boring—you don't want to hear about how close Cadel and I are. Tell me about Thekla! Is it really all fields and fields of green everywhere you look, the way they say it is? You must find our land so different." She rose and began to wander about the tent.

Saraid looked at her through the mirror. This conversation was very odd. "It's different," she agreed. "But very beautiful in its own way."

"Mm-hmm…what's this? *The Flower of Royalty B-Blossom'd*? What funny letters. Did you bring a book with you to read in the Adaiha?"

Saraid looked up and saw that Belet was holding her copy of The Book. Perrin had unpacked it and placed it on the small stand next to her bed.

"Yes," she said shortly. No way was she going to explain to this girl about her precious Book. Then a thought struck her. "Have you read it?"

"No. Is it good?" She flipped through a few pages and wrinkled her nose. "Oh. It's old. The pictures are pretty, though. I think Del might have this one." She set it back down again. "He says I should read more."

There they were, back to "Del" again. Why did Belet keep bringing him up? "What kind of books do you like?"

Belet made a vague gesture. "You know. Exciting ones. Not that he has any of those. Do you read a lot?"

"Yes."

"Oh." Belet glanced down at The Book again. "Well, I should see if Del need me. I'll come see you later."

Did she have a choice? "Thank you," she replied.

Belet gave her a tight little smile and left.

Saraid set down her comb and braided her nearly dry hair into a plait. What had that been about? Why had Belet come to see her, apart from idle curiosity and to talk about how close she and Cadel were—

Keranieth! Was that it? Did Belet think that she and Cadel— that she was *happy* to be here with him? Was Belet jealous?

"She's welcome to him," she said aloud, and went to sit down on her bed. She picked up The Book and flipped through it as Belet had. Huh. Cadel would never be interested in anyone who didn't think this was the most exciting book in the world—the talks they'd had about Count Ebroian—

She clapped The Book shut and set it down again.

# Seven

The bread of wisdom contains three main ingredients: watching, listening, and learning. But unless it is leavened with understanding, the bread will not rise.

—*The Flower of Royalty Blossom'd*

SARAID HAD EXPECTED PERRIN would come for her that morning, as Cadel had said. But it was Belet who rapped at her door.

"Heya!" she said, sticking her head in the flap. "Would you like to breakfast with me?" Today she wore robes of pale brown edged with rose, and her hair was coiled on the back of her head in a much more elegant fashion than Saraid's braid.

"Um..." Saraid was sitting on her bed, trying not to fidget. "I think I'm supposed to eat at Cadel's tent."

"Oh, did he invite you this morning? I eat at midday with him and Ha-dadai quite often—"

"Actually, I'm supposed to take all my meals with him." Belet's proprietorial air was starting to grate on her, even if the last thing she wanted to do was eat with Cadel.

"You are? I mean, of course you are." Belet's recovery was so smooth that Saraid couldn't help but be impressed. "You being a foreign guest and all. Shall we walk over together?"

Perrin arrived before they'd gone a few paces. "Good morning, Your Highness. Belet." She looked at them. "The princess is supposed to—"

"I know," Belet interrupted. "I'll take her and see if my grandfather needs me today."

"Hmm." Perrin fell into step beside them, and the three of them were silent for the short distance to Cadel's tent—Del's tent, as Belet would call it. Somehow Saraid couldn't imagine herself calling him anything so silly as Del.

Cadel emerged from it as they approached, and Saraid was sure he'd been watching for her. "Good morning, Saraid."

"Heya, Del." Belet linked her arm through Saraid's as if they were best friends and smiled at him.

Cadel hesitated. "Uh, heya, Belet. Saraid, this is—"

"We've been introduced," Saraid said. Did he think they hadn't, what with Belet practically hugging her?

"Oh. Yes, of course..." His words trailed into an uncertain silence.

Saraid watched him. Why was the usually unflappable Cadel at a loss for words? It was gratifying for a change but also puzzling. She glanced out of the corner of her eye and saw that Belet's smile had widened. She was enjoying his discomfiture too, but probably not for the same reason. Hmm. *Was* there something going on between Cadel and Belet? Because if there was, then why had he behaved toward her back in the desert as if he —

Perrin cleared her throat. "Good morning, Cadel," she said in a voice a little louder than usual. "I was just on my way to see Meyric." She put a hand on Belet's shoulder and gave her a bright smile. "Shall we go together? You said you were on your way to speak to him."

Belet opened her mouth. But Perrin was already steering her off to one side, hand still clamped on her shoulder. "How is your mother faring?" Saraid heard her ask.

Cadel turned back to his tent and held open the flap. "Saraid?"

Pox it, he was back in control again. It would have been interesting while he was still off-balance to say, "My, you two make a *lovely* couple," or something equally pointed.

Cadel led her to the table and seated her across from him. A tall, thin, elderly man appeared almost immediately with a large tray, setting plates down next to the tall copper tea urn that was already there.

"Saraid, this is Tiruus. He and his wife, Mervii, have the thankless task of keeping me fed and clothed." Cadel smiled at the man, who grinned back.

"And yer father before you, m'lord," he said. "I remember when he first came here with you —"

Cadel didn't speak or even move, but Tiruus looked at him and stopped as abruptly as if a hand had been clapped over his mouth. "Yer Highness...milord," he mumbled, turning a dull red, and hurried out of the tent with his tray.

Cadel filled her plate and they ate in silence, which suited Saraid just fine. Odd how Tiruus had scuttled away like that, but maybe that was just his way. Belet was more immediately interesting. It was clear she found Saraid's presence unwelcome, and that it had to do with Cadel. How could she explain to the girl that she had no interest whatsoever in him and that she was here against her will? It wasn't as if she wanted these command performances in Cadel's tent three times a day —

"I'm glad to see you like our food," Cadel said, glancing across the table at her empty plate.

"I was hungry," Saraid replied, keeping her tone as neutral as she could.

In truth, she *had* liked the food. The flatbread was fresh and warm, spread with a nut paste and sweetened with honey, and the yellow fruit as drippy and delicious as it had been yesterday. Despite the seeming barrenness of their land, the Adaihans certainly knew how to coax sustenance from it and make it more than palatable. But there didn't seem to be any reason to tell Cadel that.

Or anything else. Just because he had control over her movement didn't mean he had control of all of her. He'd said he
expected her to be here, and here she was. But he couldn't command her mind or her tongue. If she were cold and unresponsive,
maybe he'd get bored, ransom her off quickly instead of trying to
maintain the false friendship they'd shared before—she still
couldn't believe he wouldn't be demanding a ransom for her!—
and go back to Belet, who at least seemed to like him. Maybe she
needed to set word limits for the day and aim for the absolute
minimum of conversation with him that she could manage. Fifty
words a day? Seventy-five?

"Did you sleep well?"

Would nodding or shaking her head count as a word? She'd
have to work out the rules for this system. To be fair, a nod would
have to count as one word, since it was the same as saying *yes*. Or
maybe as half a word.

"Readjusting to sleeping by night can be difficult for travelers
in the Adaiha when their journeys are done. But I'm sure you
were tired enough last night."

Nod. Once she'd finished crying herself to sleep, she'd slept
deeply and dreamlessly. Only a lotion Perrin had brought her last
night had kept her eyes from looking dreadfully red and puffy
this morning. Or maybe she shouldn't have used it. Appearing
before him bedraggled and miserable this morning might have
been satisfying, if counter to Perrin's exhortation to appear strong
and brave.

"Were you comfortable? Did I forget anything you need?"

"Did you really—" She clapped her mouth closed. She'd been
about to ask if he really had planned her tent for her, contrary to
what Belet had said—but pox it, he'd have her up to fifty words in
no time if she couldn't control herself. And besides, it didn't
matter a whit if he had or hadn't.

"You look more rested." He rose from his chair and circled
around toward her. Today he was back in his usual dull, sand-
colored robes—evidently yesterday he'd dressed up for her. The

thought made her uncomfortable for some reason. As did the fact that he was now standing directly behind her chair.

"But your hair is all braided away again." He tugged gently on her plait. "It was so beautiful unbound."

Shivers went down her back. "Don't do that!"

"I'm sorry." A pause. "It makes sense to wear it that way during the day. But women in the Adaiha always wear their hair down in the evening."

"I am not Adaihan."

"No, you aren't. But doesn't The Book mention that showing respect for the customs of others is a valuable way of gaining influence over them?" His voice was serious and a little reproving, and his eyes were wide and innocent.

"I shall take it under consideration," she ground out through clenched teeth. How dare he quote The Book at her in order to get his way! "So what's next? Will you choose my clothes for me as well as my way of dressing my hair?"

"Would you like me to?" He held up a hand to stem her imminent explosion. "I'm joking, Saraid! But you did arrive without much baggage. If there's anything you need in the way of clothing or anything else, I will see that you get it."

"I am not in need of anything."

"That's not quite what I heard from Perrin. Now, shall we go?" He held a hand out to her. "It's a beautiful morning and I usually walk the camp at this time."

She resisted the temptation to bite his hand and ignored it instead, rising on her own and stalking past him to the tent's flap. She *had* to stop letting him get under her skin like this. And the worst part was that he had made her say over fifty words already, and breakfast was barely over.

The sun was still low on the horizon when they emerged from Cadel's tent, but the camp was bustling. Saraid half expected to see Belet loitering under the awning, but she wasn't there. She looked about her curiously as they ambled down the paths among the tents. They were of different sizes and configurations but all had awnings under which families were just finishing their morning meals. Their presence was most puzzling; this was supposed to be a brigands' hideout. But it seemed desperate Adaihan bandits spent their mornings spoon-feeding mashed fruit to their babies or bouncing their toddling children on their knees to make them giggle or smiling at their wives bent gracefully over the baked clay hearths just beyond each awning.

So, too, did Adaihan bandits keep what looked like little shops, with green and gold and blue lengths of ribbon fluttering above copper cooking pots and little packets of spices and tins of oil. That one there, with the simmering pots of towels soaking in scented water, evidently kept in practice with his blades by shaving the row of men waiting patiently in line on stools before his awning, chatting and drinking tea. And the very old men and women wrapped in cloaks and sitting out on the sunny sides of tents must still ride out a-raiding, rheumatism permitting. Saraid snorted to herself, but an unexpected twinge of homesickness lanced through her. This camp reminded her of villages she'd seen in Thekla when she was small and Mama would take them to the countryside in the summer. Both places had the same air of cozy domesticity, of good people going about their business with goodwill.

Cadel knew them all. The old women they stopped to speak to all insisted on stroking Saraid's hands, chuckling gleefully and giving Cadel meaningful looks. He joked easily with them, then an instant later had switched smoothly to discussing more serious matters with their sons or daughters. He always seemed to know minute details of everyone's lives, from whether someone's grandfather's left knee was feeling better to whether the grazing northwest of the spring would be sufficient for their goats and sheep for another few weeks. Saraid was reminded of how her guards had all fallen into the habit of deferring to his opinion or asking his advice, because of that air of calm authority, friendly but self-assured, that he seemed to possess.

A smithy was set up in the only permanent stone-built

building she'd seen so far, surrounded by children who took turns working the bellows and shouting as the smith struck sparks from a bar of glowing metal. The acrid smells of hot iron and burning charcoal pervaded the area. As they passed by, the smith shouted, "Good morning, m'lord. And my lady princess."

"Good morning to you, Faraz. How's that last load of coal burning? Hot enough?"

"Just fine, sir. Thank you for seeing it got to me." He bowed as easily as one could while wielding a large hammer in one hand and gripping tongs in the other.

The children bowed as well, then giggled and elbowed each other. Cadel made a face at them, and they giggled harder.

"Are you lord of the bandits or lord of the manor?" Saraid muttered to Cadel when they were out of earshot.

He looked at her sideways. "What do you mean?"

"You know very well what I mean."

"I'm not sure that I do. You outsiders seem to think that all we Adaihans do is prey on travelers, but you're wrong. We live here, just as anyone would. My men have homes and families, too."

He wasn't going to put her off that easily. "And the sore knees and the goats and the babies?"

"I care for everybody here, not just the Riders. They're all my people. My responsibility."

"You seem awfully young to be a leader."

He shrugged. "One does what one must."

"But you're not Adaihan."

"I've lived here for most of my life. Doesn't that make me Adaihan?"

"But you're not *Adaihan* Adaihan. And neither are Perrin or Meyric or several people I've seen this morning. It's clear from their accents." Aha! Had his smile slipped just the faintest bit? "Why?" she persisted.

"Does it matter?"

"I don't know. Does it?"

"No. Not to us."

"But why?"

"Ah. Here are the stables. I have to say hello to Silbe."

They'd come to a pair of long, narrow tents, parts of which appeared sideless. Then Saraid saw that the walls were in sections and that the tents were divided into stalls. The wall-less parts were stalls with the walls temporarily rolled up.

"Who's Silbe?" The name sounded familiar.

"My horse. You rode him here."

His horse? Oh, no. No. "Does that mean that you…"

He raised an eyebrow. "That I what?"

"That I was with…that you and I…" She couldn't bring herself to finish her sentence.

"Whom did you think it was? I wasn't about to let anyone else ride with you. Heya, Silbe." He went to one of the stalls and whistled softly to its occupant.

It had been Cadel holding her close through the long ride here. Cadel whose shoulder she'd fallen asleep against. It hadn't been Kayn's cloak that had smelt so reassuringly of him, but Cadel himself.

And it was Cadel who'd just successfully distracted her once again from a topic he wanted to avoid discussing.

She stalked past him, seated herself on an upturned bucket, and stared at the horses. Men moved from stall to stall, replenishing water buckets and shoveling out waste, and a pair of cloaked Riders trotted up, pushing back their hoods and ex-changing greetings with the workers as they dismounted. If only she could leap up and seize one of their saddled mounts and ride for all she was worth, all the way to Mauburni.

"Speaking of your clothes…" Cadel gave Silbe a final pat and came to stand by her. "If you're going to live in the Adaiha, you'll need a proper Adaihan cloak. Unless you want to borrow mine again."

*Theklan clothes suit you better than Adaihan,* Belet's voice whispered in her mind. "That won't be necessary."

"I didn't think so. But two of us wearing my cloak at the same time is perhaps a little friendlier than you'd like, though I could bring myself to get used to it. So I've already arranged for one of our seamstresses to make you a *lahart*—that's what we call them."

"I already possess a perfectly fine cloak from Thekla, thank you." It was getting hard to speak with clenched jaws.

"Which would serve you perfectly well if this were Thekla, but it isn't. You need a *lahart* here in the Adaiha."

Horses and Riders and cloaks…something in her mind clicked into place. "Very well." She rose. "If I must."

It took all her willpower not to run back to her tent and demand that they get started on her new cloak immediately. She maintained her former air of reluctance, but underneath she simmered with excitement.

She'd figured out how to get to Mauburni.

After Cadel had left her at her tent with a reminder to join him at noon—a reminder she barely heard—she went immediately to her dressing table, which held her brush and comb and the small *lumox*-wood box with her jewelry. She carried it to her bed and opened it.

Watching the horses and the Riders and trying not to listen to Cadel, it had come to her. She couldn't escape on her own. Jumping onto a horse and fleeing, the way she had daydreamed about, wouldn't work.

But bribing a Rider to guide her to the Mauburnian border might.

She upended the box and brooded over the small, shimmering pile of gold and gems. Mama's emerald earrings were certainly tempting enough, but they were Mama's. She'd use those only if she absolutely had to. Next to them sparkled the pink tourmaline bracelets the Lord Protector had sent her. She picked them up and weighed them thoughtfully in each hand. They were perfectly matched, the rare deep rose color unvarying from stone to stone.

She could offer one immediately to whomever she was bribing and the other once the border was in sight—and Lord Mutrand surely would be happy to add a further reward once she was safe in Madariv. Losing his gift would be a wrench, but The Book said that treasures were shackles if they couldn't be cast aside when necessary.

"Heya—oh!"

Saraid jumped. Belet stood just inside the entrance of her tent, her eyes wide. Had the girl even knocked, or had she been so engrossed in her plans that she hadn't heard? A sudden whisper of an idea—Keranieth help her if she was wrong, but she had to chance it—prompted her to hold up one of the bracelets as if examining it. "Come in," she said. "I was just looking at a few things." The pink tourmalines and gold caught a shaft of light and glittered. She watched Belet from the corner of her eye. "They're a gift from my future husband in Mauburni." She held up the other as well. "Wasn't that nice of him?"

Belet stepped closer to the bed. "They're amazing," she whispered.

"Here." Saraid patted the bed in invitation, then held one out to her. "Do you like it? Try it on."

Belet sat, then reverently unfastened the bracelet and draped it over her slim tanned wrist. "I've never seen anything so beautiful." She held up her hand so the jewels caught the light again. "Not here in the Adaiha."

"They're pretty enough." Saraid swung the other one around on her finger. "At least for a start. Varian says he'll cover me with jewels if I wish it. Bracelets for every day of the year. And necklaces to match, if I want."

Ah, that had worked. Belet glanced up from her wrist and shot her a look of pure envy.

"Of course, that won't happen if I can't get to Madariv." She sighed and continued swinging the bracelet back and forth, back and forth. Belet stared at it, transfixed. "I'd give a lot to be able to get there, and the sooner the better," she added.

Belet tore her gaze from the swinging bracelet. "What do you mean?"

Saraid leaned toward her and spoke quietly. "I don't know what conclusions you've drawn about me and...and Cadel and everything, but I have no desire to be here. I want to go to Madariv and get on with what I'm supposed to be doing, which is marrying the Lord Protector of Mauburni. I want to leave." She held the other bracelet out. "Help me get away from here, and these are yours. Life can go back to the way it was—for *both* of us. You can have Cadel, and welcome to him."

Belet sat back. "You mean it?" she said slowly. "You don't want to stay here with him?"

Saraid snorted. "You're jesting, right? I was *kidnapped*. I want to get out of here."

"Then go back to Thekla. I know he'd take you there."

"No. I'm going to Mauburni or nowhere."

Belet looked back at the bracelet on her wrist and was silent for a long moment. Saraid hardly dared to breathe.

"All right," she finally said. "I'll help you." She unfastened the bracelet and handed it back to Saraid. "Save your jewels. Getting you out of here is sufficient reward for me," Belet said it pleasantly enough, but her accompanying smile was cold.

Saraid felt a quick longing for Nin, who never smiled in that nasty-nice way. She almost protested that bringing her here was Cadel's idea, not hers. But there was no point in rubbing that fact in. If Belet wanted Cadel, she could have him, and her own life could get back onto the path that had been mapped out for it, with The Book to light her way. No more surprises or changes. No more infuriating Cadel with his infuriating knowledge of The Book and his infuriatingly happy-go-lucky smile and infuriatingly beautiful blue eyes—

"Very well," she said aloud. "You know Cadel's Riders. Could we use these to bribe one of them to take me there?"

Belet gazed down at the bracelets. "Maybe. Can you promise a bigger reward once you arrive in Mauburni?"

"Yes," Saraid said at once. If Lord Mutrand didn't provide one, she would. But of course he would, once he knew all she'd been through.

"All right. Let me think about some possibilities while you think about what you're going to say."

"What *I'm* going to say? I thought—"

"I'll find a Rider for you, but you have to be the one to convince him. If it doesn't work out, I don't want anyone to suspect I've had anything to do with this."

By "anyone" Saraid guessed she meant Cadel. Or her grandfather. "Only if you help with any other incidentals that might come up around my getting away. There might be things I can't take care of on my own—water and food, for example."

"Yes, yes, all right." Belet rose and went to the door, then paused. "Not that I'm delighted by the prospect, but we're going to become new best friends from now on. It'll make planning this easier."

Saraid just managed not to say, *And you think I'm delighted?* No need to antagonize her ally; with any luck, their alliance would be a brief one. "Yes, I understand."

Belet nodded and left.

Saraid let out a long breath. The Book said that one must always be open to unexpected opportunities; her gamble had paid off. If anyone would be able to find a Rider to take her to Mauburni, it would be Belet. She would surely be on her way to her new home in a matter of days—maybe a week, at most, praise Keranieth.

But a small niggle of doubt would not let itself be smoothed away. She had seen Cadel's Riders in action; would it be possible to find one who wasn't absolutely devoted to him to take her to Mauburni—?

Yes, it would. Belet, of all people, would be able to find her one. All she had to do was bide her time and muster her patience.

# Eight

Do not confuse activity with accomplishment. Some activities are, of course, worthwhile and necessary, but others are either useless wastes of time or downright harmful.

*—The Flower of Royalty Blossom'd*

THE SOMEONE CADEL HAD sent to make her *lahart* turned out to be a taciturn, middle-aged Adaihan woman named Hirra and her daughter, confusingly also named Hirra, who arrived at her tent the next afternoon. Saraid submitted to being measured and examined the smooth, tightly woven wool that would make the outside layer of the garment. The thread from which it was made had been dyed in heathered shades of tan and brown and ocher; spread out over her floor it looked like a piece of the desert captured on cloth.

"This is *idhe* cloth," explained the older Hirra. "It's woven only in the Adaiha. For lining we use a brightly colored, contrasting material: if lost in the desert, you turn your cloak inside out to help make you more visible to searchers."

Saraid remembered Cadel had put his cloak on her inside out.

So *that* was how Seinu and his men had found her so easily.

She was less happy with the lining Hirra showed her, of softer blue wool identical to that in Cadel's cloak. "You don't have any other color than this?"

Hirra shrugged. "This be what we were told to use, Your Highness."

Pox it. Saraid had begun to think that an Adaihan cloak would be an amusing souvenir of her adventure, but perhaps she'd been wrong. The last thing she wanted was something that would remind her so vividly of Cadel.

But Belet had suggested that Saraid cooperate with getting her *lahart* made while she looked for a suitable candidate. So here she was, surrounded by Hirras and breadths of fabric.

The younger Hirra remained silent down on the floor, pinning together the multiple panels of the outer cloak that her mother cut out totally by eye, without a pattern. Only when she clambered to her feet and reached for her basket of needles and thread to begin sewing did Saraid notice that her eyes were not Adaihan gold, but gray.

"You're following your mother's trade?" she asked casually, sitting next to the young woman. They weren't all that far apart in years, though now that she wasn't on hands and knees on the floor it was possible to see that the younger Hirra was pregnant.

"My family's women have been *lahart*-makers for many generations," she answered. "I'm the seventh, and gods willing, this will be the eighth." She laid a hand on her stomach and rubbed it gently.

"Just the women? What about the men? Doesn't your father make them, too? Or your husband?"

Hirra-the-Younger giggled. "My father was one of the Mauburnians who came here. He never wore a *lahart* until he met my mother. And my husband is one of Lord Cadel's Riders. No, just we women know how. Here, want to help? You can sew the straight part down here if you know how. It's good luck to put your own work into your *lahart*. Mothers hold their babies' fingers and help them make a stitch or two on their first one—"

"Hirra!" Hirra-the-Elder frowned at them. "Mind your tongue. This is milord's lady, not one of your gossips."

"I'd like to help." Saraid took the lengths of cloak the younger Hirra offered. At least it would serve to pass the time.

As she threaded a needle and tied a knot in the thread's end, she thought about what Hirra had said. Who were those "Mauburnians who came here" and gave Hirra her gray eyes? Did they have anything to do with Perrin's obviously non-Adaihan appearance, and Meyric's?

And Cadel's, for that matter?

"I've found the fatal error in your plan," Saraid announced at that evening's meal.

Cadel finished serving her a portion of a large omelet stuffed with herbs and poured her some wine before he answered, "A fatal error? Are you sure you want to tell me what it is if it is so fatal? Count Ebroian would consider that a poor decision, strategically speaking."

"Very funny. As a matter of fact, it doesn't matter if I tell you as it is nothing you can control. Do you think I didn't think of that?"

"As a rule I avoid trying to second-guess others' thoughts. It rarely accomplishes anything. So tell me, what is my error?"

She eyed him frostily. "You're not taking me seriously, are you?"

He sighed. "Saraid, there is no one in the six kingdoms whom I take more seriously than you. But I doubt you'll believe that."

"You're right, I won't. Now, your error." She leaned forward, relishing the moment. She'd thought of it that afternoon while sewing with the Hirras, and it had been all she could do not to leap to her feet and shout in triumph. If she were right, she wouldn't even have to worry about escaping. "I am expected to arrive in Madariv in the next few days. I suppose they will allow a few extra days beyond that, as accidents happen. But when I don't arrive after that, the ambassador and my husband-to-be will certainly be concerned. And each day that I don't arrive will increase their concern."

"I see." Cadel nodded slowly. "How many days have you factored in for them to allow for possible delays due to weather or just having left later than originally planned, for whatever reason?"

Why didn't he seem even a little concerned? "I would expect that in the next ten or twelve days, their anxiety at my absence will have reached the point of action."

"What action?"

"Why, to come and look for me, of course. Are your Adaihans ready for an invasion?"

"As a matter of fact, they are. But there won't be one."

Her conviction wavered. He sounded so sure... "How do you know that?"

"How do you think I have reached the position I'm in without always considering the details? I'm also a disciple of Count Ebroian." He took a bite of omelet. "Concealing your presence here, since you've chosen for now to remain, is not as hard as you seem to think."

"But what if I don't want it concealed?"

He ignored that outburst, which she realized at once was more or less what it deserved. "Think about it. Any communication between Thekla and Mauburni has to pass through the Adaiha, which I control. So as of a day or so before you joined us, I arranged it so that messengers who leave either place will be stopped and their messages read. Any to do with you will be re-written and substitute messengers sent on to deliver them. Thekla will learn that you have safely arrived in Madariv, while Mauburni will receive the news that your departure has been delayed."

By Keranieth, he was serious! "But the other group that set out—the decoy. Are you going to stop them as well?"

"Of course not. They'll arrive in Madariv as planned. The people who matter already know you're traveling separately. They knew there was a risk that you'd be later or earlier than they would. Explaining that discrepancy is their problem. As I said, we could potentially keep this up for months."

"Oh." She couldn't manage more than that—she was too close to tears.

"It doesn't have to," he said gently. "Although I hope that you will decide that this is where you would rather be. However, if you do choose to return to Thekla, I will do my utmost to make sure it is impossible for your father to find a way to send you to Mauburni."

"Why?" she cried. Tears of disappointment burned her eyes, making it hard to look at him. "Why are you so determined to keep me from going to Mauburni?"

He was silent for a long moment. "I have my reasons," he finally said. "And no, I'm not going to tell you what they are," he said when she opened her mouth. "It's not the right time."

"Will it ever be?" she asked bitterly.

"I don't know."

The rest of their meal was very quiet.

Two days later Saraid was on her way back to her tent from her morning meal with Cadel when Belet appeared at her side, looking dainty and perfect as usual. Saraid sighed to herself— daintiness had never been something she was noted for—and tried not to mind. The Book said that difficult circumstances sometimes forced difficult alliances. Count Ebroian had certainly gotten that one right.

"Isn't it a lovely morning?" Belet took her arm. Saraid couldn't help wondering if Belet wasn't taking a certain malicious pleasure in their enforced closeness.

The sun was the same white gold, reflecting off the sand and making her eyes water just as it did any other morning in the Adaiha, but Belet was digging her nails into Saraid's arm. "Oh, yes!" she agreed, matching Belet's effusive tone.

"It's too nice to stay inside. Let's walk, shall we?" Belet steered her away from Cadel's tent and down a lane of tents in the direction of the oasis pool. "I have some news," she added more quietly.

News! Had Belet found a Rider to help her escape? It was difficult to merely nod and pretend nothing out of the ordinary was happening till they were well away from the last of the tents. Then she extricated herself from Belet's arm. "What news?"

"I think I found you a Rider. He's perfect for it—an orphan, no wife or betrothed, been on patrol for a little over a year so he knows the land."

Saraid exhaled slowly, realizing she'd been holding her breath. He sounded perfect. Maybe this escape would be easier to pull off than she'd thought. "What's his name?"

"Lannu. The best part is that he's just coming off duty. If we go over to the stables, you can meet him."

"Did you say anything to him yet?"

Belet rolled her eyes. "Of course not. We agreed—that's up to you."

"Yes, all right. Shall we go meet him— Oh, I don't have any of my jewelry with me—"

"You don't want to have any jewelry with you. You have to work up to it." Belet spoke as if she talking to a backward child. "All you want to do for a few days is chat with him. Be pleasant, ask him questions, get him to trust you. After that you start talking about Madariv—ask him about it because he's been there for his training at the Eb."

The Eb? As in the Ebroian Military Academy in Madariv? How had an Adaihan youth gotten into the most exclusive military training school in the land, well known even in Thekla? "He's been there? How did—"

Belet cut her off. "Yes, of course he has. Many of the Riders have. So you start asking him questions about all the wonderful and exciting things about Madariv, and then you get wistful about wanting to see it... and *then* you work around to the bribe. Not before."

"Oh." Much as she didn't like to admit it, Belet was right. Didn't The Book say, *The greater the undertaking, the greater the preparation*? She couldn't just stride into the stables waving her jewels like she was looking to buy passage on the next coach to Ardath. "You've put a lot of thought into this, haven't you?"

"I certainly have." Belet's affable tone was ever so slightly razor-edged. "Come on, let's go before he finishes taking care of his horse and goes off to sleep." She took Saraid's arm again.

Saraid would have liked to question her further about this Lannu's having been to the military school founded by Count Ebroian in Madariv. No wonder her kidnapping had been so smooth. Between training at the Eb and their own native abilities with horses, Cadel's Riders would be a formidable force.

A professionally trained force in the Adaiha...and now it was united under Cadel. There was a lot more going on in here than anyone in Thekla had suspected. Or Mauburni too, probably. Was Lord Varian aware of any of this? Part of her marriage agreement was that Thekla and Mauburni would launch a joint mission to reclaim the Adaiha for Mauburni. Having the Adaihans united made that mission a much more difficult prospect. The sooner she escaped and warned everyone, the better.

A short distance from the stable tents, Belet paused. "I'll go in with you and show you who he is," she murmured. "Go over to him and admire his horse. That's the best way to get a Rider's attention."

Inside the cool, shadowed tent Saraid nodded to the startled stablehands they passed, answering Belet's inconsequential chatter about the different horses with her own. Nor were they the only young women there. Evidently a midmorning stroll through the stables was an accepted social event. Several Riders were there, rubbing down their horses or cleaning their tack or just lounging about, exchanging sideways looks and banter with the smiling young women...a handful of which were Riders themselves.

"There," Belet whispered and nodded toward a Rider, still cloaked and with a dark scarf looped around his neck, just unsaddling his horse. "That's Lannu. Go on." She nudged Saraid, then hurried down the tent toward an older man and threw her arms around his neck. "Oh, there you are, Dadai! I was looking for you!"

Saraid gulped, then ambled toward the unsuspecting Lannu. Now, how did girls do it in the novels she'd read, when they were trying to get a boy's attention? Not that she wanted in the least to flirt, but she had to start somehow.

"Good morning," she began, smiling brightly at him as he glanced up.

"Um, g'morning, Your Highness." He bowed uncertainly.

So he knew who she was, then. "I, uh...I couldn't help noticing your... your horse just now. He's *very* handsome." She looked at him through her eyelashes and hoped he wouldn't take fright and flee. Had that been too obvious?

The man—boy, really; he couldn't have been all that much older than she was—straightened his shoulders as he unbuckled the horse's bridle and lifted it over the animal's head. "Isn't he? And fast, too. He's a half brother to m'lord Cadel's horse, Silbe. Have you seen him?"

More of him than she'd wanted to. "Oh, no. Which one is he?"

"Over here. Heya, Jurru, take care of my friend here for me, won't you?" he called to one of the grooms. "This way, Your Highness."

Saraid followed him down the row of stalls. So far, so good. "Are you a Rider?"

"Yes, Your Highness. Just a year now." More than a touch of swagger appeared in his step.

"A year." Saraid made herself sound properly awed. "So what does a Rider do?"

"Whatever we're asked to. Mostly I'm on guard duty, making sure no one's around who shouldn't be."

"It must be rather dull work, just riding around the desert."

"Someone's got to do it, Your Highness. It isn't Madariv, mind, but it gives me an excuse to ride."

"So you've been all the way to Madariv? Is it a long journey from here?"

"Not too bad. Here you are." He paused in front of a stall and called, "Heya, Silbe."

Saraid stepped forward dutifully and exclaimed over the horse, trying not to gloat openly. This was going almost too well. It had to be a good omen.

"Then you must know the Adaiha pretty well." She stroked Silbe's sleek neck.

"Pretty well, I guess." The words sounded modest, but his smile was anything but.

"That is something, to know the Adaiha well enough to ride it without getting lost. I'll bet you know it better than anyone." The Book said that flattery could work wonders, the thicker the better. Hopefully the count knew what he was talking about.

He did. The boy positively preened. "Well, I...yeah, I suppose I do."

"My goodness." Saraid blinked, as if momentarily overcome. "Well, I ought to let you get back to your horse. What's your name?"

"Lannu, Your Highness."

"Thank you, Lannu. I'm sure I'll see you around..." She gazed at him meaningfully and he blushed.

"Yes, Your Highness. I'm, um...I'm usually here this time of day...if you happen to be around, you could...you know, stop in again," he added in a rush, bowed again, and hurried away.

Saraid looked up at Silbe. "Thank the gods you can't talk," she muttered, and left more slowly than Lannu had, trying not to skip with joy. Belet had been right. This might actually work. And Lannu seemed nice enough. She would offer him a place in her guard when she was established in Mauburni, if he wanted it.

Belet caught up with her a moment later. "And?"

"It went perfectly. He seemed to like talking to me."

"Good!" For a moment, Belet sounded sincerely pleased. "Skip tomorrow, then go back the next morning. If you're careful, you might be able —"

"Saraid!"

She looked up, squinting in the strong midmorning light. Cadel strode toward them. Instead of his usual Adaihan robes he wore breeches that clung to his long legs, high boots, and an open-throated shirt. His face was streaked with dust and sweat, and he held a long sword, its blade blunted with strips of lead.

"Looking around?" he said when he drew up to them.

"Is looking around permitted?" His clothes looked familiar, somehow. Hadn't the Mauburnians who'd come to negotiate her marriage dressed similarly?

"Of course it is." He wiped his forehead with his sleeve. "Oh — heya, Belet."

Belet nodded distantly. Pique at his belated greeting, Saraid guessed.

"I'm in the middle of a weapons drill," he continued. "My Riders practice daily, but I can't always make it."

"Some days you're busy kidnapping — I beg your pardon — *detaining* people."

"Only certain special ones." He grinned. "Want to watch us?"

Saraid gritted her teeth. "Not particularly."

Next to her Belet stirred. "We were just going back to —"

"Good," Cadel said, as if neither of them had spoken. "There's a chair and some shade over there." He gestured to a small awning set on the edge of an open area of packed-down sand. "I'll be interested to hear what you think."

What she thought was that she wished she could wrest the sword from him and give him a good thwack with it. A group of Riders leaning on their swords, some attired like Cadel, watched them curiously from the center of the practice area. Saraid ignored

BETWEEN SILK AND SAND

them and stalked toward the awning. Belet kept pace with her.

"You don't have to come if you don't want to," Saraid muttered. "I think I'm the only one he's decided to order around."

Belet shrugged. "I have nothing better to do right now."

Three men already sat under the awning, evidently watching as well. They murmured polite greetings but thankfully didn't try to engage her in conversation. Saraid seated herself on an empty stool and grimly exhorted herself to be patient. Belet choose a stool next to her, shifting it slightly before she sat.

Cadel had rejoined the group and was listening to one of their number, an older man with grizzled hair, talking earnestly and gesturing with his hands. Grizzle-Head finished his lecture, picked up his sword and called, "In pairs. Overhand parries, in turn."

In the next few minutes, Saraid found herself clutching her hands, supposed to be folded serenely together in her lap. Cadel moved with a sure, powerful grace, blocking and then attacking, as skillful with a sword as any of the other men. Evidently not being able to practice daily hadn't much hindered him.

"Good block. Milord Cadel's got a lot of power in those shoulders," commented one of the men.

"Aye," agreed another, "but it's the strength in the thighs that holds him steady. Look at them!"

Saraid did her best *not* to look, but it wasn't working. The muscles of his shoulders and chest and arms slid and bunched under his shirt, plastered to his skin with sweat. She moved restlessly on her stool. If she had seen him like this back when she thought he was Kayn, she would have been practically swooning. *But he isn't Kayn,* she told herself fiercely.

"Enjoy watching sword practice, do you?"

Saraid looked up and saw that Belet was watching her, not the practicing men. "Since I've never seen it before, yes, it's mildly interesting," she replied with as much dignity as she could muster.

Belet's eyes narrowed. "Hmmph."

Pox it, why had Belet tagged along? Being forced to watch

111

Cadel was difficult enough without being glowered at by Belet as well. Why did he have to be so good that she could only be impressed in spite of herself?

At last, after an excruciatingly long time that perversely flew by, the grizzled man called a halt. The Riders trooped back to the awning, nodding politely to her as they passed. Cadel himself paused before her, breathing hard but still grinning.

"Well?" he asked. Someone passed him a cup of water and he drank it down, head thrown back so she could see the muscles of his throat. He handed back the cup with a nod and looked at her expectantly. "What did you think?"

"Well done," Belet said before she could think of an answer. "Though Her Highness seemed a little bored. Perhaps she —"

"Thank you, Belet." Cadel's glance slid over her and back. "Saraid?"

"I think it's a very warm day," she said shortly.

"It is a warm one, isn't it? We'll be at this for a while yet. I'd let you go back to your tent but it's a long walk in the bright sun to get back there. It might be better if you stayed here in the shade and watched us till we're done, and then we can go back together." He gave her his sunny smile and turned away to pick up his sword.

Belet made an exasperated noise and rose from her seat. "I'll come later to hear about how your talk with Lannu went." She swept out of the awning, leaving Saraid alone to watch Cadel practicing with his men in unwilling fascination.

As Belet had directed, Saraid skipped visiting the stables the next morning but went the morning after that, taking care to avoid the practice ground in case Cadel took it into his head to make her sit there and watch him again.

Sure enough, Lannu was there, and had obviously made sure his hair was combed and his face washed. Saraid asked him more questions about his horse and listened as if riveted by his accounts of riding patrol in the Adaiha. The fish was nearly hooked. Her cloak would be done in another day or two, and then she'd reel him in. With the way her luck was going, she might be in Madariv in another week or ten days.

At the evening meal that night Cadel regarded her from across the table. "You've been busy, I hear," he said, tearing a piece off a disc of flatbread.

Saraid nearly choked on a bite of grilled meat. "What do you mean?" she asked when she could breathe again. Had someone told him about her visits to the stables?

"You've been helping the Hirras with your *lahart*."

"Oh." Her heart flopped once, then slowed to a less panicked beat. "Yes, I have. Is there anything wrong with that?" She took a sip from her cup. More Theklan wine. The taste was both pleasure and pain.

"Not at all. Hirra-the-Younger says you're reasonably competent with a needle. For a princess, that is." He grinned at her. "Being useful and decorative is uncommon."

Saraid rolled her eyes. "Are you waiting for me to say the same about you?"

"Do you want to? I'd be flattered if you did, but I think I know better than to expect it."

He was right about that. She'd never admit to his face just how attractive she thought—or rather, used to think—he was. The thoughts that crossed her mind while watching him practice his swordsmanship the other day didn't count; she'd probably been suffering from heatstroke. "Go to your Adaihans if you want flattery. They all think you're wonderful enough."

To her surprise, his smile faded and he looked away. "I don't care how wonderful they think I am, so long as I have their trust. It's what I've worked for all these years."

She'd never seen him so serious—at least not since that conversation they'd had about her marrying the Lord Protector, back when she still knew him as Kayn. "How many years?"

"Since I was old enough to understand what was important. And I'll be twenty-five come spring, if you were wondering." He smiled, but his eyes remained serious.

"How long have you been...whatever it is you are?"

"You may not like to hear this, but in Adaihan my title is 'Kayn.' It means something like leader or overlord." He hesitated. "Or king."

"What do you plan to do as overlord of the Adaiha?" She couldn't quite bring herself to call him *king*; it gave him too much legitimacy. "It's not as if it's a real country. Someday Mauburni may decide it's time to take the Adaiha back."

"It won't have to. When the king comes back to Mauburni, so will the Adaiha."

"That time may come sooner than you think." At least if she and the Lord Protector had their way.

"I hope so," he said quietly.

She laughed uncertainly. He had no idea what Thekla and Mauburni were planning for the Adaiha. "So will you hand the Adaiha over to the king when he returns?"

"The Adaiha will go gladly to him. Remember the curse."

"Count Ebroian's curse? Do you believe in it?"

"Well, we'll see what happens when the king returns. If it rains in the Adaiha, then we'll know."

She laughed again. "You really do believe in it, don't you? You're full of conversational surprises tonight."

He looked at her levelly. "So are you. This is the first time we've had one since you got here without you resorting to silence or childish behavior. I've mostly ignored it. I know that you're upset at your situation—"

"Can you blame me?"

"No, I can't, though I had hoped you would be a little more resilient. Believe me, if there had been any other way to keep you safe—"

She gave a polite laugh. "Oh, is *that* what you call it? Keeping me safe?"

He ignored the sarcasm oozing from her voice. "Yes, it is. Keeping you safe is my main goal. I wish I could be keeping you happier as well. I have to say that my stomach feels much better when we can converse at table like two normal people for at least a little while."

Saraid had opened her mouth to deliver a scathing response and found she couldn't. Had she really been that bad? The Book was firm on the point that anyone who claimed the title of gentleman or lady was never needlessly rude—and that went doubly so for kings and queens. And—she gulped—she *had* been needlessly rude to Cadel, when a dignified silence would have sufficed and perhaps been more powerful. Certainly her rudeness had accomplished nothing.

He was still watching her. "Now you're angry again. I shouldn't have said anything."

She took refuge in a long drink of wine, then said, "Having a mirror held up to you when you're not expecting it can be a little shocking."

"Then can we call a truce?"

Saraid studied her cup. In another few days she'd have convinced Lannu to guide her to Madariv, and then she'd be gone. She could afford to force herself to be civil to Cadel for a little while. And it was much more pleasant to talk politely while eating than to snarl and be disagreeable. Surely they could find neutral topics of conversation for a day or two.

"Yes," she finally said. "Truce. For now."

He smiled then, his full sun-coming-out-from-behind-clouds-and-melting-everything smile that was a more dreadful weapon than either his teasing or his honesty. "Thank you. A provisional truce is better than none. It's a starting point, anyway."

She did not reply. The Book said that the best way to keep a secret was to forget that you had one. She'd play along and let him think what he wanted. In a few more days it wouldn't matter.

Two days later, Two days later, the Hirras finished her *lahart*. The elder Hirra ceremoniously handed Saraid her needle so that she could take the last two stitches and tie off the thread, then motioned for her to stand.

"You must wear it so that it knows you," she said. "That is the way with a *lahart*."

Saraid glanced at Belet, who looked bored, and Perrin, who smiled indulgently at Hirra but nodded. "Go ahead. Let's see how it fits, anyway."

She slipped the cloak over her shoulders. The substantial *idhe* cloth was surprisingly light for its weight and fell into full, graceful pleats around her. The hood was close-fitting but deep and could be folded down over the face or back on itself above the forehead. Two extra deep pleats above the shoulders gave extra room when wearing the cloak while on horseback. Cadel's *lahart* had felt comforting, like a favorite blanket, but it was too long and voluminous on her. This fit her perfectly and, like all perfectly-fitting clothes, felt wonderfully right. She glanced down, rubbing her hands over the fabric. Its texture was smooth and almost velvety under her palms. "It's beautiful."

"It's all right." Belet yawned as she spoke, propped on a cushion on the rug.

Perrin frowned at her. "It is all that it should be. Our Hirras are probably the best *lahart*-makers in the Adaiha."

"Thank you, Lady Perrin." Hirra-the-Elder's face twisted into an odd expression, and Saraid realized that she was smiling.

"Will you go show it to Lord Cadel now, Your Highness?" the younger Hirra said slyly, gathering up reels of thread and putting them into her bag.

Belet sat up, her indolence vanished. "I'm sure he's busy and won't want to be interrupted for such a trifle," she said quickly.

Perrin raised an eyebrow. "On the contrary. I'm sure he'll be pleased to see it. It was his idea to have one made, after all. Go on, Your Highness."

"Should I? Now?" Giving pleasure to Cadel was not on

Saraid's list of favored activities, but showing off this beautiful *lahart* was too irresistible a prospect.

"I'll go with you. It's time I went home, anyway." Belet climbed to her feet.

"Yes, do. I'm sure your mother would appreciate a little more help in her present circumstances," Perrin said.

"She's such a bossy old witch," Belet muttered as soon as they were out of the tent. "Mamai's fine. It isn't as if she hasn't been pregnant before. Perrin just likes to order everyone around. I'll be glad when we leave for Callest so I don't have to see her as much."

Saraid bit her tongue. Belet was her ally, even though their alliance was born solely of their needs. Still, Perrin had been very kind...and seemed to be very wise.

Cadel was at the table under the awning in front of his tent, talking to Meyric. They both fell silent and stared when she approached and put back her hood.

"Hirra hasn't lost her touch, I see," Meyric said after a moment. "The *lahart* suits you, Your Highness."

Cadel rose and came around the table, not taking his eyes off her. He wasn't smiling.

"What's wrong? Doesn't it meet your approval?" she asked him.

"There's nothing wrong," he finally said, a little hoarsely.

"Then don't you like it?"

"I do like it...very much." He reached out and ran two fingers down her upper arm. "I like you in it. It makes you look like you belong here."

She was about to snap out an exasperated contradiction, but his almost painfully fierce gaze stopped her. She felt warm and a little breathless. No one had ever looked at her like...like he wanted to devour her—and made her feel like she wanted to be eaten.

"Well, the Hirras will be glad to hear you approve." Belet's voice sounded unnaturally loud in Saraid's ears. She'd nearly forgotten there was anyone there beside Cadel.

He blinked, and she wondered if she looked as dazed as he did.

"It's a very practical garment for the Adaiha," Meyric chimed in. He was looking at them both strangely, tugging on a curl near his left ear.

Saraid tore her gaze from Cadel's. "Yes, it... Excuse me." She fumbled for the clasp at her throat. "The heat..."

Belet stepped forward and almost yanked it off her. "Not really the time of day for a *lahart*," she agreed, but her delicate brows were knit in an angry line. "Come on, let's go back to your tent."

Saraid still felt Cadel watching her as Belet practically dragged her away. What had just happened to her there? She'd *liked* Cadel's reaction, liked the way he couldn't stop looking at her —

"What in the gods' name was that about?" Belet muttered, breathing hard through her nose so that she was almost snorting. "I thought you hated him?"

"I *do*."

"Could have fooled me. You two looked like you were about to jump on each other. Come on." She yanked on Saraid's arm.

Saraid realized that they weren't going to her tent. "Where are we going?"

"To the stables, to find Lannu if he's there. You've got your cursed *lahart*. Now it's time we got you out of here. I don't trust Cadel not to...to do something stupid. Or you, for that matter," she added.

Saraid didn't argue. This had been a warning that for all her anger at Cadel, she still couldn't help finding him attractive, just as she had before — and that was dangerous. She had to get away from him, the sooner the better. "I can't — not now. I need my jewelry, remember? And Perrin and the Hirras are probably still in my tent. I'll go tomorrow."

Belet tossed her hair and looked sulky, but nodded. "Tomorrow. I'll go with you."

"Don't you trust me?"

Belet met her eyes. "After what just happened? No, not really."

Saraid spent a good part of the night pondering how to approach Lannu and, the next morning, made Belet rehearse with her till she felt comfortable. That meant they were late to the stable, and most of the morning crowd had dispersed so that she was afraid she might have missed him.

But to her surprise and relief, Lannu was sitting cross-legged just in the shade of his horse's stall, braiding thin strips of leather. He scrambled to his feet and greeted her cheerfully. After returning his greeting and making small talk for a few minutes until Belet, at the end of the row of stalls, gave her an all clear, Saraid made her move.

"Lannu, I was wondering..." She paused and looked at the ground, then moved a little closer to him. "There's no one else I can trust...no one else who'll help me." She was pleased with the quaver of anguish in her voice. Nin had always said she was a hopelessly bad actress, but just now she didn't have to pretend very hard that she was upset. She blinked several times to generate extra moisture in her eyes as Belet had taught her, then raised them to his. Surely no one could resist a teary-eyed princess in distress.

He gulped. "What is it? What's wrong?"

"I...I can't stay here any longer. I don't belong here. I have no quarrel with the Adaihans...I just want to go!" There. She hadn't had to fake that, either. "You know the Adaiha, and how to get to Madariv. Will you take me there?"

"Your Highness!" He looked shocked.

"You'll be handsomely rewarded." She fumbled in her sleeve where one of her bracelets was pinned, wrapped in a scrap of *idhe* cloth, and showed it to him. The tourmaline and gold strand draped across her hand like an exotic lizard. "You may have this now, and another one like it when we reach the border. And once I'm safe in the city, you can have anything you want. Gold and jewels. A knighthood or a commission in the army."

Lannu's eyes had widened. He seemed unable to say anything; his mouth opened and closed again.

"Or land and a house, if that's what you wish. All you have to do is guide me there."

He finally seemed to find his voice. "When?" he whispered.

"As soon as possible. Tonight, if you will."

He stood silent again, eyes downcast, considering. Saraid held her breath. Dear Keranieth, had Belet chosen the right man? If he refused...

"All right," he said at last, and she breathed again. "Tonight. Meet me here at, uh, midnight."

"Thank you! Oh, thank you!" She held the bracelet out to him. He took it, perhaps a little reluctantly. But what did that matter? He'd agreed!

# Nine

One of a ruler's most valuable attributes is clarity of vision. Few men are capable of seeing their situations as they truly are. Rare is the person who can recognize defeat and understand that it is time to switch to a different tactic.

—*The Flower of Royalty Blossom'd*

SARAID LEFT CADEL'S TENT directly after their evening meal that night, pleading tiredness. She'd been distracted, but so had Cadel. He had toyed with his cup of Theklan wine, not looking at her and not speaking, then suddenly seemed to notice his plate and gobbled everything on it very quickly. On the other hand, she'd had to force herself to eat because of her excitement and uneasiness. His silence suited her just fine. After the episode with her *lahart*, she wasn't sure what to say to him, anyway.

Back at her tent, she prepared for bed as usual in case Perrin stopped by, pretended to read for a while, and blew out her lantern. Then she changed back into her clothes and climbed into bed again to wait.

Her saddlebags were already packed and hidden under the

bed—she'd just taken the bare necessities—and Belet had brought her provisions and made sure her waterskin was full. How many nights would it take to get there? Lannu hadn't said, and Belet wasn't sure. But that wasn't important. She'd last as long as it took to get out of the Adaiha.

When the night watchman made his periodic round of the camp, she waited for his quiet humming and bobbing lantern to fade away around a corner, put on her *lahart*, snatched up her bags, and slipped into the night. The moon was nearly full and she tiptoed uneasily from shadow to shadow as Belet had told her, to avoid being seen. She approached the stables with caution, in case some of the Riders were lingering there on such a fine night, but the area was dark and deserted. Had Lannu changed his mind…or worse yet, told anyone? She fought back her uneasiness. She would count to one hundred and sneak to Belet's tent if he hadn't come by then.

A low whinny halted her at sixty-seven. She peered around the corner of the stable tent and saw a *lahart*ed figure emerge from it, leading two horses.

"I didn't hear you saddling them," she whispered, hurrying toward him. "Is everything rea—"

Lannu held a finger to his lips—or where his lips would be if he weren't wearing a mask and scarf swathed around the lower half of his face. Saraid nodded and fell silent. Sound would carry on such a calm, clear night. She drew up her own scarf to partly cover her face, then took the reins of the horse Lannu handed her. A few hundred feet from the tent they paused while she buckled on her saddlebags. They mounted and set off.

It was a beautiful night. The moon cast a glittering white light on the peaks and edges of the dunes around them, bleaching the golden sands silver. They contrasted with the black shadows of the hollows, and the two created a black-and-white landscape that was lovely but confusingly two-dimensional, so that judging distance was almost impossible.

But Lannu was untroubled by the hypnotic, deceptive landscape. Saraid rode next to him, glad to let him navigate while exultation in the ease of their escape washed over her. She'd done it! She'd gotten her story back in its ordained path. No more inconvenient detours, either of her fate or of her heart.

"Did you have a hard time getting away?" she asked when they'd ridden about ten minutes.

He shook his head, then lifted his finger again in that shushing gesture. For an instant, Saraid was annoyed. Weren't they far enough from the camp that conversation was safe? But Lannu was the Rider here—perhaps there was some reason that the less noise they made, the better. And once they'd gotten past the preliminary pleasantries, what would they talk about? She'd asked Lannu to desert his people, and he'd done so. He probably wasn't in much of a mood to chat. It was probably best to keep conversation to a minimum, at least until daybreak.

Time went by, then more time, and still they rode in silence. Saraid yawned behind her scarf and wished she'd been able to get a proper nap that afternoon, but she'd been far too keyed up. This bouncing back and forth between sleeping by day, then by night, then back again was harder than she'd thought it would be.

"Shall we stop for a rest?" she called to Lannu, who rode a few paces ahead.

Without even turning, he shook his head.

At least he could have said yes or no. This silence of his was going to get on her nerves pretty soon. But he was right—they couldn't afford to rest yet. By daybreak everyone would know they were missing, and Cadel would undoubtedly send searchers after them. Now was the time to put as much distance as possible between them and the camp. Saraid straightened her shoulders, which had begun to sag. If Lannu could endure this, so could she.

Would they still arrive in Madariv ahead of the decoy caravan? Probably; she'd been in Cadel's camp several days now, but the decoy, being larger, was undoubtedly traveling much more slowly than she had been. She would try to sneak into the city and make her way to the Theklan ambassador's house first.

He and Papa had been friends growing up, and she'd called him Uncle Ithan when she was very small. She hadn't seen him in years, since she was a child. Would he recognize her now?

The moon sank toward the horizon, then past it. The sag in her shoulders had begun to affect the rest of her, but Lannu rode on, his back straight and his pace unchanging. The stars began to fade and the black of night to yield to a colorless gray. Day would come soon, and Cadel would wait in vain for her to come to his tent. Or perhaps Perrin would come in to say good morning, as she often did, and find her empty bed and deserted tent. When would Lannu's officer realize that he was missing? Or would someone notice the missing horses first? Would Cadel stomp around, shouting orders for his Riders to find her at all costs? She was sure she knew what Belet would be doing—informing Cadel that she was a spoiled ingrate who wasn't worth going after and that he was well rid of her.

She wished, though, that she'd had a chance to find out the true reason for why he'd kidnapped her in the first place. Perhaps someday, when the Adaiha was under Mauburni's control once more, he'd be captured in turn and she could come down to his prison cell and ask him...or maybe not.

And anyway, what did she care what he thought? The chances were that she'd never see him again. She could forget about him and get on with becoming a perfect monarch with the Lord Protector. Yes—starting right now she'd not think about Cadel.

At last a hint of rose suffused the horizon as they rode up the flank of a tall dune. Surely they'd think about stopping soon? She could last for longer—well, maybe a *little* longer—but their horses would need rest. She rubbed at her eyes. They felt as if they were lined with Adaihan sand.

"Lannu," she croaked—her throat was rough from having been silent so long. "I really think—"

They crested the long dune just then, and Saraid was struck dumb in mid-sentence. Cadel's camp lay before them, the still, mirror-like pool of the oasis reflecting dawn's first light. She stared at it, then blinked rapidly. Had she dozed off and found herself in the middle of a bad dream?

But her horse broke into a trot, sensing its stall and feed bucket, and there was no way to sleep through a brisk downhill trot. At the bottom of the dune she reined him in and turned to Lannu. "I trusted you! How could you do this to me—"

But Lannu had put back his hood—wait, wasn't his hair dark, not gold?—and was pulling off his mask.

It was Cadel.

For a moment, Saraid could only cling to her horse as a complex surge of emotions battled inside her—dismay and embarrassment, anger and, oddly, shame. Anger won. She took a deep, ragged breath and spat, "What are *you* doing here?"

"Sshhh! Do you want to wake the whole camp?"

Saraid bit her lip and spurred her horse toward the stables, Cadel close behind her. Tears blurred her view of the silent, peaceful scene. What had happened? Belet hadn't changed her mind and told Cadel, had she?

At the stables a lone figure stepped out from the shadows. It was Lannu. He took her horse as she dismounted and met her eyes with an apologetic grimace. She coldly turned her head. There was her answer—not Belet, but him.

Then Cadel unstrapped her saddlebags and led her back through the still-silent paths to his tent. He directed her into a seat, struck a flint to light a brazier of *faarv*, then stood before her, arms folded and *lahart* flung back over his shoulders, staring at her appraisingly. The dancing flames in the brazier shadowed his eyes so that she couldn't see his expression. She ignored him and concentrated on keeping her back straight and her face under control. Whatever happened, she must not cry in front of him.

"I can't say I blame you for trying," he said at last. "And I must admire your courage and ingenuity. It might have worked if my men were not completely loyal to me. Lannu came to me directly after your visit yesterday." He picked up a box from the table, took something from it, and tossed it into her lap. It was her pink tourmaline bracelet.

"And don't try to bribe anyone else to carry a message for you," he continued. "That won't work, either."

She ignored it and glared up at him. "So what was the point of making me ride all night? Are you that fond of torturing people?"

He glowered back. "I didn't do it to torture you. I did it because I thought it would be a good way to teach you an important lesson."

"I'm not your pupil," she snapped.

He leaned over her chair, hands planted on its arms, their faces inches apart. His eyes were a piercing, lightning-storm blue, even in the dim light cast by the brazier. "Right now, you are. And you need to learn that I am in control here."

"Fine, you're in control. You have complete power over me. Are you happy now?" She would not look away, even though his face was getting as blurry and out-of-focus as the camp had. Pox it, she wasn't supposed to cry. "What now? Chaining me in my tent? Leg-irons and handcuffs?"

The fury in his eyes faded. "Saraid, I would never do that to you."

Saraid's rage deepened, if that was even possible. "I think I have made it abundantly clear that I don't want to be here. Why won't you let me go to Mauburni?"

He turned away from her rubbing his neck. "I'm trying to save you," he finally said, his voice low.

"From what?"

"Not what. Whom." His voice was so quiet that she could barely hear him. "From your intended husband."

"What?" She jumped up from her chair. If she weren't so angry, she might have laughed.

He whirled to face her. "Quietly, unless you want Tiruus in here."

"*You* may want him in here, to keep me from throttling you!" she whispered furiously. "Are you mad? What does my marrying the Lord Protector of Mauburni have to do with you?"

He met her eyes calmly enough, though she could feel, even through the space that separated them and her own rage, that he was as taut as a drawn bow. "No, I'm not mad. And I never intended to bring you here. I knew you were crossing the Adaiha, but I hadn't planned on coming anywhere near your caravan. You're the one who blundered into the oasis where I happened to be staying on my way back here."

"I'm supposed to believe that?"

"You can believe what you like. I'm just trying to explain myself."

She crossed her arms on her chest. "Please, continue. I'm simply fascinated."

"You don't need to do that, you know." He sighed and rubbed his neck again. "I was surprised when you arrived at Hursnam's—non-Adaihans rarely end up there. There wasn't any one thing about you that made me suspicious—but a lot of little things, taken together, helped me figure out who you were fairly quickly, despite your story."

Saraid sat down again, feeling deflated. Talnith. Captain Zamas's all-too-military bearing. And just maybe, a few behaviors and unintentionally dropped snippets of information of her own. Pox it, she should have taken Talnith and gone straight to their rooms and not spoken to anyone that first morning. Then none of this would have happened. "What a prize we were, to drop into your lap like that." It didn't come out as lightly as she'd intended.

"Not as far as I was concerned." He paced a few steps, as if restless. "Having you loose in the middle of the Adaiha was an unwelcome complication. I've just finished negotiations with the Gesanthu Clan and I couldn't be sure all the bands in the clan knew about the agreements, or that some of them might not find a small group like yours too tempting not to attack. Dealing with an international incident before I was ready for it was the last thing I wanted. That's why I got Hursnam to suggest to Zamas that you needed a guide and that I was just the man for the job."

"So you could kidnap me yourself?"

"So I could keep you out of trouble. Quite honestly, I wished you damned Theklans hadn't thought you could outwit us by sending you separately and that you had never set foot in the Adaiha."

"What changed your mind?"

He stopped pacing and took a deep breath. "You did."

She stared at him.

"If you had been the maid and Talnith the princess, I wouldn't have cared as much. I probably would have turned you all around and eventually have led you back to Thekla, just to try to keep Mutrand from getting his bride...though I would have done my best to convince *you* to stay in the Adaiha with me."

"As if I would!"

He ignored her interruption. "But you were the one going to marry the Lord Protector. What did they tell you about him, Saraid? What did he tell you about himself?" He looked at her hard.

She remembered, with an uneasy feeling, some of their conversations about Lord Protector Mutrand back when he was Kayn. "How do you know what he's like? What does it matter to you?"

"*You* matter to me. Mutrand is twenty years older than you. And for those twenty years he's been able to do pretty much as he pleases. Do you think he's going to stop just because he's married to you? He wants to marry you as part of his bid to be named king. Your job is to be royal, produce heirs for him, and keep out of his way while he continues to live the life he's accustomed to."

What was he implying about the Lord Protector? "I have no idea what you're talking about," she said.

"Of course you don't. When you said that you were doing your best to teach yourself to love him sight unseen, to make his life your life, I couldn't get it out of my head. He doesn't want your love or to have you in his life helping him be the perfect enlightened monarch. He doesn't want to *be* an enlightened monarch. He wants the crown, that's all. He wants you because you're a princess who'll help him become king, and then may the gods have mercy on Mauburni. Because he won't."

"You're lying." This couldn't be true. "Father—the council— they would have said something—"

He pounded his fist on the table. "Would they, Saraid? You yourself told me how important your marriage was for Thekla. How desperate Thekla is for the Mauburnian market for its goods and crops to be restored, and to regain access to Mauburnian shipping. And you're the key." His voice softened. "To your father and his ministers, the personal happiness of one princess probably doesn't seem too high a price to pay."

Saraid glowered at his feet. Somehow she didn't want to meet his eyes just now. "Why should I believe a word you're saying?"

"Because it's true. I have"—he paused—"connections in Madariv. They keep me informed about a great many things. For example, did you know that your principal lady-in-waiting-to-be is one of Mutrand's favorite mistresses, and has been for years?"

"Which proves nothing, as there's no way for me to confirm or refute what you say. So what about you? Are you the fairy-tale hero come to rescue the princess?"

He didn't flinch away from the scorn in her voice, but she saw his hands clench. "Why not?"

"So that's why you're not asking for a ransom. What are you going to do with me, then? No matter how good your 'system' is, at some point someone will realize I'm gone. Or..." She looked at him through narrowed eyes. "Marrying a royal princess would go a long way toward making your lordship of the Adaiha look more legitimate as well. Are you borrowing a page from Lord Mutrand's book?"

He looked down at the table and adjusted a pile of papers. "If you decide that you want to stay for my sake, I would be...very pleased. But I would be equally pleased to return you to Thekla, if that is what will make you happy. I would never force you to marry me. Never." His voice was low and very serious.

"I'd like to see you try!"

"Believe me, I know better. Besides, there are much better methods than force."

She let herself snort in a way that would have given her governesses apoplexy. "Such as?"

For the first time, he smiled. "That would be my business. Now, since we both agree that you can't be forced to act against your wishes, then I will humbly beg the pleasure of your company at my tent from now on in the afternoons."

"*What?*"

"It's my poor Riders. You have them terrified, and this seemed the easiest solution to the problem. They swear they won't go anywhere near the stables in case you take it into your head to try to bribe another one of them. Poor Lannu begged for double duty for the next month because he's afraid you'll try to talk to him again. I would never force you, of course, but you see the difficulty I am in." He spread his hands in a gesture of helplessness.

Saraid became aware that she was actually spluttering. "Why, you—you—"

A loud "heya!" from somewhere outside, followed by a murmur of conversation, halted her. Cadel glanced toward the flap of his tent. "Tiruus will probably come in shortly. If you don't want him or the rest of the camp to know about our expedition last night—and I'm not sure they wouldn't regard it as an insult to their hospitality—then you might want to go back to your tent now. If you're quick enough, you can pretend you've been asleep in bed all night."

All at once her weariness seemed to catch up with her. "Pretend, nothing," she muttered under her breath. If she hadn't been able to escape, then she might as well go have a well-deserved nap.

He smiled. "Good morning, Saraid."

She ignored him and hurried out. Fortunately she met no one on her way, though she heard people stirring in their tents and smelled a few cooking fires being kindled. Once safely back in her tent she didn't even bother shedding her *lahart* and clothes but climbed straight under her covers.

Sneaking to Mauburni hadn't worked. At least she'd tried it, though, instead of sitting and feeling sorry for herself. She would just have to bide her time and, in the meanwhile, learn all she could about Cadel and his plans for the Adaiha. It was information that would surely prove useful to the Lord Protec— no, to her husband—later on.

And why had Cadel said those things about Lord Mutrand? They were lies, of course. They had to be. Papa and his ministers would *never* have consented to marry her to a monster. Still… either he was an extraordinarily good actor or he really believed what he'd told her. His voice as he talked about Lord Mutrand and Mauburni had been almost pained, as if the Lord Protector had personally harmed him in some way.

Or was this part of his plan to make her decide she wanted to stay with him?

She rolled over and poked at her pillow. Pox it, she should march right back over there and tell him that she wanted to go home to Thekla. That would show him how she felt about him!

But the memory of the silk farmers she'd seen on her way out of Thekla, singing as they planted new trees because her marriage would help restore their livelihood, caught at her. How could she disappoint them and thousands of others by turning her back on marrying the Lord Protector?

No. As much as she would have liked to run all the way home to Thekla, she couldn't. Thekla was relying on her to get to Mauburni, and she would get there eventually—she knew she would. But until she understood what Cadel really wanted, she would have to remain here, to watch and wait.

And be on her guard.

# Ten

Remember that endurance will overcome one's opponents when nothing else will, though open conflict might seem a more satisfying method of combat.

—*The Flower of Royalty Blossom'd*

"GOOD MORNING!" SOMEONE SAID, far too loudly. "You left these in my tent, and I thought you might want them."

"'S not funny, Nin." Saraid rolled over, eyes shut tight, trying to burrow deeper under her covers—and found that she was unable to move.

"I think you're trapped," the voice said, sounding amused. "Need a hand?"

Saraid woke up a bit more and realized that she couldn't move because she was wrapped in a cloak, not because Nin had immobilized her with pillows. And it wasn't Nin who'd spoken—

"Cadel!" She squirmed until the *lahart* loosened around her enough to let her unfasten it and sit up in bed. "What are you doing here?"

He was standing over her, her saddlebags slung over his shoulder and a large tray in his hands. He looked clean and rested and far too jaunty just now, in spectacular contrast to her gummy-feeling eyes and disheveled hair.

"You're supposed to take your meals with me, remember?" He set the tray down on the floor and fetched one of her chairs. "And since it was time to eat and you hadn't arrived, I figured I'd bring our breakfast here."

Saraid groaned and fell back onto her pillow. Why didn't these tents have locks on the flaps? She'd planned to sleep until noon, at least.

"I'll leave your bags on the table here if that's all right."

Pox him, he was barely able to keep the laughter out of his voice. "How long have I been asleep?"

"Not very long. Just a pleasant nap. Tea?" He bent over the tray and poured a cup.

Saraid did not tell him what he could do with his tea, though she dearly wanted to. "I've been up all night, thanks to you. The least you could do is let me get some sleep."

"And waste a beautiful day?" He didn't bother pointing out how silly her words had been—his grin was doing a fine job of that all by itself. Well, what did he expect her to say? They hadn't *had* to spend the night riding in circles in the Adaiha. That had been his idea.

Scowling, she took the cup he handed her. "Aren't you even tired?"

"Of course I'm tired. So what?" He poured himself some tea and handed her a plate of grilled flatbread spread with honey, then sat back in his chair and studied her. "Doesn't The Book say, 'Let not yesterday influence how you live today, except in wisdom gained.'"

The last thing she wanted to hear right now was Cadel quoting The Book at her. "I doubt that Count Ebroian meant it quite that way."

"Why not? And even if he didn't, it still works well. Eat your bread."

"I'm not hungry."

"Yes you are. Or you will be soon enough." He got up again and began prowling around her tent, then paused at the bar where her few clothes hung neatly from hooks and examined them, head to one side. "Hmm. You do need more clothes. Will you wear this today?" He indicated a deep aqua tunic.

She nearly choked on a sip of tea. "Why should I?"

"Why not? It's a beautiful color. Just like the sea." He turned and looked at her, still smiling, but there was an intensity in his look that made her turn away in confusion. "Would it help if I said I would think you most surpassing fair in it?" he added, more gently.

"'Let not flattery turn your head or permit the flatterer to gain power over you with honeyed words.'" There. That should fix him.

"'Understand that the gift of an honest opinion, though sincerely given, may not be appreciated by the recipient,'" he promptly countered. How could she ever have been pleased that he knew The Book almost as well as she did?

There was a rustling at the flap of the tent. "Your Highness?"

"Come in, Perrin." Cadel took the aqua tunic from the hook and laid it on Saraid's bed.

"Cadel?" Perrin stood halfway in the entrance, looking surprised. "What are you doing here?"

"Making my life difficult," Saraid muttered.

"But it's much more interesting when it is. Don't you think so?"

"For goodness' sake, Cadel, go do something useful and let this poor girl get dressed." Perrin stood to one side of the flap, holding it open and making shooing gestures. "Go!"

"Yes, ma'am." He paused long enough to look meaningfully at the tunic, then left.

"Sometimes I wonder if he's four or twenty-four. It's not always easy to tell." Perrin looked at the tray Cadel had brought and shook her head. "Unfortunately he's too big to spank anymore."

Saraid was startled into a laugh. "Don't tell me you ever spanked him?"

"Once or twice. When he needed it. Which seems to be occurring more often now than it did when he was small." Perrin picked up the tray and set it on the table, not seeming to notice her saddlebags still lying where Cadel had put them.

Saraid took a sip of tea and cleared her throat. Time to start listening and learning. "How long have you known him?"

The older woman sat down in the chair Cadel had vacated and smiled to herself. "All his life. I was his governess until his mother was—until she died, and after that I more or less raised him. His father—his father was a good man, but not perhaps the most capable one. We did our best, Meyric and I."

Meyric too? "Are you and Meyric...you know..."

"Goodness, no!" Perrin smiled, but not happily. "I lost my husband and sons many years ago."

"I'm so sorry." She thought of Mama. "Was it a sickness?"

"No," Perrin said shortly. She frowned at Saraid. "Why are you wearing your *lahart* in bed, Your Highness?"

"Oh, er, no reason. I was chilly." Saraid huddled into it so that Perrin wouldn't see she wasn't wearing her nightdress beneath it. "But I do wish you wouldn't keep calling me Your Highness." Dropping the formality might encourage Perrin to talk more, which would help with her new self-appointed role as intelligence gatherer.

"Are you sure?" Perrin seemed surprised.

"Very."

"Well." Perrin sat still for a few seconds, looking at her. "Thank you, Saraid. Now why don't I let you get dressed?" She rose, smiled, and slipped out of the tent.

As soon as she'd left Saraid jumped up and changed, grumbling, into the tunic, then poured herself more tea and sank back against her pillows, thinking about what she'd learned. Non-Adaihan Perrin and Meyric had mostly brought up non-Adaihan Cadel, who had become overlord of the Adaihans. How had that come about? And what about Cadel's parents—his dead mother and good but ineffectual father? How had she died? What had his father done or not done? If only she weren't too tired to think straight...

She was awakened again by someone clearing her throat. Hirra-the-Elder was peering at her from the flap of the tent. Beyond her was the younger Hirra, laden with a large bundle.

"Princess." Hirra-the-Elder nodded when Saraid sat up and blinked at her. "Lord Cadel sent us. He wishes you to have proper Adaihan robes made up. May we come in?"

Saraid wished she could bark out a no, roll over, and go back to sleep. But it wasn't the Hirras' fault that she wasn't being allowed to. She nodded.

The younger Hirra set her bundle down on the table and unwrapped it, and Saraid saw that it contained fabric, rose and dark blue and soft green.

"Aren't they lovely?" Hirra-the Younger was pink with excitement. "Milord Cadel picked them out. I'd never thought a man could pick out the right colors for someone, but these are perfect for you." She unrolled the dark blue and held it up.

It would be cruel to dampen her enthusiasm. Saraid got up and let the elder Hirra drape the fabric over her shoulders, then obediently looked in the mirror her daughter held up. Maybe Cadel did have a surprising ability to choose flattering colors for her. But even more obvious was the message the unwitting Hirras had carried for him. Every time she wore one of these robes, she would remember him.

"Is it to your liking?" Hirra-the-Elder asked.

Saraid hesitated. It was a beautiful color, and it did look very good on her... "It's lovely," she finally admitted.

"Then we will make this one first. Hirra, isn't there a paler shade for the underrobe in here somewhere?"

Saraid submitted again to being measured, then left the Hirras to spread the fabric all over the floor of the tent to begin cutting and went to sit on a chair set out under her awning. Perhaps reading The Book would prove soothing. And maybe she could sneak in a doze as well.

She sat down in the chair under the awning and opened The Book.

> *The loss of my most beloved liege lord and friend King Thanel is one of the great griefs of my life, and though I am humbly grateful for the trust invested in me to raise his and his dear queen's only son who too carries his proud name and guard the realm for him until his majority, it is a gift I would gladly have forgone. But since it has fallen to me, Count Varian Ebroian, to do these things, I have lain awake many nights and long, thinking on how best to fulfill my trust—*

Well, no one had ever said the prologue of The Book was its best part. Saraid's attention wandered to the illumination on the page facing it, showing a fanciful picture of Count Ebroian and the young King Thanel walking on the shore, evidently discussing weighty matters of state. By the way the boy king was glancing off to one side, she couldn't help wondering if he wouldn't rather have been chasing waves or skipping rocks than talking to Count Ebroian—

She sat back in her chair and frowned. She couldn't possibly be *bored* with reading The Book, could she? Of course not. It had to be that she was still tired from riding all night or still cross with Cadel for—well, for any number of things. Maybe she should go inside and see if the Hirras would let her help with the sewing. But that would be only a temporary fix. In a few days' time they'd be done with her sewing and then she'd—

"Good day, Your Highness," said a soft, piping voice.

Saraid looked up from The Book. A young girl stood before her, bowing formally with her hand on her heart. Like most of the Adaihan children Saraid had seen, she wore a shorter, less voluminous version of their parents' Adaihan robes and sandals, but over hers was a tabard, quartered blue and silver. She had a head full of wild brown curls and a mischievous cast to her pointed nose. Behind her stood Belet, arms crossed over her chest, her face expressionless.

"Um...good day to you." Pox it, she knew she was going to have to explain to Belet what had happened, but did it have to be right now?

"I'm Kursa. That's my sister, Bel—"

"We've already met, Kursa. C'mon, do your job." Oh, yes, it was clear Belet was not happy.

The child's eyes were a light, clear gray, and they examined her with great interest. "I'm gonna. But I've never seen a princess before." Then she seemed to recollect herself, for she stood straighter, filled her chest with a deep breath, and said in a rush, "Lord Cadel's compliments and would Her Highness th' Princess Saraid be so gracious as t'attend him somewhat later today as he is un'voidably detained on a nurgent matter a' business." She paused, then said, tentatively, "I think I got that right. Ha-dadai made me practice."

Saraid smiled. "It sounded right to me."

"Oh. Good." The girl went back to scrutinizing her. "I didn't know princesses wore braids."

"Well, this one does. Is there something else should I be wearing, do you think?"

"I dunno." Kursa sighed again. "I wish I could wear my hair in a braid. But it does this"—she shook her head so that the curls bounced—"so Mamai has to keep it short. She says it's because I got Ha-dadai's hair, but he still has his own hair, only it's gray. So I don't know what she means."

Saraid laughed. "I think she means that your hair is just like your grandfather's. Members of the same family often look a lot alike."

"But mine isn't gray." The girl scratched her nose. "If I got a new Ha-dadai, d'you think I'd get better hair? I like Lord Cadel's hair. It's pretty. D'you think he could be my ha-dadai? But ha-dadais are usually old, aren't they?"

"Usually." Saraid kept her face straight. "But unfortunately that's not how it works. I'm afraid you're going to have to keep your hair and your grandfather."

"He lets me be a page." Kursa patted the blue-and-silver tabard proudly. "He says it helps keep me out of trouble and gives Mamai a chance to rest. She's going to have a baby, you know, and it makes her feel sick a lot so she can't take care of me. And Dadai is one of Lord Cadel's Riders, so he's away a lot, so I help Ha-dadai with his work."

Saraid remembered her first morning in Cadel's tent, when Perrin had said that Meyric had his hands full with Kursa — not a semi-wild Adaihan warrior, as she'd guessed, but his granddaughter. It seemed strange for some reason — these people having everyday, ordinary problems and lives didn't match her picture of them as kidnappers and bandits.

"All right, that's enough, Kursa. You did your job. I need to talk to Her Highness now." Belet stepped forward.

While Saraid had been thinking, Kursa had leaned forward and was looking at The Book, still open to the picture of Count Ebroian. "It's so pretty," she murmured, firmly clasping her hands behind her back as if to keep herself from touching it.

Saraid stood up and set The Book on the chair, turning it so that the girl might see it properly. "You may look at it while your sister and I talk."

Belet took her arm, just as she had in the past, but dug her fingernails into her flesh as they walked away from the tent. "What are you still doing here?" she asked, hissing the *s*. "Lose your nerve?"

Saraid flexed her arm in protest. "No, Lannu did. He went straight to Cadel and told him I'd tried to bribe him. Cadel wore a mask and came in his place and had us riding in a circle all night before he finally brought me back and told me not to do it again."

Belet muttered something rude-sounding under her breath.

"Burn Lannu! I thought he'd be perfect...does Cadel know I helped you?"

"I don't think so. I certainly didn't tell him, if that's what you're wondering."

Belet scowled. "I'll have to think harder about who we approach next. There'll be a new group of Riders coming in from the Eb in a few days—"

"It won't do any good. Cadel said none of his Riders were bribable and that I shouldn't even think about getting one to carry a message out, much less help me leave. There won't be a next time."

"You're giving up just like that?"

Saraid sighed. "Didn't you hear what I said? It won't work. And I for one don't want to try it again and go for another circular jaunt with Cadel. Once was humiliating enough."

Belet was silent. "If the price is right, I'll bet we could find someone," she said stubbornly. "But if you're too worried about your dignity...or maybe you've changed your mind and aren't so eager to get away after all."

Saraid stopped walking. "Whose idea was this in the first place? I believe it was mine, if you recall. I'm the one with something at stake here."

"And I'm not?" Belet's voice grew shrill. "Until you showed up, Cadel and I were friends. I'm sure things were about to progress just as I'd hoped they would. Now he doesn't even know I exist. If I were a princess, I bet he'd still—"

"Look," Saraid interrupted. "If you can find someone to take me and guarantee it'll work, I'll gladly go. But you have to take on some of the risk this time and make the arrangements first. I'm not going to waste my time on another pointless—"

"Princess?" Kursa had come skipping up to them. She held The Book out, still open to the frontispiece. "Who's this?"

Belet dropped her arm. "We'll talk later."

"Heya, Bel—Ha-dadai says you're to go home and sit with Mamai and not hang around Lord Cadel's tent today," Kursa called after her, her light voice carrying. One or two people nearby glanced up.

Belet ignored them and her sister and stalked away.

"She's been awful cranky lately." Kursa looked up at Saraid with a troubled expression. "Mamai wants her to start looking for a husband when we go to Callest, but if she's that cranky all the time, no one'll even talk to her, don't you think?"

It was safer not to comment. "Let's sit down and I'll tell you about this book." Saraid held out her hand.

When they got back to her tent, she held The Book open on her lap. "This is a picture of the man who wrote this book. He's walking with the king, who was just a little boy. His name was Varian—see the little $v$'s the artist worked into the pattern on his coat?"

Kursa shook her head. "I can't read yet. I was 'sposed to start school but our teacher had to go to Callest a long time ago because his mother got sick, so we don't have any school. That's why I'm being a page right now."

"You can't read?"

"Unh-unh. Mamai's teaching me my letters but she doesn't always feel good enough to sit up in bed, and Belet's always busy, so I haven't learned 'em all yet. When we go to Callest, I guess school'll start again." She leaned again over The Book. "So those are $v$'s," she murmured.

"V-vee. For Varian." This was surprising. Cadel had seemed so concerned about the welfare of the people in the camp—remembering all those rheumatic knees and everything—so why had he allowed this situation to occur? Surely lessons for the small children of the camp were as important as anything else. "Over here is a $k$. It's the first sound in *king* and also in *Kursa*."

"K-Kursa!" the girl repeated. "I know that one. And C-Cadel, too."

"No, there's a $c$ at the start of Cadel. Sometimes it sounds like a $k$, as it does in Cadel, but sometimes it sounds..." She stopped, seized by an idea. "See here—why don't I teach you?"

Kursa's eyes widened. "Teach me? Really?"

"Why not? I don't have anything else to do, and your mother and sister can't right now. Would your grandfather let me, or are you too busy being his page?"

"I dunno. We need to go ask him." Kursa looked thoughtful. "Would you teach my friend Hannel too? She wants to read real-l-l-l-ly bad. And maybe Gerron even though sometimes he's a pig? And Wenru?"

"Er—well..."

But why shouldn't she teach the children their letters? True, she knew little about teaching. But she liked children—she'd always wished she'd had younger brothers or sisters but Mother had always been ill—and she loved books. Weren't those the most important attributes for a teacher? And it would give her something to do while waiting for rescue or for Cadel to realize she was a lost cause.

Kursa was leaning over the picture again. "How do you know if a word with a *k* sound at the start has a *k* or a *c*?"

"Well, as you learn to read you memorize how words are spelled, and then you can guess when you run across new words."

"How?"

"Well, you... Here." Saraid hastily flipped to another illumination. "That's the royal palace of Mauburni, in Madariv. Isn't it beautiful?" Hmm, maybe there were a few more things it was helpful to know as a teacher. But surely she'd be better than no teacher at all.

Kursa flopped onto her knees and leaned her arms on Saraid's lap to study the picture. "Oh, I know about that place. Ha-dadai says that from the tower here you can see all the way to the Isle of Rolg when the sky is clear. He promised he'll show me when we go back."

"What?"

"You *knooow*." She shrugged. "When we go back to Madariv."

Saraid stared down at the top of her curly head. "You're from Mauburni?"

"Uh-huh." Kursa turned a few pages over. "Ooh, is that the king of Nolor? He's scary looking. There's a *k* again. Does that say *king*, like it did on the other page?"

"Yes, it does. Very good. Can you find any other *k*'s?" That would keep her busy for a moment. Saraid sat back in her chair, thinking. So Meyric was from Mauburni. Was Perrin as well? And Cadel? If so, what were they doing in the Adaiha? And what about Lannu and the other young Riders who'd all gone to Madariv to attend the academy? Were they all connected? The more she learned, the more mysterious and confusing it all became.

"I wish I could read this," Kursa sighed. She scrambled back to her feet and looked longingly at The Book. "But I need to get back or Ha-dadai will be cross."

"If I have anything to say about it, you'll learn to read it." Saraid rose and looked at the sun. It was probably close enough to the *somewhat later* Cadel had requested, though she'd not caught the knack of knowing the time by glancing at the sky that these Adaihans had. Or Adaihan-Mauburnians. Cadel was going to regret commanding her to spend her afternoons with him by the time she got through questioning him today. It would serve him right, too. "I'll walk back with you."

"Can I come back and look at that book again sometime?" Kursa took her hand and looked up at Saraid through her eyelashes.

"Absolutely."

The child nodded happily. "Do you really think my hair is pretty?"

Did all small children change the subject without warning like that? "Yes, I do. I said I like your curls, and I always mean what I say," she answered emphatically.

"Do you think Lord Cadel's hair is pretty, too?"

"Um..." They were only a few paces from Cadel's tent, and Kursa's voice carried.

"I think it's pretty. Heya, Ha-dadai." Kursa released her hand

and danced up to Meyric, who was just coming through the tent's flap. "Look, the princess came with me. She's got a pretty book and she's gonna to teach me to read it."

"Kursa! I told you to come right back. You haven't been bothering her, have you?" Meyric's frown was both loving and exasperated. "Your Highness, I'm sorry if Kursa's been disturbing you. She's young, you understand."

"Not at all. We had a very interesting talk." She nodded toward the tent. "May I?"

If he was surprised at her sudden eagerness to see Cadel, he didn't show it. "Please. He's waiting for you."

Cadel was sitting at the large table in the center of his tent, rolling up a sheaf of documents when she walked in. His somber expression swiftly changed to a smile of pleasure. "Saraid! I knew you'd be beautiful in that color."

She ignored him. "I want to talk to you."

"Really?" He scooped up the rolls of paper scattered on the table and tipped them into a basket. "Are you finally admitting that we're still friends?"

When would he stop playing with words? "That's not what I meant. I *need* to talk to you."

"Oh. What about?" Cadel's servant Tiruus came in then, bearing a tray with bread and a pitcher and cups. He set it down on the table and left. Cadel glanced at it pointedly. "Don't forget that we're being civil to each other during meals."

"I'll be civil if you will." She sat down in the chair opposite him. How should she begin? "I just met Kursa."

"Kursa." He smiled. "She leads poor Meyric a merry dance. But her mother's not well and her father's one of my Riders, so Meyric's helping out with watching her."

"So she said." How should she start? No sense in tiptoeing around. "She can't read, you know."

He poured her a cup of cold tea from the pitcher. The manservant came in again with another tray. Cadel smiled and thanked him as he set out the serving bowls of dressed greens and boiled eggs and cheese and left, then turned back to Saraid. "Yes?"

"She says her teacher had to leave a while ago, and no one else has taken over teaching the youngest children."

Cadel took a plate and began heaping salad on it. He seemed to like serving her meals, and she'd learned not to argue. "That's right. Firna's family needed him back in Callest."

"And no one's taken his place?"

He paused for just an instant, spoon hovering in midair, then went on. "So?"

"Doesn't that bother you? You're the one who knows all about everyone's goats and rheumatic knees and coal. Doesn't not having a teacher for them concern you at all?"

"It seems to concern *you*." His face was expressionless as he set her plate before her.

"It's a shame that a bright little girl like Kursa can't read yet. It should bother you. In fact, I'm shocked that it doesn't."

"What do you think should be done?" Now he sounded almost bored as he served his own food. That made her angry.

"I think that someone should be teaching them. Like me."

He blinked. "You?"

"Why not? They need a teacher, and I need to have something to do when I'm not being forced to trot around at your heels." She was beginning to warm to the idea. "It's a disgrace! If everyone in the camp is your concern, what about them?"

He sat back in his chair and looked at her. "You want to be their teacher."

"Somebody needs to. It's—"

"It's a disgrace, yes. So you just said." He continued to look at her thoughtfully. "Saraid, less than a day ago you tried to run away from here. Now...this. Why? Are you doing this because of something you read in The Book or because *you* want to?"

Was that an insult or not? "Aren't I allowed to have a mind of my own?"

"That's what I'd like to know."

She sighed impatiently. "If you must know, I got the idea from

Kursa's looking at my copy of The Book but not being able to read it. Does caring if she and the other children can read count as my own idea?"

"Interesting. I thought your opinion of Adaihans was that we were all worthless brigands?"

"I never said that!"

He cleared his throat gently.

"I didn't mean it like that," she amended.

"So just I'm the worthless brigand."

"Yes—no—that isn't the point!" She was going to throw her plate at him if he didn't stop baiting her. "Do you want a teacher for the children or not?"

"Well..." he said slowly. "It would serve to keep you out of trouble."

She glared at him. "I don't get into trouble."

He raised an eyebrow, and she flushed. "I don't consider what I did 'trouble.'"

"I suppose you wouldn't." He rubbed his chin, one hand covering his mouth as he did. Pox it, was he trying to conceal a smile? "Very well," he finally said. "I doubt you can do much harm to Adaihan youth in the weeks before we go to Callest. Teach away if it pleases you."

She ignored the first part of his speech. "Thank you." The words felt awkward in her mouth, addressed to him. "Where is the school?"

"The school?"

"For the children? You know, what we were just discussing?"

He shook his head. "This is a temporary camp, Saraid. When Firna was teaching the beginners, he had them meet at his tent. That's what the teachers of the older children do here, too."

No school? "What about books and—and writing implements and—"

"Whatever Firna had, he took back to Callest with him so he could teach there. That's how it's done in the Adaiha. If you want to be a teacher, you'll have to arrange your own school."

"But—"

"Of course, if you think you're not capable…"

He was looking at her with that barely hidden amused expression again. She straightened in her chair and reached for the bread. "I'm quite capable, thank you."

"You might talk to Perrin. She'll have some suggestions, most likely."

"I'll do that."

"Or Meyric, perhaps. He—"

"I said I'll take care of it."

They ate in silence after that. Saraid avoided looking at Cadel, afraid she'd see the smile lurking in the corners of his mouth again. She'd started to fear that smile, because it confused her. Not to mention scared her. People only smiled like that when they felt in control of a situation. It certainly wouldn't be appearing on her face any time soon.

Also, Cadel's earlier question wouldn't leave her alone, because she had asked herself the same thing: why *did* she want to teach this school, when yesterday she'd been plotting her escape?

As much as she hated to admit it, she knew the answer. Cadel would not let her go forward, and she would not go back; so for now, this was her home. Which meant that these people were, for now, her people, and if she was a true princess and student of The Book, she must serve them in whatever way she could.

The thought made her uncomfortable…and as The Book said, most thoughts which made one uncomfortable were probably true. She pushed back her plate.

Cadel's voice broke into her thoughts. "Not hungry?"

"I've had enough, thank you."

"As you wish." He rang a small bell and Tiruus appeared. He removed the dishes but left the pitcher. Cadel refilled both their cups from it. "You never answered Kursa's question, by the way."

"What question?"

"About my hair."

His *hair*? Oh, no! He'd overheard that? Saraid remembered

Kursa's high, clear voice. Evidently he had. "What about your hair?" she stalled.

"Do you think it's pretty?"

A sudden picture popped into her mind—the evening at the oasis, when they'd just met—how the setting sun had lit his hair so brightly and how she'd longed to touch it. Pox it, she *had* to stop thinking of him as Kayn. "I don't care if it is or not. Right now I'd simply like to set it on fire."

He threw his head back and laughed. "Oh, Saraid. I wish you knew how—"

"How much I amuse you," she finished coldly. "You're making it quite clear."

"That wasn't quite what I'd intended to say, but it will do for now." He slipped out of his chair to kneel by hers and took her hand. She tried to snatch it away, but he wouldn't let it go. "Can't you relax with me just a little?" he asked, very quietly. "We used to tease each other and laugh together, back when we were Kayn and Nin. Do you remember?"

The longing in his voice was shockingly naked. And terrifying. Saraid stared down at her lap and wouldn't let herself remember. "We're different people now."

"Only because you want us to be."

"I can't," she whispered.

"You can't, or you won't?" he asked, then sighed. "No, never mind. Go talk to Perrin about the school. I'll see you later." He stood up and walked stiffly to his desk, where he suddenly appeared absorbed by a document lying on a tall pile.

# Eleven

*Eyes work best when they're open. Observing details enables the larger view to be understood.*

*—The Flower of Royalty Blossom'd*

"HOW DID HE TALK you into running a school?"

Perrin was sitting under the awning of her tent, sewing. She set down the tiny shirt she'd been making for Meyric's new grandchild and stared at Saraid.

"He didn't. It was my idea." Why had that come out sounding so defensive? Probably because of the skeptical look Perrin had given her, so soon after Cadel's dubious reaction. "Well, it was. I need something to keep me occupied, and Kursa told me she hadn't learned to read yet because the teacher had left. I thought Cadel was so concerned about everyone's well-being—how could he have neglected finding them a teacher for so long?"

Perrin folded up her sewing. "He didn't. He'd found new teachers twice, but for one reason or another they were unable to do the job. And what with other matters that have had him away from camp a great deal, and then your arrival—" She looked at Saraid. "He didn't tell you that?"

"Uh...no." It was suddenly easier to look other places than directly at Perrin. Why hadn't Cadel told her that, instead of letting her give him that lecture? Unless—unless it had been his way of seeing if she was sincere about helping—

Perrin shook her head and muttered something under her breath. Saraid just caught "...what he thinks he's going to accomplish I have no idea..." but didn't hear the rest as she bent to put her sewing into a basket at her feet.

"It wouldn't be a large group—several families have already left for Callest for the winter—but I expect there are still a handful of children Kursa's age who are ready to start learning," she continued in a normal tone of voice. "You'd be doing a service to their parents. Getting ready to leave the oasis for the winter is time- and attention-consuming. And it will give the children a head start once they get to Callest."

"You all keep talking about this Callest—where is it? What is it? I've never run across mention of it in my reading."

Perrin smiled. "That's the way we want it. It's a—well, I suppose you'd call it a small city, hidden deep in the center of the Adaiha. Very few non-Adaihans have ever been allowed into it, so it's not surprising you've never heard of it. It didn't even exist before the drying of the Adaiha—it's partly subterranean, built in the cliffs and caves left by a vanished river."

That sounded fascinating. "Will we go there?"

"I don't know what Cadel has planned for you. He hasn't seen fit to tell anyone." Perrin sounded faintly peevish as she spoke. "Now about your school..." She sat back, frowning and tapping her fingers on the arm of her chair. "I've got an idea of whom to invite, but I'll have to think about it a little more. Probably no more than six or eight children are left who would qualify. What do you plan on teaching?"

"Well, I..." she began, then closed her mouth. What would she teach? She'd just gone and demanded of Cadel that she be allowed to run a school. Now she'd better figure out how she was going to do it. "The very basics. Their letters and numbers, I suppose. I don't know how that's done in the Adaiha, so I wouldn't want to interfere with their later schooling by doing things too differently."

Perrin nodded her approval. "That's perceptive of you. Besides, schooling for young children shouldn't be too burdensome. They're just learning how to learn. A part of each morning is usual for this age."

Which would still leave her afternoons free to be with Cadel. A pity. "Very well."

"We'll plan tomorrow on visiting the families I have in mind. What will you charge?"

"Charge? As in, a fee? I'm not doing this for money!"

"Then you won't get any students. Adaihans are skeptics. They don't believe you can get anything worthwhile for nothing. No, don't look stubborn. It's true."

Why hadn't Cadel told her any of this? "But I don't want or need their money."

Perrin sighed. "Charge them something now. Put it aside and then quietly use it to pay for their lessons with the regular teacher in Callest. That way face will be saved for now. By the time they find out about it..." She shrugged.

Saraid understood. By the time the parents found out about it, she'd probably be long gone from everyone's lives here, and it wouldn't matter. They could be grateful or suspicious as they liked. For an instant, the thought that what she was doing here was temporary and unimportant stung. Then sense prevailed.

"All right. I'll do that," she agreed.

Within a week, it was arranged: the children invited, the fees (set by Perrin) paid, and at midmorning two days later Saraid had seven children aged five and six, including a bright-eyed and expectant Kursa, sitting cross-legged on mats in a semicircle in front of her, beneath her awning.

She'd gone with Perrin to visit their parents and had been struck by the quiet, watchful dignity of the Adaihans—as most of them were, apart from Belet and Kursa's very pregnant mother, Ahryne, who had her father Meyric's gray eyes and plump build. They seemed pleased and slightly surprised by the idea of her organizing a school, but all agreed to send their children.

For the first day, Perrin suggested she speak with each child and see what they already knew or remembered from previous lessons, if any, which seemed sensible. Nevertheless, she was still nervous as she looked at the faces looking up at her. Taking a deep breath, she said, "Good morning."

Various mumbles approximated a greeting. Then one voice said, "Are you really a princess?"

Saraid met the large brown eyes of her questioner, a small girl with braids that Kursa must envy. "Yes, I am."

"A real one?" This from a boy who evidently had the Adaihan skepticism Perrin had talked about.

"'Course she is, Fhorri!" Kursa interrupted impatiently. "My ha-dadai and Lord Cadel said so."

"Oh." The boy's thumb drifted toward his mouth. He brought it back down and sat on his hand. "Well, *my* brother's a Rider. He just got back from Mauburni."

Saraid saw a few of the other children roll their eyes at one another and remembered the day she and Perrin had gone to visit his foster family. By Fhorri's gray-blue eyes and fairer hair, she'd guessed that one of his parents hadn't been Adaihan. The poor child had lost both of them—first his father, then his mother not long after—and then his only brother, who'd recently returned from somewhere. Not Mauburni, certainly. The boy had probably just picked the farthest-away place he could think of.

"Yah, my dadai's a Rider too. And so is Hannel's." Kursa sighed dramatically. "Can we start school already? I wanna *learn* something."

*So do I. How to keep you all focused.* "I'd like to talk to each of you one by one to find out what you know. In the meanwhile I

154

made you these to look at." She pulled out a bag of squares of old saddle leather Perrin had obtained for her. Using sticky black *faarv* and sand, she'd made a letter of the alphabet on each one. "We'll use these for you to learn your letters — you can see them and feel them," she said, tracing her finger over the rough, sandy lines on one.

At the end of the morning, she was exhausted but knew what each child knew, and had to remake only six of the letters that had been rubbed clean in the excitement. As the children rolled up their mats, the boy Fhorri let out a yell.

"Vul!" He launched himself at a sturdy young man dressed in Rider's garb who was approaching Saraid's tent.

"Oof!" The youth pretended to stagger. "Stop that, Fhor. You're almost as big as me."

Fhorri beamed. "You've gotta come see my teacher. She's a princess, you know," he confided.

"A princess, huh? Whatever you say."

"No, really she is." Fhorri tugged on the young man's hand and dragged him back to her. "Saraid, look! It's my brother — the *Rider*." He spoke the last word in a reverent tone. "Tell him — tell him you're really a princess."

She smiled. "I'm your teacher, Fhorri. The princess part isn't important right now."

The young man — Vul, Fhorri had called him — looked at her skeptically, just as Fhorri had earlier, but bowed politely enough. "Not many princesses in the Adaiha."

"As I'm from Thekla, I wouldn't know," she returned pleasantly.

"Thekla?" He frowned. "The only princess from Thekla I know of —" He broke off, and the skepticism in his face faded into shock. "You aren't — you're...Your Highness! You're supposed to be arriving in Madariv any day now! The city's all decorated — they're waiting —"

What? "Madariv — you were there?"

"Yes, ma'am. I just passed out of the Eb with my class. But

you— What are you doing *here*?"

She realized that she was practically gaping at him and tried to compose herself. Madariv! Then Fhorri *hadn't* exaggerated. But how?

Then she remembered. Belet had said something about Cadel's Riders going to the Ebroian Military Academy, hadn't she? But in the heat of their planning her failed escape, she'd forgotten about it. Well, she wouldn't forget now. Madariv! Oh, wait till she got hold of Cadel later on—she would make him tell *all*.

But that would have to wait. "It would appear I've been...er, unavoidably delayed," she said. She'd almost said "detained" but her conscience would not let her lie to him. Cadel had made it clear she was free to go—as long as she went home.

"Delayed...by Cadel?" Vul's face turned red. "But the treaty with Thekla—Your Highness is supposed to be marrying the Lord Protector—"

Saraid resisted the impulse to clutch his arm and pour out her woes to this friendly young man. He was the first person to behave as if she really was supposed to be elsewhere. "Er, yes—"

"What are you calling her that for? She said we can call her Saraid." Fhorri was almost dancing in place next to his brother.

Vul put a restraining hand on Fhorri's shoulder. "You can, but I can't. Your Highness, I—I don't know what to say."

Neither did she. It was time to change the subject before both of them dissolved in embarrassment. "You don't have to say anything, really. So—er, you must be glad to be back."

"Yes, I—" He looked at her again with gray-blue eyes just like his brother's and shook his head. "I'm sorry. Maybe I should start again. Vulharu tiel-Morrel, at Your Highness's service."

"He's been gone *two whole years*," Fhorri said before Saraid could return the greeting.

"Aw, it wasn't bad. There's an awful lot in Madariv that's worth seeing and doing. I'm sort of sorry—" He bit his lip, then shrugged. "But it's nice to be with family again. Hey, I'm starting patrol today, Fhor. Want to come meet my horse?" He looked at

Saraid over the boy's bobbing head. "When you're new, they send you out by daylight. So I get afternoon duty." He bowed again. "It was an honor to meet you, Your Highness."

"You too, er...Vulharu."

"Call me Vul. It's what I got used to at the Eb. Vulharu was too Adaihan-sounding." He caught Fhorri's head under his arm. "C'mon, flea."

"Am not a flea! I'm almost as big as you." But he happily stayed glued to Vul's side as they walked away.

Saraid waved to the rest of the departing children, reassured Kursa that they'd *really* start work tomorrow, put her chair and the rest of the sand letters back inside her tent, picked up the sewing basket Perrin had lent her, and walked slowly to Cadel's tent for the midday meal, framing her plan of attack.

Meals with Cadel had been very quiet since the day she'd discussed the school with him. He didn't tease her, but was almost formally polite. It was restful for a change, but also disquieting. Under all that polite distance she could sense a tension that was evident only in his gaze, as intense and blue as ever.

Today was no different. "And?" Cadel glanced up from a sheaf of papers as she joined him at his table. "How did your school go?"

"Quite smoothly, thank you."

He nodded and resumed reading. "Did Kursa behave?"

"Kursa was Kursa, but I like her. And I met one of your new Riders. His brother is in the school." She took a breath. Would he even hear her? "So, just how many of your Riders go to the Ebroian Academy?"

"Hmm? Oh, many of them," Cadel replied, but absently, and reached for a piece of charcoal with which he scribbled a note.

"Many of them!"

"Yes."

"But—that's impossible!"

He looked up at her for an instant. "No, it's not."

"*How?*"

He turned back to his papers. "I believe I told you that I have connections in Madariv."

Yes, he had, but—but *this*? "I don't— How can you get away with it? Hasn't anyone noticed? Don't all Eb graduates go directly into the Royal Forces of Mauburni?"

"Obviously not."

Saraid seethed. He clearly had no intention of satisfying her curiosity on what was going on here. But he also had no idea how tenacious she could be. She'd find out, sooner or later. And when she got to Madariv... "He seemed sorry to have left there."

"Funny. Most of them can't wait to leave. Madariv isn't what it used to be."

"As you would know from your frequent visits," she commented sarcastically.

"Yes." He wrote something else and frowned.

Had he actually heard what she'd said? "You're jesting."

"What?" He looked up at her.

"About Madariv."

"What about Madariv?"

"That you've been there and you know it."

"Oh. No, I'm not jesting."

"But how..." She trailed into silence. It was no use asking any further questions, because he clearly wasn't about to answer them, either. But if he indeed had all this contact with Madariv, it would explain what he knew about the Lord Protector—

No. That was just gossip, surely.

Saraid finished the rest of the meal in silence, then went to her spot. Since Cadel had insisted she spend the afternoon with him she had appropriated a corner of his tent where there was a paricularly thick Nolorish carpet and a pile of cushions strategically located under a window-flap. Here she curled up and either read his books—mostly on political theory and philosophy—or did the sewing on her new robes that Hirra-the-Elder permitted her, mostly hems. It was the one luxurious spot in the tent; even Cadel's bed was a mere cot, like the ones used by his Riders,

Perrin had told her.

The Hirras had finished one set of her new robes—the rose-pink ones—and would be finished with the others shortly. Cadel had stared as if transfixed the first day she wore them, much as he had when she showed him and Meyric her new *lahart*. His obvious approval pleased her, and then confused her—why should she care? But she liked the robes, too—they were cut better than the ones she'd worn before—and pretended not to hear Cadel's soft intakes of breath when she appeared at his tent in the morning.

She rested against the cushion under the window-flap and took out her sewing. The deep blue linen had a soft sheen to it that was somehow more obvious because of the cloth's dark hue, and Hirra-the-Elder had used silver thread for the seams so that a faint metallic gleam shone from it like stars in a moonless sky. The pale blue underrobe that went with them was already done. If she hurried today, she might wear them tomorrow. Would Cadel like them as well as the others? Not that she cared, of course.

The light from the window was softer than usual. High thin clouds tempered the sun, as Perrin said they sometimes did this time of year, though this autumn had been unusually cloudy for the Adaiha. Saraid put in the small, precise stitches that the elder Hirra demanded—she'd learned to be careful after watching in embarrassment as Hirra clipped out the first hem she'd done, tsking under her breath as she did—and thought about the school. Kursa had already been tracing *k*'s in the sand next to her mat while Saraid had been talking to the other children, but some of her fellow students were either more inhibited or less eager to learn. Fhorri, for example, had seemed more interested in trying to rub all the sand from his *f* square than trying to write one on his own. Maybe mentioning that Riders had to be able to read when they went to school in Madariv would motivate him—

Meyric's slightly raised voice caught her attention. "...to Madariv now," he said, sounding worried. "It's too hazardous."

She glanced at him and Cadel, huddled over some documents at the large table. Honestly, the two of them were constantly

159

buried in letters and documents. Surely being overlord of the Adaiha didn't generate *that* much paperwork.

"I haven't been in months." Cadel's voice had that stubborn note she was learning to know well. Were they talking about Cadel's going to Madariv? It was true, then, what he'd said?

"Surely someone else could go."

"The reports from the boys who just came back concern me. It's time I went and had a look around. Next week, I think, if things hold. See to it, please, Meyric. And don't try to talk me out of it. My mind is made up."

Meyric sighed, and she heard the sound of papers being gathered. "Very good, sir. But I still think it's an unnecessary risk."

"It's not a risk. It keeps me sharp."

She stole a peek then. Meyric was already halfway to the door flap. He went through it without looking back. Cadel was once more bent over papers, brow furrowed as he read.

That conversation had been frustratingly interesting. So did Cadel visit Madariv? If she asked him outright, would he tell her? What made it so particularly risky for him to go there right now?

She needed to concentrate on finding out more about what Cadel was up to.

By the end of the first four days of school, Saraid was sure of one thing: that Count Ebroian, despite being author of a book that was written as a guide for a child king, had absolutely no idea of what children were really like.

For example, The Book seemed to assume that people would act in a way that was, generally, predictable. Five- and six-year-olds were anything but that. Why were Hannel and Kursa best friends one day and sworn enemies the next? Why could Gerron remember all the sounds of his letters one day and none of them the next? None of it made any sense, and The Book wasn't helping. Saraid felt rudderless without it to rely on, adrift on this sea of unexplainable irrationality.

Perrin seemed less ruffled. "This is the way small children are," she said calmly to Saraid after they'd separated Kursa and Hannel to prevent a threatened hair-pulling brawl. "They don't even know why they do the silly things they do most of the time. Eventually they learn by observation how to interact and behave and learn in school. We just need to do our best until they pick up the rudiments."

"Was Cadel like this?" Somehow she couldn't picture Cadel being anything but utterly self-possessed, even at age five.

"Er, no. He was remarkably rational from a very young age. But my younger son was a different matter altogether." Perrin smiled then sighed, and Saraid remembered that she'd somehow lost her family. "Still, look at Fhorri—he's settled down beautifully. Give them a chance."

Fhorri *had* settled down well. Saraid wished she could take some credit for his determination to be the first to learn to read in the class, but the real source of it seemed to be his brother, Vul. He came every midday to pick up Fhorri and walk him home on his way to patrol duty, and after the second day of class she saw them walking together and talking, looking very solemn. The next day Fhorri came to class and surprised her by being able to trace all the letters in his name and say their sounds. When she complimented him, he shook his head.

"Vul says his friends at the academy said their little brothers could read already. I gotta hurry," he said seriously. "I don't want Vul to think I'm not as good as they are."

Saraid kept an eye out for Vul that day and took him aside as the class was finishing up for the day. "He'll be reading and writing in no time, I'm sure, and it won't be because of anything I did," she said after telling him what Fhorri had said. "I wish they all had brothers like you to hero worship."

Vul shuffled his toes in the sand and looked pleased, if embarrassed. "Thank you, Your Highness. It's kind of funny to be the one looked up to. I was the same way with my dadai. Fhorri's too little to remember him—he died when he was still a baby." His shy smile hardened into a grim line.

"How sad he never knew him," she said gently. "But at least you did."

"I thought the sun rose and set on him. Still do. It's what kept me going at the academy when I first got there and was so homesick—the thought that I had to at least try to be as brave as he was."

"Was he a Rider too?"

"Um…yeah. Heya, Fhorri, let's go or I'll be late. Your Highness." He bowed shortly and turned away as Fhorri scampered up to them.

As she watched Vul's and Fhorri's retreating backs, she saw someone fall into stride next to them—a small someone with a long spill of dark hair that she tossed over her orange-robed shoulders as she smiled up at Vul. Belet had been avoiding her since the failed escape attempt—not that Saraid minded very much. Was Belet still trying to find a Rider to help her? She'd said something about looking over the new Riders just back from Madariv, which might explain why she was talking to Vul.

She shrugged and turned back to her tent. Let Belet worry about that; if Vul was willing to guide her, she'd go with him. But she hoped it wouldn't be quite yet; after all, she had to find out that Cadel was doing, himself sneaking off to Mauburni.

# Twelve

When what a man says and what he does are at odds, look to his deeds. They will tell you what are his true intentions and concerns.

—*The Flower of Royalty Blossom'd*

"LET'S GO," CADEL SAID after their midday meal the next day. "We've got some business to attend to."

Saraid looked at him warily. "We do?"

"I do, more accurately. I thought you might be interested in watching, though, since you seem to find us interesting."

"I try to find everything interesting," she said. Pox. That had made her sound like an utter prig, hadn't it?

"I think you do. Except for me, of course." He pulled a long face.

"I never said that," she said without thinking. Pox again.

He raised his eyebrows. "You do find me interesting? Is there hope for me, then?"

Ah, here was her chance. "I also find urban sanitation and the diseases of silkworms interesting."

"Which are both very important matters worthy of a great deal of attention," he said, grinning his old sunshiny smile. "I'll take being classed with them as a sign of progress." He held out a hand to help her up.

"I'm perfectly capable of walking on my own, thank you." She tossed her head and winced. A wisp of hair at the nape of her neck had caught on the chain of Lord Mutrand's portrait miniature. She reached up to disentangle it.

"Something wrong?"

Pox the ever-observant man. "No," she said, quickly dropping her hands.

"Here. Let me help you." He came up behind her and lifted aside her braid. She couldn't help shivering as his fingers brushed the back of her neck, working the fine hairs free of the metal links.

"I can do it myself." She reached up to push his hands away.

"I know you can. But I'm almost done… There." But his hands still lingered on her neck. "What are you wearing, anyway?"

Saraid cringed. "Nothing."

"Nothing," he repeated. "May I see the nothing?"

"I meant, nothing important."

"Then you won't care if I satisfy my curiosi— Ah. I see." He'd pulled the chain neatly up before she could grab at it and already held the miniature. "How touching. Is this part of your self-education in falling in love with a man you've never met?"

"None of your business!"

"That depends on who you ask." He stood a moment longer, staring at the picture of Lord Mutrand. "Not a bad likeness, but they rather flattered him."

She tried to turn and glare at him, but it was hard to move her head while he held the miniature.

"Of course, that's hardly surprising, under the circumstances." He let it drop gently. "Court painters, as a rule, know their business depends on making their sitters look good."

Saraid tucked it back under her robe. "I'm surprised you didn't confiscate it and stomp on it."

His mouth quirked into something not quite a smile. "Believe me, I was tempted. But it's your property. I have no right to destroy it. However, it's up to you to decide whether or not to have the delicacy to continue to wear it while you're my guest."

"I'm not your guest."

"But you know my opinion of the man. Wearing his miniature hardly seems tactful. Doesn't The Book say that a true gentleman—and I suppose it goes for a gentlewoman, too—avoids doing that which offends those with whom he must live?"

He looked solemn and slightly aggrieved, as if she'd insulted him, but that smile—that *infuriating*, mischievous smile—was there in his eyes.

"All right," she said through gritted teeth. "I won't wear it anymore if it bothers you that much. Which I rather doubt."

"Spoken like a true gentlewoman." He bowed with a deep flourish, then grinned. "I'm sorry, Saraid. I know I shouldn't tease you, but when you get indignant like that, it's impossible to resist."

"'Giving in to temptation is one luxury a ruler cannot afford,'" she snapped. "If you'll be so kind as to give me a moment, I'll return it to my tent."

She waited for him to tell her to do it later, but he didn't. "Very well. Come to the oasis when you're done. I'll see you there."

She stalked grimly back to her tent, where she put the miniature in her *lumox*-wood box, then stared down at it. Lord Mutrand's narrow, handsome face looked back up at her. Was she imagining things, or was his gaze faintly reproachful? The worst part of this whole episode was that she couldn't remember the last time she'd actually looked at it.

"You're letting Cadel win. He's sucking you into his life here so you'll forget Lord Mutrand and Mauburni," she muttered to herself. From now on she would take out Lord Mutrand's picture every morning and evening and look at it for a count of two hundred breaths.

She slammed the lid of her jewelry box down and thought
about staying defiantly where she was. But Cadel would probably
do something like move whatever he was doing to her tent so that
she wouldn't miss it. Besides, she couldn't help being just a little
curious—all in the interest of learning as much as possible about
the Adaiha, of course.

When she arrived at the oasis, she saw that the pond at the
heart of the spring had shrunk since the last time she'd looked at it
just a few days before. Did that mean they would be leaving the
camp soon?

Beyond the pond was a bare, flat oblong of earth, picked free
of stones and the short, scrubby plant life that grew up unchecked
in the rest of the area. Saraid had seen it before and wondered
what it was for. Now she knew. Today an awning had been set up
in it, and a small crowd had gathered beneath it, clustered
together in knots. Some had brought folding chairs or stools and
were seated, gazing expectantly at one end.

She followed their gaze and saw that Cadel was there, seated
in a chair flanked by a pair of broad, low braziers full of burning
*faarv*. He wore a white *lahart* she'd never seen him in, with the
hood drawn up over his head, and the flames and rising heat
waves of the braziers near him made him look remote and
otherworldly. He caught her eye but didn't rise or call her over.
Instead he nodded toward her and said something to Meyric,
standing next to him.

Meyric bustled over to her. "Your Highness. Won't you join
me over here?" He indicated a pair of chairs behind a small table,
set in the far corner of the awning.

She followed him. "What is all this for?"

"It's the *Kaynilhurrtha*. That's old Adaihan for "word of the
king." It's a sort of court system for the hearing of disputes. Cadel
holds them every couple of months or so, either here or at other
camps, and twice a year a big one at Callest."

"What kind of disputes?" Saraid sat in one of the chairs and
watched Meyric open a record book and check his inkwell.

"Civil ones, mostly. Actual open wrongdoing or violent dispute is generally dealt with immediately. Here you'll see arguments over property or breech of agreement or that sort of matter. Property disputes might involve grazing or water rights or sheep rather than land, but other than that, people are people wherever you go. You'll see."

"And Cadel is the final arbiter?"

Meyric hesitated. "In a place such as the Adaiha," he finally said, "this sort of justice works. Life has fewer layers of complexity than in a city—at least, fewer man-made complexities. If Adaihans were not happy with the judgments Cadel gave, they would not have accepted his lordship over them for very long."

"I see. Just how long has he been lord of the Adaiha, anyway?"

"Of the southern Adaihan clans? Since he was nineteen, when his father first became ill. The others have gradually acknowledged him since then, one clan at a time. It's a good thing he's young and strong—the pace he's set himself would have killed an older man."

"But why has he—"

"Ah, it's starting." A pair of men had approached Cadel and were greeting him in the Adaihan fashion, hand pressed to hand. Meyric dipped his pen into his inkwell and looked expectant.

And relieved. It had been clear Meyric hadn't wanted to discuss just why Cadel had gone to the vast labor of uniting the Adaiha. But at least she'd learned a little more.

The cases Cadel heard were relatively ordinary, as Meyric had said they would be. What wasn't ordinary was how he heard them. He had known each person who stood before him all his life and used that intimate knowledge as he decided each case.

It was while she listened to the petition of a group of youths to be accepted for training as Riders that she saw something else: that he wore an unconscious dignity as easily as he did the white *lahart*. A line from The Book suddenly floated up out of her memory: *A true king does not need to remind others of his position, for it ought to be obvious to all.* Except he certainly wasn't a king, she reminded herself quickly.

"That will be about it," Meyric murmured. "Ten is about the usual number he hears—"

"My lord!" a loud voice called.

The heads of all the spectators swiveled as a powerfully built, white-haired man stepped under the awning. Saraid thought she saw many of them smile to each other as if amused.

"Bahdru," Cadel nodded respectfully, not smiling.

"My lord, how long have I been in your service?" The man approached Cadel's seat, looking as though he was holding back some strong emotion.

"As long as I have been alive, Bahdru, and in my father's, too. You have been one of my most trustworthy Riders."

Bahdru nodded. "And yet someone has dared to take my horses from your own stables. Wils and Nurri—both of them were missing when I tried to go on duty last night."

Now most of the watchers were openly elbowing each other. Saraid soon understood why when Bahdru spoke again.

"I know who took them." He leaned forward eagerly. "He doesn't know I saw him, but I did. Hard to miss him when he's seven foot tall and bright red. Nurri's hidden in the cave under the pond—she's in foal again and likes the water. But he took Wils with him because none of his own horses are good enough— imagine that, King of Nolor, and he still has to come and steal *my* horse."

Saraid glanced at Cadel. Whatever Bahdru might once have been—and based on his impressive size, she wouldn't have been surprised if he had once been a Rider—he was now obviously quite out of his wits.

Cadel frowned as he glanced around the tent, and the smiles and sniggers among the spectators ceased. "Rider Bahdru, your horses will be found and whoever took them punished," he said gently. "I would ask you, however, to go home and braid new halter lines for them while we search. The old ones were probably cut, and Wils and Nurri will need new ones."

Bahdru's face cleared. "I knew you'd listen to me. If anyone can find them, it's you. I'll go home and get busy."

"Your horses aren't the only ones who need new leads. Once you've done yours, would you be willing to braid twelve new ones for me? I will excuse you from riding duty during that time. No one can braid as good a lead as you can."

"I would be pleased to, sir, if you're sure you can spare me." Bahdru's back was suddenly very straight.

"I won't be sparing you. New, strong leads are too important. I'll see that a sufficient bundle of *gsernev* fiber is sent to you tomorrow. Meyric?"

"He'll have it, my lord." Meyric scribbled a note in the margin of his book.

Bahdru bowed, then strode out of the tent. Everyone watched him, their conversations subdued as they also rose and prepared to go, but Saraid studied Cadel instead. Not everyone would have had the patience or the kindness to play along with Bahdru's delusions and find something for him to do that made him feel needed.

"How long has that poor man been like this?" she asked Meyric.

He sighed and wiped his pen on a rag, then corked his ink-well. "About four years. He hasn't actually ridden patrol in over seven, and Wils was the name of his first horse—but he's long since dead. It's very sad, but his daughter looks after him well."

Unwilling as Saraid was to admit it, his daughter wasn't the only one. She watched Cadel still sitting in his chair, chin in hand, gazing into space as everyone drifted away from the awning. But then he seemed to recollect himself, gave a small shrug, and looked at her. There was a faint question in his eyes and in the angle of his chin.

Meyric rose. "A good session." He held up his book to check that the ink had dried on the topmost page. "I hope—"

A sudden cracking, splintering sound reverberated through the air, obliterating the rest of his words. Someone shouted, but his cry cut off abruptly. It sounded like Cadel.

A strong *whuff!* of displaced air hit Saraid. "What—" she began, but her half-asked question was answered as Cadel disappeared behind billows of *idhe* cloth. The awning was collapsing.

Meyric dropped his book and dove toward the front of the tent. Other people shouted—she heard the thud of feet rushing back toward the awning, as well as Meyric's frantic, "My Lord! Cadel! Can you hear me?" muffled by the fabric.

*Of course he can hear you,* said a little voice in her head. *You're yelling loudly enough.* But another, more somber voice said, *But what if he can't?* Someone had shouted when that cracking sound happened and the awning first began to fall, and the shout had been cut off...and Cadel's chair had been in front of one of the awning's support poles—

A second billow, this time of smoke, rolled toward her. She coughed and waved it away from her face, staggering backward. The braziers! There were the wide braziers of flaming *faarv* on either side of Cadel's chair. The awning must have fallen onto them. Would the heavy *idhe* cloth smother them, or would it burn?

*Burning—on either side of Cadel's chair—*

Suddenly she beat at the cloth, trying to follow Meyric. She held her sleeve over her nose and mouth to keep out the smoke, but it was impossible to push aside the weighty folds of *idhe* one-handed. "Cadel!" she called, choking on the smoke that seemed to fill her throat with thick, dirty dust.

"Your Highness!" someone shouted, and a hand closed on her arm. It yanked her sideways.

"No—got to help—" She gasped and coughed again, and then harsh, beautiful sunlight and clear air replaced the smoke and heavy cloth, and she was blinking at Vul, who clutched her arm, looking horrified.

"Are you all right? What were you doing under there?" He almost shook her.

"Watching," she rasped. Dear Keranieth, Cadel was still there!

She wrenched away from Vul's grip and lurched back toward the semi-collapsed awning, but Vul grabbed the back of her robes.

"Oh, no you don't, Your Highness," he said firmly.

"But—"

"Saraid!" Perrin hurried toward her, looking worried. She caught at Saraid's hand and examined her. "Are you all right?"

"The awning—Cadel's under there...pole broke, I think...and the fire— Let *go* of me!" She tried to evade Vul's grip again.

Perrin hung on to her hand. "Sshh—it's all right—he's out, but he's frantic about you. Come on."

"Is he hurt?" Saraid stopped struggling and turned to Perrin, whose concerned face blurred.

"Not enough to count." Perrin reached up and wiped her eyes with an edge of her sleeve, and then Saraid understood why everything had gone blurry. Her legs suddenly felt like wax that had sat in the sun too long, and she swayed.

Perrin put a supporting arm around her waist. "Thank you, Rider," she said to Vul. "Lord Cadel will be most grateful for your assistance to the princess."

"I..." Vul hesitated, then bowed. "I'm honored to have been of service," he said, rising. "Will you be all right?"

"She'll be fine, thank you," Perrin said. "Please come with us." She began to draw Saraid away.

A throng had already gathered outside the other side of the fallen awning, beating at the smoking mass with sticks and shoveling sand onto it. Perrin pushed her way through them, half leading, half dragging Saraid.

Saraid let her, trying to make sense of what had just happened. She, who'd always prided herself on her coolness, had panicked. And for no very good reason: a few feet to the side and she would have been safely out from under the fallen cloth.

But the huge black gulf of fear that had washed over her hadn't been for herself or her own danger.

"Here we are," Perrin said brightly.

She pulled Saraid forward into the small clearing at the

crowd's center and nodded at Vul to follow. Two men were there, dirty and black-faced, one of them—in a soot-stained white *lahart*—half lying on the ground. At first Saraid thought Meyric was propping Cadel up, but then she realized instead that he was holding him down.

"I'm fine, blast it—let me go!" he was saying furiously. "I have to find Saraid—

"I'm here," she said in a small voice.

Cadel's head whipped around and he stared at her for a second, his eyes arrestingly blue in his soot-streaked face. Then he let them close. Meyric grunted as he slumped against him.

Saraid knelt by him. It felt wonderful to be off her unsteady feet. "Is he hurt?" she asked Meyric.

"No." Cadel was back to struggling against Meyric. "Are you?"

"One of the awning supports fell and struck his shoulder, and then the awning caught fire. Fortunately *idhe* cloth tends to smolder more than burn, but it makes a lot of smoke," Meyric told her. He peered anxiously at Cadel's left side. "I don't think there's any serious injury, but that will be for the healer to decide…that is, if Lord Cadel will be reasonable for a moment and let—"

"I asked if you're all right." Cadel ignored Meyric's scowl and reached for Saraid's hand.

She let him take it and didn't even mind when he squeezed it almost painfully tightly. "I'm all right. I got a little…confused, but Vul pulled me out." She indicated Vul at the edge of the crowd with a tilt of her head.

Cadel looked up at him. "Come here, Rider," he commanded.

Vul shuffled forward, looking embarrassed. "Sir… it was nothing. Her Highness…I couldn't not—"

"It was not nothing," Cadel said. Saraid felt him grip her hand more tightly. "You have my gratitude, Vulharu tiel-Morrel." He pushed once more against Meyric and clambered awkwardly to his feet, dragging her with him.

"Cadel!" Meyric jumped up and caught him as he swayed, but

Cadel ignored him and made Vul a deep bow.

"You will also have a commendation for bravery outside the lines of duty," he added. "Meyric, see to it."

Meyric's face settled into an expression of patient resignation. "Yes, sir."

Vul had turned a deep, painful red. "Thank you, sir," he muttered to his feet. "May I go, sir? I should have reported to bow practice twenty minutes ago."

Cadel nodded. "Come to my tent after practice. I would speak with you then."

Vul made him a short bow, bowed again to Saraid, and turned away. The crowd around them parted respectfully for him, then began to melt away to join the others shoveling sand on the smoldering awning. Evidently seeing Cadel on his feet again had reassured them.

"You're hurt. You didn't have to do that," Perrin scolded him gently.

"Yes, I did." Cadel let out his breath in a long sigh and leaned toward Saraid. He touched her cheek. "You were crying. Are you sure you're not hurt?"

"Oh, Cadel!" someone called. Belet trotted toward them, trying to keep up with a tall woman who carried a large bag. "Cadel, you're hurt!" Her voice rose in a dramatic squeal on the last word.

"He's standing, so he can't be too bad," the tall woman said. She halted in front of Cadel, dropped her bag, and looked keenly at him. "Sir?"

"Healer," he acknowledged. "My shoulder — it's nothing —"

"I was so worried when I heard all the shouting." Belet had wormed her way in front of her grandfather and grabbed at Cadel's arm — the left one. He grimaced.

"It's probably just bruised, but that won't help it." The healer politely but firmly pushed Belet aside. "Go tell Tiruus to fetch some hot water to milord's tent, will you? And Mervii should brew up some strong *hailsh* tea."

"But…" Belet jerked her head at Saraid. "Why can't *she* do it?"

Meyric gasped. "Belet!"

"Belet, do as Healer Derru tells you," Cadel said quietly, not looking at her.

Belet flushed. She cast Saraid a dark look and turned away without speaking.

Meyric stared after her, his mouth slack. "Sir, I… Your Highness…" he faltered. "I don't know what's gotten into her lately."

"Don't you?" Perrin murmured.

"No harm done, Meyric." Cadel sighed again. "Derru, I suppose you'd like to have a look at this shoulder now."

"Among other things." She picked up her bag. "But what I would like to know is why that tent pole decided to fall on you."

"It was an accident," Cadel said firmly. "They do happen, you know."

Meyric was frowning. "I'll have a look at the poles, milord, while you're with Healer Derru." He turned and stalked back toward the awning.

Perrin took Saraid's hand. "Come on. I think you could use a rest," she said, and led her away from the milling crowd.

Saraid meekly let Perrin and her servant, the elderly and disapproving Rabat, check her for injury and order her into a bath. Rabat scrubbed her hair and stood by grimly while she drank the five cups of tepid *hailsh* tea that Perrin insisted on for her smoke-roughened throat, then ordered her to bed. Saraid spent the next while pretending to nap while she tried to understand why she'd been so upset about Cadel.

It wasn't that she wanted to see him hurt or dead—no one deserved to die trapped under a burning tent. But her anxiety had gone far beyond general concern. It had been…personal. It had been because *he* was the one in danger.

Belet's rudeness was nothing compared to the shock of that.

# Thirteen

Shared laughter and shared peril will bind men together more quickly than any other force, so choose well those with whom you would share either.

—*The Flower of Royalty Blossom'd*

TO SARAID'S SURPRISE MEYRIC appeared at the usual time to escort her to Cadel's tent for the evening meal.

"Is he well enough?" she asked. "His shoulder..."

"Derru wrapped it well. It is bruised, but no permanent harm was done. Having you come this evening will take his mind off his discomfort." He smiled, but the expression quickly faded as they stepped into the dusk.

"Speaking of discomfort, Your Highness..." He cleared his throat. "I...I would like to apologize for my grand-daughter's behavior this afternoon. She was...overexcited by her concern for Lord Cadel."

Speaking of discomfort, indeed. Saraid looked away and mumbled, "No offense was taken, Meyric."

He rumpled his curly hair. "Thank you, Your Highness. I know you're generous enough to overlook it but...I fear I've been overindulgent with Belet. She's always been rather my pet." He coughed slightly. "She regards Cadel more as her former playmate than as her sovereign and tends to take liberties she shouldn't." He coughed again. "Some girls can harbor silly, romantic notions that have no basis in reality."

Never had she been so grateful to reach Cadel's tent. Anything was better than continuing this conversation. "It's...it's not important. I've already forgotten it."

Meyric bowed. "I thought you would like to know that we're looking into apprenticing Belet to Healer Derru. It's a useful skill to have and she might show some vocation for it...and it will give her something more constructive to do than idle away her time with me. I should have done it months ago, I see now, and for that I apologize as well."

"Meyric, truly, I understand." She'd once harbored some silly, romantic notions of her own, after all.

"Thank you." He bowed again and left her.

Saraid watched him return to his tent, just beyond Tiruus's, and realized that she really had forgiven Belet, though she doubted they'd ever be friends. Apprenticed to Derru — that would keep them out of each other's way, no doubt, which was surely for the best. But it also meant that Belet would probably be too busy to look for a Rider to help her run away to Madariv. The thought was disappointing, yet also freeing. If Belet couldn't help her escape anymore, what could she do? After all, The Book said that worrying about circumstances beyond your control did not accomplish anything. She took a deep breath and stepped inside Cadel's tent.

"Saraid." Cadel rose from his chair and came to meet her. His left arm was bound against his side and he still wore the smoky-smelling, stained white *lahart*, but his smile was as wide as ever at the sight of her. "Are you well?"

She swallowed and pretended not to notice the hand he half held out to her, as well as the feeling of relief at the sight of him that had come over her. "Yes, thank you. And you?"

"No harm done. Derru says I just need to wear this for a day or two—the sling, not the *lahart*, though by custom I have to wear it until past sundown—and then I can start using the arm again. Come sit."

She followed him and sat down at the table, wishing she could go back to her tent. Yet all that afternoon she'd been restless, wondering what was happening with Cadel. Would she ever have any peace as long as she was in his hands?

"What did you think of today—not the fire, I mean, but the rest of it?" he asked, pouring wine for them.

She hesitated. "It was... You were right. It was very interesting."

"She said I was right." He put down the pitcher and pretended to clutch his chest in shock.

"Oh, stop."

He grinned. "All right, I'll behave. I'm glad you found it interesting. It's the old Adaihan way of justice. It predates even the coming of the sand, when the Adaihans were nomads with their great flocks of sheep and cattle and the Adaiha was all grassland." He looked into his cup, swirling its contents, and asked almost shyly, "Did you think I did well?"

She swallowed, remembering Bahdru's straight back as he left the tent. "I— Yes."

He didn't reply. They sat in silence, a surprisingly unstrained one, until Tiruus came in bearing several dishes on a tray.

"Ah." Cadel looked pleased. "I asked Mervii for an entirely Adaihan meal this evening, in honor of the day. Thank her for me, Tiruus."

Hadn't all their other food been Adaihan? But now didn't seem the right time to ask. Besides, whatever Tiruus had brought in smelled delicious. She leaned forward as he served them what looked like a thick stew, with meat and vegetables cut into different shapes in a savory brown sauce. "Mm. What is it seasoned with?" She sniffed as he set a plate before her, served Cadel, and bowed himself out.

"It's *birrash*. It's an herb that grows near some oases in the eastern Adaiha." Cadel popped a chunk of meat in his mouth, then suddenly made a strange sound, somewhere between a choke and a wheeze, and snatched up his cup of wine. She watched as he drained it, then sat back, gasping.

"What's wrong?" she asked when he looked a little less paralyzed.

"*Hatsuan* pepper," he croaked after pouring more wine and drinking it down. A fine sheen of sweat had broken out across his forehead and upper lip. "I didn't see the bit of one stuck to that bite. I'd forgotten they're an ingredient in this dish. Mervii usually makes it without them for me, but maybe she thought that since I'd requested an authentic Adaihan meal..." He mopped his forehead.

*Hatsuan* peppers. Hadn't he mentioned them before? "What are they?"

"Innocent-looking little yellow pods, native to the south of the Adaiha and in the *Hatsu* region of Nolor. When cooked with other ingredients they help enhance their flavors, but to actually *eat* one..." He shuddered. "Some people are mad enough to, though. Others just grind them into paste and use them to remove rust from iron implements and to treat severe skin ailments that resist other cures."

She laughed. "They can't be that bad."

"I've even heard some people use them as bait for vermin traps in granaries, spread with honey. One bite, and the poor creatures die. In agony."

"Now you're definitely joking." She probed at her plate and found a scrap of pale yellow. "Is this one?"

"Yes, but—"

She popped it into her mouth.

"No!" He jumped out of his chair and shoved his napkin at her. "Spit it out. Or drink something." He grabbed her cup, cursed his bound arm, then put it down and seized the pitcher.

She chewed. A bright, slightly bitter taste, followed by an

increasing heat, spread over her tongue. She tensed, waiting.

"Saraid! Are you all right?" He hovered over her, holding the pitcher as if he were waiting to douse her head in case it began to smolder. "Say something!"

"Are you sure that was one?" The heat spread but didn't intensify. It was rather tasty, in fact. "Let me try another."

Cadel stared at her. "Are you sure?"

"Whatever I just ate was hardly hot at all. If that was one, I don't know what all the fuss is about. My nursery maid back in Thekla made hotter soups for me and my sister when we had colds. You know, to help clear our noses." She pushed her plate toward him. "Find me another one."

Wordlessly he set down the pitcher, picked out a slightly larger piece of pepper, and held it out to her. She ate his from his fingers, trying not to laugh at his fearful expression. "Hmm. Not bad."

He stared. "I can't believe it. Here." He took another piece of pepper, cut it in half, and gave part to her.

She ate it and licked her lips. "Yum."

Still staring, he gingerly bit into the other half...and dove for her cup. "How are you doing that?" he sputtered after drinking it down.

"I don't know what's wrong with you. They're quite good." Saraid found another piece of pepper on her plate and ate it, thoroughly enjoying the confusion and astonishment in Cadel's face. Ha. Now he knew how she felt half the time when they were together.

He peered at her mouth. "Did you put some special coating on your tongue before we began to eat?"

"No. Here." She reached across the table and began to pick the peppers from his plate. "Is that better?"

He squinted at his plate, then at her. "Did you get them all? I don't trust you not to have left one in there, just so you can laugh when my tongue catches fire."

Was it the look on his face or the way his eyes met hers,

laughing and yet still a little surprised, that made her suddenly wish she could reach up to him and tuck a lock of his hair behind his ear, just as he had to her once? Would it be as soft as she'd imagined it might be, back during those dreaming days when they rode together through the Adaiha?

"I wouldn't laugh," she said, more to herself than to him.

He didn't move, as if he were afraid of disturbing something. His eyes looked very blue all of a sudden, and very bright, and his thick lashes gleamed gold in the lamplight. She wished she could brush her fingers across them as well, to see if they were as soft as his hair, and half lifted her hand.

But just then he stood. "I wouldn't either," he said almost inaudibly, turning away from the table. She waited for him to say something further. He did, but it wasn't what she'd expected.

"I have to be away for a few days," he said, back still to her.

She couldn't help blinking. There he went, changing the subject again. Then she remembered the fragment of conversation she'd overheard between him and Meyric.

"Oh? Away where?" Yes, that had sounded properly not very interested. The Book said that a good way to interrogate people was not to fire questions at them but to appear politely bored when they spoke, because then they told you things in an effort to engage your interest.

"Around. Even with the best surveillance, there's nothing like seeing a situation for yourself. Surely it says as much somewhere in The Book." He turned and looked at her expectantly.

How did he always seem to know when she was thinking about The Book? "Um…yes, I think it does." But her words were halfhearted. Meyric had said something about Cadel's trip being dangerous, hadn't he? "So, uh…how long will you be gone?"

"I don't know. It depends. Why? Surely you won't" — he paused, then lowered his voice dramatically — "miss me, will you?"

She folded her arms.

"But you seem a little — dare I say it? — concerned."

Pox it, from now on she was going to wrap her head in a scarf during conversations with him, to keep him from making these uncomfortably accurate guesses about what she was thinking. "You have to admit that if something happens to you, my position here is difficult," she said stiffly.

"No, not really." Cadel came back to lean against the table next to her. "If anything ever happens to me, you'll be escorted back to Thekla immediately. I've already arranged that with Meyric."

"To Thekla? Why not to Mauburni? If you're gone, what difference does it make?"

"It still makes a huge difference." His voice was low and serious. "Even if I were dead, I still wouldn't want to make it any easier for you to marry Mutrand."

"You really do believe what you said about him."

"I believe it because it's true." His eyes were as serious as his voice. "Could you still become his wife, knowing what he is really like?"

"But I don't know!" Her hands curled in frustration. "You've made some vague accusations against him but that's all. I don't even know what he's supposed to be guilty of, much less whether the accusations are true."

"Saraid, listen—"

"No, you listen to me. You're refusing to let me go to Mauburni without any reason that I can see. My father and his councilors want me to go there for a very good reason—because our country needs this alliance. You, on the other hand, can't even tell me what your reasons are."

"And if I tell you how rotten and corrupt he is and what he and his cronies are doing to Mauburni? That your marrying him will only give him the legitimacy to expand his scope to destroy the country for his own gain? That your only importance to him is as a tool that can be tossed on the rubbish heap once it has served its purpose?"

A brief, distant echo of the silk farmers' song sounded in her mind's ear. "I didn't need my father to tell me anything—I saw for myself why I need to go to Mauburni. What proof can you show me of these things?"

He was silent for a long moment. "I—I've tried to spare you that," he finally said.

She made an exasperated sound. "'Oh, yes, let's spare the dainty, sheltered princess! The gods forbid she should see anything that might cause her an instant of distress.' Is that what you thought? Then you haven't been paying much attention to what I am."

He looked away. "I have been paying attention. I can respect your strength and still want to shield you if it's in my power. But tell me this, Saraid—what if I'm right? What if he *is* the monster I say he is? What will you do then?"

"I—I would require proof."

"And if you have that proof? Would you still choose to go to Mauburni? To marry him?" He reached out with his good hand to brush her cheek with the tips of his fingers. "That's why I stopped you from going there. So that you *would* have a choice. A real one."

It was her turn to look away, lest he see how his touch had shaken her. The Book said that choices had to be weighed against each other, like bags of grain. But there was no scale she knew of that could reckon the weight of her responsibility to her country.

And would her heart weigh anything at all in such a measuring?

"It's easy for you," she said, almost more to herself than to him. "You get to decide if what you want for yourself and for your people are at odds."

He didn't reply. When she finally gathered enough courage to peek up at his face, she saw that his brow was knit. He opened his mouth as if to speak then closed it again and rubbed his forehead as if it ached.

"Saraid..." he said with a sigh. "If only you—" He stopped abruptly, and a peculiar expression crept over his face. "Did you hear that?" His voice was calm, but there was an underlying tension in it.

What was he talking about? "Hear what?"

"A sort of soft click...in a pattern, like *tt...tt — tt — tt — tt...*"

She cocked her head. "I don't hear anything."

"It's behind me — there it is again...in my hood —" He had grown pale. "Saraid, do as I say. Get up very carefully — no sudden movements — and go get Tiruus."

"But —"

"Go."

The contained urgency in his voice froze her for an instant, then propelled her out of her chair and into the dusk.

"Tiruus!" she called as she ran to the next tent. "Tiruus, Cadel needs you!"

He appeared almost instantly in the flap of his tent, still clutching a napkin. Evidently he had been at his dinner as well. His wife Mervii peered from behind him. "What? Where? What's wrong?"

"I don't know — he said he heard something in his hood — clicking, I think — and then he went very still and told me to come get you."

Mervii gasped.

"*Vaungon,*" breathed Tiruus. He shoved his napkin at Mervii and dashed for Cadel's tent. Mervii ran after him.

"Please..." Saraid panted, following. "What is it? What's wrong?"

Tiruus had vanished inside by the time they got there. Mervii halted a few feet from the flap of Cadel's tent and peered at it anxiously. "*Vaungon* — scorpion rat," she whispered. "Only they make that sound."

That sounded vaguely familiar. Had Cadel told her about them once, back when they were riding together? He'd said — Keranieth, what had he said? "That's... They bite, don't they?"

Mervii nodded. "The mothers are deadly venomous. But what is one doing here? Most of them have had their young by now and are getting ready to go into cold-sleep till the water comes back with the longer days." She stared at the tent, wrapping her arms around herself.

Saraid stepped forward. Mervii put a restraining hand on her arm and hissed a warning, but she shook it off. She had to see.

The scene that she saw when she lifted the tent flap the merest crack seemed almost normal. Cadel stood where she'd last seen him, leaning against the table by her chair. Tiruus stood behind him, wrapping his gloved right hand in one of Cadel's robes and not taking his eyes off the back of Cadel's head.

"Easy, milord," he murmured. "I can see her now — she's in the hood of your *lahart*."

"No heroics. Use a cup and try to scoop her up. I don't want you to risk a bite. Mervii would kill me if anything happened to you." Cadel's voice was steady, but in the lamplight she could see that a fine sheen of perspiration dewed his forehead. She was sure that she'd barely moved the flap, but suddenly his eyes darted to her as if he could see her standing there, taut with tension. *No. Stay,* he mouthed.

"And she'd kill me if anything happened to you, along with the rest of the Adaiha, so we'd both be dead men." Tiruus took one of the cups from the table and sidled closer to Cadel. He raised his arms out to the side, then slowly brought them in, toward the back of Cadel's neck. "Be still...I think I can just..." With surprising deftness, he brought the cup to Cadel's head and clapped his wrapped hand over it. "There! Got her, milord."

Cadel didn't move. "Are you sure?"

"She's clicking away in here." He set the cup on the table, the wadded robe firmly over it, and fumbled at his belt with one hand before producing a long, thin knife. Working its tip under the robe, he probed with it in the cup, then shoved it down. "Hah! She'll not trouble you again," he said with grim satisfaction.

"Saraid, you can come in now." Cadel's shoulders sagged as he sat down.

She pushed aside the flap. "Are you...are you all right?"

"That was a bit closer than I'd like to be to a *vaungon*." He closed his eyes and smiled crookedly.

"That was closer than anyone'd like to be to one," Tiruus said. He left his knife in the cup and came over to stand behind Cadel. "I'm checking your hood, milord, in case she'd left a nest in there."

"Odd place for one to nest. Not very close to water." Cadel leaned forward and let Tiruus peer gingerly inside the hood of his *lahart*.

"No, but 'tis a quiet enough place for it. You've not touched this *lahart* since the last *Kaynilhurrtha*." He finished examining it and let it fall. "Eh, nothing."

Cadel sighed. "I'd like to know how she got in there. Saraid, would you please pour me some wine…the unoccupied cup if you don't mind."

She ignored his weak jest and reached for the wine pitcher. Her hands shook as she filled a cup and handed it to him. He looked at her sharply. "Are you all right?"

What would he do if she put her head in his lap and asked him to stroke her hair until her beating heart slowed and her fear leached away in relief that he was safe? "I'm fine," she said, feeling her face grow warm. "Just a little startled."

"I am, too," Tiruus said. "Look, milord." He held out the cup that held the dead *vaungon*.

Cadel took it, frowning, and stared into it. Saraid looked as well, trying not to make a sound of disgust at the bloody mess inside. Through the blood she could see the creature's sand-colored scales and the frill of dark fur that ran down its spine and long tail, and the tiny swollen teats on its underside. It was strange and exotic and even pitiable in death, but— "What about it?" she asked.

"Look at its front feet." Cadel's face had gone curiously still.

She squinted at the *vaungon's* tiny, curled claws. "What am I looking for?"

"Her feet had been bound. You can just see the remains of

thread looped around them, there…and there." He handed her the cup and pointed with his good hand.

She wrinkled her nose and set it on the table. "Why would someone do that? And how could they without being bitten?"

Tiruus rubbed his cheek, shadowed with silver stubble. "'Twouldn't be hard. You could slip a loop of twine round her jaws to keep 'em closed and then tie up her feet…and then slip off the loop and leave it somewhere till she chewed through her bindings…like in the hood of someone's *lahart*."

Cadel took a drink of his wine. "Interesting," he said softly. "Do you think that's what happened?"

"Aye, milord, I do. As you said, what's a *vaungon* doing here…and like that?" He held his hands up in front of him, wrist to wrist, and waggled his fingers.

"Milord!" Mervii pushed through the tent flap. Saraid had forgotten about her and wondered what had delayed her, then saw Meyric close behind her and, to her dismay, Belet as well.

"What happened?" Meyric almost lunged for Cadel. "Are you—"

"I'm fine. Tiruus and Saraid have everything well under control." He rose and smiled at Meyric, and Saraid saw him reach behind him and try to conceal the cup with the dead *vaungon*. He didn't want them to know, then.

But Mervii was quicker. "By the blessed gods, it *was* a *vaungon*!" she declared, snatching it up.

Cadel tried to take it from her. "Mervii, no harm done. We're all—"

"Her feet had been bound," Tiruus said. "Look! Somebody had put her into Lord Cadel's *lahart* like that."

Saraid heard Cadel curse under his breath as Mervii, Meyric, and Belet clustered over the cup. Then Meyric looked up at him, his eyes wide.

"Sir…" he said slowly. "First the pole…and now this."

Mervii and Belet gasped. Saraid wanted to, but didn't.

"Get rid of that, please." Cadel took the cup from Mervii and handed it to Tiruus. "What do you mean?"

"Er..." Meyric looked at them all and hesitated, and Saraid guessed that he regretted having spoken.

Belet made an impatient sound. "I'll tell if you won't. He and Dadai looked at the poles once the fire was put out. Someone had cut the one over Cadel's head and wedged it back into place with a long string tied to it. A good sharp jerk on the string was enough to bring it down. Whoever did it probably thought it would burn in the fire, but it didn't."

"It would appear, sir, that the intent to harm —"

"Oh, *Ha-dadai*." Belet groaned and turned to Cadel. "Don't you see? Someone's trying to *kill* you."

# Fourteen

Self-knowledge may be the best knowledge there is, but gaining it can be a frightening experience. Be brave.

*—The Flower of Royalty Blossom'd*

SARAID WAS AWAKENED EARLY the next morning by a hard little poke to the back of her shoulder.

"Aren't you up yet?" someone said, sounding scornful.

Who—*oh.* "Good morning to you, too." Saraid squinched her eyes tightly shut for a moment, then opened them and rolled over with a sigh.

Belet stood by her bed, arms folded on her chest. "I have to be up at dawn to go to Derru from now on." She sniffed. "I don't have the luxury of lying abed till all morning."

"As I have a school to teach, neither do I." Saraid sat up. "Was there something you wanted? Because if you're done being offended by my sloth, I'd like to get out of bed and get dressed."

"I'm here to apologize to you for my behavior yesterday afternoon," Belet said sulkily. "*Ha-dadai* said I had to."

Saraid turned her head to hide her grimace. Was this Belet's idea of contrition? Still, she was obeying her grandfather's order

…in word if not in spirit. "I accept your apology. Now, if you'll excuse me—"

"I also wanted to tell you that I may have found someone to take you to Madariv."

"Oh?" Saraid rose and went to her dressing table so that she could keep her back to Belet—and her face averted. "That's good news."

"I'm still feeling him out, so don't pack yet. I want to make sure that this time it works."

"Yes, so do I." Saraid reached for her brush and swept it through her hair a few times. Had that sounded enthusiastic enough? "I don't want a repeat of what happened with Lannu."

"Good. Then maybe Cadel will survive to his next birthday after all."

Saraid almost dropped her brush and turned to stare at Belet. "What's that supposed to mean?"

"Hmm? What?" Belet looked at her with wide, innocent eyes. After a few seconds, they narrowed. "It means that before you came, Cadel didn't have tents collapsing on him or *vaungona* hiding in his clothes. And I can't help wondering if, once you're gone, he won't anymore."

Saraid took a breath, and another. "I don't particularly care for you either, Belet. But I don't permit my dislike to cloud my judgment. You have no reason to think I wish any harm toward Cadel just because I want to leave his camp. And I should like to know how I would have had the wherewithal to saw through a tent pole I didn't even know existed or find a creature I'd only heard talk of." She paused, then added, "Besides, I thought you were worried that I returned his feelings for me? Which is it? Do I love him or hate him?"

Belet's hands half rose, as if she were going to carry out her earlier threat. "I must go to Derru's." She turned and stalked out of the tent.

Saraid closed her eyes and consciously loosened the too-tight grip she had on her brush. Belet had all but accused her of trying to kill Cadel. Of all the ridiculous... Surely she didn't believe it? Or had the girl decided to hate her so much that she'd blame anything on her? People saw what they wanted to see and thought what they wanted to think, as The Book said. She'd just seen an excellent example of that.

She toyed with her brush, gazing at her *lumox*-wood box on the table. Could it be Vul that Belet had been talking about as a possible guide to Madariv? She'd seen them together several times, his head bent toward hers as they walked together, absorbed in conversation.

It seemed hard to believe that he would be willing to leave behind Fhorri, even if he did seem to have enjoyed his time in Madariv. If he wouldn't go with her, then what? She'd have to stay here indefinitely — with Cadel —

She hastily resumed brushing her hair.

A few days later, Saraid was reading to her pupils. It was a nice way to end each morning's schoolwork and ease the children into a quieter mood as they left for home. Besides, it gave her a break as well. Her sleep hadn't been as restful as it could have been lately; her thoughts whirled and darted and stung like mirkflies, and even her dreams, when they finally came, were strange and perplexing.

"Now, what the thief didn't know was that the horse he'd stolen from the poor man was a talking horse, one who had been born in the gods' stables and had come down to live among men to learn what they were like. As the thieves rode toward their hideout in the foothills of the Tigertooth Mountains, they laughed and boasted of what they would do for their next robbery, and the horse listened carefully to their words—"

"But horses can't talk. I've never heard a horse talk before." Fhorri's face had gone red with indignation.

Kursa sighed. "So? Everyone knows horses can't talk." For a

moment she sounded exactly like her older sister. "But this is a make-believe story. You're *supposed* to pretend they can."

Fhorri looked abashed but held his ground. "But they can't. Me thinking they can won't change that."

"I *know* it won't. It's just a *story*."

Saraid put a braided strand of thread in the book and closed it. Maybe story-reading hadn't been such a good idea. But she'd always loved to be read to; most of her little school did as well, apart from the single-minded Fhorri. "Why don't I find a different story to read right now?" she asked brightly. "I can finish the horse story after school is done, and those of you who didn't care for it don't have to stay—"

"*Hold!*" a loud voice bellowed. Before Saraid could pinpoint where it had come from, a whole chorus of shouts followed it.

"What is it?" she said, standing.

"Sounds like near the practice ground." Kursa had bounced up onto her toes, as had all the other children. "Can I go look?"

"No." Saraid stepped out from under the awning to look in that direction, but too many tents obscured her view. "Whatever it is, I'm sure we'll find out soon enough. Now, about that story..."

She returned to her seat and found a story in the book of tales about how a queen of Nolor had taken her dead husband's place and ridden into battle against Mauburni in ancient times. Fhorri still looked disbelieving but held his peace, and the queen's exploits were fortunately exciting enough to keep the children's attention. Still, when she dismissed school, they all fled, too curious to stay behind and hear about the talking horse.

Saraid was just as curious but forced herself to put away the school things and get ready for the midday meal with Cadel as usual. He would undoubtedly know what had happened and, after a certain amount of teasing, would probably tell her. So she smoothed her hair, straightened her robes, picked up her basket with her embroidery and book, and went to Cadel's tent.

Meyric was not in front at his table, which was unusual but not unheard of. What was more unusual was the babble of voices coming from within the tent. Saraid pushed aside the flap and looked inside.

A crowd hovered around Cadel's table, blocking it from view. Eight or nine of Cadel's Riders stood around looking worried and talking in low voices. Meyric and Tiruus were there, and Mervii bounced on the balls of her feet, muttering and looking for a way past the Riders. Above them Saraid heard Perrin's voice.

"Nonsense. It happens all the time. Cadel is too young to remember, but the same thing happened to my husband, and he was the kingdom champion nine years running and the King's Own Bowman—"

Saraid couldn't stand it any more. "What has happened?" she asked loudly.

The hubbub faded away as everyone looked up at her in surprise. Then the Riders inched back from the table, and Meyric turned toward her.

"Your Highness, it's quite all right…the eye wasn't touched, thank the gods—"

"Whose eye?" Saraid craned her neck to look around him.

Cadel was seated at his table, though she still couldn't see much of him. The healer Derru was bent over him, and Perrin seemed to be behind him, her face calm but her posture all but shouting her worry. Belet stood next to Perrin, scowling, while Derru did something…she couldn't quite see what…

"Is that Saraid?" Cadel said. "Enough for now, Derru. Let me see her."

"It's lucky enough that you can!" Mervii cried shrilly and burst into tears. Tiruus mumbled an apology and led her out of the tent.

Derru sighed. "Only for a moment. I still need to finish closing that cut." She stepped aside.

Saraid approached the seated Cadel. He looked whole and unharmed apart from a vivid red line, oozing blood, that stretched from near the end of his right eyebrow up toward his hairline. The whole upper side of his face was starting to turn an ugly purple, and Derru tsked and pressed a wet cloth back against it. "Keep that on it unless you want your eye to swell shut," she commanded. "It's going to be bruised badly as it is."

"I know." Cadel meekly held the cloth in place. Blood streaked the side of his face and the shoulder of his shirt. "It's all right, Saraid. I was just in the right place at the wrong time."

She stood next to his chair but didn't reply. The cut seemed to be clean and straight but the sight of Cadel's blood seeping from it...all that blood... She swallowed hard and asked, "What happened?"

"Archery practice," Perrin said before he could speak. "His bowstring snapped as he drew his bow. It doesn't happen often, but it happens. Accidents do, you know." She shot a stern glance sideways at Belet, who looked away. "And the eye is unharmed. Face and scalp wounds bleed a lot, even not very serious ones."

Perrin's voice sounded like it was coming from very far away. Or was it muffled by the pounding of her heart in her ears? The only thing that was clear was Cadel's wound—covered now, but it hung large and red and bloody in her mind's eye. She had heard of men being killed by breaking bowstrings before, when the tension released by the snapping string shattered their bows into fatal splinters—

"Saraid? Are you all right?"

Who had spoken? Derru? Perrin? "Yes. Excuse me." She turned and hurried past Meyric and the staring Riders to the tent flap. Behind her she heard someone say something and Cadel reply in a firm voice, "No, let her go."

The noonday sun must be unusually harsh today, because her eyes burned and watered uncontrollably as she ran from Cadel's tent, and her throat felt achy and tight. Not even shielding her face from it as she stumbled along seemed to help much. Surely once she was back in her tent they'd feel better.

But even the cool shade of her tent didn't ease them. She scrubbed at her face with a handkerchief. Where was that lotion Perrin had given her the morning she arrived when the sun had dazzled her after being blindfolded so long—

Oh, pox it. The Book said that honesty with one's self was even more important than honesty with others. If she was going to be honest, then she would have to admit that it wasn't the sun making her cry, but Cadel.

She threw herself on her bed and buried her face in her pillow. The *vaungon* hadn't hurt him and the fire and the falling pole in the tent had barely scratched him. But that wound on his face today, and all the blood—and the thought of what might have happened if that string had caught him an inch lower... She pushed the picture out of her mind. It hadn't. He'd be all right. But for a moment her fear had nearly paralyzed her.

All right, if she was going to be *strictly* honest—she couldn't be anything else, not with Mama's copy of The Book sitting right there on the table by her bed, practically staring at her—she'd been more than a little in love with him when he was Kayn.

But being infatuated with Kayn had been safe because Kayn was going to leave her when she got to Madariv, and she would have gone on to be the Lord Protector's devoted wife. Being in love with Cadel—ah, that was different. And emphatically *not* safe. Because if she wasn't careful, she'd never want to leave him.

"Stop it, Saraid," she said aloud. It was no use letting her mind wander down that path. Thekla's claim on her came first.

She sat up, wiped the last tears from her eyes, and reached for The Book. It had helped her through the bleak months after Mama had died and had given her something to hold on to over the last year as she contemplated leaving Thekla. Now it would help her put her love and desire for the most charming and lovable man in the six kingdoms—even if he *had* made her ride all night after her escape attempt and teased her too much. She knew it would.

But as she leafed through each chapter of The Book, curled up on her narrow bed, Count Ebroian seemed anything but helpful. Where was the solace in passages like *Virtue is a gift in and of itself. The reward for doing as one should is the knowledge that one has done right*? Would that be her reward for giving up a chance at love with Cadel? Being able to say, "The Book said I was right?"

She flipped to another chapter. *The knowledge of having done one's duty is what enables a just man, be he ruler or peasant, to rest his head peacefully each night upon his pillow.* Ha. Maybe that explained why her sleep had been so wretched lately. She'd been too busy thinking about *not* doing her duty.

She clapped The Book shut, resisting the urge to throw it on the floor by her bed. Once not so very long ago she'd gloated over passages like those, nodding smugly as she read them to herself. But it was easy to be virtuous when there was no other choice. She closed her eyes and sighed. For the first time, Count Ebroian had failed her.

When Saraid's eyes opened again, The Book was gone, and so was her tent. She blinked, then understood why. Evening had fallen, and her tent was dark. She'd been reading The Book, trying to find some word of compassionate advice, and ended up sleeping the afternoon away.

A murmur of voices somewhere outside her tent made her lift her head and listen. One of them was Cadel's. He was talking to someone, but his words were too quietly spoken for her to decipher. Then a glow of light made her squint as someone carrying a small lantern lifted one of the door flaps. She quickly laid her head back down and closed her eyes, forcing her breathing back into something like the slow, deep rhythm of sleep.

Someone was in her tent. She heard a quiet clink of something being put on her table, and then another, slightly louder one. A pause, and then The Book, which still lay under her hand, slowly slid out from underneath it. The curiosity was getting to be too much for her.

"Mmmm..." She exhaled and stretched, then opened her eyes.

Cadel was just putting The Book down on her bedside table. A lantern on the larger table behind him silhouetted his form and left his face in shadow. She pretended to blink sleepily up at him. "Cadel? What're you doing here?"

"Coming to see what kept you in your tent all afternoon and half the evening. I can hardly say anything, though, since I slept a good part of it as well, thanks to Derru and her potions." He turned his head slightly, and she saw the white bandaging wrapped around his forehead. His injury! She'd nearly forgotten, wrapped as she'd been in her own unhappiness.

"You should be resting, shouldn't you?" She pushed herself up to sit. "I'm sorry I made you come out to check on me."

"I've rested enough. And I figured you might be hungry by now since you didn't have anything at noon or dinner, so Tiruus made you up a tray." He gestured back at her table.

"Oh. He didn't have to do that." She stood up.

"Yes he did." He reached up and brushed a stray lock of hair off her cheek. "Come on, sleepyhead. Eat."

"But you—"

"Have already eaten, thank you." He went to her table and pulled out one of the chairs. She went to it and sat. He pushed the tray toward her and sat down opposite her. The lantern's light enclosed them in a small golden circle within the shadows of the tent.

"How…how do you feel?" she asked after obediently uncovering the plate on the tray. Greens dressed with herbed oil and two meat turnovers, redolent of onion-grass, steamed gently up at her. Her stomach suddenly woke up and growled.

"All right. My head aches and I'd rather not dance the shield-clashing dance right now, but that's about it. No more blood and bother." He shrugged.

"Oh. I—I'm glad." She took a large bite of turnover.

"Yes, I think you actually might be," he replied, so softly that she wasn't sure she heard him. When she looked up at him, he was sitting back in his chair, staring at her thoughtfully. The bandage looked very white against his tanned face. "Eat," he commanded again.

Saraid ate. It was much easier to do that than to think of something to say just now. But was he going to sit there and watch her eat her supper? She stole a look at him. He was watching her closely, like one of Keranieth's priests studying the wheat grown in the temple fields for signs of the goddess's will. It was disconcerting, but she was too hungry to care. Much.

But when her plate was mostly empty, her unease grew stronger. When she was done eating, she would be free to talk. As she patted the corners of her mouth with the napkin, she braced herself. She had been trained in a royal court, where making polite, pointless conversation was practically an art form—yet she could not think of one thing to say.

He pushed his chair back and stood up. "That's better. Mervii will be pleased."

"I don't think she likes me." The look Mervii had given her as she fled the tent that afternoon had been far from friendly.

"She doesn't like change. Don't worry about her, she'll come around. An empty plate is the quickest way to her heart." He picked up the tray, smiled at her, then turned toward the tent's door flap and vanished through it.

She stared after him, feeling oddly flat. Pox it, she was being ridiculous. She'd just been worrying that he'd want to talk and that she wouldn't know what to say if he did. She should be glad he'd left quietly.

She rose and went to her dressing table and picked up her hand mirror. Ugh. She should have known. A complete mess. She'd been sitting there being stared at by Cadel with a head full of wispy ends curling every which way. She set the mirror down, pulled her braid over her shoulder and untied the cord that bound it...and felt it slip suddenly through her fingers.

"Oh!" Her voice came out squeaky with surprise.

"Let me, please," Cadel said quietly.

Her heart was beating too fast. Just from surprise, of course. "I thought you'd left."

"I did. And came back."

She felt movement and a soft tugging. He was...Keranieth, he was unbraiding her hair. "I can do that myself!"

"I know you can." His hands moved swiftly, un-entwining the sections of hair. He was so close behind her...she shivered.

"Cold?" he asked softly.

"No...er, yes, just a little."

"Almost done." His hands were at the nape of her neck, separating the last strands of her braid. His fingertips brushed her skin and she nearly gasped aloud. And then he leaned past her and picked up her brush from the dressing table.

"Cadel," she whispered.

He lifted her hair and eased the brush through it. "Shh. It's all right."

But it wasn't all right. Her maid had brushed her hair for her for years and she'd barely noticed. But this wasn't chubby, comfortable Jora. She was so exquisitely aware of Cadel's every movement that she could feel him everywhere; her hair was like a conduit, funneling the touch of his hands over her scalp and down her spine, into her middle and down to her toes. It was terrifying. It was also more delicious than anything she'd felt before, even when he occasionally caught a tangle. Somehow the quick little tugs of pain made the rest even more pleasurable.

How long did he stand there, sliding the brush through her hair? Long after even the smallest snarl had been smoothed away and only the sweeping rhythm of his hands remained, sending wave after wave through her. When at last he leaned over her again to put her brush down, she turned to look up at him. His face was half-shadowed from the lamp off to the side but she could still see his expression, unsmiling and intent, and the way his eyes reflected the lantern's light. She felt as though she were balanced on a cliff. One tiny push, even a breath of wind, and she'd tumble all the way into them.

"All ready for your rest," he said softly. "Good night, Saraid." He looked at her a moment longer, then turned and left her tent.

# Fifteen

One may not always like the contents of an overheard conversation. But like a bitter medicine, one is usually glad it has been taken in.

*—The Flower of Royalty Blossom'd*

AFTER A RESTLESS NIGHT, Saraid awoke in the morning feeling unsettled. She lay in bed for a few minutes trying to figure out why. Nothing in particular was happening today, was it? No, just the usual round of school and meals with Cadel—

Cadel. The memory of last night came flooding back over her. His eyes in the lantern light. And his hands on her hair—

Keranieth, she was going mad.

She threw aside the covers and quickly dressed. What had he done to her last night? She'd been ensorcelled, transfixed—

She had to get out of here before he made her forget everything she was supposed to be doing. Last night had made that absolutely clear. Her country needed her: Thekla's prosperity was in her hands. She'd prepared for this all her life—Mama had seen to that. She couldn't shirk her duty now, when she was so close; somehow, she had to put Cadel behind her and get to Mauburni.

As far as putting him behind her—she would begin that at once. She would go to Cadel's tent for breakfast, just as always. But today she would erect a barrier of frost around herself so thick and cold that he'd never be able to melt through it.

She finished dressing, humming the song the silk farmers had sung, and made her bed, smoothing the quilt till it lay straight and wrinkleless. Then she straightened her robes on their hooks, dusted her dressing table, and aligned the Nolorish carpets on the floor so their edges were perfectly parallel. Unfortunately, after that she couldn't think of anything else she could do to delay going to Cadel, so she put on her *lahart*—slowly—and slowly walked to his tent.

But before she'd reached it, Kursa came running up to her, wearing her silver-and-blue tabard.

"Saraid!" She pushed her curls out of her eyes. "Uh, I mean, Your Highness. *Ha-dadai* sent me—you'll be dining in your tent until Lord Cadel gets back."

"What?"

"You *know*. From his mission." She sidled closer. "I can ask Ha-dadai if he'll let me eat with you if you're lonely or something. Mervii cooks good."

Saraid put her hands on the girl's shoulders. "Kursa, start again. What are you talking about?"

Kursa blew out her breath in an exasperated puff. "His *mission*. He left last night. Well, it was last night when he left the first time. The second time it was nearly dawn 'cause it took them a while to find another girth for Silbe after the first one broke—"

It was far too early in the morning to deal with Kursa's narrative style. "Kursa, I'd love it if you ate with me. Let's go back to my tent, shall we?" She took her hand. If she could intersperse her questions for Kursa with mouthfuls of food, she could at least slow her down and try to make some sense out of this. Cadel gone? Now? Without telling her?

Tiruus arrived at her tent with a tray just as they did. "Yer Highness." He bobbed his head respectfully. "Did Kursa tell you?

I'll be bringing yer meals till milord gets back."

"Thank you, Tiruus." She held the tent flap open for him. "Um...where did he go?"

Tiruus set the tray on her table and turned to look at her, his dark eyes gentle. "He didn't tell you, then? Eh, that's like him. Hates good-byes, he does. He's off on one of his scouting trips that he likes to take now and again. He goes different places. I expect that he'll be back in a week or ten days. Maybe more, maybe less, depending."

His scouting mission...to Madariv, as she'd heard him and Meyric discussing? *I still think it's an unnecessary risk,* Meyric's voice echoed in her mind. "I see. Thank you, Tiruus."

"What about Silbe's girth, Tiruus?" Kursa hung on to Saraid's arm, bouncing. "Tell her about that. They said that Lord Cadel was galloping up a dune and it snapped right there and he fell hard, and he was like to break his neck if he'd been a little farther along to the old lake bed where it's hard and rocky, but he was on sand and he rolled—"

Tiruus frowned at her and muttered something that sounded like "nosy little baggage." Saraid touched his sleeve. "Please tell me."

He glowered at Kursa again, then shrugged. "More or less what little tattle-tongue here said. They weren't all that far gone when the girth on milord's saddle let go. He wasn't hurt, so they came back for another and left again. 'Tis nothing to worry about."

Kursa glowered back. "He could have been killed, Belet said. And she said that it looked like someone had done something to it so it would break on purpose—"

"What?" Saraid must have squeezed Kursa's hand too hard because she yelped and pulled away.

Tiruus looked as though steam were about to pour from his ears. "But he wasn't killed, was he? Now get back to yer grand-father, you little vulture. I heard him tell you not to dawdle."

Kursa's lower lip stuck out belligerently but she bowed and

left. Tiruus watched her go, then turned back to Saraid.

"What about the girth, Tiruus?" she asked before he could find something else to speak of.

Defeated, he sighed. "I don't know, Yer Highness. Meyric said it looked like the stitching holding the buckle had been filed down, so that it would break with use but not right away. Didn't see it myself, so I can't say. And I'm trying hard not to let news like that get around. Milord Cadel's the heart and soul of us, and if folks got the idea that someone was trying to hurt him…" He shook his head. "It could get ugly."

"I understand." The tent, the *vaungon* – though not many knew of that – the snapped bowstring…and now this. Surely it was just a string of bad luck, but to the Adaihans, living in the shadow of danger, it would appear in a much more sinister light.

"Er…" Tiruus cleared his throat. "Yer Highness, if you've time this morning, you might step in to see Lady Perrin. She's not well."

Keranieth, everything was going wrong this morning. "I'm sorry to hear that. Of course I'll go, but I don't want to disturb her if she's sick."

"Nahh. Disturbing is what she wants at times like this. You'll see." He went to the door flap, turned, and nodded toward her table. "You eat now. I'll be back for the tray."

Saraid sat down and poured herself some hot palm-mint tea, curling her hands around the cup to warm her fingers. Mervii had made her favorite grilled flatbread spread with nut paste. She picked up a piece, then put it down again.

Cadel had left for a week and hadn't said good-bye. He hadn't even told her he was going. He could have last night, when she'd nearly swooned as he brushed her hair; he must have left shortly after that. And then the incident with the girth – just an accident of course, just as the tent and the *vaungon* and the bowstring had been…

Maybe it was good that he was gone. It would give her breathing space. Thinking space. Keranieth and all her maidens knew she needed it. But first she'd do as Tiruus had asked and visit Perrin.

It was odd not to see Perrin seated under her awning as she usually was in the morning, sipping her tea and watching the sky "in case it looked like rain," she'd joked to Saraid once. Hmmph. Nothing was right this morning, just because one man had temporarily gone away.

Perrin looked up from her pillows as Saraid entered. Her maid, Rabat, hovered over her, refolding a wet cloth. She gently pushed Perrin back down with a murmur of admonishment and put the cloth on her forehead.

"I'm sorry you're not well." Saraid crossed to her bedside and knelt beside it. "Tiruus told me."

"Tiruus should stop being such a busybody. No, I'm not ill, child. Rabat, bring a chair so Her Highness can get off the floor." Perrin smiled weakly at her. Her pale blue eyes looked bleary and red.

"It's one of her headaches," Rabat said. "Don't tire her out, please, Your Highness. She needs her rest."

"Oh, stop fussing, you old mother hen. I'll be all right. Eventually." She closed her eyes and sighed.

"She gets them every time Milord Cadel goes away," Rabat muttered under her breath to Saraid as she brought a chair. "Almighty sick headaches that knock her down like this till he gets back safe."

"Which he always does, so you would think I'd be less foolish by now," Perrin said, eyes still closed. "Thank you, Rabat. I'll be fine."

"Just a few minutes, mind," the maid whispered to Saraid, and left.

Saraid sat down in the chair. "When did he leave?"

"Last night. He stopped by on his way out." Perrin sighed and winced as she moved her head on the pillow.

"He didn't tell me."

"I'm not surprised. Good-byes aren't easy for him. He does it for me because he knows I'd be livid if he didn't, but he hates doing it. Plus, considering where he was going—" She stopped and looked guilty.

"To Madariv."

Perrin opened her eyes. "He told you?"

"Well, sort of. He said he had to go away for a bit, and I, um, kind of figured out the rest."

"I hate it when he does. The risk...especially now..."

Especially now—since she, the Lord Protector's bride-to-be, was here. "Why is he there, anyway?"

"He thinks it's important that he himself go there periodically. I don't know the details," Perrin said, closing her eyes again, and this time there was a distinct air of evasion in the gesture. "Gods, my head hurts."

Saraid took the cloth off her forehead and refolded it so the cool side was against her skin. "I'm sorry. Is there anything I can do for you?"

Perrin's mouth quirked. "Not right now. Perhaps later I'll feel well enough to get up."

"I'll visit you after school." The disapproving Rabat had stuck her head back inside the tent and was frowning ferociously at her.

"Yes, do that." Perrin hesitated. "You might find the children a little difficult today. It always seems like the entire camp feels off when Cadel goes away."

Perrin was right. The usually smiling mothers who walked with their children to school were today still-faced and silent. The children themselves were their usual friendly selves, but more fidgety and inattentive than usual.

At midday, Kursa did not leave with the rest of the children. "I'm staying here with you," she announced as Saraid was tidying up, gathering the leather letters to see which would need repair that day. "Lord Cadel said I should make sure you weren't lonely while he was gone."

"Oh, he did, did he?"

Saraid straightened and turned. Belet stood there, holding a tray and looking annoyed. "Tiruus was busy, so I'm doing Mervii the favor of bringing your food." She shoved the tray toward Saraid. "Though I don't know why you couldn't have fetched it yourself."

Kursa eyed it. "Uh-huh, he did. He told me yesterday. So I'm gonna stay here an' eat with Saraid so she won't—"

An odd expression overtook Belet's face. For a few seconds, she looked almost horrified. "You certainly are not!"

"But—" Kursa's face crumpled.

"Absolutely not!" Before Saraid could react—not that she could do much holding a tray full of food—Belet had grabbed her sister by the arm and yanked her away.

"It would be all right with me if she stayed," she called after them. Poor Kursa looked as though she was about to cry, whether from disappointment or her sister's nails digging into her flesh.

"No. My mother's expecting us." Belet was already several paces away.

"Don't worry," Kursa shouted defiantly. "I'll come back lat— ow! Don't do that, Bel!"

Saraid carried the tray into her tent and sat down at her table. What was with Belet? Just because she herself didn't care for Saraid didn't mean she had to keep Kursa from being with her. It would have been nice to have some company while she ate the salad and cheese Mervii had sent for her. There would have been enough for Kursa—Mervii had heaped her plate with the tiny greens that grew around the oasis.

After eating she took the tray back to Mervii, who accepted her thanks with a curt nod, making it clear that she was not in a mood to chat. Kursa was nowhere to be seen near Meyric's tent, and Perrin was napping, according to Rabat. The camp seemed un- usually quiet and the afternoon hung before her, silent and empty without Cadel.

Nonsense! She was perfectly capable of keeping herself busy without him. First she'd take a brisk walk and then go back to her tent and find something useful to do, like writing out more practice pages for the children to trace in the sand for tomorrow's lesson. Then she'd work on the length of embroidery she'd started, patterned from a design from the margin of one of the pages of The Book, and maybe read through it and find those passages about doing one's duty and adhering to one's decided course. She straightened her *lahart* on her shoulders—the day was cool as the sun shortened its course—and strode down the path.

It wasn't long into her circuit of the camp that she noticed something odd: the number of unfriendly glances coming her way. Faraz, the smith, waved to her pleasantly enough, but his wife, bringing him a pitcher of cold tea, turned her face away when Saraid greeted her. After that, she paid close attention: whenever she met someone's eye, she would smile and nod politely, but fully half looked away and ignored her greeting. It was unsettling, not to mention strange: on any of her previous rambles she'd seen nothing but smiles. Of course, on all of those she'd been accompanied by Cadel, but even so…

Well, everyone was probably worried. Hadn't Perrin said they were whenever Cadel went away? It was just like the way the mothers had been this morning, bringing their children to her for school—but that had felt odd, too.

Her path had led her near Cadel's tent. Maybe she should stop in and borrow one of his books to read later. Surely Meyric wouldn't mind. And she could sit for a moment—she felt tired and a bit off, all of a sudden—

"Danger? Cadel's safer in Madariv than he is here these days, thanks to Princess Bitch from Thekla."

Saraid froze. That had been Belet's voice.

"Why do you say that?" an unfamiliar female voice wondered. "She's a nice enough girl, seems like."

"Oh, yes, *seems* like," someone else said with a sniff.

That had been Mervii. The voices were coming from Tiruus's tent, next to Cadel's. Saraid edged closer.

"Haven't you noticed?" Belet went on. "Nothing ever happened here before she came. Then we had the tent falling at the *Kaynilhurrtha* and that bowstring breaking and finding the *vaungon* in his hood —"

"No!" gasped the unknown voice. "A *vaungon*?"

"Yes!" Mervii squeaked. "Right after the *Kaynilhurrtha*, when they were dining. My Tiruus saved him from it. And now this breaking girth...Belet's right. Nothing like this happened before *she* came."

A burning, leaden feeling began to churn in Saraid's stomach. They couldn't be serious. Belet and Mervii didn't really think that she —

"But why?" the unknown woman asked. "He thinks the world of her, I thought. He brags about her school to everyone who'll listen —"

He did *what*?

"—and goes on about how good she is with the children and how they love her till he's fairly glowing."

Keranieth, was he really saying that?

Belet snorted. "Yes, a pack of five-year-olds are rare judges of character. The fact remains that until this Saraid showed up, Cadel was safe. She didn't want to come here — you know that. In fact, she hates it here. She tried to run away a while ago but it didn't work."

Mervii made a shocked sound. "I didn't know that!"

Saraid closed her eyes. *Pox* Belet! She wasn't going to own up to her own part in the escape attempt, that was certain. Her face suddenly felt hot and sweaty and her head dizzy.

"Oh, yes. She tried to bribe a Rider, but it didn't work."

"Goodness," said the woman. "Why?"

"Why? Because she hates Cadel, that's why. So what I'm wondering is, what relation do all these accidents have to the fact that she hates him? What's going to happen to him next when he comes home?"

"You don't mean...you think it's *her*?"

"Well, I don't know for sure. But I'm sure she's more than capable of doing something dreadful."

That was it. No wonder people in camp—especially the women—had been looking at her oddly just now. Belet was spreading horrible lies about her. Well, that was going to stop now.

She took a deep breath—funny, but it seemed as if her chest would only expand halfway—and started around the side of the tent to the door flap. She was going to call Belet out in front of the whole camp if need be and stop these rumors once and for all.

"Belet!" she called, reaching for the flap. But her voice sounded funny—not so much a shout as a breathy gasp. The heavy burning feeling in her stomach flared into a bonfire, and sweat ran down her forehead into her eyes so that she couldn't see.

"Be—" she tried again, desperately, and fell to her knees because her legs didn't seem to belong to her anymore.

Voices saying nonsense syllables yammered somewhere above her—or was she really hearing them at all? Then the bonfire in her stomach rushed up her throat and out, all over the sand before her...but it still burned...sweet Keranieth, it burned even though her face was now cold and numb...

Just before the world went black and red with the flames, she caught a glimpse of Belet's face far, far above her. It was smiling.

Perrin was there. Every now and then Saraid would sense her calm presence when she woke from the nightmares, or feel her gentle hands bathe her face with a cold cloth or hold a cup for her to drink from or a basin for her to empty her insides into.

Belet was there as well—or was she? That could have been the nightmares. Once she thought she heard Perrin sending Belet away, saying, "I think you've already done enough, don't you?"

She tried to tell Perrin just what Belet *had* done, but her mouth wouldn't work properly and instead she slipped back into sleep. And once she thought she heard the healer Derru talking to her, asking her what she'd eaten, but somehow the words had changed shape in her ears so she couldn't be sure she'd actually heard them.

But at some point the black and red nightmares of fire and pain faded away and sleep became soothing instead of torturous and haunted. She swam up out of unconsciousness a few times, long enough to drink small cups of a cool, chalky-tasting potion that Perrin held for her, and promptly fell back asleep.

When she finally awoke—really awoke—Perrin was there, reading by the light of a lantern at her table. Saraid watched her for a moment through slitted eyes as she turned the pages of a book, her thin face all hollows and edges in the oblique light.

"What are you reading?" she croaked. Her throat was dry and her lips felt shriveled and cracked.

Perrin looked up. There were dark smudges under her eyes but her smile was as warm and gentle as usual. "I wondered if you might not waken tonight. I'm reading your copy of *The Flower of Royalty Blossom'd*." She held up The Book. "I hope you don't mind. It's helping me understand a great deal that was unclear before."

Understand a great deal of what? But thinking too much right now would just make her head hurt. Then Perrin's words sank in. "Tonight? What night is it?"

Perrin closed The Book, poured something into a cup from a pitcher on the table, and brought it over to her. "Drink," she commanded, helping her sit up. "It's just water for now. Derru will be bringing more medicine for you in the morning."

The plain, cool water tasted like the finest Theklan wine. She drank it down eagerly, then asked again, "How long have I been sick?"

Perrin turned to refill the cup. "This is the fourth night since you were taken ill," she said. "But you need to rest another day at the least, possibly two."

Keranieth's tears! "Four nights?"

Perrin handed her the refilled cup without replying. After

she'd emptied it a second time, Perrin brought her chair closer to her bed. "If you don't mind, I'd like you to try to remember when you got sick that day. What happened?"

Saraid lay back against her pillow. The water seemed to have loosened her up, made her feel less thick and sluggish. "Nothing, really. I got up, then talked to Kursa and Tiruus. He brought me breakfast but I wasn't very hungry. I came to see you, held school, then Belet brought me a tray from Mervii and I ate and went for a wa—"

"Belet brought your tray?" Perrin interrupted.

"Yes. She said Tiruus was busy and that Mervii had asked her to. Why?"

"Nothing. Go on." But there were grim lines creasing Perrin's forehead.

"I went for a walk and I—" She remembered the conversation she'd overheard among Belet, Mervii, and the unknown woman, and hesitated. Should she tell Perrin what she'd heard Belet say? "I heard Belet and Mervii and was going to go in to talk to them when I got sick. And that's pretty much all."

"Pretty much all?"

"I—I think so."

"I see." Perrin sat for a moment, staring at the ground. Then she rose briskly. "Well, you seem better but let's not push matters. I suggest you get some more sleep. I'll see you in the morning." She put the chair back and bent to get the lantern.

"Perrin?"

"Yes?" She paused, her expression wary.

"Thank you for taking such good care of me."

Perrin's face softened. "Cadel wouldn't have expected anything else. But I didn't do it just for him. Sleep, child. I'll see you in the morning."

It was another two days before Saraid was steady enough to get out of bed. Derru brought her more of the chalky-tasting medicine and Perrin would only let her eat broth and plain flatbread until her stomach felt less tender. Kursa was allowed to visit her in occasional, very brief intervals and loudly hoped that she'd be better *soon* so they could have school again—like maybe tomorrow. Meyric came, and Tiruus, but not Belet, for which she was grateful.

And Vul came. Saraid was surprised to see his earnest face peeking through her tent flap at her the second day.

"Lady Perrin said you were better," he said, stepping in. "I brought you this." He handed her a small cloth bundle and smiled shyly.

"That's so nice of you, Vul—oh!" The cloth revealed a sand-colored object, slightly smaller than the palm of her hand—of stone, it looked like, but in the shape of a many-petaled flower. "What is it? It's beautiful! Did you make it?"

He grinned. "No, the Adaiha did. It's an *ansohrrvii*—a sand-blossom. They form in certain places, usually where there was a river once, a long time ago. No one knows why." He pulled up a chair and twitched his *lahart* out of the way as he sat. "They say that they're flowers that somehow missed Count Ebroian's curse. When they bloomed the first spring after the Adaiha became a desert, he turned them to stone but let them stay since they seemed so determined to grow."

"I like that story. It sounds like something he would do." She smiled down at the stone object. "Thank you for bringing it to me."

"You're welcome. Fhorri asked me to find it for you. Don't tell him I told you, but when he heard you were sick, he was worried he'd done something bad and that it was your way of deciding not to teach anymore."

She laughed. "Oh, no! Tell him I can't wait to get back to teaching him. I'm much better. The...you know...the vomiting is over, and the burning feeling and the numbness and all."

"The... Your Highness." He was frowning. "Was that what was wrong with you?"

"Yes. Is it some common disease in the Adaiha? Derru wouldn't say. She just looked stern and gave me some vile-tasting white potion to drink."

Vul shook his head. "I don't know that I should say, then."

"What?" Now that she thought about it, Perrin had been mysterious as well, asking her questions about the day she'd gotten sick. "If you know what I had, I wish you'd tell me. Don't I have a right to know?"

"Your Highness, I don't know that I know anything," he said slowly. "But what you had...well, it sounds like what happens to someone who's eaten *ruuish*."

"What's *ruuish*?"

"It's a plant that grows around oases in this part of the Adaiha, little dark green leafy thing. Healers use it—it makes a good poultice for wounds, helps reduce pain by numbing the flesh—but it's poisonous if you eat it. Even the goats know better and won't graze on it. But you couldn't have eaten any of that. It just seems a funny coincidence, that's all." He looked at her questioningly.

"A coincidence—yes, that is funny." She returned his look, but in her mind's eye all she could see was Belet, carrying a tray of salad for her lunch—and refusing to let Kursa eat with her that day.

# Sixteen

Of an equal difficulty with gaining self-knowledge is being able to admit when one is wrong. It is a rare man who can with any honesty.

—*The Flower of Royalty Blossom'd*

SHE WAS STILL THINKING about it two days later when the children came back to school. They were almost comical in their eagerness to hug her and ask if she was feeling better. Some of their mothers seemed to have thawed as well, but not all of them. Saraid was equally polite to both groups. It was easier, somehow, now that she knew their frostiness was due to Belet's lies, not to anything she'd done.

Belet herself had done a creditable job of vanishing; Saraid had not seen her since she'd rejoined the living. Kursa brought herself to and from school unlike before, when Belet had often accompanied her, and when Saraid walked with her back to her tent on the second day, Belet was not there, the coward. She would not be able to hide forever: Cadel's camp was too small for that. What would she say to Belet when they finally met? Something along the lines of, "Was there any particular reason you tried to poison me?" Not that she knew for sure that Belet had, but it certainly appeared that way.

And it looked like Perrin shared her suspicions. She'd taken to lingering at Saraid's tent after school was dismissed until her midday meal was brought, and if anyone but Tiruus brought it, she practically picked apart every item on the plate. Saraid let her, but neither of them discussed why; it was somehow just too large a matter to discuss. But while Saraid felt better knowing Perrin was watching over her, it just added to the general tension, growing thicker every day that he was gone, created by Cadel's absence.

Three mornings after school resumed Saraid awoke early after yet another restless night. She groaned and rolled over, hoping that she could fall asleep again before she woke up too thoroughly. As she did, her foot struck something on the end of the bed.

She sat bolt upright. In the dim early light she could see a large lump, like a canvas-covered package. She stared at it for several seconds, trying to figure out where it had come from and what it might be. Only one person would have dared to sneak into her tent during the night and put it there —

She threw the quilt aside and launched herself at it.

The lump turned out to be a sack, tied closed with a length of coarse twine. She picked at the knot impatiently and finally got it undone. Inside the sack was another sack. She muttered a word Fhorri had taught her and assured her was something very bad in Adaihan and set to work on that knot too. That one proved less difficult, and she quickly had it open. She yanked it off and peered inside.

It contained a half-dozen small slates, framed in smooth wood. And two bundles of pieces of chalk in a rainbow of colors. And even a half-dozen small books of fables and fairy tales, bound in sturdy waxed linen.

Saraid jumped out of bed and wrestled off her nightgown, then seized the closest set of robes and dressed hurriedly. There wasn't much water left in her washstand but she made do with it, shivering as she splashed the coldness on her face. She could do a proper wash later on. She reached for her hairbrush on the dressing table and stopped. There was a small bag there, but this time of silk velvet, not rough canvas.

She sat down on the stool before the table and undid the small ivory toggle that held the bag closed, then shook the contents into her hand. A long strand made of lustrous, moon-white beads fell into her hand, making her gasp. Pearls! They were rare outside of Mauburni—she'd seen them for the first time only when the Mauburnian envoys had come to see Papa back in Thekla. They came from a type of sea creature that only lived off the Isle of Rolg, Ambassador Rathal had told her. These pearls were not as large as the ones he'd worn, but they were of a more delicate hue—truly like a strand of little moons. Interspersed among them were long beads of deep blue lapis lazuli, beautifully carved in a stylized pattern of waves. It was a breathtaking piece of jewelry, fit for a queen. Saraid gazed at it for a long moment, trying to decide what to think, then tucked it carefully back in its bag, flung her *lahart* over her shoulders, and fled the tent.

She rehearsed possible things to say to him as she strode through the early morning dimness. She could say, "Thank you for the school supplies." Or "You've been gone ten days and I've been worried sick." No, change that to "The camp's been worried sick." Should she mention the necklace? No. There was no way she could, not without blushing and stammering. What did he mean by such a gift?

But when she stalked into his tent, all her theoretical speeches fled.

Cadel was indeed back. And evidently fairly recently; saddle-bags still lay on the floor where they'd been dropped, and his *lahart* was thrown over a chair. Cadel himself was at the back of the tent. He'd obviously just washed—his hair curled damply and dripped water down his bare shoulders and back—and he was busily shaving in front of a small mirror, humming as he did. A towel was wrapped around his waist. It was all he wore.

Had that funny tight feeling that gripped her throat been audible? Probably it had, for Cadel's hand froze and he looked back at her in the mirror. His eyes widened, then crinkled into *that* smile.

"Saraid!" He sounded surprised, but she knew better. "How nice. You're here in time for breakfast."

In plenty of time for breakfast. Only now did she remember that the sunlight had barely begun to touch the tops of the tents as she hurried past them. Breakfast would not be for a while yet.

"I thought it was—that I was... I'm so sorry..." She stepped back, reaching one hand behind her to find the tent flap. It wouldn't be a dignified retreat, but *any* retreat was all she wanted right now.

"Don't leave. I'm glad you're here."

He turned, and she had another view of his smooth, muscled chest. Pox it, where was the tent flap? Of course, she could just stop staring at him and turn to look for it—and she would, very soon. "But you're busy—I can come back later—"

"No. Please stay, won't you?" He phrased it as a question, but there was no mistaking the command in it. He gestured at the chair pulled up to his desk, a scant distance from where he stood. "Sit here so we can talk."

The Book was silent on the topic of nearly naked men, although a line about naked truths in chapter six came uncomfortably close. She sidled past him and could smell soap and clean Cadel. Pox it, this was worse than watching him practice his swordsmanship that day. Had he seen her nostrils flare as she breathed in his scent? Was that why his smile had suddenly grown wider?

"I missed you," he said, rinsing his straight razor in a bowl of water and lathering more soap on his face. The cut on his temple from the snapped bowstring was much smaller now, and the swelling had gone down.

"I'm sure you were too busy to think of anything but what you were doing," she said, stiffly perched on the edge of the chair. That towel was wrapped carelessly low on his hips. If he moved too quickly, it would catch on the edge of the washstand and fall right off him. The mere thought made her close her eyes.

"Not at all. You were always there in my thoughts. In one way or another." He scraped the razor across his right jaw.

"What's that supposed to mean?" If only she could look somewhere other than at his bare torso and at the way his muscles moved as he shaved. It made it very difficult to think straight.

"Whatever you want it to." He smiled into the mirror as he checked his face. "Did you like the souvenirs I brought you?"

"Um…I'm very grateful for the slates and the books. And so will the children, I'm sure. They can't wait to start practicing writing properly." He was working on the left side of his face now and shifted his stance slightly. Saraid held her breath, but the towel stayed in place.

"Good." Another peek at her out of the corner of his eye. "So did anything happen while I was gone? School all right?"

Thank the gods he hadn't asked about the necklace, too. "Fine, thank you."

"Excellent," he said, putting the razor down and wiping his face off. Saraid breathed a sigh of relief—maybe he'd put some clothes on now—but to her dismay he went back and re-soaped the right side of his face. "I always miss patches, you know. Tiruus does a much better job, but I didn't want to bother him," he commented cheerfully.

Blessed Keranieth, would he never finish shaving and get dressed? "Look, why don't I come back when you're—"

"But it's nice to have you here with me." He began humming, finished the right side of his face, and then went over the left again. She thought that would be it, but it seemed that he had yet to do his upper lip. And regrettably, staring at a semi-nude Cadel wasn't getting any easier, even after all this time. He was breath-takingly beautiful—quite literally, as she felt as if she weren't quite getting enough air.

"There we go." He wiped the razor and put it in a box, then patted his face with a damp cloth. "There's nothing better than getting clean after a hard ride. Are you all right? You're looking flushed."

"I'm fine."

"Are you sure?"

The Book said that you shouldn't lie when you could tell the truth, even if that truth was not the one sought. "If you must know, I was a trifle indisposed while you were gone."

He paused and turned to look at her. "Indisposed how?"

"It was just a stomach fever. Nothing you want to hear about."

He frowned. "I want to hear everything about you. What happened? Did Derru take care of you?"

"Yes, and Perrin. You don't need to trouble them. I'm fine now. Just a little tired."

"Hmmph. I'll talk to them later." Cadel walked past her chair, his towel-clad hip just brushing her arm. He stopped and turned back. "You're wearing your hair down. Is it for my benefit?"

"No!" she said indignantly. "I just...forgot."

"Oh. Because you were so anxious to see me?"

She opened her mouth, then closed it on the crushing denial she'd been about to deliver—because it would not have been the truth. She *had* been anxious to see him, and...and if she was to be honest, she had missed him. And what was more, she realized that with him back, she felt safe again. But she couldn't let him know that.

But what if she did? She'd been stuck in this defy-Cadel-at-all-costs pattern for so long that it seemed as though she couldn't behave any other way toward him. But she could. She had a choice. Her hostility—her real anger toward him—had long since faded. And while she wasn't entirely sure what had taken its place, she did know that she didn't have to be controlled by something as blind and mindless as habit. Or, for that matter, pride.

"As...as a matter of fact, I *was* anxious to see you," she said, lifting her chin but not turning to look at him.

He was silent so long that she wasn't sure he'd heard her. "Well," he finally said. "I suppose it was over some issue that I neglected to take care of before I—"

"No," she interrupted. "It wasn't that."

Another pause. "Ah," he said, softly. "What was it, then?"

"It was..." She swallowed. "I mean...I'm glad you're back... safely."

He didn't reply, but moved away. After a moment she heard the rustle of cloth as he dressed. Praise Keranieth for small favors. But what was he thinking right now? Was he pleased? Did he believe her?

"Saraid," he said.

"Yes?"

"Thank you. That can't have been easy for you." He came around the table to face her, dressed in his usual robes. "I won't assume it means anything beyond the face value of the words...but thank you just the same."

There wasn't even a hint of teasing in his voice or eyes, which were dark and serious. That was a relief, and so was being able to let down her guard with him, even slightly. But somehow she'd hoped for...oh, something more than his restrained thanks.

Then again, why should she? She'd been prickly to him for so long that he was probably still looking for thorns. An intelligent man did not try to embrace a thorn bush, and Cadel was almost alarmingly intelligent. And just as he had said to her before, whatever happened between them was up to her.

So what if she reached out and took his hand? Just held it in hers for a moment or two? Would his restraint crumble away? Would hers? Or was her duty to Thekla and Mama still too strong, the duty that decreed she should make her way to Madariv and the Lord Protector at all costs and not let herself admit that she

was falling in love with Cadel—

"Here you are, milord!" Tiruus appeared in the tent flap with an enormous tray in his hands and an even more enormous smile on his face. He dropped the tray on the table and enveloped Cadel in a tight, back-thumping hug. "We can all start breathing again now you've come back. How is the news?"

Cadel returned the hug but glanced at her before he spoke. "Guardedly optimistic, Tiruus. Give my love to Mervii, will you? And tell Meyric I'll need him for most of the morning. Gods, that smells good. I'm ravenous."

When the children arrived for school that morning, they were back to their usual bouncy, chattering selves. They were also nearly beside themselves with excitement when she produced the slates and chalk for them, and waited anxiously while she shared them out. They became so absorbed in copying and recopying their names that they were all still bent over their improvised desk—a long board resting on two baked-mud bricks—when school ended. Vul quietly joined Saraid where she sat watching them.

"You look much better today, Your Highness. There's color in your face again, if you don't mind my saying so." He glanced down at his brother, whose brow was furrowed in concentration as he formed his letters. "But I think everyone's feeling better this morning."

Everyone except him, that was. She thought about asking if there was a reason for the shadows under his eyes and the air of tenseness that hovered around him like a cloud, but decided not to. "I feel better, thank you."

"Well enough for an adventure?"

She opened her mouth, glanced at him, then closed it. Belet had done it after all, then. She'd recruited Vul to help her escape. In another night or two or three, she'd be leaving her school and

Kursa and Perrin. And Cadel. She cleared her throat, trying to clear the sudden lump of dismay that had coagulated there. "An...adventure? What kind of adventure?"

"Dune sledding!" He grinned. "I thought it would be fun to go one of these nights. The moon's getting full again, and there's nowhere near Callest that's as good for it as there is here."

"Dune sledding?"

"Uh-huh. It's kind of childish, but...you know." He shrugged sheepishly. "That doesn't mean it still isn't fun. While I was out on patrol I spotted some dunes east of here that look like they'd be great—nice and gentle on one side, leading up to a steep face on the other. I'm getting a group of us together—want to come?"

Sledding on sand! She hadn't been sledding since she was small and they'd visited the Salann Hills one winter. But dune sledding sounded better—no cold, wet snow to work its way under her clothes. And in the Adaiha, by moonlight—it would be beautiful. "It sounds fun—"

"Great!" he interrupted. "I'll let you know what night we choose."

" —but I think I'd better discuss it with Lord Cadel first."

"Oh. Oh, right." He turned a dull red. "I'd forgotten—I'm sorry, Your Highness."

"Don't be sorry. I'd like to go." What would Cadel say if she asked him? After all, she'd be going with members of his own guard. It wasn't as if she'd be able to escape or anything. "I'll ask him about it."

"Sledding?" Cadel said that evening when she brought it up over their evening meal. He'd been practically conjoined with Meyric all afternoon, catching up on camp business, and looked tired. No wonder, if he'd been riding all night and hadn't slept that day. She'd wanted to scold him into taking a rest but hadn't been able to find the words to do it.

Now he drummed his fingers on the table, a faraway look on his face. She picked up her cup and took a drink of wine.

"Very well," he said suddenly. "Tell him we'd love to go."

She inhaled a drop of wine and coughed. "We?"

"Of course. I haven't been sledding in years. I used to be pretty good, you know." The tired look around his eyes seemed to have lessened.

"You're coming, too?"

"Why shouldn't I?"

Because despite his smiling cheerfulness, she'd never seen him do anything so frivolous. "I'm not going to try to run away again, you know," she said stiffly.

"I know that, because you're still here."

"What?"

"Saraid." His voice was gentle. "I've been gone for ten days. You had plenty of time to plot and carry out another escape attempt, presupposing you'd been able to find someone to help you. Which is highly improbable but not impossible. So I assume you've given up the idea."

By Keranieth's toes—it hadn't ever even occurred to her to think of fleeing while he was gone. Not once. Yes, she'd been sick for a good portion of that time, but still— "I see. Your going was a test, then."

"Of course not. I had serious business to transact in Madariv. But I was very interested to see what you would do. Anyway..." He nodded to a large and battered brass tray balanced on a wooden stand. "See that tray over there? Bet you just thought that was a beat-up old table, huh? That won me several races back when I was young." He grinned happily. "It'll be fun. You'll see.

# Seventeen

When offered the opportunity to try a new activity, take it. Any knowledge is useful, and even the most frivolous game can offer insight.

*— The Flower of Royalty Blossom'd*

SARAID WAS UNPREPARED FOR Vul's dismayed reaction when she arrived at the stables four nights later, trailed by Cadel dragging his enormous tray. She hadn't seen Vul since the day he invited her to go sledding; Fhorri had delivered the message that that night would be the night for them to go.

"Are we late?" she asked him, pulling her *lahart* more closely around her throat. The evening air was chilly and clear, and the light of the rising moon made apparent the stunned look on Vul's face.

"Late? Uh, no..." He swallowed, then nodded toward Cadel, who had just disappeared into the stable to get Silbe, and asked her in a low voice, "He's coming, too?"

"Yes. I didn't have a chance to tell you—he decided he wanted to go when I told him. It's all right, isn't it?"

"What? Oh...yes, sure it is. I just never thought..." He shrugged and smiled, but the smile was definitely forced.

Cadel emerged some moments later leading Silbe. He'd some-how managed to strap his outlandish tray to one side of the horse's saddle. "It's probably easier if you mount first," he said to her. "Let me give you a leg up."

"I have a horse for her, milord," Vul said.

Saraid glanced at the group of waiting sledders — she recog-nized several young women about her age as well as Vul's fellow Riders — who were waiting, some already mounted. Several of them were riding together, but not all.

"Why can't I ride on my own?" she said under her breath to Cadel.

"Riding in the desert at night can be tricky unless you're used to it," he replied. "The shadows do strange things."

"You didn't seem terribly concerned about it when we rode with Captain Zamas." Nor the night she tried to escape, but she couldn't say that right now.

"That was different." He glanced at Vul and his friends, who were watching them curiously. "You don't want to hold everyone up, do you?"

She wasn't going to let him win that way. "No. But I want to ride on my own."

He looked at her, head tilted to one side. "Very well. But before you go, you have to tell me why you won't ride with me. Is it because you're afraid of me?"

"Of course not!"

She couldn't see the expression in his eyes — the moon was behind him — but his voice was quiet. "Then is it because you're afraid of yourself?"

Saraid's breath caught in her throat.

"Well?" he asked softly.

"I'm not afraid of anyone," she said, and reached for the edge of Silbe's saddle.

Cadel made a step out of his hands and helped her up on the horse's back, then climbed up behind her. "Thank you," he said to

Vul. "But we won't be needing a mount for Her Highness."

"Heya!" someone shouted. Saraid turned. Belet was dashing toward them, her robes hitched so she could run. Pox. Well, she was going to have to face her sooner or later.

"Couldn't...get away," Belet panted as she arrived. "Had to — Cadel! What are you doing here?"

"Heya, Belet. I believe there's a horse all ready for you." Saraid felt him nod toward the horse Vul still held.

Belet cast him another surprised look — she ignored Saraid completely — and went quickly to Vul. They exchanged a few murmured words, then Belet mounted the horse he held and they all left.

The night air was almost unnaturally clear, so that the edges of the dunes in the moonlight looked crisp and close. Around them Vul and his friends laughed and chatted, and one girl with a lovely voice was convinced to sing while the rest provided the choruses.

How Vul knew where they were going she had no idea, but after riding eastward for what felt like a long time he shouted and pointed. A range of mighty dunes reared up among the gentler dunes around them, like islands rising from the sea. They had gentle slopes on one face, then dropped at a much steeper angle on the other.

Cadel stared up at them pensively. "I haven't been to these dunes in years. They must have grown, though — they look as big now as they did when I was fourteen."

"You know them?"

"Why shouldn't I? You know the countryside around your home, don't you?" He swung off Silbe and helped her down. Around them the others were doing the same, putting hobbles on their horses to keep them from straying, loosening saddle girths, and giving them water bags. Then they took up their trays and tramped up the gentle side of the first of the dunes.

"Now what?" Saraid asked when they reached the top.

A loud whoop answered her. One of the youths had flung his

tray down, thrown himself onto it face first, and was shooting down the steep face of the dune. Another, then five or six followed him, some sliding face first, others seated on their trays.

Cadel bent and tied a short length of cord to one of the handles of his tray, then sat down on it. "Sit behind me and put your arms around me," he commanded.

She hesitated, but this looked like too much fun to risk missing. She sat down cross-legged behind him on the tray and gingerly rested her hands on his shoulders.

"Saraid." He sounded somewhere between amused and exasperated. "Have you ever been sledding before?"

"Of course I have! On snow, but it's mostly the same thing."

"Then you know sitting like that won't work."

She bit her lip. He was right, but she *couldn't*—no. It was time to prove that she wasn't afraid of him. She uncrossed her legs and slid them around him, then wrapped her arms around his middle.

"Much better. Ready?" Cadel asked.

Saraid narrowed her eyes as she peered over Cadel's shoulder at the steep slope below "Ye—" she began, but before she'd finished speaking, Cadel had pushed them off. Cheers from the top of the dune followed them.

Unlike sledding on snow, they moved slowly at first, until momentum took over. The growing wind in her eyes made her squint; it mixed with the *shuuussh!* of their passage down the sand in her ears. She held more tightly to Cadel, feeling his muscles tighten as he leaned one way, then the other, to guide their course down the hill. A breathless laugh rose in her throat; she swallowed it back but another took its place. How long had it been since she'd done something like this just for the fun of it? The Book contained one or two passages about relaxation and amusing pastimes, but nothing about plain fun.

As they slid to a stop, Cadel looked over his shoulder at her. "Want to go again?"

"Yes!"

He grinned. "You sure?"

She put out her tongue at him, and he laughed.

They slid twice more down that dune. All the tension seemed to lift from her midsection, and she felt deliciously light and free. Around her the others were laughing and chattering as well, and even their horses seemed amused as they watched and touched noses with each other. The moon rose higher, and the dips and hollows in the dunes changed subtly as it progressed across the sky.

"All right," Cadel said after their third run. "Next run, you steer."

"You mean you're steering this thing?" Saraid nudged the tray with her toe. "I would never have guessed."

"Yes, I'm steering. Sort of. Impudent wench." He flicked her gently with the cord. "You use your weight to lean toward where you want to go, and that helps guide you."

"Let's go try that one." She pointed to a dune two peaks away. "It looks even steeper."

"All right." He handed her the tray's cord. "Good idea, actually—no one else is on it, so you can't get us into any collisions."

"Hey!"

He laughed and began to run. "Beat you to the top," he tossed over his shoulder.

"No fair! I have to drag this!" She leapt after him.

Cadel continued to run for a few yards more, then stopped and waited for her to catch up, taking the tray back from her. They trudged through the sand to the deserted dune in companionable silence, Saraid stealing glances at him now and again. Cadel was nearly always—as far as she had seen—sunny and cheerful. But underneath there was a sense of watchfulness, of calculation, even. Tonight that feeling was gone. Like her he was in the moment and simply having fun.

At the dune's peak he poised the tray and patted it. "You sit, and I'll push us off from behind. Don't forget, lean in the direction you want to go in. Ready?"

Saraid settled herself and gripped the cord tied to the handle.

"Mm-hmm."

Cadel sat behind her, his legs to either side snug against her and one arm tight around her middle. She was acutely conscious of him almost wrapped around her. Then as he pushed them off, the thrill of the ride took over.

Riding in front was even more exhilarating than she'd thought it would be. The wide slope spread before her, open and free, all hers, and the cool night air rushed past her ears and blew the tendrils of hair back from her face. Cadel was probably getting tickled unmercifully by them. She grinned to herself and tried an experimental lean to the right. Their trajectory did not change. Impatiently she leaned farther—

—and she was half-somersaulting, half rolling down the slope, Cadel close behind—no, nearly overtaking her; they were going to crash—but all the while she was laughing, tears starting in her eyes and her breath coming in giggling, gasping snorts. Near the bottom the slope gentled and they rolled to a halt, tangled together, Cadel half atop her. She turned her head and saw the empty tray slither to a halt, spinning ludicrously. The sight made her burst into fresh laughter.

"By the gods, that's what you consider steering?" He propped himself up on one elbow and frowned at her with mock ferocity.

There was sand in her nose. She sneezed, then grinned at him. "It's what you told me to do."

"It didn't sink in far, did it? And to think I'm letting you teach school in my camp."

"Hah! It sank in just fine. It was your tray's fault. It isn't balanced."

"Not balanced? I beg to inform you that tray's perfect for sledding...when it's got a competent driver, that is."

"It is not! It's warped and all full of bumps and dings. I'm surprised this is the first time we fell."

"We didn't fall because I know how to steer it."

"We didn't fall because you got lucky." She was still grinning. "Now get off me so we can slide some more."

"Not till you apologize." He loomed over her, pinning her arms down.

"For what?"

"For insulting my very fine tray." Below his scowling brow, the corners of his mouth twitched.

"I didn't know your tray was so sensitive about its shortcomings." She wriggled her wrists experimentally.

His grip on them tightened. "Do you want to lie here all night?"

"If you're going to be that way about it..." She sighed theatrically. "I'm sorry I insulted your tray. I'm sure it is a most superior...er, vehicle."

"Thank you." He clambered to his feet and held out his hand to help her rise. She reached to take it, let him pull her up, then yanked her hand out of his and gave him a shove. He tumbled back down again.

"Even if it's perfectly wretched for sliding!" she finished triumphantly, plopping herself down on his stomach and grabbing his wrists. "Now who wins?"

Cadel laughed. Before she could react, he'd squirmed and twisted his arms up and around her and forced her back down, holding her in place with the weight of his body. "I do," he said.

"No...fair! You're...bigger...than me—" She writhed and tried to free her arms, but it was no use. "All right! You win." She went limp beneath him.

But something had changed. Cadel's face was very close—so very close that she could feel the heat and moisture of his breath on her cheek. All at once she was aware—so very aware—of the weight of his body pressing down on hers.

"Saraid," he whispered, his lips almost touching hers. His face filled her field of vision, blocking out the bright moonlight above, and his scent drove any other thoughts but of him out of her mind. Her body was melting, shifting, to get closer, to encompass him. *Yes*, it murmured—*oh, yes*—

"Cadel!" The shout ripped through the night air, jarring her out of the moment. A low beat of running, gliding footsteps and other voices followed it, talking in loud, excited tones. Someone was coming. In a second they would find her and Cadel entwined at the bottom of the dune.

Cadel stiffened. "No," he muttered. He closed the distance between them and kissed her.

She closed her eyes, and instantly the world consisted only of feeling—his hands gripping her shoulders and his mouth on hers, sweet and hard and seeking. She heard herself say, "oh" deep in her throat, felt her lips soften and part under his—

"Lord Cadel! Sir!"

Her eyes flew open. Cadel pushed himself up and stared down at her, then pounded the sand with one fist before climbing to his feet. Even in the moonlight she could read the anguish in his expression as he held out a hand to help her up. "Saraid," he said, almost pleadingly.

"They need you." She still felt the warmth of his lips on hers.

"But I need *you*."

"Heya!"

She looked past him. A pair of the young men who'd come with them, one of them a Rider, had just crested the dune and were loping down it in long, sliding strides. "Milord!"

Cadel rubbed his face with one hand, then turned to the Riders. "What is it?"

They skidded to a halt in front of them, kicking up a plume of sand. "It's one of the Border Watch," the Rider said. "He was on his way to the camp to see you. Lisnam sent word—they've just done a rescue. Twelve at once, sir!"

"Twelve." Cadel sighed. "Did Lisnam get to them in time?"

"Just. One of the twelve was Master Elliv." The Rider's voice had gone oddly flat.

Cadel's face seemed to close in on itself. Without speaking he turned and broke into a run.

Saraid stared at his retreating back for a moment as the pair leapt to follow him. Then she slid down the rest of the slope to get the forgotten tray and hurried after them.

She'd let him kiss her.

No. She hadn't *let* him. She'd thoroughly enjoyed everything about that kiss, every touch, every pressure, every last sensation — everything except its hasty ending. In that kiss she'd sensed a release and peace that had seemed so close; she'd felt like a drowning person who'd fought fiercely, then given up and gone under, only to find that the air was where she thought the water had been.

Cadel and another man cloaked in Rider's garb were talking intently when she got to them, surrounded by the sledders. She touched Vul's arm. "What's going on?"

Vul's forehead creased. "I'm not sure if it's my place to tell you, Your Highness."

Just then, Cadel said loudly, "Let's go. Mabila and, er, Yann, you come with me."

Vul stepped forward. "Sir, let me come, too."

"Cadel!" Belet pushed past the other sledders. "Me, too. I can help. I've got my bag with me."

Cadel frowned and opened his mouth, then nodded. "I forgot you were training with Derru. All right, you and Vul as well. The rest of you head back as quickly as possible and send out horses and supplies enough for twelve. Now."

The group scattered, murmuring, and hurried to the horses. Cadel turned to her, his face softening as their eyes met, just for a moment before his mouth thinned in a grim expression. "Something's come up that I have to see to," he said, his voice clipped. "I want you to return to camp with the others. I'll be back in a day or two. You can ride with—"

The words came out before she had time to think. "I want to go with you."

His brows lowered, and he turned to the Rider. "We have water for the horses. Go take care of yours before we go. I'll be along in a moment."

The man nodded and turned away. Cadel took her by the

shoulder and pulled her a short distance away. "Saraid, you don't understand. This isn't a pleasure trip anymore."

"I'd guessed that."

He rumpled his hair and frowned. "By 'not a pleasure trip' I mean we're going to ride hard for the rest of the night, then work even harder after that trying to save people who're on the brink of death. If they aren't dead by the time we get there."

"I'd like to help save them." So that was what had been meant by a rescue. But whom were they rescuing?

"People who likely have been tortured then dumped in the Adaiha to die," Cadel said, as if he'd heard her unspoken question. His voice had gone harsh.

She swallowed. "You're not going to frighten me off. I'm going with you."

"Saraid—"

"I said I'm not frightened. What are *you* afraid of?" she asked quietly.

He stared at her for the space of a few breaths. "All right," he finally said. "Don't expect to be comfortable. We'll have work to do."

"I understand." She met his gaze squarely. "Will you tell me the whole story?"

He hesitated, then nodded. "Once we're on our way. Come on. Somebody take my tray for me," he called, hurrying to Silbe.

Saraid waited until they'd been riding for a while before venturing to speak. Cadel's face was grim and set, and apart from urging Silbe on frequently, he did not say a word. Vul and the other Riders were equally silent.

"Is it far, where we're going?" she asked.

"We'll get there midmorning if we can keep up this pace. Would that it were sooner," he added, under his breath.

Saraid waited, but he didn't say more. "It sounds as if you knew one of the people who—who'd been found," she said.

"Yes."

"Cadel, please tell me—"

"What we're going to see," he said, sounding as if he were keeping some deep emotion in check, "is the result of how your erstwhile husband-to-be likes to keep the peace in Mauburni."

"What?" She sat up straighter.

"When somebody offends Lord Protector Mutrand, either by disagreeing with him or by being too successful or popular or by not giving him what he wants, he has a unique way of dealing with them."

"No," she whispered.

"They disappear, sometimes right off the street. Or if His Grace the Lord Protector has taken a fancy to their property, a little charade will be performed — a trumped-up charge brought against them, false witnesses produced — you get the gist, I'm sure. Then they're brought out to the Adaiha, usually after his jailers have had a little fun with them, and are left to die. Their property is forfeited, of course."

Saraid clenched her hands, but the bite of her nails into her palms was only a distant pain. "How long has this been going on?" she asked in a small voice.

"Years. Adaihans have helped these people when they've run across them, but a few years ago we started a Watch that keeps an eye out for them. We manage to find many of them in time, but not always. It depends on how badly they've been hurt before they're dropped. There's a very small oasis — hardly more than a place where a spring bubbles up from bare rock — that we use for one of our Watch base camps. It's only half a day's ride from the area where Varian's thugs like to abandon a lot of their victims. We do our best to save them there and then send them on to Callest." He sighed. "Rest if you can. You'll need it." He pressed her gently against his shoulder.

"What about you?"

"I don't get to rest."

"Not ever?"

"Not until... No, I don't." He sighed again.

Saraid rested her head on his shoulder and closed her eyes.

The feeling of him so close reminded her of where they'd been not long before, tumbled into each other's arms three-quarters of the way down a dune—not a memory likely to lull her to sleep. She listened to Silbe's muffled hoofbeats and tried to think of something from The Book—a single line, even—that covered what was happening to her right now. As hard as she tried, she couldn't.

# Eighteen

The sight of human frailty or mortality can be shocking to the young, who think they will live forever. But it can also contain lessons in compassion and wisdom.

*—The Flower of Royalty Blossom'd*

IT WAS ALMOST NOON when they arrived at the Watch camp. A clump of small tents clustered at the foot of a low rock face; near it stood an awning under which horses dozed on their feet. A short distance away, a row of small stone cairns faced east, toward Mauburni.

Cadel didn't pause. As soon as Silbe came to a halt he slid to the ground. Saraid dismounted stiffly after him. A pair of Riders emerged from one of the tents and came to them, murmuring greetings and bowing to Cadel. He nodded curtly. "I've brought an apprentice healer. Belet, do what they ask of you. Where is Master Elliv?"

"Milord." One of them stepped forward. "I'll bring you to him."

"He still lives?"

"In body, yes. But in spirit..." He shook his head. "Yarl, take their horses." He glanced curiously at Saraid but did not speak.

"Come with me," Cadel said to her. "It may not be pleasant."

She swallowed. "I understand."

They followed the Rider to one of the tents. Within it three people lay on pallets while another Rider watched over them, going from one to another to sponge their faces or drip water into their mouths.

Cadel knelt beside one of them. "Master Elliv. Nice of you to visit us here in the country, man," he said quietly, forcing a smile.

The man on the pallet opened his eyes. They were sunken and dull, and he seemed to be having a hard time focusing them. "Lord Cadel?" he whispered.

"You're safe now. You'll be all right." Cadel gently pushed him back down as the man struggled to sit up. "We got to you in time."

"No—Mutrand—my son—Elliv—he..." The man broke into hoarse, hacking sobs. Cadel reached for his hand, then froze. Saraid, peering over his shoulder, saw why. Master Elliv's hands were wrapped in layers of bandage, but the bandaging was curiously short. Either his hands were curled into fists under them, or—or— She quickly turned her head away, her stomach churning.

Cadel's face had gone very white, but his voice was still calm. "Are you in pain? Did they give you something?"

"Hands...don't matter. My son— They— Right in front of me— How he screamed! Why didn't I die, too?" Master Elliv sobbed. Saraid saw that his face was dry. Of course. A man who'd nearly died of dehydration and blood loss would not have any moisture left in his body to spare for weeping. Somehow, the thought of being deprived of tears to mourn his own son was almost as bad as the physical injuries he'd suffered.

She could see Cadel's jaw clench, but his hand was steady and gentle as he rested it on Master Elliv's leg. "I know you wish to have died, my friend. But I'm glad you did not." He looked up at the Rider, who knelt nearby. "Gorra, can't you give him something to make him sleep?"

The Rider shook his head. "Not until we get more water into him, m'lord. He can't very well drink if he's unconscious. But he's been resisting. I think he's trying to die."

Cadel pressed his lips together, then stood up. "Saraid, see if you can get him to drink. I need to check on everyone else."

"Me?"

"He always used to have a soft spot for a pretty young woman." A brief, pained smile crossed his mouth. "I'll bet you can do it, if anyone here can." He ducked out through the flap and was gone.

"All right," she muttered, squaring her shoulders. She'd asked to come, and by Keranieth, she'd not flinch now. "How much must he drink?" she asked the Rider, who'd been watching them with interest.

He pointed to a large pitcher by the man's head. "If you can get that into him, I can give him *dontur* tincture enough to sleep two hours. Then we'll need to wake him and give him more to drink and change the *ruuish* poultice on his hands, but after that he can sleep six."

*Ruuish* poultice. A nervous laugh rose up in her throat but she choked it back. Instead she crouched next to Master Elliv, who was tossing his head from side to side on his pillow. "Master Elliv," she called gently, touching his cheek.

He half opened his eyes, then blinked and opened them farther.

"My name's Saraid. Will you let me help you drink a cup of water?" She gave him her prettiest smile.

Some of the fog seemed to clear from his eyes. "What's a girl—doing here?"

"I came with Cadel. Here." She shifted around until she sat behind his head. "If we lift you a little, you can rest your head on my lap at just the right angle so drinking will be easy. You won't have to keep sitting up."

"Saraid," he whispered. "Not— You came—Cadel? Saraid...?"

He was still staring up at her but hadn't refused, so she motioned Gorra over to help lift Master Elliv and prop him up on a pillow in her lap. "You're... What you...doing here?" he demanded, gazing up at her.

"I am presently Lord Cadel's...guest," she said, accepting a fresh damp cloth from Gorra to place on his forehead.

"Guest." Master Elliv made a short, sharp noise that she realized was a snort of laughter. "M-Mutrand's bride is Cadel's guest. Good...for him." The long speech seemed to tire him. He gasped for breath and said, "How?"

A sudden inspiration struck her. "I'll be happy to tell you, sir," she said. "*If* you'll drink what's in this cup."

He made his strange laugh again. "You're...clever as he is. Tell me."

Saraid made him drink two cupfuls, sip by sip, before she would corroborate that she was indeed *that* Saraid. In the meanwhile her legs went from pins-and-needles to totally numb, but she didn't stir. If Cadel could face this man smiling, she could put up with a little discomfort.

"Thought you delayed...leaving Thekla," Master Elliv said after drinking another cup. Gorra was nodding at her approvingly. "That's...what we heard."

"That's what Cadel wanted you to hear." So his plans had worked. Did they ever not?

"And you're...his guest." Master Elliv actually chuckled. "He's...amazing. If anyone...deserves the crown...he does."

Crown? What crown? "Drink," she commanded, glancing into the pitcher. The poor man's mind was starting to wander; best get the rest of this into him so that he could rest.

After Master Elliv had drunk his last cup, laced with juice from the *dontur* vine, and drifted into sleep, Saraid carefully slipped from beneath his pillow. Gorra helped her to her feet. "Thank you, Your Highness," he said. "Milord was right about your being able to distract him. At least he has a chance at living now."

"Who is he?" Saraid looked back the sleeping man.

"He was the Master of the Ebroian Military Academy at Madariv and a friend to Lord Cadel and Lord Cadel's father before him. He's the one who helped get us all into the Eb." Gorra swallowed. "He was also the best swordsman I ever saw and taught the advanced classes in rapier. But he'll never hold a sword again. All his fingers were cut off, just below the first joint."

Saraid's stomach clenched again. "Why?"

"From what I could gather, it was because he refused admission to the Eb for the nephew of the Lord Protector's...er, friend. The entry requirements are strict, and exceptions aren't allowed. At least, they weren't. That will likely change, now that Master Elliv's gone."

"And his son? Why did they kill him?"

"Who knows? To send a message, I suppose. Life grows ugly in Madariv, Your Highness. You don't know how glad I am that I finished at the Eb when I did. First time I've been glad I'm not twenty in a long time." He chuckled, but his face was grim.

Beside him, one of the other injured men stirred and made a strange guttural sound. Gorra turned to him at once. "Easy, lad. More water?"

The man made the strange noise again, and Gorra lifted him up and helped him drink. He seemed to have a hard time swallowing; much of the water ran down his chin, but the Rider patiently held the cup till he'd had enough, then eased him back down again and blotted the spilled water. After the man's eyes had closed, Gorra sighed. "No tongue," he murmured to Saraid. "That's what happens to people who dare to publicly disagree with the Lord Protector."

She winced and nodded to the third man. "What about him?"

"Badly beaten. Maybe he was a craftsman who sold the Lord Protector an inferior product or a footman who spilled his soup. We've seen both." He looked at her kindly. "Why don't you go get a breath of air? You're not looking well. Now that Master Elliv's sleeping, I can deal with these two."

Saraid staggered out of the tent on her still-numb legs. She wished her ears were as numb so she wouldn't have to hear about any further atrocities. Mauburni was not ruled by a Lord Protector, but by a monster. Cadel hadn't told her a hundredth of this.

Yet even if he had, she was not sure she would have believed him. This had to be witnessed to be believed. And dear blessed Keranieth, she had seen it.

Cadel was not in the first tent she looked in. That one was also occupied by injured people—two men and a woman—being tended by another Rider. Saraid did not want to know what had been done to them.

She found him in the last tent, helping another Rider wrap a limp figure in a linen cloth while Belet watched, pale-faced. His eyes were suspiciously bright, but his hands were steady as he carefully tied the sheet closed at the body's feet. "I'll get the men I brought to help me bury him," he said to the Rider. "You two stay with them." He gestured to two other people on pallets. Both were, mercifully, asleep. Or unconscious.

The Rider puffed his cheeks and blew out gustily. He was white-haired and weathered and looked distinctly annoyed. "No. You'll go get some rest, milord, and they'll bury this one."

"I'm fine, Lisnam. Save your doctoring for the ones who need it." Cadel rose and was about to pick up the body, then saw her. "No, Saraid. You don't need to be here for this."

The man he'd called Lisnam stood up also. "Your Highness." He bowed. "I'm trying to convince Milord Pighead here that he's done enough."

Cadel raised an eyebrow at him but didn't reply. "How does Master Elliv?" he asked her.

"Asleep for now. I bribed him into drinking what he needed."

Lisnam looked relieved. "Thank you, Your Highness. I'll check on him shortly." He looked pointedly at her, then at the tent flap.

She caught his intent. "I could use a moment's quiet, Cadel." Which wasn't, by any means, a lie.

"She's far wiser than you are. Either go with her or I'm going to hold your nose and make you drink your own dose of *dontur* tincture." Lisnam crossed his arms on his chest.

Cadel sighed and rubbed his eyes. "All right, Master Equally Pigheaded. You win, damn you. Come on, Saraid."

"Use the rest tent," Lisnam called after them. "I'll send someone with a jug of cold tea for you."

"I'll fetch it if you don't need me here." Belet rose. "Is it cooling in the spring?"

Lisnam nodded, and Saraid's heart sank. The last person she wanted to sit and drink tea with right now was Belet, but Cadel was already leaving the tent. He led her to another, one blessedly empty of injured people, and gestured her in.

"Go on. I'll be back after I check on everyone."

"No you won't." Belet appeared behind him, lugging a green ceramic jug. "You heard Lisnam. Sit for a minute and drink some of this. You need a rest."

"I will, later. Thank you, Bel—"

"Now. Please tell him, Saraid. He'll listen to you." She held the jug out.

Saraid began to reach out to take it—and hesitated. The last time Belet had brought her something to eat or drink, she'd been ill for days.

But Belet wasn't even looking at her; her gaze was fixed on Cadel. Reassured, Saraid took the jug; Belet surely would never risk harming him. "Come on, Milord Pighead," she said, taking the jug.

"Thank you." Belet was still looking at Cadel with that peculiarly intense expression. Then she turned away and hurried back toward the tents of the wounded.

Cadel sighed. "Damn you as well." But he followed her into the tent.

She found some cups on a low table and filled two from the jug. "Drink," she said, handing one to him.

He rolled his eyes at her and took a gulp, and then another.

"All right. But you, too. Sit." He sank down onto the canvas floor against a cushion. She sat next to him and sipped from her own cup.

"Thank you for helping Elliv," he said, after a moment of staring into his tea. "Was it too bad?"

"No, not..." She swallowed. "Yes. Why didn't you tell me?"

"I did. On the way here."

"No. I mean before this. What—what Lord Protector Mutrand is doing."

"Would you have believed me if I had?" He took another long drink, watching her over the rim of his cup.

Which was exactly what she had said to herself. "I'm not sure," she replied, looking at her hands. "It was... I had no idea anyone could do that to another human being. Master Elliv...and the man with no tongue... He wasn't much older than me, I don't think."

"Saraid..." Cadel was gripping the cup too hard. As she watched he carefully relaxed his fingers. "I didn't want you to see this, when you asked to come with us. But then I decided that you couldn't deny it if you'd seen it with your own eyes." His voice lowered. "I'm sorry. It wasn't a kind thing to do." He put down his empty cup and held out his arms to her.

Saraid's breath caught. Back in the dunes, they'd embraced mostly by accident. But to go to him now would be intentional.

She was so very tired. Tired because it been a full day since the nap she'd taken yesterday afternoon. But tired of struggling, too. Tired of looking for reasons to resist Cadel. Just now, they were both weary and saddened by what they'd seen.

Slowly, stiffly, as if she were crossing a miles-wide chasm, she set down her still-mostly-full cup and moved into the circle of his embrace. As his arms surrounded her she rested her head on his shoulder and felt his heartbeat pounding in his throat. Or perhaps it was her own heart she felt, racing at his closeness.

He didn't try to kiss her again but held her gently, stroking her hair.

"Gorra told me about Master Elliv," she said when she thought she'd mastered her breath. "About what a swordsman he is—was."

"And what a friend to me," Cadel added.

"I...I'm sorry."

"I am, too."

"No—I mean...I'm *sorry*. I didn't believe you when you said the Lord Protector was a monster. You were telling the truth."

He didn't answer, but his arms tightened around her. She sighed and closed her eyes. Peace. Peace such as she hadn't felt for weeks, despite the horrors she'd seen today.

But it would be at best a temporary peace. Thekla would not let her rest for long, and the question of doing her duty to her country had grown bigger and thornier. Much, much thornier. Marrying the Lord Protector would enrich Thekla, true—but it would also enable him to grind Mauburni further beneath his heel. Had Father and the council known any of this about the man they sought as an ally—and as her husband?

*Had they known and sent her anyway?*

She buried her face against Cadel's shoulder.

"You're not pulling away from me," he whispered after a while. "You could if you want to. I told you before—I'll never force you."

"I know."

"Saraid...when we were sledding and fell off and I...you know..."

Her face felt like it had caught on fire. When he'd kissed her.

"You didn't pull away then, either."

"No, I... No."

"Why not?"

Trust Cadel to always cut to the heart of the matter—and to make her face it. Because he'd accomplished precisely what he'd set out to do. He'd danced around her and trapped her in her own words and managed her quite nicely, all the while silently showing her his true worth and waiting for her to realize that they were meant for each other.

"I...I didn't pull away from you because I couldn't," she finally said. "Or... No. I didn't want to. I wanted you to kiss me. I think I have ever since we met, but I've been too busy telling myself that I didn't love you when I do—"

Cadel made a soft noise, almost like a snort.

"Don't you dare laugh at me! Do you know how hard it is for me to admit any of this to you?" She lifted her head off his shoulder to frown at him.

But instead of smiling down into hers, Cadel' eyes had rolled back into their sockets and his head lolled. As she stared he collapsed, sliding slowly sideways against her till his head rested on her breast. She caught him instinctively as his weight settled limply into her.

"Cadel?" she asked, shrugging her shoulder against him.

No answer, except for his quiet steady breathing. He was asleep.

For a moment, she was indignant. How dare he nod off while she was declaring her love for him?

But the feeling of him against her, big and warm and solid, was too wonderful. She squirmed into a slightly more comfortable position against the cushion at her back and looked down into his face cradled against her. In sleep he looked boyish, all those stern lines smoothed away. She stroked his hair back from his forehead—and yes, it was just as thick and soft as she'd always thought it would be, just luscious to run her fingers through, and kissed his brow. Ha. Now she had something to tease him with—falling asleep just when she was admitting he was right. She wouldn't let him forget it.

Not that she'd forget it, either. In the time—not long!—since they'd left to go sledding in the dunes, she'd gone from refusing to ride with Cadel to feeling her heart swell as she held him sleeping in her arms. Was this what life with him would be like? To be able to stroke his hair whenever she wanted, to spar with words and then close their battles with kisses...to know, eventually, that words weren't necessary because the knowledge of him was bone-deep inside her?

She rested her cheek on the top of his head. Funny how he'd just passed out like this. Maybe the amount of strain he'd been under was just too much, even for him. Keranieth knew how tired *she* was, how limp and sluggish she felt now that the emergency was over. It would be so nice to let go as well and join him in sleep.

But she couldn't quite drift off. It might have been that her right foot was tingling uncomfortably, tucked as it was underneath her, or that when she closed her eyes her head had begun to spin. Or it might have been the faint rustling coming from the front of the tent...she lifted her head to look and felt a wave of dizziness ripple unpleasantly through her.

Belet was peering in through the flap at her. "Is he asleep yet?" she mouthed.

"Out cold," she whispered. Oh, please let Belet leave so she could sleep, too...but wait. How did she know he was going to—

"About time," Belet said in a normal voice, and stepped inside, tossing her hair back from her face and smiling at her. But there was no warmth in her smile, only a satisfaction that verged almost on gloating. She was carrying a coil of rope in one hand, and in the other a long knife.

# Nineteen

Even if one's heart is pure and conscience clean, doing the wrong thing for the right reason is still doing the wrong thing.

—*The Flower of Royalty Blossom'd*

"BELET," SARAID SAID, OR tried to say. But her mouth had suddenly gone dry and dusty-feeling, and another wave of dizziness made it hard to focus her eyes.

"But why aren't you out? Didn't you drink any of the tea?" Belet let the coil of rope slide to the ground and came over to peer at her.

"T...tea?"

Then she understood. The tea they'd drunk, that Belet had brought them. Cadel had drunk a full cup of it, while she'd only sipped at hers. Which was why he had collapsed...and why she was feeling dizzy and light-headed. She'd been right to hesitate to accept the jug from her. If only she'd refused it. "What did you put in it? Why?"

Belet rolled her eyes. "What do you think? A good double dose of *dontur* tincture—what you gave Master Elliv. I suppose it's slightly easier having you awake. It means I won't have to carry you. Assuming you cooperate, that is. But I think I can arrange that." She tapped her fingernails on the blade of the knife and smiled again.

Saraid stared at it. She wouldn't panic, even though she was half pinned down by Cadel's unconscious weight—drugged, not sleeping, so there was no chance he could do anything— "Don't you dare hurt Cadel!" She struggled to sit up.

"Hurt Cadel? Why should I want to do that? He's perfectly safe. You, on the other hand…" Belet drawled her words.

"Bel!" The door flap twitched aside, and Vul walked in, wrapped in his *lahart*. He looked from Belet to her and frowned. "What's going on here?"

Saraid closed her eyes in relief for just a second. "Vul," she croaked. "Please, help… Cadel's been drugged and I can't… She has a knife… Help me—"

Vul came to stand by Belet. "Curse it, put that knife away! I thought we agreed we weren't going to have any of that."

Belet pouted. "I was just having a little fun." She slipped the knife into a sheath at her waist. "Did you have any trouble with Lisnam?"

"Not a bit. They swallowed the story whole. You're to tell Healer Derru to send out more supplies, by the way. Too bad she won't ever get the message. I already have the horses. Even got someone to saddle them for me. We'll just need to head west a ways then circle back east." He knelt next to Saraid. "How much tea did you have? Can I help you up?"

There was something strange going on here, but she wasn't quite sure what. If only her head weren't feeling like an entire swarm of Choderian bees was buzzing in circles inside it. "You know about the tea," she said, enunciating carefully so that the words didn't slip away.

"We thought it would be the easiest way, Your Highness." He slid his arms round Cadel's chest and lifted him off her, then let him fall carelessly to the ground before taking her hands and pulling her to her feet. She swayed and began to fall, but he caught her with a steadying arm. "Steady on, Your Highness. I'll help you. Bel, did you get her *lahart*?"

"Yes." Belet jerked her head back toward the door.

"Good. Let's get her into it and we can go. The horses are ready, but I don't want to leave them too long. How long is Cadel likely to sleep?"

"Most of the afternoon, if he drank that whole cup. More likely till sunset, since he was already tired out."

"So he'll be out at least until the supplies arrive from the camp. Good. They'll be too busy to notice we're gone. That buys us some extra time."

"Gone?" There was something not right—*very* not right—going on here. If only she weren't so dizzy— "Where're you going?"

"It's not just us. You're coming with us." He spoke soothingly, as if she were a small, unreasonable child. "We're going to Mauburni, just like you've been wanting to. The Lord Protector's waiting for you there, remember? Won't you be glad to finally see him?"

To *Mauburni*? "No!"

Vul paused. "Bel?" he asked, sounding uncertain.

"It's the *dontur* tincture. It makes people confused sometimes before they sleep," Belet said impatiently. "Come on. Carry her if you have to."

"Don't listen to her!" She did her best to focus on his face. So Belet had found someone willing, eager even, to bring her to Madariv. How ironic. But somehow it didn't seem very amusing just now. "I want to stay here!"

He sighed. There was something different about him—he seemed taller, more authoritative, and less the shy country boy. "I'm sorry to hear that, Your Highness. I'd been led to believe that you were more than willing to go. Not having your cooperation will make this a lot more difficult." He glanced at Belet.

She shrugged. "Give her more of this, then." She bent and picked up the cup of drugged tea Saraid had set down when

Cadel had held his arms out to her. "Another gulp or two and she'll be out."

"No!" Saraid tried to jerk out of his arms and nearly fell over again.

He caught her and twisted her arms behind her, but gently. "I didn't think I'd have to do this. Is that why you insisted on the rope?" he said to Belet.

"I thought it couldn't hurt. And here." She pulled a scarf out of her sleeve. "Better cover her mouth, too."

"Stop—don't want to leave!" Saraid fought them as well as she could. But Vul already had her hands behind her, and not being able to stand because of the dizziness that washed over her in waves made any real resistance almost impossible. If only Cadel would wake—but Cadel still lay where Vul had left him. So close—yet he might as well be back in the camp with Perrin and Meyric.

"This is for the best, Your Highness, really it is." Vul finished tying her arms. "I'm just glad we're leaving before one of our scout parties finds this camp. They're mostly trained to kill first and ask questions later. I'd really hate to see anything happen to you after you were so kind to Fhorri."

"One of *our*...?" She stared at him. "But you're Adaihan— you're one of Cadel's Riders—"

He looked faintly uncomfortable, but also proud. "That's what you were all supposed to think. But I'm not his." He jerked his head over at Cadel's still form. "If he has his way, we'll all end up dead fighting a war we'll never be able to win. My father already died for him. I don't need to as well."

"Fighting what war? What do—"

Before she could say anything further, Belet had tightened the scarf over her mouth. She pleaded with Vul with her eyes.

"The Lord Protector will be so pleased to see you. I'll be proud to bring you to him myself." And he picked her up, slinging her over his shoulder. "Go see if it's all clear, Bel. The sooner we get to Madariv, the better."

Saraid's mind raced—though stumbled was perhaps a better description—as she bumped uncomfortably against Vul's back after Belet declared the way was clear. The diffident, slightly raw youth, so proud of his status as a Rider, whom she thought she'd known was gone. Or maybe he was still there—only along with them, he'd been a Mauburnian spy as well.

And Belet. How she must have gloated when she approached Vul and found him more than willing to take her to Madariv. The thought made her feel slightly sick.

They must have originally planned to spirit her away from the sledding trip. No wonder Vul had looked so dismayed when Cadel arrived to go with them. They couldn't have known that this trip to the Border Watch camp would take place, but coming here, so much closer to Madariv, had only played right into their hands.

One point remained confusing. Vul had made it sound as though Belet were coming with them. But she would never want to do that. Surely having a clear chance at Cadel was the whole reason she was helping Vul spirit her away to Madariv. Keranieth, if only she weren't so groggy maybe she could figure out a way to stop them. But bound and gagged, she was powerless.

A soft snorting and a dull, impatient stomp of a hoof on sand told her they'd reached the horses Vul had mentioned. He bent and let her down, holding her steady against him.

"How are we going to get her on a horse?" Belet asked. "She's so useless she might as well be asleep. We could always roll her in a sack and tie her across the saddle, I suppose." There was an edge of pleased malice in her voice.

"Enough, Bel. This is your future queen. You don't have to like her, but you can at least be civil." Vul whistled quietly. At once the horse next to them knelt.

"Here we go, Your Highness. Nice and easy..." He started to guide her onto the saddle. She shook her head violently and immediately wished she hadn't as a wave of nausea overtook her. Vul took advantage of it to push her onto the saddle, and Belet held her down while he wrapped a length of rope around her in several loops and secured it to the saddle, then tied her feet to the stirrups.

"I'll retie your hands in front so that you can hold on to the saddle. But you're on here about as firmly as you can be. *Hizzarr!*" he murmured to the horse, and it stumbled awkwardly to its feet.

She tensed, but Vul was unfortunately right: she was in no danger of falling off. "Besides," Vul continued, "I'll be riding with you. Prann is strong enough to carry both of us. You'll be quite safe, Your Highness."

Safe. Tears welled up in her eyes. She'd felt safe when Cadel had held her, back at the camp.

"Let's go, Bel," Vul said, nodding to the other horse, then turning to check the girth on Prann.

Belet didn't reply.

"Bel?" Vul looked up.

"I...I don't think I'll be coming," Belet said. She had begun to back away from them.

"Not coming? What are you talking about?" Vul sounded stunned. "Of course you're coming. We've been talking about this for ages. We'll live like lords in Madariv once we've brought Her Highness to the Lord Protector—probably *be* lords, he'll be so grateful. Wouldn't you like to be Lady Belet? We'll have—"

"Yes, I'd like to be Lady Belet. But not as *your* lady. I never promised anything about that." Belet's voice was cool.

"What are you saying?" Saraid felt Vul shift slightly against her leg. He was sliding one hand under his *lahart* toward his waist.

"I'm staying here. I never wanted to go to Madariv. I just wanted to get rid of her. Once she's gone to Mauburni, Cadel will come to his senses and finally notice me. At least he'll be safer. No more falling tents or *vaungona* in his clothes or snapping bowstrings—"

Vul's stealthy motions ceased. "What?"

"Who else would have wanted to do those things to Cadel? Everyone else in camp loves him." Belet was almost in tears now. "Don't believe her when she says she wants to stay with him. I heard her talking to him, that first day when she came. She hates him."

Saraid wiggled her jaw against the gag to try to dislodge it and answer her accusations. When she'd overheard Belet say the same things back at camp to Mervii and the unknown woman, she'd assumed she was merely trying to stir up trouble. But it seemed she'd come to believe her own words. Almost in spite of herself, Saraid felt a sudden pity for her.

"Everyone loves him except me." Vul sighed. "*I'm* the one who did those things, not her. Except for the bowstring. That really was an accident."

"You!" Belet stared at him. Saraid wasn't sure if the flush on her face was from her own emotion or from the light of the setting sun.

"After you suggested we escort the princess to Madariv, I stopped trying—this seemed to be more likely to succeed. Besides, I thought you and I..." He stared at the ground between his feet, shuffling the coarse sand with the toe of his boot. "I didn't realize that you felt that way about Cadel, or that you hated her so much..." He trailed off, then looked up at her keenly. "Did you hate her enough to feed her a plateful of *ruuish*?"

Belet flushed again. "Yes, if you must know. I thought it would be funny."

"Funny," Vul repeated slowly. "Would it have been funny if she'd died or taken permanent harm?"

"I don't care!" Belet stamped her foot. "We're even. You tried to kill Cadel and I wanted to kill her. Take your precious princess and go to Madariv. I'm going back to C—"

In one fluid motion, Vul was next to Belet, clutching her arm. The blade of his knife just pressed into the side of her neck. "And tell Cadel everything once he wakens?" he said. "Let him know there's someone loyal to Mauburni who knows that he lives and where he is? I don't think so."

"Let me go, you—you traitor!"

Vul's jaw clenched, and he moved his knife ever so slightly so that it just nicked her, sending a tiny trickle of blood down her throat. She froze.

"Smart girl," he murmured. "Did you feel that?"

"There's something on the blade." Her eyes half closed, and Saraid could see her chest rise and fall with her breathing.

"Yes. Nothing fatal, but nothing you'd like very much if you had more of it. I can't afford to leave you here, Bel. It's too late. You shouldn't have tried to lie to me." He let go of her arm but still held the knife in place at her throat and fumbled with his free hand in the pouch at his waist, producing a length of cord. "Hands behind your back, please. And don't try any tricks."

Slowly, she slid her hands behind her. He tied them and removed the knife from her belt. "Any other surprises like this?" he asked.

She glared at him and shook her head.

"I hope not. I like you a lot, Bel, but I'm not going to let you ruin my plans." He patted her down, nodded, and lifted her easily onto the other horse. Then he came to stand by Saraid.

"I'm sorry, Your Highness, but you'll have to ride on your own while I look after Belet. I'll lead your horse, but if you can stay awake, it might be safer for you. Do you understand?"

She stared at him. He gestured for her to bend her head and loosened the gag. "I don't expect you're capable of much noise right now," he said. "So you might as well be comfortable."

He was right. Her mouth felt dry and thick and she wished she could drink the entire jug of Belet's drugged tea and go to sleep and forget that this was happening. "Please let me stay," she whispered. "You and Belet...you go..."

He looked at her steadily. "Do you really think that's still possible, under the circumstances?"

"I swear I won't say a word—"

"Really, Your Highness?"

She closed her eyes.

"I didn't think so." He tied a leading line to her horse's bridle, then mounted the other horse behind Belet. "Now...let's go. We've wasted enough time."

They left camp at a walk, maintaining a slow, quiet pace for a while as the afternoon waned. When Vul judged they were far enough from the camp to ensure that no one would be able to see them change course, they began to move back eastward.

"The moon will be up later," Vul commented. "A good journeying night."

"He'll be angry as a singed lion when he wakes," Belet said. "You know he will. He'll curse your name and the day he ever heard it—"

"It won't matter much, Bel. We'll be practically on the border by then," Vul said. It was clear from the exaggerated patience in his voice that he was struggling to keep his temper in check.

Saraid was struggling to stay upright on her horse. Sleepiness washed over her in waves so that she'd suddenly jerk awake and realize she'd dozed for a few seconds. It was one more misery to add to her list. Talking was the last thing she wanted to do right now, but it might help keep her awake—and help her think of some way to escape or convince Vul to change his mind. The Book said that knowledge was the most powerful ammunition. Oh, what wouldn't she give for her copy of The Book just now—for anything familiar and comforting.

"Why?" she asked into the silence.

He glanced back at her. "Why what, Your Highness?"

Was he being evasive or polite? "Why do you hate Cadel? Why are you doing this?"

"Why shouldn't I hate him?" he said after a moment, staring ahead. "He killed my parents."

"What?"

Belet made a snorting noise. Vul ignored her.

"My father was a Rider," he said after another pause. "He was Adaihan, but he loved Cadel's father and Cadel himself — he was a Rider for Cadel's father before I was born. He was...you know those people who seem bigger than everyone else, even if they aren't? That's what Dadai was like — he had a loud voice and a big laugh, one of those laughs that made everyone else around him laugh too. He used to sing all the time — you could hear him riding in from patrol, singing as loud as he could. My mother would lift her head from whatever she was doing when she heard him and smile. He loved her so much — she was from Mauburni. She used to tell me stories about how wonderful Madariv was and how she missed it, but then she'd say that home was where Dadai was.

"And then he was killed when Fhorri wasn't quite three." He spoke quietly, but his voice thrummed with pain. "Cadel was there. They were out on a longer patrol and stopped for the night to camp near some rocks. During the night, a *vaungon* — a scorpion rat —"

"I know what a *vaungon* is." A knot tightened in her midsection.

"They like to burrow near rocks at night because they absorb heat during the day, so in the winter Adaihans usually avoid sitting or camping near them. But they decided to camp there because the rocks offered shelter from the wind and it was early enough in the year that Cadel and the others didn't think the females would be breeding yet."

"Including your father?"

He went on as if he hadn't heard her. "One crawled into his blankets and bit him when he shifted in his sleep. He was still alive in the morning, but just barely. Cadel tried to get him back to Callest, but it was too late."

Saraid couldn't stop herself. "So that's why the *vaungon* in his hood."

"Of course," he said, expressionless. She looked away.

"My mother died about a year and a half later, when the lung fever came through," he continued after a pause. "She didn't seem to want to fight it. I think she was glad to die, with him gone."

"I lost my mother when I was young, too," Saraid said quietly.

Vul turned to look at her. "Then you should understand what I lost."

"I understand that I don't blame anyone for her death."

He scowled. "That's easy for you to say."

"But—why did you let Cadel send you to the Eb if you hate him so much?" Belet asked curiously. "If I hated someone, I wouldn't accept anything from them."

Saraid remembered her bracelets. No, she wouldn't.

Vul jerked around to glare at her. "Cadel owed me!" he spat. "It was the least he could do to make up for killing my father!"

"But your mother would have been taken care of—that's part of the Riders' compact!"

"I'm wondering how you could leave Fhorri. You were all that he had left," Saraid put in.

Vul was looking distinctly cross. "Fhorri didn't need me. Our uncle—Dadai's brother—took us to live with his family. They spoil Fhorri rotten and I don't think he remembers he ever had another father than Andursa. But I remember. And I wanted to go to Madariv, because my mother loved it."

"And get away from your uncle," Belet put in. "Everyone knows you and he don't get along."

His back stiffened. Belet's comment had obviously hit a nerve. "I wanted to go to the place she loved, even if she couldn't be there with me. I'm happy to be going back because I hate the Adaiha. There's nothing in it for me."

"Including Fhorri? You're just—abandoning your little brother? He worships you!"

Another pause, slightly longer. "He doesn't need me. He'll forget me soon enough."

Any sympathy she might have felt for him evaporated. "Did the Lord Protector give you much when you decided to turn spy for him?"

"I never had the honor of meeting him," he replied stiffly. Ah, that, too, had hit home. "Only one of his ministers. And it was damned difficult to convince him I wasn't lying about the whole thing. They even put me in prison for a few months, waiting to see if I'd break down. I didn't."

"So they sent you out here to be a spy."

"Yes."

"Just you."

His voice was carefully flat. "You can stop needling me, Your Highness. I know they're testing me. If I went back to the Adaiha and never came back, all they would be out was some money. But if I return to them with something valuable—real, solid evidence of Cadel and his plans or something like that—then they'll know I'm telling the truth. I'll have a career and a life with them, a good life. Finding you and bringing you to them is the best thing that could happen to me."

He'd given this a lot of thought. She supposed she ought to admire him. "You're a good actor, by the way."

"Your Highness." He held his mount back so they were riding side by side. "This isn't personal. I like you, really I do. I think you'll be an excellent queen for Mauburni. It's where you belong. Not here in the desert, living in tents. I'm doing the right thing, bringing you to the Lord Protector."

Belet snickered. "Well, *I* thought so."

Saraid looked away. Vul sighed again and let her fall behind him on the lead line.

They rode all through the evening and into the still, moonlit night, pausing twice to eat a quick meal and rest the horses. Despite the fact that she hadn't eaten in Keranieth knew how long, Saraid's stomach rebelled at the thought of food and she could only nibble at the cheese rolled in flatbread that Vul gave her. The water was more welcome and she drank deeply. Maybe if she consumed enough, she could slow their pace by demanding relief stops every other dune they crossed.

But would there be any point? No one back at the Border Watch camp would miss them. From the brief exchange Vul and Belet had had, it appeared that he'd told Lisnam and the others that he and Belet needed to return to camp on some pretext. They'd assume she was resting, same as Cadel; no one would notice her missing until he woke up. Vul would have a whole night's lead on them.

As they rode, she saw Belet nod, then give in and let her head fall back onto Vul's shoulder. She felt envious for a moment — whether the dontur tincture was still affecting her or if genuine need for sleep had taken over — but being able to nap would have meant riding with Vul, which was out of the question. She would never ride double with any man but Cadel —

No. She couldn't think about Cadel now. It hurt too much.

When the gray predawn had lightened into full morning, Vul stopped near the base of a low rock cliff. Over the last while, Saraid had noticed more variety to the terrain, fewer dune fields and more rocks. They were approaching the hills that marked the border between the Adaiha and Mauburni.

"This looks like a good spot. The horses need to rest and so do we," he said, setting Belet down and coming to untie her from her saddle. "We'll sleep for a bit and then get going again. I assume I can leave these ropes off you now, Your Highness."

"What about me?" Belet flapped her hands behind her. "My arms hurt. Why does she get to go free and I don't?"

Vul ignored her. "There's a couple of blankets in here," he said, unbuckling his saddlebags and rifling in one till he pulled out a gray woolen blanket and handed it to Saraid. "That spot over there by the base of the rock will give you a bit of shade. I'll sleep over here with Bel —"

"Well, well," a voice said. "What have we got here?"

# Twenty

A commanding officer not only leads his men, but serves as their model for behavior in all that they do. Know the commander and you'll know his men.

*—The Flower of Royalty Blossom'd*

BELET SQUEAKED. SARAID LOOKED around her wildly for the source of the voice. Next to her Vul drew his sword, but he looked just as confused.

"Ha!" The voice let out a short, sharp laugh. Another joined it, and another, until a whole chorus of laughter rained down on them. She looked up and saw them.

A line of perhaps a dozen men crouched on the top of the rock cliff a scant twenty feet above them, just visible in the growing morning light. They all held bows, nocked with arrows and aimed straight at her and Vul and Belet.

A man rose from his crouch. The first rays of the sun glinted on his sword as he drew it and leaned on it casually. "Well, looky here what we've found, boys," he said, and she knew he'd been the one who'd spoken. He wore tan-gray, but breeches and a tunic rather than robes, and his cloak was short. By that and by his accent, she knew he wasn't Adaihan. That could only mean one thing.

"Put up your weapons," Vul called, sounding relieved. "We mean you no harm, *Platron*."

The man cocked his head. "*Platron*, eh? What're you knowing about *platrons*, desert rat? And what's that you've got in your hand? A bunch of flowers?"

Vul looked sheepish but started to put his sword back in its scabbard. "I'm a soldier of the Eb same as you, *Platron*."

"Oh, no you don't, boyo." The man on the cliff—she had to assume that the title *platron* meant he was the patrol's commanding officer—gestured lazily with his sword to a spot below him. "Put it down over here, along with any other little toys you might have." He turned his head slightly, not taking his eyes off them, and grunted a word of command. Half of his archers rose and scurried out of sight. The other half remained where they were, bows still drawn.

Very slowly, Vul walked to the bottom of the cliff, unstrapping his sword belt and laying it down on the ground. He added the knife at his belt, and one from his boot.

"Just one boot?" the officer called.

Vul bent, glowering slightly, and removed Belet's knife from his other boot.

"Good boy. Now step away from your pretty little horses, all of you, just in case you've got something else sharp and pointy-like hiding under your saddles." There was a note of derision in the man's voice that made Saraid uneasy.

The half-dozen soldiers who had disappeared were now there beside them. Evidently there was a path leading down from the top of the cliff. Five of them kept their bows trained on Her and Vul and Belet while one went to fetch Vul's weapons. "Got 'em, sir," he called.

The officer nodded. "Keep on them. We'll be down." He jerked his head, and the group on top of the cliff vanished as well, reappearing quickly to join their fellows.

The officer looked her and Belet and Vul up and down in silence, then slowly paced toward them. "Three little Adaihans," he said, "wandering all alone. Running away from home to go to the big city? Or just sneaking away for a little quiet time together? Though I can't believe a prawn like you could keep two girls happy—"

"You filth," Belet spat. "How dare you—"

The *platron* bent and lifted up her bound hands. "Oh, ho!" he chortled. "Needed convincing, did you? Or do you Adaihans just like to play nasty games with each other?"

"*Platron.*" Vul stepped forward. Instantly half a dozen swords were pointing at him. He held his hands up appeasingly. "I *am* a soldier of the Eb. I completed my course with the 317th class this past summer."

The *platron* shrugged. "Is that supposed to convince me?"

"And received a special commission from Minister Walset." Vul raised an eyebrow, waiting for the *platron's* reaction.

It never came. "Should I know him?"

"He's second assistant to Lord Arnine!" Vul said indignantly. "I'm on an important mission for the Ministry of Intelligence and mustn't be detained. I request that you aid us and bring us to Madariv at once."

The *platron's* lips twitched. "Hoy there, lad. You've got a bug in your brain, haven't you? Can you prove you're working for this Minister Whosit?"

"Of course I can." Vul started to reach beneath the neck of his robe.

"Drop those hands!" The *platron's* sword swept toward his throat.

Vul dropped his hands. "In the pouch around my neck you'll find the minister's warrant with his seal," he said, his voice shaking only a little.

The *platron* motioned to one of his men to step forward. "Cover him while I see what this sprat's going on about." He stepped behind Vul, reached for the back of his neck, and fished up a small pouch of waxed linen. Vul moved his head to enable him to remove it, but the *platron* cut the cords on the edge of his sword. Vul's jaw tightened, but he kept silent.

The *platron* opened the bag and pulled out a tightly folded square of paper. He made a show of unfolding it, then peering at it closely. Some of his men sniggered.

"Well—" he finally drawled. "Very impressive. Nice seal this Whatsit's got. Very pretty." He let the page flutter to the ground, then stepped on it. "Very pretty indeed—but not an official government one. Anyone could have written this. Your auntie, for all I know."

"Look, you!" Vul turned and lunged toward him, then stopped when the point of the *platron's* sword again touched his throat. "This is Her Highness, Princess Saraid of Thekla. I'm trying to get her safely to the Lord Protector in Madariv and you're not letting me!"

The officer's dark eyes widened, then narrowed. Then, to her dismay, they crinkled into further laughter. "Princess of Thekla? Boys, did you hear that? We've caught us a princess, wandering around in the Adaiha! And who's this?" He nudged Belet. "The queen of Choder?"

The archers lowered their bows and crowded closer, elbowing each other. "Where's yer crown, then, Princess?" one of them called.

"You'd better believe she's the princess!" Vul growled. "And why shouldn't she be in the Adaiha? She had to cross it to get to the Lord Protector, didn't she?"

"Ah." The officer forcibly restrained his laughter. "You mean this is *that* princess? Lord Mutrand's bride? Pardon me, Your Highness, but where's your retinue? Or did you just slip away from your royal retainers for a little breath of fresh air...or fresh meat?" He leered at Vul and poked him in the midriff.

"Stop that!" Vul aimed a punch at the *platron's* face. But the officer had neatly kicked him in the groin before his hand was halfway across the distance between them. Vul crumpled to the ground, white-faced and gasping. Saraid's uneasiness blossomed into fear.

"No!" Belet said, dropping to Vul's side.

"Do something with him," the officer said dismissively to a pair of his men, then yanked Belet to her feet.

"Don't touch me," she snapped.

For a moment, he stared at her. "A right haughty piece, aren't you? Maybe you are a princess. Or was that your friend, here? Hey, boy!" he called to Vul, who stood swaying between two soldiers. "What's it like to swive a princess? Is she better than a common bawd? Does she have a gold-plated—"

His last word was lost in a shout of laughter from his men.

Saraid pulled her *lahart* more tightly around her. "*Platron*! He's telling the truth. I am Saraid Kasantranieth, Princess of Thekla of the House of Kasantranieth," she said, putting on Full Royal Mode. "My father is King Lygon of Thekla, Honored Fifth of the Name in the House of Kasantranieth—"

"House of Kasantranieth?" The *platron* pretended to consider. "No, ain't been to that one yet. Of course, there are a lot of whorehouses in Madar—"

"How dare you!" She lunged and tried to slap him, but he caught her wrist and twisted it around her, pulling her back against him.

"Be reasonable, girl. What do you expect us to think? That you're a really a princess, or a horny Adaihan chit off with her boyfriend for a bit of fun?" he said in her ear.

"Right now I am not convinced that you're capable of thought." Saraid heard her voice shake and tried to steady it. "But what I would expect of the Lord Protector's border guards is courteous, honorable behavior."

"Oh, I see. Well, let me tell you something, Your *Highness*. This is a desert. Deserts are mighty dry places, and a man works up quite a thirst out here. You boys thirsty?"

Uproarious laughter punctuated by calls of "Dry as a bone!" and "Perishing o' thirst!" answered him.

"And the problem we have, now, is that you and your friend here are just like a couple of long, cool, glasses of water set before thirsty men. Do you know how long we've been on duty in this shit-pile of sand?"

"It's not any of my concern."

He went on as if she hadn't spoken. "It's been five months since any of us have clapped eyes on Madariv…or even on a stinking village full of peasants where you can't tell the difference between the girls and the pigs if your eyes are closed. So we'd be happy to take you to Madariv…eventually. Boys, according to Mistress Princess here we're supposed to be courteous and honorable," he said over her head to the soldiers. "So I trust you'll have the courtesy to give your commanding officer the honor of being the first to show her just what a border guard can do with his sword."

The soldiers cheered.

Saraid's sense of what was happening around her seemed to shift, so that it all appeared to be occurring very slowly. She tried to twist out of the officer's grasp, but her held her too tightly. *I'll have bruises on my arms tomorrow,* she thought, then realized that they would probably be the least of her pains. The officer had grabbed her braid and was bending his head toward hers—pox it, was he going to try to kiss her?—and she scrunched up her face in disgust and turned her face to one side—

—which was how she saw the arrow from nowhere embed itself between his shoulder blades. He gasped and stiffened, then toppled forward, knocking her to the ground. She hit it hard, gasping for breath.

"Saraid!" she heard someone shout above the din that erupted around them. She heaved at the officer's inert weight and tried to shove it off her. She was unarmed, but maybe she could take the dead man's blade or get to Vul's confiscated weapons. With a final grunt of effort she rolled out from under the man, then scuttled sideways away from him and toward the cliff face. One of the Mauburnian soldiers nearly toppled onto her, gurgling blood from an arrow in his throat, and she cried out in horror and swerved away from him.

More arrows hissed deadly paths toward the Mauburnian soldiers from somewhere off to the left, and death cries mixed with angry shouts and the thud of horses' hooves thundering toward her. Saraid pressed back against the rock face, trying to make herself as inconspicuous as possible.

A snorting, blowing horse halted in front of her, and a cloaked, masked figure leaped off its back. She dodged to one side, but the tall figure had caught her by the arm before she could take more than one step. She opened her mouth to scream, but the man had scooped her up in his arms and held her tightly against him.

"Blast it, Saraid, what were you *thinking*?" a furious voice said in her ear.

She gaped up at her captor. Cadel's eyes looked back at her from behind the mask. They were glittering blue and icy with anger.

"Cadel...oh gods, Cadel..." She threw her arms around his neck and buried her face against him. To her shock, he reached up and almost yanked her arms away.

"Are you all right?" he asked, his voice rough.

"Y-yes...Cadel, how did you—"

He shoved her toward the horse. "Up. Lie low on him."

She mounted the horse—it was Silbe, she realized now—and lay low against his neck. The rough hair of his mane chafed her cheek but she didn't care. She was safe, both from the horrible Mauburnians and from Vul. Somehow, Cadel had found her. He was upset now—of course he was—but once this was over she'd be able to tell him what had happened and they could go on from where they'd left off, when he'd fallen asleep in her arms and she'd told him she loved him.

Cadel had looped Silbe's reins over one arm and was easing out of the battle and up the gully, sword drawn. Behind her Saraid could hear the grunts and curses of battling men, the clash of weapons, the thud of bodies as they fell, and hoped she'd never have to hear those sounds again.

They soon reached the top of the gully. Saraid started to lift her head, but a short "down!" from Cadel made her quickly drop it again. It seemed a long time before they stopped.

"Off." Cadel's voice was still harsh. She slid off Silbe's back quickly.

They were in a boulder-strewn field a few paces from a group of cloaked Riders, all busy. Two were pitching a small tent, and another fed fuel to a small fire while another poured water from a skin into a pot set atop it. Others tended to horses or rummaged in bags. They looked so safe and ordinary that Saraid wanted to cry. She turned to Cadel and held out her arms. "Oh, Ca—"

Her words evaporated in her mouth. Cadel wasn't standing there, waiting for her. He wasn't even looking at her. He had swung up on Silbe again and, as she stared at him, turned away and cantered back toward the gully. His back was straight and his shoulders stiff, and he didn't turn to look at her. In a few seconds, he had disappeared down the sloping path.

Cadel had just ridden away from her.

Her throat had gone tight, as if she were choking on her own breath, and the cheerful morning sunlight fractured into prisms. She'd faced the horrors of the maimed people at the watch camp, been kidnapped and carried off into the desert, then threatened with bodily violence. But only this had made her cry.

"Cadel!" she shouted. By Keranieth's silver crown, he was going to listen to her. "Cadel, it wasn't my fau—"

"Your Highness." Someone touched her arm. She whirled, rubbing the back of her hand across her eyes. It was Lisnam, the doctor from the Watch camp.

"Healer," she acknowledged. A chill, distant note in his voice warned her not to say anything further.

"You are unhurt?" He would not meet her eyes.

She managed not to laugh bitterly at his question. "I am unharmed, thank you. It's not what you think—I didn't—"

But he had already turned away, returning to the fire to join a pair of Riders setting out small vials and flasks.

Her breath caught again. She could go after him, tell him what had happened—

If he would even listen.

One of the Riders had risen to talk to Lisnam. Now he came up to her, putting back his hood—and this time, she nearly did collapse. It was no Rider, but Perrin.

"Saraid," she said. Her voice was cool, too, but her eyes were concerned and pitying. They completely undid her.

"Perrin!" she wailed, and threw herself into her arms.

"There, child. It's all right." Perrin seemed surprised but returned her hug. "We were so worried about you."

"Y-you were?" Saraid drew back to look at her.

"We came after you, didn't we? Even though..."

Some of her hurt kindled into anger. "You don't think I left because I *wanted* to, do you?"

"Ah." Perrin nodded. "I told him that might be the case, but he wouldn't listen. I think we have to have a talk so you can explain what happened."

The morning sun was suddenly too bright. Saraid closed her eyes against it. "Cadel thinks I ran away from him?"

"I'm afraid he does. He thinks you planned this with Belet and Vul. But you say you didn't." Perrin's voice went up ever so slightly.

"No! Vul and Belet forced me! Vul was a spy for Mauburni— he told me as we rode—and Belet was helping him because she wanted me gone so she could try to catch Cadel."

"A spy?" That seemed to take Perrin aback. "Oh, dear, we *do* have to talk. The tent's for any wounded, but we can at least go find someplace a little more private." She took Saraid's arm and turned away from the rest of the Riders, who were studiously ignoring them, then stopped. "You're sure you're all right... physically?"

"Yes. Cadel— You arrived in time. It's just..." She blinked hard at the tears that had welled up again. "Why are you here?"

"I came with the supplies to the Watch camp, to help with the injured. I've picked up some little skill in nursing over the years. When we arrived, we found out you were missing. I decided to ride on with Cadel to find you."

"How did you find us?"

"It was a still night with plenty of light, and your trail was easy enough to follow, even with Cadel still half-unconscious. Now come along, child. We've got some sorting out to do here before everyone leaves."

"Leaves for where?"

Perrin's eyes got that pitying look again. "Before we go back to camp. And before you leave for Thekla. Cadel's sending you back. You leave at sunset."

# Twenty-one

Neglect not the study of history, and remember that not all history is written down. Often it is those unwritten stories that are the most important and true.

*— The Flower of Royalty Blossom'd*

SARAID LET PERRIN GUIDE her over to a group of small boulders and seat her on one, then watched while Perrin returned to the fire and made them both mugs of tea. She knew she was sitting on a rock warmed by the morning sun, bathed in light, but she felt frozen and numb, as if she'd been locked in a stone cellar for days.

"Why?" she croaked when Perrin returned and handed her a cup.

Perrin did not require an explanation. "Because you'd already tried to leave once with Belet's help — yes, we knew about her helping you that time — and…well, how do you think the situation looked? The sledding trip and then all of you begging to come along to the Watch camp…Belet suddenly having to return to home at once and the drugged tea she brought, which Cadel drank and you barely sipped —"

"He fell asleep in my arms…just before I told him I loved

him." Saraid started to wrap her arms around herself, then realized she was holding a cup. Where had it come from? Everything felt disjointed and dim, as if it were happening to someone else and she was hearing it described from across a noisy room.

"Oh, dear," Perrin said again, but this time with a frown. "Drink that before you drop it. And tell me more about what happened."

"It was Belet and Vul. Belet brought us *dontur* tincture that Lisnam had been using." Saraid took a gulp of tea. It scalded her mouth yet somehow made her start to shiver. "All those things that happened to Cadel were Vul's doing—the tent and the *vaungon* and the saddle girth. He hated Cadel and wanted to go back to Madariv." She stumbled through what had happened, speaking in disjointed phrases, saying things as they came to mind, circling around the huge blackness that Perrin's words had made: *He's sending you back to Thekla.*

At some point she must have stopped talking, because it had grown quiet. Perrin was looking at her thoughtfully.

"And you say you love him now," she prompted gently.

"I...I think I did back when I didn't know who he was...but I couldn't believe it. I had to go to Mauburni, for Thekla. But he made me love him. Everything he did...everything he was...I fought it...but it caught me anyway. And then to have the truth about the Lord Protector laid out so starkly—"

"Mmm. Do you love him enough to stay here with him in the Adaiha?"

Saraid thought of Cadel's back as he'd ridden away from her, straight and implacable. "Does it matter? H-he doesn't want me now."

"Stupid child." Perrin smiled to remove the sting from her words. "Do you think he's actually stopped loving you? If he had, he wouldn't have ridden like a possessed man after you even though he could hardly stay in the saddle, so that he could send you safely home to Thekla rather than let you go where everyone else that he's ever loved has died horrible deaths."

"What?" A little of the fog in her brain melted away. What was Perrin talking about?

Perrin considered. "Except for his father. And even his father might·have been said to have died there, at least in spirit." She sat up straighter on her rock, as if she'd made a decision. "I'm going to tell you a story. Cadel made me swear never to tell you, but when you've reached my age, you'll learn that some promises are better broken."

"But—"

"Let me speak. My story concerns a king and his family. His kingdom was a beautiful and important country, a country with a mighty navy and merchant fleet and a long history and tradition centered on the sea. The king was of an ancient lineage; his family had ruled in line unbroken from parent to child for over four hundred years.

"This particular king had never expected to come to the throne. He spent his youth sailing and fishing rather than learning history and how to rule his country. He had three healthy, robust elder brothers, after all. He was no more likely to become king than his favorite horse was.

"But life can do strange things. So it was that suddenly, in his early twenties, after a lifetime of not preparing for it, this young man became king.

"Now, he had good intentions and was at heart a decent young man. But he'd never learned subtlety or to look at situations on more than a surface level, and his advisors tended to be men whom he liked to go sailing with, rather than men who could give him advice on how to rule his country. So affairs began to—well, slip a little—though the outward prosperity of the country seemed unchanged.

"In time, the king married. He chose a lovely young woman, the daughter of one of his nobles, and they loved each other dearly. But again, he did not choose wisely. Other nobles were affronted that he'd chosen her and not one of *their* sisters or daughters. The girl herself, though kind and good and generous, was as guileless as her husband and had no more idea of how to be a ruler."

"She'd never read The Book, then," Saraid couldn't help muttering.

"No, she hadn't," Perrin said. Her smile was sad. "I doubt she'd even heard of it. So some years passed. It took a while for the queen to conceive, but at last she found that she was pregnant. The king was overjoyed, and to celebrate he decreed an amnesty and honors to be bestowed. He asked his ministers to draw up a list of persons to receive them, and as a result, a certain wealthy man who had been cultivating and giving expensive gifts to these ministers received a knighthood and entrée to the king's court. This wealthy man was of humble origin and had worked hard to gain his wealth. He looked forward to what he thought was his just reward for his labors.

"But he had counted without the snobbery of the nobility. You see, he had earned his fortune mining and selling seabird guano as fertilizer—a much-needed commodity in that sandy-soiled country but a difficult background to live down. He was ignored when he went to court, or worse, giggled about and pointed to behind his back. People would sniff the air when he walked by, as if the scent of guano somehow still clung to him. Even the king joined in, referring to him as Sir Whiffy. It was not so much malice as thoughtlessness, but it cut the man to the quick. Perhaps he was a little mad, or just one who bore a grudge. But he swore he would get his revenge on the king and his nobles.

"The queen in due course bore the king a handsome, healthy son, and life seemed perfect." Perrin paused for breath. "He was such a beautiful baby," she said, half to herself.

"I thought this was a story?"

Perrin went on as if she hadn't spoken. "But outside the king's protected, comfortable existence in the palace, matters were far from that. As I said before, he was not an astute administrator and tended to let others see to what he should have been watching himself—and some of those he trusted were not deserving of his trust. So he had no idea of what the new wealthy knight he'd carelessly teased was up to.

"Buying expensive gifts for government officials and cultivating members of the lesser nobility were perhaps not too concerning. But raising the foundation of a private army on his country estates was a different matter, as was buying large amounts of weaponry and food interests like mills and fishing fleets. And his new friends—former working men like himself who'd struck it rich and younger sons of the old nobility with too much time on their hands—were only too willing to listen when he began to drop poison in their ears about the king, calling to their attention his weaknesses. Those who listened to him, lulled by his flattery and gifts, began to believe him. The court and the halls of government became places of shadow and suspicion.

"But the people of the capital city began to notice something: food prices began to rise as the man's agents, disguised in something very like the king's livery, bought it up and created an artificial shortage. No one starved, but the price rise was enough to cause discontent among the city's inhabitants. The man sat back, watched his plot unfold, and bided his time until the right moment came."

Saraid again opened her mouth to speak, but Perrin ignored her.

"It came late that year. Prices remained high and bread supplies low due to both a poor harvest and his manipulations of the market, and there was much unrest. At the same time, the queen gave birth to her second child, a darling little princess. The king was delighted and wished to declare another public holiday, but his ministers warned him that the public mood would not permit it. Astounded, the king asked why, and those of his ministers who had not been bought off explained the food situation. When the king inquired angrily why he had not been told before, his honest ministers replied in surprise that the king's agents had been buying up the food and it was presumed to be on his own orders. The king denied any knowledge of the matter, declared that it was to be thoroughly investigated, and commanded his ministers to report on the matter in two days' time.

"The king awoke early the next morning and decided to go out and talk with the early morning market people instead of waiting to hear his ministers' report. He went in disguise, with only a few guards to accompany him. This impulsive act saved his life, for shortly after he left, squadrons of the man's soldiers descended on the palace and the governmental buildings and began to lay them waste in a bloodbath. Many of the nobility whom the man had been unable to corrupt to his cause were killed that day, though not a few either escaped or were safely away on their estates. At the same time that he ordered the slaughter in the palace and in the government, the man sent messengers into the city, promising plenteous food and drink and reward to those who joined him and death to those who opposed him. The king and his tiny entourage heard this proclamation with amazement, and the king would have laughed it off and challenged the messenger had the messenger not pulled from a bag the head of one of his most trusted ministers. His guards counseled secrecy and the king reluctantly agreed, for he had left his wife and children still asleep at the palace and greatly feared for their safety.

"Meanwhile at the palace, the attackers were about to reach the royal apartments. The prince's governess was an early riser and was awake when the first of the man's soldiers broke into the palace. She was able to hurry her little pupil into secret passages she knew of, for she had been the daughter of the previous king's household steward and grew up there. However, she was too late to save Queen Elladis and her infant. Both were killed before her and the prince's eyes. They saw the man himself kill the queen. The man's nephew, for he was not married and had no sons, was there as well. He grabbed the tiny baby girl by the feet and dashed her brains out against the wall."

"Perrin..." She wanted to shake her head, to try to impose some order on her whirling thoughts. "What are you telling me?"

"You know your history. I'm sure you've guessed whose story

this is by now," Perrin said gently. "Would you like me to go on? Or do I need to?"

Saraid groped for her hand. "What happened after...after you saw the queen killed?"

Perrin did not blink at her use of *you*. "Cadel and I hid in the walls till nightfall—he never once complained of being hungry or thirsty, though we had nothing to eat or drink—and then we slipped out under cover of darkness. Madariv was in an uproar, and I decided the best thing to do was to leave the city and go to my husband's estate in the country. Friends risked their lives to hide us, and then I had word that my family had also been killed and our estate taken by the new Lord Protector.

"But we also heard rumors that King Galleron had survived and fled into the Adaiha, and so we did as well. After nearly two months, we were able to find him once again. But he was a broken man. Though many from his court eventually joined us in the Adaiha—you've met several of them—he was never able to rally himself or others to try to retake his country. Ever since, we've pinned our hopes on his son. He has the drive and intellect his father lacked, though he has his father's physical prowess...and his mother's beauty and sweetness—" She smiled and blinked back tears. "Look at me. Nearly twenty years, and I still cry when I think about it."

"Why didn't he tell me who he was?" Saraid cried. "Why keep it a secret from me?"

"Because he had nothing to offer you but himself. He wanted to try to make you love him for who he was—not as an outcast from his own land. And he didn't want you to think he wanted you just because you were a princess." Perrin pulled a handkerchief from her sleeve and dabbed at her eyes. "The pair of you—sometimes I wasn't sure who would throttle whom first—or who would kiss whom first. You and he were meant to be together, as far as I can see. I wanted to make sure you had a chance to find that out before either of you did something irevocable and never admitted that you love each other."

*Something irrevocable.* "But he already said that he doesn't …that I should go—"

"Of course he said that. What do you think it looked like to him, your disappearing while he slept? He may be the overlord of the Adaiha and in a good position to retake his throne—"

Saraid drew in a sharp breath. "Retake his throne? You mean, he's going to try to oust the Lord Protector?"

Her astonishment seemed to surprise Perrin. "Why else would he have gone to the trouble of uniting the Adaiha? Of course he wants to retake his throne. But please remember that though he may be lord of the Adaiha, as a man in love he's utterly defenseless."

Her head had started to hurt. King Cadel. "But what do I *do*?"

Perrin leaned forward and took her hands. Though her eyes were kind, they were also implacable. "I can't tell you that. Nobody can tell you that. But once you decide, you must be the one to tell him."

"Ahem." Lisnam was standing several paces away. He did not look at Saraid, but addressed himself to Perrin. "I could use your help, Lady. They're bringing up the wounded."

Perrin nodded and rose. "How many and who?"

"The Mauburnians were killed to a man. We lost two—young Vul was one of them—and five wounded, not too badly." His eyes slid briefly over Saraid, then returned to Perrin. "The girl Belet was hit with an arrow. A lung may have been pierced. I won't know till they've carried her up and I've seen her."

Saraid gasped. Vul had kidnapped her and Belet had hardly been her friend, to state it mildly, but still—she thought of Meyric and Kursa. And Fhorri, little Fhorri with no parents, who worshipped his big brother the Rider.

Perrin had turned pale. "What of Cadel?"

"Unhurt but busy supervising the burial. He wants us to be gone by nightfall, even the wounded if possible. Another Mauburnian patrol may happen by, considering where we are. I must go." He wheeled around and strode back to the tent. Saraid could see two Riders approaching it with a laden makeshift stretcher.

"Isn't there anything I can do?" she said, catching at Perrin's hand.

"There are lots of things you can do. And you have until sunset to figure out which ones. I must go help Lisnam." She squeezed Saraid's hand and let it go.

# Twenty-two

Avoid making decisions when tired, hungry, or overcome by physical or emotional discomfort. When possible, eat well and get a night's rest before you do. Sleep especially clears the mind of fog and shadows to a remarkable degree.

—*The Flower of Royalty Blossom'd*

SARAID STARED AFTER PERRIN. The rightful king of Mauburni was alive and well—and the love of her life. And she'd been awful to him for weeks, telling him she preferred Lord Mutrand—dear Keranieth, the one who'd murdered Cadel's infant sister as callously as one would swat a fly.

She needed to think, and to do it in a quiet place away from the bustling Riders. Beyond the rocks where she and Perrin had sat were more rocks and another low rock face, remains of terraces cut by a long since dried-up river. She trudged along it till she found a hollow in the face, not quite a cave but deep enough to shelter her from the worst of the sun, drew her *lahart* around her, and huddled inside it, chin on her knees.

Cadel thought she had run away from him again. He hadn't heard her tell him she loved him or felt her hold him tenderly as he slept. Perrin was right—from his viewpoint, it did look suspicious: the drugged tea brought by Belet, her previous co-conspirator, which he drank and she just sipped at; her and Belet's and Vul's eagerness to come along to the Watch camp which lay even closer to the Mauburnian border. And worst of all, the only people who could vindicate her—Vul and Belet—were either dead or unable to communicate right now.

What could she say to Cadel that would make him believe her?

She could point out that she hadn't run away while he was in Madariv. He himself had said that. But the fact she hadn't then didn't mean that she hadn't planned to do so in the future. The Book stated in several places that the absence of something was not the equivalent of its opposite.

Oh, what she wouldn't give for her copy of The Book right now. Would Count Ebroian, the most brilliant statesman of his day, know what to do if he were in her position? Ha. He probably never would have gotten himself into such a predicament.

Besides, The Book had failed her, beginning that night when Cadel had brushed her hair. She'd thought less and less about it after that night, stopped thinking about her life through its lens. The irony was that Cadel was forcing her to resume that path she'd once chosen, with The Book as her guide, and go back to Thekla. Maybe Father would let her go live on his estate in the country, and she could ride and raise *lumox*-trees and make her own silk and be an eccentric maiden aunt someday to Nin's children. Or she could be even more virtuous and self-sacrificing and make whatever political marriage Thekla asked her to. Except to Lord Mutrand. Not him. Not when the rightful king of Mauburni lived—

No. Thinking about Cadel hurt too much, just as it had when Vul was carrying her away from him. That had been bad enough, but somehow, this was worse. Everything hurt too much right now, and there was no comfort anywhere.

She let herself slump sideways, curling up on her side, and

pulled her *lahart* around her. Outside the sun rose higher over the Adaiha, but she kept her eyes closed against it. Darkness was all she wanted just now.

A sandy beach; blue water and pale gold sand, and in the background the towers and bastions of a large structure, whether castle or fortress she couldn't say. The scene looked familiar, but she couldn't place where she'd seen it before; she had never seen the ocean in real life, but she was quite sure this was a seaside beach. She was walking with someone, a tall man with graying hair and a hawk-like nose who also looked familiar. He wore a black tunic embroidered with gold thread in a heraldic pattern, with little *t*'s cleverly worked into the design—pox it, why couldn't she remember?

The sun was warm on her shoulders and the sea sparkled off to her left, somehow looking both warm and cool at the same time. She stared at the toes of her high-laced riding boots as she walked down the damp sand and wondered if her companion would mind if she took them off and splashed barefoot through the shallows—well, maybe not splashed. He probably wouldn't care for salty splatters of seawater on his immaculate tunic and polished boots. And besides, the hem of her Adaihan robe was getting wet enough as it was, just walking here. She sighed and kept staring at her toes.

"Don't worry. You'll have plenty of opportunity to enjoy the water once you arrive in Mauburni." The man's voice was slightly hoarse, but his tone was kindly enough. "I have always been a firm believer in the health benefits of sea-bathing, so long as the people you do it with are trustworthy and don't get between you and the shore."

Suddenly she knew with whom she walked and why he seemed so familiar. She remembered Kursa gazing longingly at a certain picture in her copy of The Book, tracing the little gold *t*'s in the man's coat. "I know. You mention it a couple of times in The Book. That's why I tried to learn to swim before I left Thekla."

"Well done." Count Ebroian nodded his approval. "Embracing your new land's customs as your own is to be commended."

"You say that, too." Saraid glanced at Count Ebroian again. He walked with his hands clasped behind his back and wore a silver chain around his neck from which hung a heavy seal. The state seal of Mauburni, which he would wield until he gave it over to the young king he'd raised to manhood. "You say a lot of things. Sometimes it's hard to remember them all."

"Why would you possibly want to remember everything I've said?" He looked at her with a humorous quirk lurking at the corners of his mouth, and she realized he reminded her strongly of Perrin.

"Wasn't that what *The Flower of Royalty Blossom'd* was for? Didn't you write it as a sort of rulebook for King Thanel to grow up by?"

The humor in his smile deepened, but his eyes were compassionate. "A rulebook? Gods, no. There's no such thing as a rulebook for life. Is that what you think it is?"

"Well...yes. At least I did once. Now I'm just confused."

"My dear." He took her hand and patted it. "We're all confused. Some of us choose to write books to try to make sense of our confusion."

"You, confused? But you're Count Ebroian. You're the one who put Mauburni back together again after the war. You're the least confused—"

"Trying to rebuild Mauburni and bring up an orphaned boy to rule it was a daunting task for one man to fulfill. The Book, as you call it, was my way of organizing my thoughts so that I could do my task. It was where I tried to write down what I'd learned so I could pass it down to my pupil. But it was just one man's knowledge. It was knowledge that I had found useful in my life and times—but that doesn't mean it would necessarily be useful in everyone else's. A rulebook? Never."

"Well, er...so how am I supposed to know what to do?" she asked in a small voice.

His voice was solemn. "The only way to know what to do with your life is to live it—to learn, to observe, to contemplate— and then to make the best decisions you can."

"Yes, but I'm a princess. I don't make decisions—I have duties."

"To whom?"

"To Thekla, of course."

He raised an eyebrow. "A duty isn't a duty until you accept it as one. And only you can decide if it is a duty you can live with. You accepted your 'duty' to go to Mauburni and marry because at that time, you felt it the right thing to do. Since then, your knowledge of the facts and of yourself has changed. You have to make new decisions. That is what being a responsible human being is about."

"Even if it goes against what others want?"

"Whose life are you living? Yours or theirs? If you truly feel what they want is wrong, then yes."

"But what if I make a wrong decision?"

He sighed. "Everyone makes wrong decisions sometimes and suffers for them. There's no such thing as surety. Look at the Adaihans, deciding not to help the king when he called them. They made the wrong decision and have duly suffered for it."

Saraid glanced sharply at him. The Adaihans believed that Count Ebroian had been a wizard and had called the sand down on them. Did he know that? Had it just been lucky coincidence for him that it had stopped raining in the Adaiha?

But Count Ebroian's face was bland and guileless as he went on. "All you can do is try your hardest to learn, so that when it's time to make those decisions, you make the best ones you can... and understand that even the best decision can have unintended consequences." His forehead wrinkled. "Do you know the story of the grateful stonemason? Didn't I put it in The Book some-where?"

"No."

"Ah. Let me tell it to you, then. One day a man—a common laborer—was walking through a narrow alley in the city and came upon a robber attacking a stonemason. The thief was about to stab the poor mason with one of his own chisels when the laborer bravely drove him off. The mason was filled with gratitude and offered to build his savior a fine new house to repay him. The laborer of course agreed, and the mason set to work the very next day. Every evening after working at his lowly job, the laborer went to see what progress had been made on his new house. One evening as he stood gazing up at it, the mason, who was up on the roof laying slates, waved a greeting at him. His movement dislodged a loose slate, which fell off the roof and onto the laborer's head, killing him instantly."

Saraid gasped and stood still. "That's a terrible story!"

"Dear me, is it? Hmm. Maybe that's why I didn't put it in The Book." Count Ebroian shrugged. "But it proves my point. The man who saved the mason did what he thought was the right thing. How was he to know that it would eventually result in his own death? And how was the mason to know that his generous gift would prove so horrible? Neither of them could know. They did what they thought right, and most of the time they would have been right. All you can do is look at as many sides of an issue as you can, make your decision with what you have, and hope for the best."

Saraid resumed walking. "And what about love?"

"What about it?"

"Well...I'm just afraid that I'll let my...you know, personal feelings cloud my decision making."

"How can they not? Your personal feelings are part of who you are."

"I know, but—"

"Trying to understand why one loves is almost impossible,"

he said, smiling again. "Don't bother. Do you love Cadel?"

"Yes. Yes, I do."

"There you go."

"But I don't know if he still loves me! What do I do? What do I say to him?"

"You could try telling him the truth."

"You make it sound so easy. He thinks I ran away from him. How can I make him—"

"You can't *make* him do anything, my dear. He has his own decisions to make as well, don't forget."

"But what if he sends me back to Thekla?"

"Then you can decide to go, or you can try to convince him otherwise. It's your—"

"—my decision," she finished, a little sourly. "I think I'm catching on."

"I knew you would."

"But what if I do stay and I turn out like the stonemason and bring bad rather than good to Cadel, even if I don't mean to? Or what if—"

"Saraid, Saraid. Don't forget the unintended consequences we discussed. What if you renounce him and he goes into battle against Mauburni and takes foolish risks because the loss of you has made life less precious to him? Speaking of Cadel..." He glanced up at the sky. The sun was lowering to its rest, and the surface of the water glowed like beaten silver in its oblique light. "It's getting late. You have some decisions to make, I think."

"But there's more I want to talk to you about! What about Mauburni? What are Cadel's chances of taking his throne back? What should I—"

He held up a hand, smiling. "After the conversation we've just had, you expect me to answer these questions?"

Saraid sighed. "I suppose not. But it certainly would be easier if you would." She looked at him sideways. "You're nothing like I'd expected you to be after reading The Book."

"Literary conventions in my day were rather restrictive. If

one plans to be a future classic, one must write to the part." He gave her a crooked grin. "Perhaps you would someday do me the honor of writing a foreword to a future edition."

"Saying what?"

"Why, whatever you decide it should, of course. Though you may be busy with your own writings by then. Farewell, my dear." He bowed in the old-fashioned, elegant way with one hand on his heart, then turned and began to walk back the way they'd come.

"Wait!" Saraid tried to fall into step with him again but somehow he quickly moved away from her, though his pace never varied. In a moment, he was gone, leaving her to blink after him, alone.

Saraid blinked again and rubbed her eyes. Where was the beach? And the silver-washed sea?

She scrambled to her feet, and then she remembered: the Adaiha. Perrin. Cadel. She'd come here for some quiet to think about what to say to Cadel, and she must have fallen asleep. Not a surprise, after the events of the last two days. But the dream she'd had—it had felt so real, talking to Count Ebroian. They'd been walking together on the shore, just like the picture in The Book. She glanced involuntarily down at her feet.

The hem of her robes was oddly darkened, as if the fabric were wet. A line of powdery white edged the damp part. She bent and rubbed it with her fingertips; it brushed away, like dust.

Or fine salt.

Tentatively she licked her finger, then stared at it in confusion. *Had* she been dreaming, or had it been something else? Had she somehow been walking with Count Ebroian, talking and watching the setting sun turn the water to silver—

The setting sun! Dear Keranieth, she'd slept—or something— the afternoon away and still hadn't decided what to say to Cadel.

But if she didn't do something fast, he'd do it for her. She straightened her *lahart* over her shoulders, brushed back the wisps of hair that had escaped from her braid—she could not remember the last time she'd been able to comb it—and hurried back over to the little camp.

The fire had burned low, and soft voices could be heard in the little tent. Nothing was to be seen of Perrin; she was probably in the tent, tending the wounded. A short distance away, a group of Riders sat or lay in a rough circle, talking or napping, wrapped in their *laharton*. One or two had risen and were gazing at the eastern sky, where a thick band of clouds seemed to absorb light from the setting sun like a gray sponge. She hurried over to them.

"Lord Cadel—have you seen him?" she asked breathlessly.

They glanced at each other, looking uncomfortable. One muttered something under his breath, but the rest remained silent. Saraid waited in agony. These must be the Riders designated to bring her to Thekla at nightfall. Her heart felt as if it had forgotten how to beat.

Finally, one of the recumbent ones sat up and pulled off his hood. It was Gorra, from the Watch camp. He looked at her meditatively, then said, "Aye, Your Highness. Last I saw, he went in that direction." He pointed east toward a low hill some way off.

Her heart thudded painfully in her chest and made it hard to speak for a second. "Thank you," she whispered, and turned away.

"Your Highness—" Gorra called after her.

She turned back. "Yes?"

He looked at her, then down at his hands. "I don't know what it is you want. But we love him and believe in him, even if you don't. Please don't hurt him more than you already have."

Tears stung her throat again, and she swallowed hard. "I'll try not to."

# Twenty-three

SHE SET OFF TOWARD the hill, walking briskly. If only her mind was as determined as her pace.

Duty and love. Thekla and Cadel. She had the time it took for her to walk from here to the hill where he sat to decide which she would choose. Her feet lagged for a few steps, but a glance back at the sinking sun spurred her on. If she didn't hurry, he would decide for her.

*What do I do?* she wanted to shriek aloud. What was right? Nothing was what it had seemed to be. If Father and his council were here and knew what she knew about the Lord Protector and about Cadel, would they change their minds? If Count Ebroian were writing another chapter of The Book right now, what would he say? She'd relied on them both, but neither was of any help now. There was no Count Ebroian walking behind her, watching. At least, she didn't *think* so.

If The Book had one main theme, one message, it was that duty took precedence over everything—even one's deepest personal wishes. She'd tried to finesse that by making her duty into her desire, convincing herself that Thekla's advancement was all she cared about. She'd tried to take it even further by making herself fall in love with the Lord Protector so that her commitment to Thekla would be more complete—and more *hers*. Hah. So much for her purity of sacrifice—she had done her best to make it into no sacrifice at all under cover of virtue.

But wasn't that human nature? Weren't people inherently selfish beings? The priests of Keranieth in the great temple back at home in Thekla were supposed to live lives of utter dedication to the goddess and to each other, and as a result the stories and jokes about their bickering and petty selfishness were known everywhere.

But that wouldn't excuse her. People might be at heart selfish, but they also knew that right and wrong existed and that they could choose between the two. It was time for her to do what was right. What *she* knew to be right.

She climbed to the top of the hill. Cadel sat cross-legged on the rocky sand with his back to her just below the hill's crest, chin on fist, facing east toward a distant line of hills—the ones that separated the Adaiha from Mauburni, she realized. Mauburni, his true home. What must it have felt like for him to make those secret journeys to Madariv, to see the royal palace and remember what had happened there?

"Who is it?" he said without turning around.

"It's me." Her voice was quiet enough that she thought she'd have to repeat herself, but his back straightened so quickly that she knew he'd heard. He didn't stir, but it felt as if he'd moved several yards away from her.

"Your Highness should be getting ready to leave," he said, not turning. "I apologize if you were not informed we'd break camp just after sunset. I'll send your belongings on from the summer camp with my fastest Rider. He should meet you before you cross back into Thekla."

The remote courtesy of his words hurt far more than anger and shouting would have. It also made her realize what she wanted to say to him. Would he listen?

She waited a few breaths to make sure her voice didn't tremble. "I thank you, but that won't be necessary."

"No?" He didn't sound particularly interested. Pox it, he would be soon if she had anything to say about it.

"No. And we won't go anywhere until you've heard what I have to say."

He didn't reply. Maybe he needed his own pause to regulate his voice. That was a good sign. "I won't prevent Your Highness from speaking, but I would ask that you keep it brief," he said at last, still icily polite. "Time grows short."

"I will take as long as is necessary." She stared at the clouds the Riders had been watching massing over the eastern hills, looking darker and closer from this vantage point, then down at the top of his head, shining red-gold in the rays of the setting sun. This would be easier if she could see his expression, but there was no way to maneuver him to face her now. She'd have to trust in the strength of her words. "You don't have to trouble yourself about having my bags sent on to Thekla, because I'm not going there."

Pause. "I'm afraid I can't permit Your Highness to go to Madariv."

"Who said I was going anywhere? I'm staying here, with you."

Another pause. She filled it, before he could deny her. "I never had any intention of leaving you. They kidnapped me—"

He shifted suddenly as if he would speak, but she pressed on.

"Vul and Belet kidnapped me. They had it all planned. Vul had turned spy while he was at the Eb. He told me so himself. He wanted to bring me to Madariv to please his masters, and Belet wanted me gone because she wanted you for herself. You..." Her voice shook again, but this time she ignored it. "You fell asleep just as I was telling you that I love you, back at the Watch Camp. Belet had drugged the tea she brought us. I had put my cup down when...when you held me, but you'd already finished yours and that's why you slept. I'd had just enough to make it easy for them to take me—"

He held up one hand. "Please," he said in a strangled voice. "Don't lie to me, Your Highness."

She stamped her foot. "I'm not lying! I didn't want to leave you then, and I won't leave you now...Your Majesty."

He jerked and leapt to his feet, whirling to face her. "Who told you?" he demanded, lunging toward her and grabbing her shoulders. His eyes were no longer icy. Instead they burned like the heart of flame under his ferociously frowning brows.

"What, I'm not clever enough to have figured it out on my own?" Of course she hadn't been, but that didn't matter right now. And she wouldn't betray Perrin's confidence.

"I see," he said softly, after glaring at her for a few heartbeats. "It's The Book again, isn't it? 'He's the rightful King of Mauburni and I must marry him so I can do my duty for Thekla.' I knew this would happen if you found out."

"Do you think I'm that single-minded—no, never mind, don't answer that," she amended. "Your being the rightful King of Mauburni doesn't matter—and it hasn't changed how I feel about you. I fell in love with you back when you were only Kayn, the Adaihan wanderer. Then I got in my own way and messed everything up. But you're right—I *do* want to do my duty to Thekla—"

He dropped his hands from her shoulders as if they burned. "That is why I'm sending you back. Now if you're quite through—"

"—but I'm going to do it *my* way." She grabbed the edges of his *lahart* and twisted the cloth around her hands so he couldn't escape. "You're going to listen to me and stop this stupid pride thing and admit you're wrong. If I can do it, by Keranieth, you can, too."

"Saraid—"

"Listen." She gave him a little shake. "I was sent to marry the Lord Protector because helping him become king in Mauburni seemed to be in Thekla's best interest. I know now that it isn't, and that the rightful king still lives—but no one in Thekla knew that before. Maybe it would have changed things, or maybe it wouldn't. But I know the truth, and now *I* have to decide what's best for Thekla—and I've decided that Thekla shall acknowledge you as king and ally itself with you. Through me." She lifted her face, pulled him to her by his *lahart*, and kissed him. "Will you marry me, Your Majesty?"

He gripped her wrists and tried to push her away. "I'm not Your Majesty. I'm an Adaihan brigand who'll never amount to much. You said so yourself."

"No. You're the king. You were one before I came here and you always will be. The Adaihans know that. And so do I, now." The last rays of the sun made a halo of his hair—*no, a crown*, she thought giddily. *Even the light knew who he was.* "You're the rightful king of Mauburni, and as a princess of Thekla I will marry you."

A low, rumbling sound rolled toward them on a sudden gust of cool wind, but she was too intent on him to pay much attention. She kissed him again, grazing her lips softly against his unyielding mouth.

"Saraid...don't..." A shiver ran through him.

"Cadel," she murmured, letting her hands slide up his chest to his shoulders.

"No," he said hoarsely.

She kissed him a third time, catching his denial with her lips and brushing it away. "Yes," she whispered. "I want to be at your side when you return to Madariv to take your rightful place as king. Because that's what we're going to do."

She felt his lips tremble under hers before he pulled his head back. "You want to marry Mauburni, not me," he said harshly. "So you can still do your duty to Thekla."

"Shh." She touched a finger to his mouth. "Of course I'm doing this purely for Thekla's sake. The fact that I love you with all my heart has nothing whatsoever to do with it."

His eyes widened. He lowered them quickly, but not before she saw the startled joy in them. It was time to move in for the final stroke.

"Cadel, you *vehdron*." She pronounced the Adaihan word with Perrin's Mauburnian intonation. "It's wonderful that you're the true king of Mauburni." She took his hand and placed it over her heart. "But don't you understand that you rule here as well? You won it back when you were Kayn. I was just too contrary to admit it."

"Your contrariness makes other peoples' undying resistance look downright spineless," he muttered, but didn't try to pull his hand away.

"I know. So you might as well give up, because there's no way you're going to be able to get rid of me now." She smiled up at him and ignored the fact that his face had gone blurry. "I *love* you," she added in a whisper.

"Saraid." He touched the tear that ran down her cheek. "Say it again."

"I love you," she shouted, and kissed him hard.

"Oh, gods...Saraid—" He pulled her against him.

Another rumble, much louder this time, rolled across the sky, and something wet landed on Saraid's head. She broke their kiss and glanced up, startled. Another something splashed onto her cheek, and another, and then a dozen more. She blinked in confusion, then understood what they were.

Raindrops.

It was raining in the Adaiha.

She drew in a quick breath and looked at Cadel staring wide-eyed up at the sky, drops of water that might be either rain or tears running unchecked down his cheeks, so she, too, turned her face up to feel the rain on it and gazed up at the clouds—the *beautiful*, gray, lowering clouds.

It was raining in the Adaiha.

Behind them she heard a sudden hubbub of voices, then an exclamation—and then a clamor of shouts and whoops of joy as the rain reached the Riders on the dunes behind them. Cadel glanced over at them, and a smile tugged at his mouth—and then he was laughing too, shaking the rain out of his eyes as he pulled her to him once again and kissed her long and hard, and Saraid was sure her heart would explode with happiness. They stood enfolded in each other's arms on the dune and let the cool rain fall on them, soaking them, and listened to it drumming on the sand under the jubilation of Cadel's Riders.

It was raining in the Adaiha.

The king of Mauburni had returned.

# Acknowledgements

The first incarnation of *Between Silk and Sand* was written back in (I can hardly believe it) 2003, when I finally sat down at a computer to see if this writing thing I'd been thinking about doing would actually work. It weighed in at 120,000 words and, quite honestly, was terrible — an utter stinker.

But it told me that I could actually write an entire book from start to finish, so there was that. I went on to write other books and was published with those, but the story I first started telling in 2003 wouldn't leave me alone. So I wrote it again four years later...and again a few years after that. And every time I (re)wrote it, friends who read it would tell me they loved Saraid and Cadel and that they had to be introduced to a wider audience (as well as showing me that the story still had a ways to go.) If it weren't for these wonderful people, this story might well have languished on my hard drive forever — so for pushing me to make it better and to persist, I will be forever grateful to Janet Halpin, Regina Lundgren, Sarah Dotts Barley, Nandini Bajpai, Wendy Cukauskas McDonald, Anne Bingham, Rose Green, Robin Prehn, Hilary Sierpinski, Vonna Carter, Ena Jones, Cyndi Marko, Robin Lemke, and Larissa C. Hardesty. Thank you, all of you. Words are my trade, but I simply can't find any strong enough to communicate my thanks and love.

In the "showing me that the story still had a ways to go" department, enormous thanks also are due to Sarah Dotts Barley, Bev Katz Rosenbaum, and Sherwood Smith, all of whose extraordinary editorial discernment taught me so much and made this story exponentially better. Your guidance helped me get out of my own way (always an issue!) and made this story something I can start to be proud of. Both this story and I are the better for the experience. And enormous thanks are also due to Amy Knupp of Blue Otter Editing for kindly correcting my often idiosyncratic punctuation and generally making the mechanics of the story better. Any remaining solecisms should be laid solely at my doorstep.

Dave Smeds, author and gentleman and graphic designer extraordinaire, created the perfect cover for *Between Silk and Sand*, bringing the story to life in one breath-taking image. I cannot thank you enough for this beautiful thing! Thank you too to Vonda N. McIntyre for creating the elegant and functional ebook versions.

Thank you also to everyone at Book View Café for all your help, support, and camaraderie in bringing this book to life. I am proud to be a part of you.

Last but never least, thanks are due (of course) to the most awesomest gal pal writer friends in this or any other known universe: Jen Clark Estes, Larissa C. Hardesty, Ena Jones, Katie Kennedy, Robin Lemke, Cyndi Marko, Deena Lipomi Viviani, and Holly Westlund. You are some weirdly, wonderfully improbable combination of wise old grandmother, comforting mom, stalwart sister, and giggly best friend. Thank you for your sanity, silliness, support, and shenanigans.

# About the Author

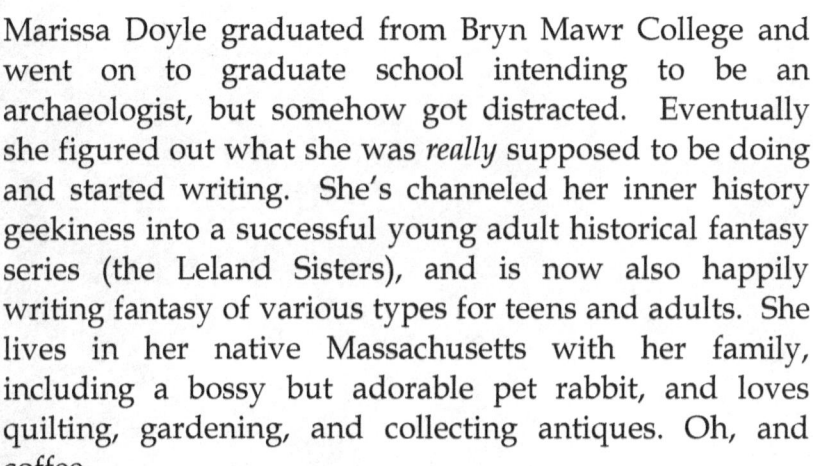

Marissa Doyle graduated from Bryn Mawr College and went on to graduate school intending to be an archaeologist, but somehow got distracted. Eventually she figured out what she was *really* supposed to be doing and started writing. She's channeled her inner history geekiness into a successful young adult historical fantasy series (the Leland Sisters), and is now also happily writing fantasy of various types for teens and adults. She lives in her native Massachusetts with her family, including a bossy but adorable pet rabbit, and loves quilting, gardening, and collecting antiques. Oh, and coffee.

Please visit her at her website, www.marissadoyle.com, and at her history blog, www.nineteenteen.com.

Thank you so much for taking the time to read *Between Silk and Sand*. If you enjoyed it, please consider telling your friends or posting a review on the site where you purchased it or on your favorite social media site such as Goodreads or LibraryThing. Word of mouth is an author's best friend and much appreciated.

## Connect with me
## (because I love hearing from readers!)

Website: www.marissadoyle.com
Blog: www.nineteenteen.com
Facebook: www.facebook.com/marissadoyleauthor
Twitter: www.twitter.com/marissadoyle
Pinterest: www.pinterest.com/mdoyleauthor


Sign up for my newsletter and get the latest info on sales, new releases, and other fun stuff!
http://eepurl.com/bVDwlf

# ABOUT BOOK VIEW CAFÉ

Book View Café Publishing Cooperative is an author-owned cooperative of over fifty professional writers, publishing in a variety of genres such as fantasy, romance, mystery, and science fiction.

BVC authors include *New York Times* and *USA Today* best-sellers; Nebula, Hugo, and Philip K. Dick Award winners; World Fantasy Award, Campbell Award, and RITA Award nominees; and winners and nominees of many other publishing awards.

Since its debut in 2008, BVC has gained a reputation for producing high-quality e-books, and is now bringing that same quality to its print editions.

www.ingramcontent.com/pod-product-compliance
Lightning Source LLC
Chambersburg PA
CBHW030530120726
47904CB00005B/1704